PRAISE FOR NANCY BAKER

The Night Inside

"Studded with passages of dark lustre . . . truly original."

—Publishers Weekly

"Baker has here contrived a riveting story, and her compromised heroine, a historian whose plunge into the past remakes her life, is a strikingly drawn and hauntingly memorable figure."

—USA Today

"Baker has obviously thought about what surrendering to the dark side means that lifts this book up above the vast . . . morass of romantic vampire fiction."

—Quill & Quire

"It's almost impossible not to finish *The Night Inside* in one frenzied, chocolate donut munching sitting. It's also impossible not to root for its feisty, feminist vampiress heroine."

—Charles Busch, author of *Vampire Lesbians of Sodom*

"Terrific . . . The unrelenting tension between the monstrous and the human propels this unique tale of gripping suspense."

—Katherine Ramsland, author of *The Vampire Chronicles*

"The metamorphosis is achieved in a highly charged ritual as sensuous as any written: this is consummation as bloodbath, as mutual blood-letting and blood-sucking . . . breathless, lingering, erotic . . ."

—The Globe and Mail

Blood and Chrysanthemums

"Baker's style combines, or alternates between, traditional realism and fantasy; realism with its developed, motivated, complex characters; plots which attempt to reflect life as we live it; and straightforward, transparent prose—and fantasy, with its more stereotyped characterizations; stylized story lines; and formal, sometimes poetic language. The latter style is more prominent in the parts of the novel which flash back to ancient Japan, where the prose lilts gracefully."

—*Toronto Star*

"Nancy Baker writes about the vampires next door . . . they bicker over petty, everyday things. They are jealous when a partner flirts with someone. They worry about paying the rent. . . . 'They're Canadian,' she says."

—*The Vancouver Sun*

"Baker evokes the various figures from Japanese culture familiar in the West—yakuza, samurai and medieval court ladies and their pillow books—but she goes beyond clichés and invests these characters with a solidity and poignancy. . . . Ardeth's nocturnal cross-country hitchhiking trip is particularly noteworthy for its undercurrents of violence and loneliness."

—*Paragraph*

A Terrible Beauty

"A polished and enchanting tale . . . It is, in a word, breathtaking."
—*The Ottawa Citizen*

"Baker's prose is lush and sensual . . . she has a real gift for making the fantastic seem plausible and investing the mundane with eerie significance."
—*The Sunday Sun* (Toronto)

"*A Terrible Beauty* is modern Canadian Gothic. . . . Nancy Baker shows her mastery of the form—the mysterious letter, the journey into the wilderness, the shadows that hide from the flickering firelight—and her real affection for a good ol' fashioned vampire yarn."
—*The Telegraph Journal* (Saint John)

"Baker's narrative is seductive and compelling. Like Rice, she transcends the horror genre."
—*Province Showcase* (Vancouver)

COLD HILL SIDE

NANCY BAKER

FIRST EDITION

Cold Hillside © 2014 by Nancy Baker
Cover artwork © 2014 by Vince Haig
Cover design by © 2014 Samantha Beiko
Interior design by © 2014 by Alysha DeMarsh / BUNGALOW

Distributed in Canada by
HarperCollins Canada Ltd.
1995 Markham Road
Scarborough, ON M1B 5M8
Toll Free: 1-800-387-0117
e-mail: hcorder@harpercollins.com

Distributed in the U.S. by
Diamond Comic Distributors, Inc.
10150 York Road, Suite 300
Hunt Valley, MD 21030
Phone: (443) 318-8500
e-mail: books@diamondbookdistributors.com

CIP Data available upon request.

ISBN 978-1-77148-310-0   eISBN 978-1-77148-311-7

CHIZINE PUBLICATIONS
Toronto, Canada
www.chizinepub.com
info@chizinepub.com

Edited by Sandra Kasturi
Copyedited and proofread by Michael Matheson

Canada Council   Conseil des arts
for the Arts   du Canada

We acknowledge the support of the Canada Council for the Arts which last year invested $20.1 million in writing and publishing throughout Canada.

ONTARIO ARTS COUNCIL
CONSEIL DES ARTS DE L'ONTARIO
50 YEARS OF ONTARIO GOVERNMENT SUPPORT OF THE ARTS
50 ANS DE SOUTIEN DU GOUVERNEMENT DE L'ONTARIO AUX ARTS

Published with the generous assistance of the Ontario Arts Council.

Printed in Canada

COLD HILL SIDE

NANCY BAKER

ChiZine Publications

For Richard

And I awoke and found me here,
On the cold hill's side.

—John Keats,
"La Belle Dame Sans Merci"

CHAPTER 1

Teresine

Tonight, I woke and did not know where I was.

Or rather I knew and was wrong.

When I opened my eyes and lay in the darkness, the sounds I heard were the rush of the water beneath my family's hut, the air was warm and still, and I could smell sweat and dust and the heavy sweetness of jessamine.

Then the water was nothing but the wind probing the shutters, the warmth of the air was only my breath beneath the blankets and the perfume was the thin smoke from the braziers that burned on either side of the bed.

I knew where I was then, at home in my bed, in my mountaintop house in Lushan and not in far off Deshiniva. At the realization, I wanted to weep—though I still do not know if it was from relief, or homesickness, or merely an old woman's emotional fragility.

Whatever the reason, sleep was well and truly banished. There was nothing to do but push my protesting bones from the bed, wrap myself in my robes and poke the dimly glowing braziers back to life. I considered going to the workroom, to play with the tiles of colour laid out on the mosaic I will never finish. It was to be my legacy, my gift to Lilit to tell her everything I have never been able to say. But I have rearranged it a dozen times and always there is something missing. I played with it because I was not ready to tell the truth and so obscured in colour, pattern and symbolic figures what could never bear the weight of messy and shapeless reality.

I was never an artist anyway, only a restorer—and there is no way to restore what has been broken over the years of my life.

So I huddle here, feeling the cold as I have not in a long time, and hope that these words will serve me as my stones did not. I must at least try to leave some record of the truth for those who might have to bear the consequences of the choices I have made.

Lilit asked me once about Deshiniva. Did she have grandparents there, aunts and uncles, cousins? Would we ever go there? What was it like?

What could I tell her, then or ever? I could not speak of it, was afraid to for fear of what might come out of my mouth once I began. So I refused to answer.

"I'll go there myself then," she announced, eight years old and stubborn as her mother when the mood took her. We were on the patio of the house, overlooking the great drop of the valley. The sky was the bright blue of high summer, burning away the fog and mist until only the highest peaks were still wreathed in the white of their perpetual snows.

Lilit sprawled on the flagstones, playing with the painted cards Urmit had given her, laying bright patterns on the grey rock. Some claimed to be able to read futures in those cards but if Lilit were constructing a fortune there, I could not see it.

Amaris sat in the shade cast by the overhanging roof. There was a ledger book open in her lap and several more piled beside her. I did not look at her; the pinched, dissatisfied line of her mouth still had the power to distress me, for all I swore that she had chosen her life and I was not to blame for any of it. It was enough that she had come and not sent Lilit with a servant. She had grown up here in this house but always seemed a guest in it. I guessed that she was grateful for the wall of important, complicated Kerias family work between us.

"You will not go anywhere," Amaris said. "Why would you want to go there? It's a poor, ugly place . . . full of poor, ugly people." I felt her glance towards where I sat in the sun. "That's what your great-aunt told me once, when I said I wanted to go visit my mother's family. Why would I want to go to see such poor, ugly people, she asked me."

"I never said ugly," I replied. "Poor and stupid, yes."

"All of them?" Lilit asked tentatively, looking from her mother to me curiously. Trying to reconcile that statement with what she knew of us, I guessed, or unwilling to consider it a judgement on herself.

"Of course not all of them," I admitted. "Some of them are rich and stupid." I looked at her open, curious face. Her skin was lighter than her mother's, honey instead of copper, but even in the bright sun her hair was the rich black of Deshiniva. Her eyes were hazel, a common enough colour in Lushan, with its odd, mingled heritages. But I still shivered sometimes when I saw them—and that made me harsh. "Trust me in this, child. There's no family worth finding and no way to find them."

"I could. Maybe you're wrong."

"You could certainly stop at every poor hut all the way down the river and ask who had a daughter named Teresine, a daughter named Keshini. But Teresine what, Keshini what? We were too poor to have last names. What does a peasant need with a last name? Every village probably has a child named Teresine who disappeared down the river to the city and was never seen again. Every village probably has a child named Keshini who—" But I stopped myself in time for that.

"You found her. You found your sister," Lilit pointed out after a moment of thought. I was grateful she had not pursued my slip and asked exactly what Keshini had done. Amaris looked at me, narrow-eyed and angry. She had long since decided where the blame for her mother's early death lay. I put my hands up to shade my eyes and stared out over the valley.

"I did," I conceded, at last. "But I knew where to look."

So here is a place to start. It might be only my cowardice that makes me believe so, my fear of finally setting down the words I have hidden from everyone for so many years. But there is truth in the old saying that the beginning holds the ending—and this story begins in Deshiniva.

What do I remember?

I remember the river: that wide, muddy vein that ran down the length of Deshiniva and gave it much of its life. The Deshi begins somewhere in these mountains, but I did not know that then. I only knew that the river was the place we lived. Our village was nothing special. A cluster of huts, some on stilts above the water; a road to the fields won back from the jungle every few years; a society of aunts and uncles, cousins and second cousins, and faces known since birth. We were poor but no poorer than most of our neighbours so we did not notice it most of the time. Only when the great merchant barges or a lord's pleasure boat passed did we glimpse a different world than the one that had been ours for generations.

The river was our life but it was also our death. Each year it would rise, swollen with the snow we never saw and the rain we suffered under. I remember lying on the floor, my eye to the crack in the board beneath me, watching the detritus of others' lives flow beneath me. Broken boats, rags, wooden bowls swirled by in the water. Animals floated past, held aloft by struggling limbs or the bloat of death. Once, when the river swallowed the lower half of the hut, we sat in sodden misery on the roof and I saw an arm wave once above the waves and then vanish again. No one remarked upon it for there was nothing we could do. We waited until the river fell again and then dug the silt from our hut and went on with the work of living.

I was the fourth daughter in the family of ten. I do not think any of us were ugly; I have hard proof enough that the world did not think me so. Whether my parents were stupid, I do not know. For years I was torn between ascribing their actions to ignorance or malice. I do not know which it was and I never will. But I have no strength left to hate them for what they did. If they had not done it, I would not be here now.

Down the river, far away, was Jayasita, the capital city. Strangely enough, it is water I remember there as well, though the house I lived in gave no glimpse of it beyond a fountain that burbled in the courtyard. Our masters there did not trust us so close to water especially those of us from up the river, and in that they were not wrong, at least in my case. When we saw the river, it was always from the decks of barges or the terraces of the palaces. And always at night, when the water was black but for the silver sheen of the moon and the reflected glow of the lanterns. I would lie back and close my eyes and for a moment, the lap of the waves on the sides of the boat would be the water against the stilts of the hut. Sometimes the sound comforted me. Other times, it made me want to weep.

It was hot in the city. In my early years in the mountains, I missed that heat, for all I had cursed it on the long days of summer when the air would not move and the sweat would coat your skin if you dared to try. On the hottest days in Lushan, when people shed their heavy robes and turn their faces to the sky, like flowers seeking the sun, it would be considered cold in Deshiniva. It always made me laugh but I am a creature of the mountains now. When I went back to Deshiniva forty years ago, I revelled in the heat for two days, then longed only for a cool mountain breeze.

Water. Heat. And green. That is the other thing I remember of my homeland. The shadowed green of the jungle, the dusty familiarity of the herbs in my mother's pots, the flower-starred gardens of Jayasita. Deshiniva is green in a thousand shades that do not exist here.

COLD HILLSIDE

And here I live in a world where the only water is the silver slip of a stream through the rocks, where the braziers give heat and the sun, so close in the blue sky, only burns, and there could be a thousand words for grey and not exhaust every nuance of it.

I bought this place with blood and grief and bitterness. I bought it for myself and for you, Lilit, whether or not you ever read these words.

I bought it because I thought it might protect your mother and then you from the danger I brought upon us all.

CHAPTER 2

Lilit

She woke and knew at once that she had made a terrible mistake.

In the faint light of the guttering candle, the cracked and whitewashed roof above her was not the roof of home. The bed was not her bed. It smelled of stale flesh and the thin mattress did nothing to soften the hard wooden edge against which she was pressed. Worst of all, it was not empty.

Lilit put her hand against the dull throb over her temple. *Fool*, she thought. *You fool.*

She shifted carefully, leaning on the edge of the bed to lever herself to her feet. The man beneath the tumble of blankets stirred and she saw his honey-coloured hair spread across the pillow. She remembered that hair in the lamplight of the tavern. It had drawn her eyes and the handsome, fine-boned face beneath it had held them.

Fool, she thought again and, shivering in the pre-dawn chill, found her clothes on the floor. She dressed as quickly as she could, leaving the laces of her undertunic undone. The man moved again and turned his face into the light. She froze but his eyes did not open.

Without the haze of drink—or because of the haze of her hangover, she was not sure which—he was not so handsome now. Or perhaps as handsome, but less otherworldly. Part-fey, he had hinted with a mysterious air she had found charming—something to be found only beyond the iron. His every word had suggested danger and every smile had promised forbidden pleasure.

Oh Mother, Lilit thought. *I am a fool. And I cannot even remember his name.*

A quick stoop to tug on her boots and she slipped out the door into the dim hallway. Through the thin walls of the guesthouse, she could hear snores. What had *they* heard, last night? She pulled her hat down over her eyes and slunk out of the door, grateful for the darkness that still held the streets. Somewhere a dog barked and she flinched.

Around the corner, she paused to finish wrapping her boot laces around her calves, tuck in loose shirttails and fasten the last clasps of her coat. Her head was still throbbing and her mouth felt dry. She wanted no more than to go home, throw up, and crawl into bed—her own bed—for the next several hours.

She hurried through the streets towards the gate. It was almost dawn, she could see the line of light limning the edge of the eastern mountains, and the gatekeepers would be preparing to open the city. They had to be—or she would never make it back to the Kerias clanhouse before slipping in undetected would become impossible. Her only good fortune lay in the fact that, while her mother might believe her capable of numerous failings, drunken tumbles with half-blood outcasts would not be the first thing that would occur to her.

And she had a plausible excuse, if required. She and the other Auster apprentices had been celebrating. A simple case of youthful exuberance and energy, that was all. They had lost track of time, the gate had closed and there was nothing to do but fill the hours beyond the iron until dawn. And if she asked what they were celebrating?

Better to stay silent and let her mother do her worst, Lilit thought with a sigh. A lecture was a small price to pay for the prize that was finally before her.

She rounded the last corner and trudged up the road towards the gate. The sky had brightened and she could see the dark bulk looming before her. There were other ways into the city, or so she'd heard. She'd never had a reason to need one and now, even if she could remember the details of any of the rumoured secret ways, she was far too tired to go scrambling over roofs or crouching through forgotten sewers. There was nothing to do but go to the gate and wait for them to open it.

There was a guard there, a long-faced man with tired eyes. He watched as she approached but said nothing, not even when she paced back and forth a few times and stamped her feet against the cold. "Will it be long until they open?" she asked at last, politely, and he squinted at the sky for a moment.

"A few minutes," he replied. She nodded and wandered to the edge of the gate. She'd never been this close to it when it was closed. It was more forbidding than she had expected. The stone blocks that shaped the frame were heavy, darker above than below, for the oldest portion of the gate dated back to the building of the city by the Agyaresh and the upper part had only been built when the Euskalans came to settle there. The wooden doors were black with age and oil so that the iron bands covering them were barely visible. Iron was set into the blocks around the frame and beneath the doors as well. There was no ornamentation in stone, wood or iron; the gate looked functional and foreboding.

There was another gate, farther up the hillside city, at the door to the palace grounds. There, the iron was wrought into black lace filigree and the symbols of the old Euskalan empire. Of course, no one that the second gate was meant to keep out should have been able to pass the first gate at all, but experience had made the Euskalans very careful. Lilit thought of the gates and of the man sleeping in the guesthouse below them and shivered.

The guard sighed and rapped on the gate. Lilit heard the metallic clang of bolts moving and then the smaller door set into the gate opened. A woman's head emerged. Beneath her helmet, her gaze was suspicious. "It's not time," she said.

"Almost," the guard countered. "So let the girl in. Her pacing is bothering me."

Lilit almost protested but sensibly kept her mouth shut and tried to look contrite. She was certain she could manage it; the woman's stare made her feel young, foolish and guilty of much worse than an anonymous midnight coupling. "Clanhouse?"

"Kerias." There was no point in lying, she decided, but could not let her own House bear the blame alone. "I'm apprenticed to the Austers."

"Rest of *them* came staggering back before the gate closed," the guard confirmed. Lilit felt her cheeks growing hot and stared down at the cobbles.

"Mother," the woman sighed and pushed the door open a little farther. "Come through then and go home."

Lilit thanked them both profusely and slipped through the door. It too was edged with iron and she made sure to touch it as she passed, knowing the woman was watching her. "Next time, don't be late." She accepted the advice with a respectful nod and hurried up the street. There would be no next time, she vowed. At least not until after the fair. Until then, she'd keep her patronage for bars on this side of the gate, no matter what the other apprentices did. She would not give her mother any pretext for denying her the right to go to the fair.

It was one of the constants of their tangled relationship; every year she would ask and every year her mother would refuse. Every year, Lilit would stand in the courtyard and watch the small, select group of cousins and aunts depart. Her mother would stand at her side, her hand on her shoulder like a weight to hold her there.

When Lilit was younger, she saw only the injustice of it. After each fair, she would be forced to endure weeks of her cousins beginning each sentence with "When I was at the fair . . ." Even while she complained of it, to herself or any sympathetic ear she could find, she knew that it was an exaggeration. Not all her cousins were allowed to go. Not all her aunts chose to (or were allowed to, though that was never discussed openly with the cousins, and thus was much gossiped about). Only those who were level-headed, sensible, and clever bargainers were to be part of the House delegation. That was what the aunts, and Ursul Keriassa Dorath, who was House Head, told them. No one had ever disgraced the House by scandalous behaviour at the trading fair and no one ever would, if her mother and aunts had anything to say about it.

What irked and baffled Lilit in equal measure was that she was—as far as she could tell—level-headed, sensible and a passable bargainer. (Well, present behaviour excepted, of course.) She was praised by her aunts for her even temper, relied on to keep her less responsible cousins out of trouble and generally considered the kind of child adults love and other children hate. She could not claim any virtue in this—she had not set out to be any of those things. It was merely that the things she enjoyed doing did not set the household on its ears and, as far as she was concerned, the less her aunts mistrusted her the more they left her alone to do what she wanted.

They let her do just about everything—except go to the fair. In that they deferred to her mother, who was adamant in her refusals.

"For the Mother's sake, Amaris," she once overheard her aunt Tannis say, "Lilit is seventeen. She's a good girl. She's twice as trustworthy as mine and Canisbay's survived two fairs now. When are you going to let her go?"

"Not this year."

"It's better if they go," her aunt said. "The truth isn't nearly as romantic as what they conjure in their heads. You're better to send her now and get it done."

"No." When her mother spoke in that voice, even her elder sister-in-house backed off. She had asked her mother that year, as always, but waited a day or two to do it. As always, the answer had been no.

Even appeals to her great-aunt Teresine had failed. "Girl, if I ask your mother to send you, you'll never go," was all she said. "Besides, she's right, for once. There's no reason for you to go to the fair." So there was no help from that quarter.

Then, last year, she had quietly gotten herself an apprenticeship with the Auster gem cutters. It wasn't unknown for members of one House to apprentice in another, though it was somewhat unusual for the apprentice to be the one asking, not the mother. But Jerel Auster had looked at her hands, looked at her sketches, and then given her broom and told her to sweep up the room. By the time her mother discovered what she spent her days doing, it was too late for her to gracefully demand that her daughter resign her position. She had been obliged to swallow her anger and settled for telling her daughter to behave herself.

And now, Lilit thought with a grin she could not repress, now she was finally going to the fair, chosen along with two other apprentices to accompany the Auster delegation. She knew she was going as nothing but a back to carry things and hands to assemble tents and hold horses but it didn't matter. She was *going*.

By the time she reached the street that led to the Kerias clanhouse, there was light creeping through the shuttered windows of the houses around her and the narrow cobbled way was no longer empty. She passed the rattling cart of the night-soil collector, making the rounds of the clanhouses, and two sleepy-eyed girls putting on their aprons in the alley beside the bakery. When she looked up, she could see the sun had cleared the ridge and touched the top of the palace, where the gold spires gleamed against the red roof and the silk pennants flared in the wind.

The gate of the clanhouse was closed. Iron formed the family crest on the polished wood and was beaten into the shapes of leaves along the lintels and stoop. Lilit stood still for a moment, then sighed and grasped the iron knocker. Two quick raps, a pause, and two more, to let those inside know it was tardy Kerias out there. After a moment, she heard the rasp of the bolts and the door opened.

It was her cousin Teril who'd drawn door duty and she gave Lilit a conspiratorial grin. "Interesting night?" she asked.

"The Austers know how to drink," Lilit replied, grateful it was Teril at the door and not Teras. The younger sister had never quite forgiven Lilit for an unfortunate prank when they were children.

"Better than you do, obviously."

"I only hope their heads hurt as much as mine does."

Teril laughed and Lilit winced. "Go on to bed. I never saw you. Just remember, I'm particularly fond of turquoise—and it is my name day soon."

"I'll remember—though I'm not sure you'd want one after I got through with it."

"I'm not fussy," Teril assured her. Lilit nodded and told herself she should be grateful that Teril didn't have a heart set on rubies. It wouldn't be so hard to find time to work on a turquoise pin and she could always buy one from the Auster shop if necessary. And it *was* nearly Teril's name day, so she couldn't even truly count it as blackmail. At least, not entirely.

She climbed the stairs as quietly as she could, slipped through the empty corridors and at last, at last, reached the sanctuary of her third floor room. Her clothes abandoned on the floor, a quick gulp or two of water from the jug on the stand, and then she crawled into her own, blessedly empty bed. It didn't even matter that the sheets were almost as cold as the room.

Fortunate fool, she thought muzzily as she slipped down into sleep, *you made it. Nothing can stop you now.*

You are going to the fair.

CHAPTER 3

Teresine

By rights, the next thing I should relate is how I came to leave that village on the river and go to the great city of Jayasita. But I cannot write those words, not yet, perhaps not ever. I do not know if this story will make any sense without this part of my past but I know I cannot tell it yet.

And without those words, how I met the Sidiana Sarit will make no sense and so how I left Jayasita cannot be told yet either.

So I will write what I can of the journey north and of my first sight of the city of the Sidianas, the city that was to become the true home of my heart.

The Euskalans from far-off Lushan—I now among them—travelled by boat from Deshiniva, north along the coast. The sailors were veterans of this route but to Sarit and me it was new and fascinating. The two of us would sit on the bow of the ship, watching as each new wonder came into sight. The shoreline slipped past, changing from sand to black rock to the green walls of jungle to cliffs of white stone crowned in golden grasses. The water changed colour beneath us and, once, dolphins raced and played beside the ship.

All this delighted Sarit, aware even then that it was the only time she would ever leave the mountains. As for me, my wonder was always edged in worry, unable to believe I would not wake and find myself back in the city once again.

Sarit . . .

Even now, even after so many years have passed, I miss her. I can count on one hand the people I have truly loved in this life and she is the first. (You are there, of course, but you know that. You are the last.) I gave her my fealty kneeling on the deck of the ship the day I left Deshiniva and I gave her my heart in the same moment.

How to describe how she seemed to me then, a year older than my sixteen years, born to power in a world I could barely imagine? She was golden, from the bright helm of her hair to the tawny glow of her skin, so different from the bronze of the Deshinivi. The crew of the ship and the guard who accompanied her, men and women alike, bowed to her, laughed with her, loved her. I had seen only one woman who held power and none of us loved her. I had not thought power and love could ever meet.

She did her best to explain it to me, when my grasp of Euskalan became strong enough to understand it. It was a still night and the ship was moored in a cove, sheltered from the sea. We lay on the deck, gazing at the stars that seemed to sway like lanterns above us with the gentle movement of the ship. "My mother is the Sidiana," she said. "The queen, in your language, but it doesn't mean exactly the same thing."

"So you will be Sidiana when she is gone."

"Probably."

"Only probably? Who else could be?"

"Any one of my cousins—or sisters, if I had them. We're all sisters-in-house of the royal clan. In theory, whichever one of us is best suited becomes Sidiana when the time comes."

"Who decides?"

"Well, usually the ruling Sidiana picks someone to succeed her—but the House Councils have to approve the choice. Most of the time, the Sidiana will choose her daughter but not always. My mother was a cousin."

"Your mother chose you?"

"In this case, I'm the oldest daughter, so right now I'm the heir. But if I do something utterly disgraceful or don't mind my lessons, or the House Council doesn't trust me, then someone else will rule."

"What would you do then?" I asked, mystified. I knew enough of the royal houses of Jayasita to know that such a suggestion would lead to exile or imprisonment at the least—but mostly likely to a knife in the dark.

"Oh, I wouldn't like it much, I admit that. They've been training me to be Sidiana since I was a child and, if I have to undergo all the suffering, at least I want to have some of the privileges. But I would find some other way to live. Marry into one of the trading Houses and run that, I suppose. Or join the Asezati and devote my life to learning." She laughed at that then sobered. "I would go, if they asked me. That's the most important thing they teach you about being a Sidiana. What you want doesn't really matter. You do what you do for the good of the city."

I nodded, though I did not really understand it. Later, in the lessons I learned from the Asezati, I understood it better. It grew from the Euskalans peculiar history of exile, struggle and rebirth—and from the bargain they had made to survive. Women ruled in Lushan but no one ruled absolutely. The theory was that only the best, wisest and most honourable would become Sidiana. It did not always work, and bred everything from vicious political infighting to several violent coups, but I can truthfully say that, during my time here, it has been everything that the founders hoped it would be. Sarit would have made them proud, for she had learned her lessons well. Raziel even more so, I think, for she had to learn that those lessons were more than words.

We left the sea and sailed up the Mekarasi river, until the cataracts made travel on water impossible. From there, the royal party went on horseback. I had never ridden a horse before, which meant a good deal of amusement for the others and a great deal of pain for me. By the time we crossed the rich plain of Srihanese, my thighs had stopped hurting and I had learned several new Euskalan curses. The mountains waited for us at the other end of the plain, always seeming to be only a day or so away. It took us a month to cross, partially because Sarit had to stop to pay her respects to the local rulers and once to visit a group of Euskalan engineers hired to build an aqueduct for the Maraj. They were all men, which surprised me, much as the fact that most of Sarit's guard were women had earlier astonished me. I later learned that the city's wealth, so necessary for its survival, sprang from the trading skill of its women and the architectural prowess of its men. A Euskalan-built aqueduct would stand a thousand years, they said, and a Euskalan-built fortress would never fall. Certainly, Lushan never had—at least not since the fall of the Aygaresh, the original and reputedly non-human builders, who had vanished uncounted years before and left it to turn slowly to a ruin that the Euskalans reclaimed.

We reached the mountains as the autumn did and our pace was quicker then, for there was some fear the high passes might close if we delayed.

I had never seen anything like the mountains. At first, they disturbed me, for all their beauty. I disliked being cold all the time, which I was, despite the layers of clothing Sarit lent to me. I felt trapped by the great bulks surrounding us—I could not see enough of the sky and it made me claustrophobic. The white peaks looked pure and remote and alien, a place that mortals were not supposed to trespass, the home of gods who might punish those who dared to do so. As we climbed, it seemed the weight of the mountains towering above me lay on my chest, crushing the breath from my body. It was just the mountain sickness, Sarit assured me. All newcomers felt that way in the beginning but it would pass. It did, but it took so long that some of the others in the party were making plans for how to leave me. Some people never could learn to live that high and they feared I was one of them.

We climbed the last high pass and began the journey down to the plateau. The scree slopes gave way to scrubby pines, fading grasses, and even the last, lingering blossoms of glossy rhododendrons. There were villages here and the people came out to watch our party pass and wave to Sarit. They were darker than she, most of them Newari, the original people of these mountains. They owed some fealty to the Euskalans in the city but it had very little impact on their daily lives, Sarit told me. Trade with the city had enriched them and, naturally enough, over the generations the two groups had intermarried, though the villages tended to remain inhabited mostly by Newari. "Some Euskalan men go to live with their wives in the villages," Sarit told me with a grin, "but men who marry Euskalan women come to live in the city."

"Why?"

"Because Euskalan women don't like to be told what to do," answered Duhoth, one of the soldiers who rode with us. He made me nervous, because he was male, and large, and young, and passably attractive. I gathered from the guard gossip I overhead that he had dallied with more than one serving girl on the journey.

Sarit laughed. "Neither do Euskalan men," she pointed out.

"Whatever you say, Sidi," he replied with an extravagant bow, quite a feat on horseback.

We stayed overnight in one of the villages, hosted by the mayor and given his best bedrooms, while he and his family stayed elsewhere. The next day, Sarit promised, we would come to Lushan.

We followed the river that ran bright and cold down the centre of the plateau. It was early afternoon before we reached the far end and we turned left, into the last half-hidden spur of the valley. At first, the city nestled at the end of it was nothing more than a smudge against the mountains. As we grew closer, it gradually took shape in the clear air, turning from the suggestion of a shape to a collection of colours to a city before my eyes.

Even from far away, I could see the white walls of the palace, bright beneath the sun. Against the gleam, the deep windows made regular patterns, the only ornaments on the smooth planes of the walls, which Sarit told me rose nine stories from their lowest point to their highest. In the centre of the wide wings, the building that held the great hall was red. As we drew closer, I could see that the colours interpenetrated, white banding the top of the red hall, red topping the sloping white walls.

The palace stood on a treeless hill. The bare rock was furred with rusty moss and a soft furze of stubborn grasses. Between the city and the palace ran the zigzag road carved into the side of the hill. Where it was not lined with buildings, it was edged in walls the same white as the palace. Flags fluttered everywhere, bright red and purple and yellow. The dark symmetry of the palace windows were curtained in the same hues. On the roof, I could see gold gleaming on the endless round knobs that crowned the palace.

Closer still, I noticed a darkness at the heart of the white walls and the red brick. When we reached the city, I saw that the lintels of the doors and windows were all touched with iron, sometimes carved into shapes, sometimes plain and unadorned. At the great gate to the city, the weight of all of it seemed to be gathered. The gates there, soaring above the road, were banded and surrounded by iron. I realized that to enter the heart of Lushan, one must always walk over and under iron.

One must always pass the test.

CHAPTER 4

Lilit

Lilit did not tell her mother until the night before the caravan left for the fair.

She waited until Amaris was alone in her office, just before the nighttime meal. Amaris was studying her ledgers as usual, no doubt in preparation for the departure of House Kerias's own delegation the next day. Teras was going, and two other cousins, and her aunts Bizat and Sitra. With them went the fruits of twelve months of carefully managed trade, the goods of Lushan bartered in the far-off cities of the south for the treasures that might strike their customers' capricious fancies. The rest of what House Kerias had laboured all year to acquire had already gone to the palace to be tallied and included in the tribute with which the Euskalans bought their sanctuary.

Lilit hovered in the door a moment and then, when her mother looked up, ventured far enough into the office to stand behind the one chair. "Is everything ready?" she asked. Her mother nodded, her expression neutral. *She thinks I will ask her again*, Lilit thought, *and she is preparing herself to refuse me again.* She took a deep breath and committed herself. "I've come to tell you I'm going to the fair this year. With the Austers."

For a moment, Lilit thought she saw a flash of fear in her mother's eyes, then it was gone, replaced by cold fury. "I do not give you leave."

"I do not require it. I am apprenticed to them, not you."

"I forbid it."

"You cannot, not this time."

"You cannot go."

"Mother, I am going. You cannot stop me—and I don't understand why you ever wanted to."

"And you do not understand anything about it. The fair is—" she stopped and Lilit saw her hands were shaking "—the fair is not for us."

"Why not?" Lilit asked, for this was the first time anyone inside the family or without had suggested her foreign Deshinivi blood would deny her anything.

"We are not Euskalan."

"I am. I am as much Euskalan as Deshinivi."

"Lilit, trust me. I am your mother. I know what is best for you, and for this House. I know you want to go but trust me. Wait a year or two." Lilit frowned; her mother rarely asked her for anything she could command instead. *She cannot command this*, she thought, *and so she is reduced to asking.* For a moment, the beseeching look on her mother's face almost swayed her.

"The Austers are counting on me," she said firmly. "I don't need your permission, Mother. I'm telling you out of courtesy, that is all." She managed a smile. "You don't have to worry—I've heard the lectures a dozen times. I'll be careful." Surely this was enough, the rituals of refusal and rebellion enacted, and her mother would surrender and wave her away. Her punishment would be the chill she knew so well and that was all.

"And if I said that if you went with the Austers, then to the Austers you belong, from this day on?" Amaris asked at last.

"Then I would say that's not your choice, but the decision of the House Head."

"It would be the decision of your mother."

"Is that the price? If I go, you'll renounce me?"

The silence stretched, colder than the air, and then Amaris shook her head. "No. Go to the fair and have done with it."

"Thank you," Lilit said and retreated quickly, before her mother could change her mind. In the hallway, as she hurried to the great dining hall, she wondered what she would have done if her mother had held to the threat to banish her. Would she have had the nerve to call her bluff? For bluff was what it was, at least until Amaris became House Head. At least as far as the official House was concerned. *As far as Amaris's heart . . . I was banished from that long ago*, Lilit thought. *And I do not even know why.*

There was a time, she remembered, when she had thought her mother's love the sure and steady centre of the world. There were the three of them, mother, father and Lilit, a small knot of shared life in the larger grain of House Kerias. Then five years ago, her father had moved out of the rooms they shared and claimed back his old place. There were no harsh words or raised voices, at least in Lilit's presence. Hendren was still Amaris's husband, still Lilit's father. Husband and wife might meet a dozen times a day in the Kerias compound; they were as polite and considerate of each other as brother and sister might be.

With only the two of them left, Lilit realized how much of the warmth of the little suite of rooms had come from Hendren. Amaris laughed less and found fault more. To Lilit's young eyes, she changed from the mother she knew to the woman she was at Great-Aunt Teresine's: a sharp-tongued stranger. For the first time, she glimpsed the depth of the ambition that drove her mother—to become House Kerias. She also wanted Lilit to be House Head in her turn and Lilit had only to have the briefest intimation of that to reject it utterly. For a time, their contest of wills shook the walls with shouts or froze them with icy silences. In the end, Lilit petitioned for a room elsewhere in the compound and received it. Her mother gave up their suite to a cousin expecting her first child, and found another place, conveniently closer to Great-Aunt Ursul.

You cannot blame me for being stubborn, Lilit thought to the memory of her mother's cold gaze, as she heard the bustle and clatter of the assembled inhabitants of House Kerias about to sit down for the feast before the fair. *I come by it honestly, your legacy as much as my skin and my hair.*

The dining room was warm from the fires of the kitchen beyond and the bodies settled around those tables. Hangings of felted wool lined the walls, the red and purple knotted crest of Kerias bright against the grey stone and the smoke-darkened ceiling. There was a ranking to the seating but it was a subtle and flexible one. Great-Aunt Ursul presided at the head table, attended by her sisters and the elder sisters-in-house. Amaris usually sat there, as well. The companions of the aunts, husbands or otherwise, sometimes joined them, but custom did not require it. They were often found at their own table along the wall. The next generation of sisters and their children, Lilit's cousins, shifted and shuffled among the rest of the tables. One of the centre tables was reserved for the youngest, who were old enough to eat unattended and happy to be free to make mischief without an adult on either side.

Lilit saw her father sitting with some of the other men and almost went to join him, despite the unspoken custom that kept that table to one gender. But her mother would arrive eventually and she decided she had best not offer her any more provocation for one evening. There was a spare cushion beside Teril, who had apparently been abandoned by Teras for the company of the other chosen. Her cousin saw her eyeing the empty space and waved her over. "Sit down," she urged. "You look worse than you did the other morning."

"I was talking to my mother," Lilit admitted and Teril laughed.

"I suspect I look the same after I've been talking to Aunt Amaris, too. Or after she's been talking to me, which she mostly does to lecture me about something I've done wrong. Luckily, I've had practice with my own mother."

"Aunt Charlot? I don't think I've ever heard her even raise her voice," Lilit protested, glancing at the broad, cheerful face of Teril's mother as she sat at the head table.

"You're not her daughter," Teril replied. "And she doesn't have to raise her voice. She just gives you a sad look and shakes her head."

"My father is the one who does that. Then he gets this disappointed look in his eyes and you want to go out and climb the Mother Mountain or something equally dramatic to prove you are worthy of his blood." Lilit looked over at her father and sighed. She suspected she would be treated to a look of considerable disappointment when she told him about the fair. Then again, he had carefully avoided voicing an opinion on the matter one way or another.

A movement from the front of the room caught her eye and she saw her mother, her plain working coat replaced with her fur-trimmed brocade, slip into her place at the head table. With House Kerias now complete, the servants began to troop in with the meal. Covered bowls of rice appeared on each table, followed by baskets of flatbread, pots of curried meats and vegetables, sauces golden with saffron. A collective sigh echoed in the room as the lids came off and the scents of the spices rose into the air.

Lilit heard the scrape of spoons on porcelain from the children's table behind her, then Great-Aunt Ursul rose and clapped her hands. "Tonight," she began, "we celebrate the bounty of the summer. We eat what the earth has given us and what our work has brought to us from all the lands below. But first, we must remember those who came before us, who brought us from the shadow of war and the end of the empire. We must remember those who suffered and starved and wandered, driven here to the roof of the world. We must remember how they came to this city, this last refuge, and the price they paid for it. Tomorrow, our House joins the others, joins our Sidiana, in paying this price. Sometimes there are mutterings that it is too high." There was a nervous cough and a whispered shush. "We all muttered such things, especially when we were young and had not been to the fair. Your children will likely mutter them in their turn. But here is the truth; the price is the price. This House, House Kerias, has always met it. This House will always meet it. Those who came before us had a terrible choice to make. When you chosen ones go to the fair tomorrow, especially those of you who go for the first time, ask yourself: what would you have done? What better deal would you have made?"

In the silence, she looked around the room at it seemed as if her eyes commanded all the others to meet them and await her judgement. At last, she shifted the goblet of water from the table before her. "We drink this water in memory of the ancestors, who had nothing else to drink, and whose wisdom brought us wine."

"To the ancestors," Lilit said, along with the assembled souls of House Kerias.

"We break this bread in memory of the ancestors, who had nothing else to eat, and whose wisdom brought us this feast."

"To the ancestors." Despite the suggestion of deprivation, the bread was warm and tasty; House Kerias saw no point in wasting resources making bad bread.

"Tomorrow, when you go to the fair, be as wise as they were. Be as careful as they were. Come back to us, over the hills and under the iron, and be home."

"Over the hills and under the iron," the Kerias aunts and uncles, daughters and sons, echoed. Lilit felt a small hollow ache inside. The words were not for her, not truly. Across the city, the Auster aunts and uncles, daughters and sons, said the same words and they were not for her either. She set down her cup of water and sighed. She would be wise. She would be careful. And she would come back, even if she could not come home.

"Lilit," Teril said impatiently and her voice jerked Lilit from her thoughts. "Pass the bread while it's still hot."

The food was good, the wine sweet, and the buzz of family voices echoed warm and embracing around the room. Lilit resolved to enjoy it, kept her eyes from the head table, and did. She did not tell Teril about going to the fair, though she longed to pry every last scrap of information from her cousin. She needed to tell her father first and did not want him to hear it from some well-meaning aunt before she could speak to him.

Her chance came at last, as the celebrations began to wind down. The little group of family musicians were arguing about the next tune to play and the servants were insisting there was no more apple pudding in the kitchen, no matter who was hungry. The children had been herded off to bed some hours earlier and now the chosen fair-goers were being given warning looks, as if they too were children up past their bedtime. In sympathy, Great-Aunt Ursul told the musicians to put away their instruments and the servants to consider the night done.

Lilit saw Hendren rise from his seat, bid his brothers and brothers-in-house goodnight and then start for the door. She followed, took the back stairway two steps at a time (a manoeuvre that left her panting in the hallway for a moment) and found him lighting the lamps in his little reading room. "So, little one, what can I do for you?" her father asked, settling onto the long padded bench that lined one wall. She sat down beside him.

"I wanted to tell you myself. I am going to the fair tomorrow." He looked surprised. "Not with Kerias. With the Austers."

"Ah. Have you told your mother?"

"Tonight," Lilit admitted and caught his faint smile.

"What did she say?"

"She was angry—but she cannot forbid it." She gave him a careful glance. "I thought for a moment she might banish me."

"She would not, not ever," he assured her. "There are things—this is an important time for her. You must remember that and be—" words left him again and one hand waved meaninglessly, as if the answer were in the air and needed to be caught "—patient," he finished at last.

Lilit thought all the patience had already been on her side, but she did not say it. She remembered her mother's voice: "The fair is not for us." Her father had never said such a thing, not even when he had upheld Amaris's earlier bans, and he was the House's expert on the fey. She knew the fair was not only for pure-blood Euskalans; there was hardly a family in the city that would qualify if that was the case. Great-Aunt Ursul herself looked a good deal more like a Newari tribeswoman than a Euskalan House Head. But the Newari had lived in the mountains for generations—their stories even held that they had seen the last Aygaresh builders of the city—

so perhaps the fey were accustomed to them.

"She said the fair was not for me, because I am not Euskalan," she said. "Because she is Deshinivi."

"That is ridiculous," Hendren said.

"But mother has never gone to the fair, has she?"

"She went once, before you were born. It did her no harm." His voice was calm but she thought she saw a shadow lie briefly across his face, a darkness that had no source in the flicker of the lamp.

"Why doesn't she go?"

"She does not like to travel." Hendren touched her cheek gently. "Now that you have finally found a way to go, are you afraid?" Lilit shook her head then nodded then shrugged. Her father laughed. "That's as it should be. It's not without its risk, this thing we must do. But it is something I cannot imagine having missed. Some people even learn to like it, or so I've heard said," he added with a smile. "So go, with my blessings at least."

"That is more than enough," Lilit said and when he held out his arms, went into them as if she were still a child.

As she went to leave, a sudden thought made her turn at the door. "Was Great-Aunt Teresine one of the ones who liked it? She used to go all the time, with Sarit and Raziel, didn't she?"

"That is something, little one, you would have to ask her," her father said and the shadow lay in his voice this time.

Lilit nodded and closed the door behind her. She had asked her great-aunt about her experiences at the fair, more than once, but Teresine would never answer. She sighed and walked towards her room. Tomorrow morning it would not matter, she thought. Whatever her great-aunt had done and her mother had refused could not stop her. Tomorrow she would go to the fair and discover for herself the salvation and the curse of the Euskalans.

CHAPTER 5

Teresine

At first, I almost hated Lushan. I would not have traded it for the life I left behind, of course, but I had no love for it.

It was cold, even when the sun was highest in the sky. It smelled strange, the fragrance of tallow candles, incense and dung fires clinging to everything, underlying the perfumes of wet wool and human flesh. Inside the palace, the rooms were full of a gloom that held none of the comfort it did in Deshiniva, where it was a welcome respite from the heat. Even the sunlight was strange, a bright white light that turned shadows stark and hard-edged.

I had grown accustomed to the Euskalans from the journey but an entire city of foreigners was altogether more daunting. The people in the streets ranged from the Newari, almost as dark as I was, to the golden grace of Sarit's seemingly endless stream of relatives. All of them dressed in black wool, brightened by vivid sashes and embroidered hems and the flashing jangle of bangles, iron amulets and luck signs. Black felt hats shaded their eyes and they all, men and women alike, wore loose trousers beneath their robes. Similar attire was quickly acquired for me; I found it itchy but at least it kept me warm. I kept my old clothing though, the long skirt and short buttoned top in which I had escaped Jayasita. Sometimes I wore the top beneath my robes, for the soft feel of the thin cotton on my skin, for the feel of home.

That first day, entering the city, I felt none of that, of course. That came later, after the initial bewildering wonder of it had faded and the city was not a mysterious new world but the place I lived every day. It was not until much later that it became my home.

Before we reached the city proper, and the great iron gate that guarded it, we passed through a quarter of whitewashed buildings, their doors and shutters bright with complex painted designs that yielded at lintels and stoops to the inevitable iron charms. Some buildings appeared to be houses, others shops fronted with awnings and tables of goods. From other doors drifted the sounds of laughter and the clatter of dishes. The people we passed glanced at us without any overt sign of interest, though one or two bowed their heads as Sarit rode by.

I tried not to stare but Sarit caught my curious glances. "This area is rather more exciting at night," she said mischievously, leaning from her saddle towards me to keep her voice low. "They say all the most . . . interesting . . . bars are here. My older cousins were always giggling about it and then whispering in the most infuriating fashion when I came into the room."

"Here?" I echoed, looking around but seeing nothing but a demure matron selling peppers and a man drawing water from a well between two houses.

"It's outside the iron," Sarit replied, as if that explained it, but then we turned onto the road up to the gate and the chance had passed to ask her more. The guards at the gate recognized her and there were polite bows and genuine smiles as our group filed past them. This time, I gawked openly at the gate and the guards stared almost as openly at me. As we rode beneath the heavy iron lintel, I looked at Sarit and found her watching me. The relief that flared briefly in her eyes made me twist awkwardly in the saddle and gaze back at the gate again.

We were inside the iron now, I thought. I had understood enough of the story of the founding of the Euskalan city to realize the source of Sarit's relief. For all the trust she had shown me, for all the oaths I had taken, this was the only test that mattered. I was human enough to pass the iron gate. I did not want to think of what might have happened if, for some unimaginable reason, I had been unable to.

The streets on this side of the gate looked much the same as those "outside the iron," though they were more crowded, the buildings rising higher, the shadows lying longer. As we passed, people waved and Sarit waved back. The occasional head would bow but nothing more than that. I thought of the progress of the lords of Jayasita, with the peasants dropping to the ground to put their faces in the dirt, and was astounded all over again. At the top of the hill, we reached another open iron gate, this one more ornate than intimidating, and then we were in the palace itself.

The courtyard was crowded with people, who burst into cheers as we appeared. They were on us in a rush, hands reaching for the reins, my travel companions tumbling off their horses to be swept up into the embraces of husbands, wives, lovers, mothers, and children. I sat still, overwhelmed, suddenly alone, as a broad-hipped, broad-shouldered woman with a crown of silver-shot blonde hair enfolded Sarit in her arms. I closed my eyes and felt something in my heart crack. I would never feel my mother's arms around me again. I knew I should not want to, should resent the betrayal, knowing or otherwise, my mother had committed but the longing was deeper than reason. It was like a bone-deep ache, a yearning no more deniable than hunger or thirst or weariness. It made me want to weep, which I had not done since the first dreadful night in Jayasita. It was my first lesson in the treacherous needs of the heart.

"Teresine. Teresine." I opened my eyes and Sarit was standing beside me, grinning, her eyes wet with tears. "This is my mother, Kelci. Mother, this is Teresine."

The woman smiled. I saw Sarit in that smile and in the spread of her cheekbones. That gave me some courage, enough to clamber awkwardly down from my horse. "Sidiana," I said, remembering the title, and began to sink into the obeisance I had learned in Jayasita but caught myself in time to turn it into a bow.

"Teresine. Welcome to our city."

"Thank you, Sidiana." Despite her smiles, I could not look at her or meet her eyes. I stood with my head bent, managed to answer the one or two questions she asked me and was grateful when her attention returned to her prodigal daughter.

Sarit introduced me to dozens of people in the crowded courtyard but their names washed over me and out of my memory in the same moment. The only one I remembered was the toddler who slithered through the crowd to cling to her leg; her sister, Raziel.

Finally, we were free to enter the great palace. I had passed some of the time in the courtyard staring up at the rise of the four-storey whitewashed walls, patterned with red brick and the heavy black lintels of the windows. The palace had looked much larger on our approach to the city, I thought, then realized we had curved around behind it on our journey up the twisting streets and so had entered from the side that faced the great mountain. Built as it was on a hill, the face that presided over the city itself was nine stories high.

COLD HILLSIDE

I expected that the Sidiana and her family would have rooms at the top of the great building but Sarit led me down into the lower palace instead. A laughing entourage of travellers and family drifted in our wake, and Raziel had been hefted briefly into her sister's arms. Amid the bustle, I managed to ask the question. Sarit laughed. "You'd think so, wouldn't you? It would be more dramatic and the view is wonderful. But it's much warmer down here, especially in the winter. The upper chambers are for the treasury, the temple and the great hall. The barracks are at one end of the first floor and a kitchen at the other, then there are the offices of the administrators, then chambers for the council and other officials who live here, then we live on the next floor, then the nursery and school and then there's the library and audience chambers, which open onto the courtyard." She paused to deposit the protesting Raziel back onto her feet. "Sometimes in the summer we sleep on the top floor for the breeze but in the winter," she shivered theatrically, "you'll be grateful for a room against the mountain, with no windows for the wind to howl through."

I eyed her suspiciously. Sarit had heard me complain of the cold more than once and I knew she was not above teasing me on the subject. I thought the nights we had passed on the way to the city were more than cold enough for me.

Still, the room they found for me, down the hall from Sarit's in the corridor she and her cousins shared, seemed warm enough. It was small, with room only for a bed on a platform against one wall, a wooden chest of drawers with bright brass finishings and a screened corner for private ablutions. It was, as Sarit had promised, on the mountain side and so had no windows. After a quick set of directions Sarit was gone, promising someone would come with clothes for the feast.

"Rest," she said. "Because we won't get any tonight!"

So I was left alone in the little room. I closed the doors, grateful suddenly to be alone, and looked around. A bronze bowl of water had been left behind the screen, so I stripped off my travel-stained clothing and managed a quick, shivering wash. My pack was also there, borne by one of the entourage, and I scrounged for my cleanest clothes and dressed again. I looked in each of the drawers to discover they were empty of everything but a sweet, green smell that was oddly comforting. The thought of putting my scant cache of grubby belongings in there seemed faintly presumptuous.

On top of the chest was a little shrine; a statue in white stone of a woman, her face serene and remote, her hand raised in benediction, her sculpted robes flowing like water around the delicate points of her toes, and a small bronze smudge-pot with the lingering scent of incense. I had heard Sarit speak of her, the old goddess of the Euskalans, whose grace now lingered high on the sacred Mother Mountain that loomed over the city. "Jennon," I said experimentally, looking at that distant face, with its hint of a smile, and wondered if I was expected to worship her as well or if they thought I would keep my old Deshinivi gods. They did not know I did not pray to them either and had not since the night my slavery became absolute. I do not say I did not still believe in them; I did not have enough strength of mind to reject them completely. But they had abandoned me and so I abandoned them. Perhaps they deserved to have me pray to the Euskalan's white-faced goddess.

After a moment, I sat carefully on the bed and bounced experimentally. The mattress seemed thick and welcoming. I lay back for a moment, noticing the heavy felt draperies that framed it. When they were pulled, it would be like a nest, I thought.

The next thing I knew someone was knocking on the door; a servant to dress me in black wool and a scarlet and purple sash and escort me to the feast.

Despite everything I had seen, I was still surprised by the informality of the banquet to celebrate Sarit's return. The braziers and the bodies of the people squeezed around the long low tables generated enough heat for the Euskalans to shed their robes to reveal sleeveless tunics in a startling range of colours, from vivid orange to evening-hued blue. Kelci was in white and there were pearls in her ears and wrapped around her wrists, luminous in contrast to the iron rings and bracelets that every Euskalan wore.

There was little ceremony. Kelci spoke a few words of welcome to her daughter and those who had voyaged with her and then the travellers gratefully dove into the selection of covered dishes that made their way around the table. There were rapturous sighs and second helpings, as if somehow the food consumed in the days since we crossed the pass did not really count as their own. This feast meant they were truly home, it seemed.

Sarit took time from her own lip-smacking indulgence—and a steady stream of well-wishers stopping by to interrupt her gluttony—to point rather indiscreetly to various members of her mother's court. "That blonde woman with the coral cuff, that's Maudrian. She was the captain of the palace guard and is now on the council." I dared a much more careful glance; Maudrian looked grim and competent and I recalled Jayasita gossip about the Royal Guard with trepidation. It was not a great step from soldier to spymaster and killing in war was not much different from killing for expediency.

"The man beside Mother," Sarit went on, oblivious to the dark shift of my thoughts, "is Neith. He's her lover." That was another surprise. I knew Sarit's father had died some years earlier and her mother had not remarried. "He used to be a soldier himself, years ago, but he retired to his clanhouse and she met him in the market one day and that was that." If Maudrian still looked martial, Neith did not. He looked soft and settled and nothing to fear.

"Do you like him?" I asked.

"Well enough," Sarit said with a shrug. "He's smart and rather funny and doesn't try to tell me what to do, which is all one can really hope for." And a good deal better than the fortune many girls had with their mother's new husbands but I said nothing.

We were both surprised some hours later, when Neith materialized at my side. "The Sidiana wishes your company, Sidi Teresine," he said formally. I glanced at Sarit and saw the flicker of her eyes from the man to the thinning crowd in the room.

"I thought she had retired," she said and the man nodded.

"She has. She has asked to see our guest in her chamber."

Sarit shifted, as if to rise, and he shook his head. The faint trace of a frown shaped between her brows then vanished. "Go on," she said and touched my arm briefly. "I'll wait for you here." The touch terrified me, as did the gentle tone in her voice, though I think she meant both for comfort. She thought I was afraid; worse, she thought I had cause to be.

But I had no choice. I rose and followed him from the room. To my surprise, he led me up rather than down, through corridors where the flicker of oil lamps seemed to sink into the wooden walls, the soft, patterned carpets. A doorway glowed ahead of us and voices drifted from it, though I did not understand the words. When we stepped into the path laid by the light, Neith held out his hand to usher me into the room.

The Sidiana waited there, settled cross-legged on a dais. There were three other women there, seated on the low benches that lined each of the walls. Maudrian was there as well, her back to the wall beside the door.

"Ah, Teresine. Please come in." Kelci's voice was warm, devoid of any threat, but I knelt and put my forehead to the bright carpet, as I would have to any lady of Jayasita. It smelled of smoke and cold and a strange, alien musk. "Sit up, child. Please." I sat back onto my heels and looked at her. "My daughter speaks well of you."

"The Sidi Sarit is very kind." Oh, it was coming back to me now, the caution I had let slip a little during the ride north. I felt my fear ease; this was a game I knew how to play.

"She is," her mother agreed. "She says you stowed away aboard her ship." I nodded, uncertain what she wished to hear. "That showed considerable courage. Or desperation." She tilted her head a little and the light caught the broad planes of her face. She no longer looked soft and motherly, but as strong and solid as the mountain. "Where are you from?"

"Deshiniva, Sidiana."

"But not Jayasita."

"No, Sidiana. I was born north of the city, on the river."

"And your family? Are they living?"

"I believe so, Sidiana."

"Do you have brothers and sisters?"

"Four brothers and two sisters, if it please you, Sidiana."

"What does your family do, to live?"

"They are farmers. We were very poor, Sidiana." I admitted the last, to forestall further questions. I did not know what she wanted, or expected, but there were things I had no wish to say to anyone, least of all to this woman on whom my future depended.

"You did not go back there. You stowed away on my daughter's ship instead. Was that because your family was too poor?"

"I could not go back." I knew she wanted more but this was a miser's game; what she did not ask, I would not answer. The fewer words I said, the fewer I might have to regret. I would give her no ammunition to use against me but no lies in which to trap me.

"What were you doing in Jayasita?"

"I was working. I was . . ." I swallowed, for the smoke from the lamps seemed to clot in my throat and burn in my eyes. ". . . a slave."

"Which you did not wish to be."

"No, Sidiana."

"So you ran away and swam to my daughter's ship." I nodded and kept my eyes on the floor before me. The carpet was red and gold and indigo, the colours knotting and unknotting in sinuous rhythm. "Why that ship, of all that must have been in the harbour that night?"

I could answer this, for I had told Sarit already. "I saw it at the dock the day before. I saw the women sailors and the women soldiers. I saw them laughing. I thought . . . I thought they were the most beautiful people I had ever seen. I told myself I would go away on the ship or I would die."

"Your life in Jayasita must have been very hard, if you would choose death over it."

There was no question, I told myself. I do not have to answer. But I knew that she was asking and would ask again in words that left no doubt. I put my forehead to the floor and waited.

"Sit up," she said patiently and I had no choice but to obey. "Look at me." Her eyes were like Sarit's, a strange blue that was no more than a wash of colour around the pupil. It made their gazes similarly disconcerting. In Deshiniva, only blind people had eyes that were not dark. But the Sidiana was far from blind. "My daughter vouches for you but she is young and her heart, her goodwill, are not constrained. Mine are. There are those who think they might take this city—or its tribute—from us. On the ship, it was possible for those charged with the safety of my daughter to watch you. If we take you into the city, into our home, into our hearts, that will no longer be feasible. So I must know what I am being asked to shelter. Tell me what you ran from in Jayasita, that you feared death less."

I swallowed and tasted bile. I could feel my skin burning and knew it must be clear to her. If I wanted to stay in Lushan, I had no choice but to tell her the truth. I suppose I had always known that the safety, the happiness I had felt over the last month would bear a price and now I knew the coin required to buy it. To my own surprise, I even understood why she demanded it. Silk scratched and whispered to my right and I remembered the other women in the room, the man still waiting by the door. "I will tell you, Sidiana," I said hesitantly, "but must it be before all of them?"

She glanced at her companions but I did not risk it. I guessed their reluctance from the way her brows drew together. At last she nodded.

"Kelci," Maudrian protested.

"You stay. And Neith." She looked back at me. "What is said in this room goes no further," she promised, as the other women rose and left. I heard the soft thump of the door closing behind them and swallowed again.

I could not watch her while I spoke. I closed my eyes and told her what she wanted to know. I did not have the words in Euskalan; I used others, resorting to clumsy definitions. But she seemed to understand.

"Child," she said at last and I opened my eyes. Her face had changed again, softened, and in astonishment I saw the gleam of tears in her eyes. She leaned forward to put her hand against my cheek, her skin cold against its heat. "You are welcome to Lushan," she said and then there were tears in my eyes as well and I closed them as her touch vanished.

Neith took me back to the room where Sarit waited. She did not ask me what had happened. I suppose she took my presence for her mother's approval and that was enough for her.

Later, I realized it had been my first lesson in the necessities of power and the price that it exacted, on both the powerful and the powerless.

It would not be my last.

CHAPTER 6

Lilit

The next morning, Lilit was at the Auster compound before dawn. She was early, but some of the house-sisters were already up, having been deputized to get the horses from the stables outside the city. In the old days all the great Houses had included stables within their compounds but over the years that space had been claimed for human use. Now the only horses within the city belonged to the Sidiana and the royal household. The rest of the Houses kept their own stock outside the city or hired mounts from the stablemasters there. House Kerias prided themselves on taking only their own horses to the fair; the Austers considered horses a waste of good coin and hired theirs.

One of the Austers, the only one not grumbling at the early hour, was Toyve, who shared Lilit's apprentice duties in the workroom. "I'm off to get the horses," she said. "Come with me, before someone sees you, or you'll be stuck packing boxes. I could use a hand with them." She dropped her voice with a conspiratorial grin. "The other two they're sending with me left their wits in the bottom of the arrack jug last night."

Horses seemed preferable to packing and Lilit joined Toyve and the other sleepy-eyed young Austers on their way out to the stables. A trickle of torch-bearing apprentices from various Houses flowed down the streets and out the gate. The stables lay on the plain beside the shallow Lake Erdu, where the shaggy, stocky mountain horses could graze on the tough grass.

Lilit followed Toyve and the others into the low-walled compound and a scene of such chaos that she could not imagine how the caravan could possibly leave before the snows came, let alone that day. Stable urchins darted through the shadows in a manner that seemed determined only by which stablemaster was shouting the loudest. The servants of a dozen Houses jostled in the torchlight and a sea of horses jostled back, snorting discontentedly. Lilit saw Teras and two more of her cousins in a knot of animals, shaking their heads and yelling at the boys who tried to thrust reins into their hands.

"Hiya, out of my way, you lumps. I want better beasts than you," Toyve cried, pushing her way through the horses, and smacking the occasional equine rump. Lilit trailed after her, accepting the leads tossed her way until she was dragging three reluctant animals in her wake. To her astonishment, the madness settled itself surprisingly quickly and soon she was watching Toyve inspect the tack and hooves of a dozen suddenly quiescent horses.

The mountains were edged in pale light, the spaces between them brightening from black to grey, as they led the little herd back up through the city. Mounted, the journey went quicker and they were trotting into the Auster compound just as the grey became blue. The household was truly in motion now; carefully packed bags waiting to be strapped to the backs of the horses, last-minute instructions being traded, a line of children perched on the upper balconies, watching their elders with curious or envious eyes. Just like at home, Lilit thought as she stood to one side, and felt a pang of loneliness. High above the city, the great bells of the temple boomed; once, twice, three times. The bronze echoes faded and for a moment there was silence in the courtyard.

"Time to go," announced Dareh Auster. Toyve's clever, daunting mother had been leading the Auster delegation to the fair for ten years; Lilit had seen her pass at the head of the family procession in the years she had watched Kerias ride out without her.

There was a flurry of embraces, a tear or two. Lilit busied herself with collecting the horse assigned to her, a brown beast with a rolling eye and a sullen look she mistrusted. She found her place at the end of the little procession, beside Toyve and the other chosen Auster cousin, Colum. He gave her a brief smile and she remembered this was his first trip to the fair as well. The thought gave her a brief moment of comfort she clung to with more fierceness than it warranted. Then a great cheer went up from the household, the gates opened, and they were moving out onto the cobbled streets. Door and windows opened, neighbours leaned out to wave. Lilit heard voices rising from other streets and the great bells tolled again, to signify that the Sidiana and her party had begun their journey down the palace road.

COLD HILLSIDE

Toyve grinned madly at her and she felt her own smile, no doubt equally manic, spread across her face. She waved at the people who waved at her and felt suddenly light, as if she could lift from the back of the plodding horse and soar into the brightening sky like the hawks that circled above the city.

This is the best day of my life, Lilit thought dizzily, and the sun slipped clear of the horizon at last and touched the city with gold.

Five hours later, she was tired and thigh-sore and well and truly weighted to the earth once again. Even the view had paled. She had never seen the mountains that stretched ahead of them and, coming over the pass, she had been dazzled by their white-plumed heights and jagged shoulders. But in the last two hours they had not changed and it seemed she had reached the limit of her awe, or else the limit of her ability to enjoy that awe while her muscles cramped and the small of her back ached.

She twisted in the saddle to look at Toyve, who rode behind her in their single-file trek up a long, scree-sloped defile. "How much farther?" she asked and the other apprentice laughed.

"Two or three hours. We're making good time. Do you want to go back already?"

"No," Lilit replied, "but I think you got the thinnest horse."

"That's the privilege of the person who has to choose them," Toyve said. "Besides, you had the better choice at the tavern the other night."

It took a moment for Lilit to realize what she meant. When she remembered, she was grateful the shadow of her hat would likely hide her blush. "I should have saved my luck for horses," she said and Toyve's laugh rang again, turning heads up the line.

At last, they reached the site of the first night's camp. Lilit slid off her horse to discover her legs had turned to stiff, heavy stalks that seemed to have no connection to the rest of her body. She leaned on the saddle for a moment and watched the rest of the party. As at the stables, what appeared to be chaos soon shifted into bustling order. Most of the sixty members of the fair delegation had made this journey before, of course, from the armoured and helmed guards to the Sidiana herself. Each House was entitled to send six representatives; by custom, three of those places were reserved for the younger members of the household. The meadow in which they camped had been used for generations and the ground held the pattern of the past in firepits of stone. Tradition had established the placement of each House; the royal delegation in the centre, the others in a circle around them.

Through the crowd, Lilit caught a brief glimpse of her Aunt Alder, her hands sketching instructions to the circle of Kerias delegates. She felt another sharp stab of longing and then Colum appeared beside her. "It's easier to settle the horses if you actually let go of them," he said mildly and, embarrassed, she straightened and handed him the reins with as much dignity as she could muster. Toyve staggered past, one pack on each shoulder and Lilit hastened to help her.

An hour later, she looked around and discovered that all the work was done; the tents erected, the horses tethered, their precious cargo stowed away, the fire started and the tea already simmering. Dareh Auster emerged from one of the tents and paused to cast a critical eye over their section of the camp. At last she nodded and, when she was gone, Lilit and Toyve let out their breath in simultaneous sighs. "Now what happens?" Lilit asked.

"We make dinner, the aunts meet with the Sidiana, we clean up dinner, the aunts tell us to go to bed early, which we never do, then it's tomorrow before you blink and time to pack everything up again."

"And tomorrow we reach the fair?"

"If we get a good start, and the weather holds, we should be there just before dark. Then we work the next day to have everything ready. . . ." She paused dramatically.

"And then?" Lilit prompted, though she knew quite well what happened next. Or at least, what her father had told her happened.

"And then the fair begins," Toyve said with a grin. Lilit sighed and accepted that her fellow apprentice took far too much pleasure in her superior experience to do more than dole out information in tantalizing tidbits. "But right now, we'd better get the meal started."

After dinner, true to Toyve's prediction, the senior Austers made their way to the great royal tent in the centre of the camp. Once they were gone, Toyve set out in search of the best "fire, wine and company." After a few moments, she reappeared and signalled to Lilit. "House Silvas," she announced. "Leave Colum to finish up here and let's go."

"But—" Colum protested but his cousin waved her hand dismissively. "You're the youngest. You clean up and guard the tents." His look turned grimly mutinous and Toyve sighed. "One of us will come back later and you can have your turn."

"I can stay," Lilit said, unwilling to be the cause of dissension between the cousins. "The later turn will do."

Toyve gave her a curious look then shrugged. Colum grinned in gratitude and hurried off after his cousin. Lilit sighed and began to clean the dinner pot.

Dareh, Kay and Hazlet returned before Toyve did. Dareh looked around the neat campsite, nodded to Lilit, who sat beside the fire with the last cup of tea, and vanished into her tent. Hazlet, who had been Silvas before he married Kay, said "Go on then. Send one of the others back to keep watch."

"Send Toyve," Kay suggested with a smile.

Lilit nodded, bowed quickly, and set off through the camp. As she neared the Silvas firepit, it seemed that all the apprentices from the camp must be assembled there, crowded in a laughing circle around the fire. She wondered how the senior Silvases felt about the business. Maybe the Houses took turns, so that each had to suffer the exuberance of the junior members in equal measure.

She searched the firelit faces until she found Toyve and Colum, ensconced in the second row on the far side of the circle. With muttered apologies, she squeezed through the ranks and leaned down to tap Toyve's shoulder. "Here already?" the other apprentice asked.

"Your family is back. Kay sent me—and told me to send *you* back," Lilit said.

Toyve sighed loudly and surrendered her place. "Send Colum when he starts yawning," she instructed, ignoring her cousin's outraged look, and disappeared through the knot of apprentices behind them. Lilit looked around the circle curiously. The assembly appeared to be waiting for something to happen, though at the moment there was no more than chatter between neighbours and the occasional shouts across the circle. She saw Teras and the rest of Kerias to her right; her cousin caught her glance and waved.

"What happens now?" she asked Colum, who shrugged.

"So far, it's been mostly singing and stories," he said and offered her the wineskin tucked into his lap. It held wine, she discovered, but it seemed well-watered and she decided a mouthful or two would be safe enough.

It was altogether too easy to imagine an ignoble end to her first fair if she wasn't careful.

"What's next?" asked someone across the circle.

"Burden's Bane!"

"Wine in the River!"

"City in the Clouds!"

Lilit could not quite determine how the decision was made, or who made it, but a bright-eyed young woman with a lute was pushed forward, and, after a fumbling tuning of her instrument, she launched into the old ballad about the scholar Burden and the unanswerable riddle. Lilit had always heard there were a hundred verses, each more far-fetched than the last, but they only made it to twenty-five before the collective will sputtered out and the musician waved her lute in surrender and retreated to her place. She played "Wine in the River" next but stayed carefully seated.

When the echoes of it had died, someone called for a story. This elicited another flurry of suggestions, for both tales and tellers. At last, a dark-haired man rose and stepped into the circle. He paused to add another branch or two to the fire and then looked around the flicker-shadowed faces.

He told the story of the child Iskanden and the tiger, how the young emperor-to-be had tricked his way out of the beast's claws and come home dragging its skin. Ten years later he had worn the skin as a cloak over his armour as he conquered the known world.

"But that is the old world. The great cities are gone, and the armies, and the riches of far-off Euskalan. So what story should we tell of the new world?"

"Anish and the North Wind," someone suggested.

"The Drunken Monk!"

"Tam and Jazeret."

"That's an old story, Vash," a girl objected.

"But it's a good one. And it's got—"A cry of warning went up from the crowd and the apprentice stopped himself. It was considered bad luck to say the name of the fey on the way to the fair. "—*them* in it."

"Tam and Jazeret it shall be then," Vash agreed to a ragged cheer. The woman beside Lilit made a faint sound of protest and Lilit could not help her sideways glance. The woman returned it, shaking her head in reluctant surrender, but said nothing.

COLD HILLSIDE

"Once, in the place not here and a time not now," Vash began and the chatter around the circle died, "there was a girl named Jazeret, who lived in a land that touched the borders of *their* realm. The people who lived there were mostly accustomed to it, and took all sensible precautions, but the reputation of the place was such that most folk from other lands avoided it. So when the news came that a troupe of entertainers were coming to the village, well, everyone for miles around resolved to make the trip to town. Jazeret's father, who did not trust towns, refused permission for her to go. She begged and wheedled and cajoled but all in vain. She was forced to listen to her friends tell stories about the tents going up and the show that would be put on and the treats to be purchased and know that this would all happen without her. When, at last, the night of the great event came, she was resolved to be there. So she told her mother she was going to look for mushrooms in the woods and, once out of sight of the house, ran down the road towards the town.

"Now the town was some distance away and Jazeret could hardly run all that way, so it was twilight and she was footsore and tired by the time she rounded the last bend in the road. There, she stood still, for she could hear the music and laughter from the village green, and see the great white tent glowing in the moonlight. It was so beautiful that she found her strength again and ran the rest of the way into town.

"The green was crowded with people. They were a smiling, laughing, joyous whirlpool that sucked her in and spun her round through all the delights of the fair; the apples coated in syrup, the fortune-teller who promised love for a coin, the jugglers and acrobats. Then she was whirled into the tent and the greatest wonders of all: the beautiful, foreign women who stood on the backs of white horses as they pranced around the ring, the lithe and graceful men who leapt and twisted from ropes, the sinuous, eerie twisting of the contortionist. In the end, Jazeret was breathless with enchantment.

"Outside, in the cool evening air, her mind was still awhirl with colour and spectacle. With all that dazzle in her eyes, she did not see the young man until she stumbled into him. Then she did—and he was dazzling too. 'Hello,' he said. 'My name is Tam.'

"Love can strike like lightning, so they say, and it struck Jazeret right then and there. It struck Tam, too, for lightning, while not always fair, is sometimes kind. Being young, and lightning-struck, they drifted through the rest of the fair in a dream and drifted into the darkness as the townspeople slipped home to their beds and the troupe closed the curtains on their gaiety. In the darkness, they pledged their love and sealed it and made the vows that lovers do, when lightning strikes them.

"But in the hour before the dawn, when it was still night but only barely, Tam told her that he could not stay. She wept and begged and cursed him. 'What can I do to hold you here?' she asked.

"'I would stay, if I had will in this. But I do not. For I must be home before dawn or face my lady's wrath.'

"'And who is your lady,' Jazeret asked angrily, 'that you must fear her wrath? Who is she that you love more than me?'

"'Not more than you,' he promised. 'But I am bound and I must go.'

"'When will I see you again?'

"'Never,' he said and turned away. But he turned back and dropped to his knees beside her and whispered, 'Be at the crossroads as the dawn comes. If your love is true, then claim me.'

"Then he was gone and Jazeret sat alone and thought on what he had said.

"At dawn, she was at the crossroads, sitting on a log by the side of the road. At the first touch of light in the eastern sky, she heard bells and horses' hooves. The air was full of perfume, sweet and cloying, and she was suddenly afraid.

"They came out of the east, riding away from the dawn. She saw the foreign women and the graceful men and the slant-eyed contortionist. In the centre of them was a bone-white horse and, on its back, a woman it hurt Jazeret's eyes to look upon. Behind her, on a horse as black as night, was Tam.

"*I cannot*, she thought, as they drew closer.

"But when they drew near, she stepped onto the road. No heads turned, no horses slowed. Jazeret breathed, the air hot and burning in her mouth, and waited for Tam. When he passed, she put her hand on his ankle and said, in a loud, trembling voice, 'I claim you.'

"There were no bells then but thunder and the world went black around her and the perfume changed to the scent of carrion. 'If you claim,' said a voice as cold as ice, 'you must hold.'

"Jazeret gripped Tam's ankle in both hands. 'I will hold.'

"The shape in her hands changed, no longer cloth and flesh but cold scales and heavy muscle. Something hissed in her face but she did not let go. Then her hands were full of fur and claws and a roar rocked her backwards but she did not let go. Feathers and thorns and fire all shaped themselves in her grip. She felt as if her skin were melting, her bones breaking.

"But she did not let go.

"At last, the cold voice said, 'Enough.' Then the thing in her hands was another human hand and she opened her eyes to see Tam's face. 'Have him, if you will. Though wanting is always better.'

"The voice echoed for a moment then was gone. The sun broke over the horizon and Jazeret saw that the road was empty but for her and Tam.

"And there they lived till the end of their days, in the land on the border, in the place that is not here and a time that is not now."

With the final, traditional phrase, Vash bowed to the assembly. As the cheers arose, Lilit heard the woman beside her snort in disgust.

"Didn't you like it?" she asked, glancing at her neighbor, a woman a few years her senior.

"Oh, Vash tells it well enough," the woman said, gathering herself up to leave. "But the ending's wrong."

"Why?"

The woman looked at her. "Because it's happy." She read Lilit's confusion on her face. "Don't they teach you children anything anymore? With them, there are no happy endings."

CHAPTER 7

Teresine

If this were a tale, having passed the Sidiana's test, I would have been welcomed into the heart of Lushan without the least tears or trouble. This being life, it did not happen precisely in that fashion.

Most of the Euskalans treated me with a casual acceptance that excused my errors with their language and my months-long tendency to get lost in the labyrinthine streets. Later, when it became apparent that Sarit intended to place me firmly within the circle of her influence, some grew kinder and others crueller. To my surprise, the instincts honed during my time in slavery in Jayasita proved very useful. I could generally tell who was genuinely friendly and who was not. The court, like all courts, seethed with intrigues over everything from the succession to who Kelci invited to dinner.

At first, it seemed like my life in the palace was nothing but work. No one in my village had ever been expected to learn anything but how to farm and fish, how to cook and bear children. I did not know how to read or write my native tongue—what use would it have been to teach me, after all? But I was expected to learn to do both things in the Euskalan language, and so spend a good portion of each day with children half my age, crouched over a slate board, drawing the sharp scratches of the Euskalan letters or using their complicated numbering system to calculate barrels of wheat received or sheep breeding in a meadow. At least for the other things I was somehow expected to master—Euskalan history, the intricacies of politics and economics—I was allowed to sit with Sarit and her cousins. At first, those classes were nothing but a blur of unknown names involved in incomprehensible actions but gradually they too began to make sense.

After a year, I was allowed to abandon my young classmates and spend all my time with my contemporaries. To my surprise, I actually missed the children, who at least were honest in their friendship or enmity, unlike some of Sarit's cousins. (I gradually came to understand they weren't all children of Kelci's brothers and sisters but that "cousin" was the term used to denote anyone who belonged to the Euskalan extended households. I, of course, was never a cousin.) As Sarit had told me on the journey north, in theory any one of them could be named the next Sidiana. The rest would form the core of her counsellors. Therefore they were educated together, a group of girls and boys between the ages of fourteen and twenty, and forged a bond comprised of equal parts of friendly—and not so friendly—competition and co-operation.

Into this complicated world, Sarit cast me and abandoned me. Or so it seemed to me, that first long winter. She was there, of course, and we spent hours in each other's company. But she seemed never to see the petty cruelties or cuts I endured. The taunts I learned to ignore impassively, the challenges I discovered how to defuse by being better than my challengers.

Some years later, I asked her about it. "I knew," she said. "Of course I knew. I know you used to cry sometimes, in the night. I did, too, because I could not help you."

"Why couldn't you?" I asked, though I already knew.

"Because my mother told me I should not. She saw more clearly than I did what you might be to me—the one person in the world I could trust above all others. I think she also saw what you might be in yourself, for yourself. And she made me see that you could not become any of those things if I interfered. You had to earn the respect of my cousins, so they would see it was your own virtue—and not my favour—that gave you your place. And it worked."

I did not argue with her, for she was mostly right, if not about my own virtue then about the situation. If I was destined by my name and my skin and my accent to always be not quite Euskalan, she could not change that, not by stratagems or fiat or the force of her considerable will. But it reminded me again of what I had learned from her mother on my first night in Lushan; that the things that made great Sidianas made uncomfortable friends.

Yet she was my friend, for all that. I have made it sound grim and miserable, my first year in the city, and it was not always so. I remember the first days of winter, when the snow still delighted me, and we flew on wooden sleds down the hills by the lake, our shrieks of laughter rising to the sky. Later, she took me skating and the metal blades sang across the black ice. She showed me the hot springs beneath the palace, the source of the warm water that flowed from the miraculous taps in the bathing chambers. More than one chilly night, we'd huddle in the shelter of her room or mine and talk about the lives we would make for ourselves. Her certainty balanced my apprehension, my fear of believing in any future at all when only months ago I had dreaded the thought of one. In time, I came to believe that in this cold, new world, I might become anything I chose.

Power in Lushan was an intricate dance between the palace and the great mercantile Houses, between the Sidiana and her advisors. Beyond the inner core of the Sidiana's counsellors, the House Council was the most powerful force in the city. Nominated by the Houses, confirmed by the Sidiana, the ten women and men (though they were mostly women in all the years I knew) were vital to the management of the tribute and the running of the city.

The decisions of both levels were administered by the palace bureaucracy, which drew its leaders from the royal cousins and the children of the Houses. The most favoured of these were trained in the temple by the Asezati. Before the fall of their long-ago, far-away empire, the Euskalans who had founded Lushan had been the core of a university. The nature of their bargain with the fey had forced them to master other disciplines but what they had been lingered on in the Asezati. They occupied one wing of the temple of Jennon at the base of the palace hill and they had trained generations of High Priestesses, poets, philosophers, ministers of state and the favoured daughters and sons of the city.

Sarit planned that I would learn from them, pass through their tempering fire, and come back to her, sharpened and honed and ready to serve.

I planned to survive them, because that was the price of being what she wanted me to be.

CHAPTER 8

Lilit

It all went very much as Toyve had said; they went to bed much too late, the aunts woke them much too early, and they were travelling again, bleary-eyed and subdued, shortly after dawn. Lilit was certain her mount had grown wider and lost what little flesh lay over its sharp spine during the night and wondered if, rather than worrying about persuading her mother to let her go on the journey, she should have been spending her time practising her riding.

Their journey took them on a winding path around the shoulder of the snow-capped mountain, up a trail so steep they were obliged to dismount and lead the horses, and then out onto a plateau where, improbably, some remnant of summer seemed to linger. The grass here was still green and blue mountain poppies still blossomed with stubborn vigor. Lilit shaded her eyes and looked along the valley to see the crevasse that split it in two, a sharp, jagged crack in the earth that ran from one side to the other.

Lilit felt her breath catch and forgot about the pain in her thighs. It was real, she thought dizzily, it was all real. Tomorrow, on the far side of that gorge, she would finally see for herself the thing her cousins gossiped about and her mother had denied her.

But between this moment and that there was, as Toyve had promised, a great deal of work to do.

They arrived at the edge of the gorge as the sun touched the edge of the mountains. The night went much as the previous one had, but the mood at the apprentice fire was more subdued and ended much earlier. No one wanted to face the day of the fair—or their House Heads—the worse for drink.

Despite her doubt that she could sleep on the night before the fair itself, Lilit did not wake until she heard the royal horn summoning the

Euskalans to assemble. She and Toyve scrambled up from their huddle of blankets and donned their robes, shivering in the raw morning air. Muttering curses, they took turns over the pan of water, breaking the thin layer of ice that covered it, and washed their faces. "Mother," Toyve gasped as they headed for the door. "Our iron. We have to take off our iron."

They did so, the haste of it mitigating the strangeness somewhat. Still, Lilit's wrists and fingers felt naked without her bracelet and rings, her ears light and fragile without earrings. "Shoes," Toyve reminded her and they dug in their packs for their special soft-soled shoes. They felt like house-shoes on her feet, insubstantial and cold. Hats jammed over hastily brushed hair, they dashed from the tent.

The Auster delegation trooped with the rest of the camp to the edge of the gorge, Lilit eager for her first glimpse of what lay on the other side

Where there had only been an empty plain the night before, she could see a great pavilion topped with the long flutter of a flag. In the sunlight, both glowed a rich, impossible gold, like the spires of the palace. It seemed as if even the breeze now carried the tang of magic—for she knew the guards would swear they had seen no one erecting that great pavilion—and she felt a thrill of mingled anticipation and fear spiderwalk down her spine.

"They're almost ready to set the bridge," Toyve said and pulled Lilit towards the edge of the gorge. She looked down cautiously. She could not tell how far it was to the bottom, with its silver ribbon of river, but it was far enough that she had a moment of terrifying vertigo and stepped back. Fixing her eyes resolutely on the far side instead, she waited for her heart to stop pounding. It would be a fine thing if she got this far and then could not cross the bridge.

There had been talk once of building a permanent bridge across the forty foot gorge. The challenge of it had appealed to the city's engineering guild but the fey had forbidden it, so the engineers had to settle for solving the problem of restringing the old bridge for each fair. They could not do it once and leave it, for wood and rope would never survive the long winter—or the fey's displeasure. The easiest solution of all would have been to find another, higher pass and come down into the valley on the far side but the fey had forbidden that as well.

The Euskalans had settled for building a stone hut in which to store those bridge components that would survive the winter and bringing the rest of the materials for each fair.

The Engineers Guild was rightly proud of their creation, though that made the process no less harrowing. Following a great deal of inspection and muttered conversations, a series of short ladders, each fitted to slide out and overlap the next was fastened together. Braced into rock and wood brackets, it was extended by rope pulleys and lowered carefully across the gap.

Lilit found it hard to watch as one of the engineers crawled carefully across the linked bridges, trailing the ropes that would form the fragile hand rails for the rest of them. The bridge shuddered and swayed beneath him, as if it were a live thing. When he reached the other side, a cheer went up from the assembled Euskalans and Lilit let out a breath she had not even been aware she had been holding.

The other engineers began the process of settling up the rail anchors and using the system of rope pulleys to ferry the corresponding materials to their compatriot on the far side. The drama complete, the crowd drifted away, though Lilit guessed that more than one of them shared her own thoughts—that soon it would be their feet on that perilous path, their hands gripping the swaying ropes. "No one's ever actually fallen off the bridge," Toyve told her as they walked back to the Auster campsite. "But a few people have gotten stuck in the middle."

"What happens then?" Colum asked.

"Someone has to go and get them to move. It's very embarrassing. Or so I hear," she added hastily. "My advice is—don't look down."

The knowledge they would have to cross the bridge soon seemed to weigh on all of them, even Toyve, and there was little enough talk as they finished assembling the packs they would need to carry across the gorge. Balancing the unfamiliar weight took a little practice and Lilit was grateful for the time to pace up and down in the camp with the burden of cloth and spikes on her back. Dareh, Kay and Hazlet arrived and took up their own packs. In this, the apprentices were not left to do all the work; experienced hands were required to assemble the fair booths and, Lilit suspected, experienced bridge crossers made the whole thing seem less terrifying.

"I know that you are thinking about the bridge, those of you who haven't done it before—and perhaps those of you who have," Dareh said to the assembled Auster delegation. "I know that you are thinking about that pavilion over there and everything it means. But here is what you must remember: none of us know what it means. None of us can know the fey. What we can know are the rules that keep us as safe as it is possible to be amongst them. If we follow them, and Jennon smiles on us, then this House stands for another year, a little stronger than the year before.

"There can be no iron at the fair. There is no excuse for forgetting that. If you have to check ten times and I have to ask you another eleven, then you will do it and you will answer me honestly." The severity of her voice made more than one apprentice look down at their ringless fingers in sudden doubt.

"We have to be gone, every one of us, by midnight. There will no lingering, no forgetting, and no falling asleep. Do not leave the fair and do not walk, not even a step, towards the other end of the valley."

"There is no reason for you apprentices to speak to them—that will be done by those of us with experience. If by some mischance," her look suggested that such a mischance was unlikely and extremely unwelcome, "you are spoken to, you will be polite. You will refer to them as "Lord" or "Lady." You will not stare. You will not meet their eyes. And under no circumstance will you be alone with one.

"Am I understood?" There were hasty assents and a few furtive pattings of robes and checking of earlobes for stray iron. "Then we shall go and make this House proud," Daren concluded and turned to lead them towards the bridge.

"She makes that speech every year," Toyve whispered to Lilit. "It scares me every time."

When the Austers reached the gorge, Lilit saw Raziel herself was waiting there, to offer a smile and encouragement to each knot of nervous apprentices as they passed. She felt a sudden unease; irrational but undeniable. She did not want Raziel to see her, to notice her. She did not want there to be another thing that set her apart when she had begun to fit herself into the weave of a household that was not her own. She put her head down and shifted a little, to find the shadow of Toyve and her pack.

The line moved forward, the bridge monitors sending people across in a steady but controlled stream. At last, they were there. She heard Raziel greet Dareh and the other senior Austers, heard their cheerful replies. "Who did you bring this year?" Raziel asked and Lilit felt her stomach drop as if the bridge already swayed beneath her.

COLD HILLSIDE

"Toyve, Colum, one of Dillian's boys, and Lilit, apprenticed from Kerias."

Lilit could not help it; at her name, she looked up and met the eyes of her great-aunt's oldest friend, the woman who ruled Lushan. An expression came and went across the Sidiana's face, so quickly she thought it must be a trick of that same light. If pressed, she would have said it was dismay but, as no one else seemed to notice, she told herself it was nothing at all. Raziel's salute to her was no different than that she offered Toyve and Colum, her smile no fraction warmer or colder. Gratefully, Lilit bowed her head and passed her, for a moment feeling as if the bridge was the lesser challenge.

She changed her mind once she stood at the edge of the gorge. The wind had risen and she could hear it whistle through the chasm before her. When she risked a look down, she could see nothing but the rock falling away into shadow. The bridge made its own sounds, the creak of the wood and groan of ropes, the footfalls of the people who dared the journey ahead of her. The engineers had fastened boards across the ladder spans to bridge any gaps and create a stable pathway but it still looked far from steady.

Toyve went first and Lilit saw her take a deep breath and step out onto the bridge. The man timing their crossings waited until she was a third of the way across before signalling Colum to proceed. Lilit took his place, at the spot where the bridge overlapped the rock edge of the gorge. The man, an engineer from the Zelan House, spared her a glance and a reassuring smile that managed, for all he must have been repeating it, to seem genuine. "It's not as bad as it looks," he said. "Just walk. That's all."

It seemed sensible, if somewhat obvious advice. She repeated it under her breath once or twice and then, too soon, he said: "Your turn."

She swallowed and stepped forward, reaching out the grasp the rope rails. The first few steps were surprisingly easy, the wooden bridge bouncing almost pleasantly beneath her feet, the ropes steady beneath her hands. "Just walk," she muttered and smiled. A few more steps and she felt the wind for the first time. It tugged at her hat, teased its way through the heavy folds of her robes, and seemed intent on tipping her pack off balance. The bridge seemed to slew beneath her feet, riding the waves of the wind with a rhythm she could not match or master.

At the midpoint, she had a moment of panic, when she felt the bridge jump beneath the tread of the next person to begin the trek. "Just walk," she said, to the wind, to the ropes vibrating against her palms, to her racing heart. "Just walk." She kept her eyes trained on the torches flaring on the far side and took another step, then another. Before her heart had even slowed, she was at the edge of the gorge and then the ground was beneath her feet, solid and steady.

Toyve and Colum had waited for her and grinned as she came towards them. "What did I tell you?" Toyve said. "It's not so bad."

"You just walk," Lilit agreed and laughed when they did but felt a faint twinge at the thought she would have to make that journey again and again. She could do it, would do it, but she doubted she would ever actually be able to think of it as nothing but "walking."

"Come on," Toyve said. "Aunt Dareh is generally sympathetic about the first crossing. But she'll still expect the booth up before midday."

After the passage across the bridge, the work of assembling the Auster booth was a relief. Lilit had never assembled one before and so was relegated to holding ropes and pounding pins but the tasks went quickly enough and theirs was not the last one up.

As they walked back to the bridge, Lilit looked around curiously. The booths had been set up in the shape of a T, the two rows crossing at a point some distance from the bridge. Each booth was similar, a canopy, a sheltered storage area, a table assembled to display the shining treasures of Lushan's magpie merchants.

Beyond them all, beside the gorge, the Faerie Queen's pavilion stood. There was no movement or sound from it but Lilit suspected she was not the only one who could not help glancing furtively at it.

Back on the far side, Lilit and the others shouldered the packs that contained the treasures the Austers gambled would bring them fortune at this year's fair. Through the crowd assembling in the camp, Lilit saw Teras and her aunts in their house best, with the sashes in the Kerias colours around their waists. She felt a surge of longing and looked away. In the centre of the camp, the soldiers had gathered, to take charge of the tribute they had guarded through the mountains. Lilit had always imagined ornate chests that required two men to carry them but the reality was much more prosaic. The treasure took up no more than two moderately sized boxes, themselves deceptively plain, polished wood. But then the sun struck one and Lilit saw the gleam of red and knew the boxes alone were likely worth more than whatever she carried on her own back. The wood of the Jascander came only from the Idoniat archipelago. Five years of hard travel might bring you there and back, or you might take that road and never be seen again.

Lilit noticed that the entire camp seemed subdued, the bustling chatter of the previous morning damped to a whisper. Then it was her turn to cross the bridge again, and its sway, and her mantra of "just walk" occupied all of her attention.

At the Auster booth, they hung the House banners and set out the intricately carved boxes that held the creations of Auster studio. Lilit examined the necklaces and bracelets, amulets and earrings. Her fingers touched the opalescent mother-of-pearl inlay and felt the hard facets of red garnets and tourmalines the green of the fey banner. To be able to do such work, she thought with awe, that was why she had left House Kerias, why she swept the workroom and bore Jerel Auster's sharp tongue, and melted and reassembled her own flawed creations. House Kerias was richer, but the Austers were artists, and she would pay more than her mother could ever imagine for a chance to be one of them.

When her work was done, she left the Auster booth and wandered down the row, looking at what was on display from the other Houses. There were counters spread with furs and woven silks and she could smell the dust from leather-bound books and the heady scent of spices. Most fascinating were the two booths of the Vinerets, who specialized in strange devices found in the bazaars of a dozen countries far from the mountains. She saw odd instruments in bronze and bone, glass and gold, as beautiful in their making as they were mysterious in their purpose.

No one knew what moved the fey to covet these things. Indeed, Houses had risen and fallen on the shift in fey fashions, that decreed that from one fair to the next some previously desired human ephemera was now utterly without interest. No one knew why the fey chose to buy such things, when, to all appearances, their magic could conjure them from thin air. But they set the rules and, from whatever perversity of their own, abided by them.

Some paid in solid Lushan coin. No one knew where they got it but it was real enough and did not turn to leaves or stone the following morning. Some paid in other things as precious or whimsical or mysterious as what the Euskalans brought themselves: fabrics as fine as a whisper, devices of strange metals and stranger functions, painted icons of gods no Euskalan could identify.

There were tales of mortals who had bargained with the fey for other things, traded their blood or dreams or children for the magic that the fey could work, but such stories always ended badly.

With them, there are no happy endings. The words echoed in Lilit's mind as she came to the end of the row. She looked across the valley, towards the far mountains that enclosed it. The land here rose slightly, curving over the long stretch of grassland and then, she supposed, falling away again. Somewhere beyond that rise was the Border Court of the fey. It was said they stayed there during the fair, for a night or a day or a month. In the beginning, some of the Euskalans had explored that end of the valley. They had found nothing but the jumbled ruin of a city even more ancient than the one on which they founded Lushan. The next year the fey had forbidden any approach to that end of the valley.

She shivered suddenly and turned her back to the empty landscape to face the reassuringly human bustle behind her. Halfway back to the Auster booth, she met Toyve. "It's nearly time," the other woman said, her eyes bright and eager, and together they hurried on.

As the sun touched the edge of the mountains and the sky to the east turned lapis, studded with the first bright gleam of stars, Lilit felt something brush her skin, like a breath of wind. She paused and looked around. Toyve took a step or two more then stopped and looked back at her. "What is it?"

"Don't you feel it?" Lilit asked. "The wind?"

"What wind?" Toyve asked and gestured at the pennants that hung limp, hiding their crests.

"I don't know. There was a wind and the air feels . . . like sparks. Like when a storm is coming," Lilit explained, turning to find that secret caress of breeze again. There was nothing but the still, cold air, suspended in the moments before twilight.

Toyve opened her mouth but whatever she might have said was lost in the sudden belling of horns. The sound rang across the valley and shattered into echoes. "The fey," Toyve whispered and her cold fingers closed around Lilit's. "The fey are here."

CHAPTER 9

Teresine

I did not necessarily like my first months at the Asezet school but I survived it far more easily than many of my fellow students did. For the daughters and sons of the court and the great Houses the relentless regime and demanding discipline of the Asezati might be a shock, but I had survived more than one initiation into an unknown world. I was accustomed to being ignorant of things a Euskalan child would know and well-practiced at focusing my attention on one task and ignoring whatever distractions others might put in my way.

For me, the worst part of the first year in the school was that I was required to move there. Lushan was not so big that we students could not have all easily lived at home but the Asezati wanted to wean us of our families and comforts. I was already well weaned of that, I thought, but my separation from Sarit was more painful than I had anticipated. I had even become attached to my little palace room and resented the small bed in the cold dormitory at the school. For that first year, we were to belong to the Asezati utterly and even family visits were forbidden for the first few months. I heard more than one student crying in the night but I never did, though some nights I lay on my cold bed, my eyes screwed tightly together to keep the tears at bay. I had cried enough, I told myself. It had done me no good, in either Jayasita or Lushan.

Even the habit of manual labour came back to me, though I had been spared any duties more onerous than cleaning my room in the palace. I found it relatively easy to rise before dawn and go about the school lighting the braziers, or breaking the ice on the well and drawing water, or sweeping the corridors and courtyard. My hands rediscovered their calluses and my body its strength. My uncomplaining habits gained me some currency with the Asezati, though they might despair of my learning, and even won me some friends among the other students.

It was easier to bear the bone-chilling cold of winter morning chores when your co-workers were competent and, if not cheerful, at least not miserable.

Once our various hours of assigned tasks were complete, the regimen was not unlike that of the palace, with the exception of our new hours of prayer and meditation. In the dark temple, smoky with incense and oil lamps, we knelt in rows behind the monks, reciting the ritual prayers to the figure of Jennon, who glowed ghostly white on her pedestal. Strangely enough, I found praying more difficult than the daily chores. I felt myself an exile from all heavenly powers, invisible to both divine love and divine wrath. I would say the words required of me, and bow in time, and click my iron prayer beads with the rest, but my mind would be elsewhere. Sometimes it was on my studies, sometimes in the palace, imagining the life I was missing. Sometimes it slid inexorably back to the past or fidgeted in anxious boredom about the present. But once in a while, it seemed as if it was nowhere at all, as if I were beyond the temple, beyond myself, beyond even time itself.

My second year at the school, while the schedule of work, study and prayer had not relaxed, the control over my precious free time had, and so I was able to rush off to the palace more often to see Sarit. Her formal studies were now complete and she was learning the business of governing by assisting her mother or other officials with their duties. She had also decided to embark on a different, and more private, series of "educational experiences."

This I discovered when she insisted I meet her one night outside the school. Even this part of the adventure took considerable subterfuge on my part, as the Asezati's relaxed discipline did not extend to students sneaking out in the night. But it was certainly done nonetheless and a promise to take the early-morning scullery shifts of one of the senior students gave me the secret to the best way to accomplish it. So on the appointed night, I left my student robes in my room, donned my old black coat and pants, and slipped through the garden to the old stable. It was now used for storage but the hayloft remained, packed with the bulk of barrels and chests. At the back of the loft, where it bordered an alleyway, there was an old door, the senior student had assured me. The top half of the door had been firmly sealed but the lower half had been pried open by generations of adventurous students.

COLD HILLSIDE

One could get out on one's own but a co-conspirator was needed to get back in. I would have to trust Sarit would be able to boost me high enough to open the little door and I was strong enough to haul myself back into the loft, else the evening's adventure would come to an ignoble end, at least for me.

Sarit was waiting for me by one of the public wells in the little square below the palace. She was alone; neither cousins nor guards in evidence. Her coat and trousers were as plain as my own and the bright gold of her hair was tucked up beneath a knitted hat. She hugged me in welcome then hurried us down the street. "Where are we going?" I managed to ask.

"Outside the iron."

"Why?" For the first time, I had misgivings. I was accustomed to Sarit doing what she pleased but I had learned enough from my various teachers to realize that, even for her, especially for her, her choices would have consequences.

"Don't worry, Tera. I've done this before."

"Done what?"

She laughed and tucked her arm through mine. Her smile was wicked and conspiratorial. "Had an adventure. Had fun. It's like the journey south. We only have one chance, before we grow too old and too responsible. So we do this while we can."

"We?"

"The Sidianas," she said. "It's the same reason we have our children young. Because when we are older we cannot take the risks."

There were a dozen flaws in her arguments, I thought, not least of which was if she caused too great a scandal she would never be Sidiana. But this was her world, not mine, and I did not yet know exactly what she defined as "having fun." And whatever she intended to do, I could not leave her to do it alone.

We passed the great gate without incident. Keeping its inhabitants inside the city had never been its purpose. Outside the interior city, the streets were bustling with residents about their business, visitors from the outlying villages there for the next day's market, and those who had come to the district's taverns to drink cheap arrack and revel in the slightly disreputable atmosphere.

Outside the iron, it was said, anything could happen.

As I followed Sarit through the crowd, I felt the dark surfacing of old memories. The feel of these streets was not so different from those that led to the House of Falling Leaves in Jayasita. It was colder here, the babble of voices spoke a different tongue, and the scent of despair, as pungent and unmistakable as rotting refuse, was not so strong, but I recognized it just the same. I suddenly wanted to return to the clean quiet behind the gate.

Our journey ended at a tavern but Sarit passed by the front door and led me instead to the alleyway beside it. A set of wooden stairs took us to the upper floor. She knocked on the door and we waited. At last, a panel slid open, revealing a pair of dark eyes. I saw their gaze flicker over us then the panel closed and, after a moment, the door opened. "Welcome," the woman said and smiled. I recognized that smile, its opaque, professional warmth, though the woman was a stranger.

The upper floor of the tavern was one great room, centred with a stove of stone and copper, and dimly lit by candles and braziers. The slatted windows below the roof were open, to let the smoke escape. They also let the night's chill enter but it was not strong enough to conquer the heat of the bodies who filled the room. I recognized many of them; the pack of palace cousins, the daughters and sons of the great Houses. There were even one or two of the senior students at the school.

Someone waved from across the room. Sarit pulled off her hat and her hair tumbled out, drawing gold from the candles at it fell. "Come on," she said with a wide smile and led me through the crowd.

It was not as bad as I had feared, though the muscles in the back of my neck were as tight as bow strings for the whole of the night. The children of the Euskalans played at decadence, content with the safe simulation of it. They flirted and drank and gambled, with no real fear of the consequences. If there were others in the crowded room with darker knowledge, they stayed away from Sarit and so I was content as well.

"Do you see that woman over there? The one with the coppery hair?" Sarit asked me at one point, gesturing with her chin towards a far corner of the room. I looked, as discreetly as I could, and saw a woman a few years our senior. Her hair was indeed redder than the Euskalan norm and her skin was brown from sun or birth. "That is Jenet Kalins. It is said her mother feared she'd fail the iron test and so left the city to bear her."

"Just said? Or is so?" I asked and looked back at the woman. There was nothing special about her but her hair, though the cluster of young men at her table seemed to think otherwise.

Sarit shrugged.

"Who knows? She will not say."

"Because she is much more interesting that way, no doubt," I said dryly and Sarit laughed.

"The boys think so, it's true."

"It's an easy thing to take off your rings and bracelets and just as easy to put them back on. Has anyone ever actually failed the iron test?"

"Not in years. I have a faint memory of one test when I was a child; a woman weeping, a baby crying." She sighed, sobering. "It's easy to forget that when we first came here, dozens of children were taken a year. There is a grave chamber, up the side of the mountain, where they buried what was left in their place. My mother took me there when I was young, to show me the bones."

"What did they look like?" I asked, in spite of myself. She shuddered.

"The bones of babies," she said quietly. "Their babies look just like ours."

"Then how did they know—?" I began, then stopped, appalled at my own suspicions. I had always thought, somehow, that the changelings looked . . . different.

"They knew. They did not even need the iron for that." She shook her head slightly and then drained her cup. "Enough of this. We need some more wine." She raised her hand and the server who brought it bowed and smiled and she smiled back at him.

His name was Somchin and he was pure Newari, from a village up the valley. He had dark, liquid eyes and black braided hair and the strong shoulders of a farmer. If he knew who Sarit was, he did not say, and neither did she. There was no place for them to go in the crowded room (though that did not stop other couples, who seemed quite content with the shadowed corners) so they made do with the alley, underneath the steps.

I was unwilling to wait in the heat of the party and Sarit was unwilling to have me wait in the alley so we compromised. A low stoop ran around the outside of the building and I sat there, midway between the mouth of the alley and the tavern door. I put my back against the wall, wrapped my arms around my knees and watched the moon rise over the mountains.

There were many things about the Euskalans that still seemed unfathomable to me. One was their attitude towards sex. In my village, where poor families like mine packed ten into a single-room hut, sex was no mystery. I had heard most of my younger siblings being conceived. But no one spoke of it, as if silence could impart the privacy that proximity took away. In the city, sex was commerce and art and power, made coarse in rough alleys or mysterious in the moonlit gardens and flower-strewn palaces. But whether among the rich or the poor, it was the delight of men and the duty of women. Men chose; women were chosen. If a woman were beautiful and clever, she could make a weapon of it, but it was a weapon she could only use if the men consented, through their weakness and need.

In Lushan, it was different. Women chose as much as men, or more. The Sidianas bore children to one man or many and each child's birth was just as honourable. As in Deshiniva, marriages were an alliance between families as much as between individuals but what happened before such alliances was accepted without question. If Sarit wished to have sex with a Newari villager, that was her choice and none would criticize her for it. It was assumed she would not choose to bear a child from such a coupling (the Euskalans had ways to prevent that, both before and after the fact) but if she did, that too was allowed.

There was only one union that was forbidden, only one kind of offspring that was not accepted.

There was a sudden thump, as the door of the tavern opened and fell back against the wall. Light spilled onto the cobblestones, accompanied by a babble of voices and the faint sound of singing. There were shouts, someone swore and the door closed again, leaving only the cloud-shrouded moon to illuminate the street. Someone was left standing there, a dark shape. I heard the sound of a flint striking then a flame flared briefly. There was the sudden tang of cinquegrass smoke in the air.

The shape shifted to lean against the wall a few feet from me. I stayed very still, watching the glow of the cinquegrass pipe. At last, a man's voice said, "Do you want some?"

I shook my head then said aloud, "No, thank you."

Despite my refusal, he moved to sit beside me. I heard the creak of leather and the sharp thud of metal on rock. "I am," he said after a moment, "too old for these games." His voice held an accent I had not heard before. I wondered if I dared to venture down the alley and see if

COLD HILLSIDE

Sarit's sport was done. The moon cleared the cloud suddenly and seemed to flood the street with light. I could see the stranger was hardly ancient, though undoubtedly twice my age or more, to judge by the lines around his eyes and the faint gleam of silver in his brown hair and close-cropped beard. The moonlight touched the complex arrangement of leather and metal that crossed the broad chest and I realized that he must be a soldier. He was looking at me with equal curiosity and I returned my gaze to the blank whitewashed wall across the street. "Strange place to be sitting," he ventured at last.

"I am waiting for someone."

"Someone in there?" He gestured towards the door of the tavern and I shook my head. "Ah, someone from upstairs, then." I shrugged. "A few of my boys are up there, too, I suspect. The women are prettier, and better born, they say." His words ought to have offended me but I was too tired. Besides, they were true. "Why aren't you up there then?"

"I am not better born," I answered sharply because I was not about to tell this stranger the truth, because I wished fervently I was back in the cold comfort of my Asezati bed.

"You're pretty enough though." He leaned forward and tilted his head to examine me more closely. "Not Euskalan, either, not with that look, that accent. Where are you from?"

"Deshiniva," I admitted. "And you?"

"Isbayan." I had never heard of it, did not know whether he meant a city or a country or a people. "Our king wanted a bridge and bought it from one of your traders. Soldiers came with the engineers. I thought, why not? It seemed an interesting enough life. Better than ploughing fields at home. Have my own troop now." I wondered if it was drink or cinquegrass or his own nature that made him so forthcoming. "You like it here, little Deshinivi?"

"Better than Deshiniva."

He laughed. "Colder though." I could not help my nod, my smile. "I don't like it here. Glad we don't have to actually set foot here more than once every few years. Too cold, too . . . haunted. In Isbayan, we had sense enough to stay away from *them*."

He paused to strike a flame against the faltering cinquegrass in his pipe. The light from the flint flared off his face. There were women who might think him handsome enough, I imagined. His hands were steady.

This time when he offered it to me, I took it. I drew a careful breath of smoke and managed not to cough. "It's too cold here," he said, as I handed it back. "Too high for me. I can't breathe." He took a long, slow inhalation. "Your friend male or female?"

"Female."

"Maybe she's with one of my boys." I shook my head and he laughed, but it was not a happy sound. I felt the brush of his hand against my hair and I stared at the white wall, as if it could swallow me, shelter me. "This is a cold place, little Deshinivi," he said again. His fingers were callused but warm on my cheek, my chin, as he tilted my face towards him. His mouth tasted like arrack and cinquegrass. Mine tasted like ashes. My blood was like thunder in my ears, as if it could pound hard enough to escape my body. As if I could escape my body through it. I closed my eyes and drowned myself in the darkness behind them.

Then his mouth left mine and I could feel him withdraw. "A cold place," he said again and, when I looked, he was leaning against the wall as if he had never moved.

We sat in silence until Sarit appeared and called me away.

CHAPTER 10

Lilit

They were in the centre of a storm of sorts, a flurry of instructions and running feet and nervous apprentices being shooed into place. In less time than she had imagined possible, they were in the assigned position beside the Auster booth, a discreet pace or two behind the senior Austers, hats straight, hands folded, respectful and silent. Before she slid into place, Lilit had dared a glimpse at the end of the alley, across from the great pavilion of the Queen. She had seen Raziel there, her hair a crown of gold in the last rays of the sun, and the soldiers ranked behind her with the tribute boxes at their feet.

Something shivered over her skin, a wind that did not stir the banners, and then she heard the sound of hooves on the hard-packed ground, the jingle of harnesses, and the faint whuffs of equine exhalations. It was hard to breathe, as if the air had grown too thin, and there was a spice in it, a fragrance that it seemed perilous to inhale.

She was grateful for the black brim of her hat that shadowed her eyes and let her cast a careful glance upwards while seeming to stare obediently at the ground. She knew Toyve was doing the same thing, and every other apprentice along the alley. The first horses passed before she could quite focus on them and she saw only a blur of high-stepping, coppery creatures with black waves of mane and faceless figures on their backs.

The riders that followed had faces, though some of them were half-concealed by helms of hammered gold or veils in gossamer silk. As each passed, she could only add another brief impression to her image of the fey. They came in many colours and their garments were a shifting tapestry of fabrics and jewels. She knew that their features must vary, knew some were male and some were female, knew some had beards and some were smooth-shaven but it seemed as if her eyes would not see any one of them clearly and so they ran together, becoming one face, beautiful and remote as the plume of snow on the top of a mountain.

Her head spun with the sight of them and she felt Toyve's fingers dig hard into her elbow.

Then the last of them had passed and she could breathe again, the air once more holding only the smell of the tents and the mountain air. "Are you all right?" Toyve asked and she nodded. Dareh Auster was gone, following the procession of fey towards the pavilion, and the three apprentices crept to the edge of the tent. Hazlet, left to watch the wares and the junior Austers, let them edge their way around the ropes and poles to a better vantage point.

The fey had assembled before their Queen's pavilion, in ranks three deep, forming a corridor that led straight to where Raziel waited. The horns sounded again, three notes that lilted like a song through the twilight, their echoes a perfectly harmonized refrain. Lilit shivered, every part of her skin suddenly too tight, and her heart beat so hard she thought it must be visible beneath all the layers of her robes.

To her astonishment, the fey horses bent their beautiful, impossibly thin legs and knelt like courtiers. Their riders flowed from their backs and bowed in waves of silk and velvet. Beyond them, Lilit saw the panels of the pavilion draw back. Suddenly, she wanted to close her eyes, to turn away, and not look at the thing she knew must emerge from the pavilion. There were creatures one was not supposed to look at for fear of losing one's soul. The Faerie Queen must surely be one of those.

She remembered Vash's story of Tam and Jazeret. *A woman it hurt her eyes to look upon.*

But she could not move, not even to blink.

At the mouth of the pavilion the Faerie Queen appeared. In the fading light, she burned like a star, cold and white and perfect. Her hair was a fall of untouched snow and her dress was sculptured ice. Lilit could not see her features clearly, only the shadows of her eyes and the line of her mouth.

The last echoes of the horns faded.

The Queen turned and vanished back into her pavilion.

Behind Raziel, the soldiers lifted their burdens and followed their Sidiana into the black mouth of the Faerie Queen's realm.

Lilit blinked, took a breath, and fainted at the foot of the Auster tent.

When she awoke, it was to the sound of Toyve's voice ordering Colum to make some tea and Hazlet's awkward patting of her hand. She opened her eyes to the shadows of the Auster tent. "She's awake," Hazlet said and then Toyve was at her side.

"Are you all right?"

"I think so. I'm sorry," she said and levered herself up from the pack she'd being lying against. "I don't know what happened to me."

"The sun," Hazlet suggested confidently though Lilit thought she saw the faintest touch of uneasiness in his eyes. "The excitement."

"I'm sorry," she said again. "I'm not generally the fainting sort."

From outside the tent, she heard the sudden flourish of horns, their melody different than before. Toyve looked up, out towards the street, her face suddenly eager. "It's beginning."

"The Queen has accepted the tribute," Hazlet explained. "Now the fair has truly begun. Toyve, make sure everything is in order in the front. Dareh will be here shortly. And you," he looked at Lilit and patted her hand again. "You rest here for a few minutes."

"I'm fine. I can help."

"Fine help it'll be if you faint again. And even Dareh would not care to explain to Amaris Kerias sa Keshini how her daughter came to fall ill in our care. So stay here."

In truth, she was glad to obey him. Her knees felt wobbly and there was a churning sickness in her stomach. Perhaps it had been the sun, she thought. Or the excitement, or the kalashba she'd eaten the night before. One of those must be to blame for her faint and for her knees and the itch in her skin that had not gone away.

After a few moments, the curtain at the front of the tent parted and Dareh Auster leaned inside. "How are you?"

"Better. I am sorry for the trouble. I think Hazlet was right. I was too much in the sun today." Lilit met Dareh's measuring gaze innocently.

"Make some tea then. There is a bottle of coldwine in the pack. Bring that and the cups you will find there to the front as well."

Grateful for a task, Lilit set to work. But when the tea was ready, and the bottle and cups set upon the trays, she heard the murmur of voices outside the tent and paused to glance through the flap in the curtain. Dareh was there, with Hazlet by her side, talking to two fey women. Lilit saw their long white fingers gliding over the jewellery on the counter.

When, the next moment, Toyve and Colum slipped through the back of tent, Lilit thrust the tray into Toyve's hands. "You take it," she said hastily. "I might drop it."

Toyve stared at her for a moment then went, stepping gracefully through the curtain. If Dareh Auster cared that her assistant had changed, she gave no sign of it, then or later. Lilit stayed at the back of the tent, willing to let Toyve be her aunt's hands and messenger. The other girl came back from each encounter breathless, whispering to Lilit and Colum about the fey who stopped and the booth, what they purchased—and with what. By mid-evening, the Auster purses were heavy with coin and the small pile of other goods the fey had bargained with was growing and Lilit had managed to avoid leaving the tent by claiming the duty of listing and packing it all.

An hour or two later, Dareh sent her and Colum back to the camp, carrying a discreet bundle of their booty. Much to his dismay, Colum was delegated to remain in the camp for the rest of the night as guard. "I could stay," Lilit protested. She did not want to plead illness before Dareh but she'd be perfectly happy with an excuse to stay within the safety of the Auster tents. Dareh gave her a long look then shook her head.

"I need your neat hand here for a while. Colum's writing looks like chicken scratches in the dust."

Dismissed, they slipped out the back of the tent. For a moment, Colum lingered longingly at the edge of the passage midway, looking at the flow of figures there. "Come on," Lilit said impatiently. "You know we can't go that way." For which she was entirely grateful, though she did not admit it.

After Colum and the treasures had been safely stowed, Lilit made her way back, skirting the backs of the other booths and their forest of tent pegs and ropes. Back here, the itchy restlessness was less and her skin felt like skin again. She turned into the passageway between two booths and stopped, blocked by the presence that barred her way. The light from the torches flared like a halo around a patch of man-shaped darkness but she knew it was not a man who waited there.

She managed a bow. "Lord Fey," she said softly and kept her eyes down.

"Mortal." His voice was smooth and dense, like velvet, with the sheen of an accent she had never heard. It stroked the shivers in her skin back to life again.

"Please excuse me." She began to back away.

"No. Do not go." She stopped, torn between courtesy and caution, Dareh's warnings echoing in her mind "Look at me."

She lifted her gaze. The fey was taller than she, though barely. His hair was blacker than the night around them, and cut close to his narrow, elegant head. His skin was as black as his hair but his eyes were pale, the irises the colour of ice tinged only faintly with green. There were no lines around those eyes, or around his mouth, but she could feel the weight of age of him, as if the long years were all compressed within him until his form was denser, more present, than human flesh could ever be.

"What is your name?"

"Lilit Kerias sa Amaris."

"You are not Euskalan."

"My father is, Lord. My mother is from Deshiniva."

"Ah. Teresine."

The name sounded like a charm, in his velvet voice, but it shocked her into silence for a moment. At last, she managed to say, "She is my great-aunt."

"Great-aunt," he echoed. "So much time has passed. Your great-aunt, is she well?" Lilit nodded dumbly. "I still visit her mosaics once each season. You must tell her that. Tell her that Bastien remembers her." He smiled, but, on his almost-human features, the expression conveyed nothing she could understand. "Tell her others remember what the Queen chooses to forget."

She nodded, barely breathing, afraid to breathe. Nothing he said made sense to her but she did not want him to notice that and stop talking. In his own way, he was more informative than either her mother or great-aunt had ever been. At least now she would know what questions to ask.

"You will do that?"

"Of course, Lord Bastien." His smile faded and he reached out to touch her cheek with fingers cool as stone.

"Be careful, Lilit Kerias sa Amaris."

He was gone before she could ask him why.

She stood in the shadowy shelter of the passageway for a moment. Should she tell Dareh Auster about the encounter? As apprentice, she owed the woman an accounting of any dealings with the fey that might affect the House. But would this? The fey lord had spoken only of Lilit's own family, not that of her employer. Despite all that had driven her to the Austers, Lilit knew there were things in her life that were not their concern. None of them had ever commented on her connection to Teresine and she would prefer none of them did.

Whatever happened, she could not linger forever in the shadow of the booth, she told herself, and made herself move forward. Toyve snatched her up as soon as she appeared and put her to work in the back of the booth. Her next hours were a flurry of unpacking and packing goods, making tea, and risking the occasional glance through the curtains. She saw the fey pass in groups or alone, heard the ring of their voices, and the wintry music of their laughter. More than one stopped at the Auster booth and bargained with Dareh in tones of suspicious concentration or distant amusement. It was a game to them, said the popular wisdom, a novelty they indulged in once a year.

How do we know, Lilit wondered. *How can we know? How can mortals know anything about them at all?*

The fey lord who stood before the spread of Auster treasures looked up suddenly. His green gaze pierced the crack in the curtains and pinned Lilit like a butterfly to the shadows. Even her breath stopped; for a moment she feared her blood would freeze in her veins. Something flickered in his eyes, the corner of his mouth twitched and Lilit's blood leapt back to life, filling her head with the sound of thunder.

He looked back at Dareh Auster then, and the twitch became a smile, and the bargain was concluded. Lilit shivered and backed away from the curtain. *All the warnings are not enough*, she thought dizzily. *They warn you endlessly not to look too long at the fey but they never tell you how much worse it is when they look at you. No wonder my mother did not do this more than once. How could anyone bear to?*

She returned to Toyve, to the work that kept her hands busy, to the chatter than touched only part of her mind. The young Austers felt none of her unease, the tension that fluttered between excitement and terror. To them, this was the adventure she had always dreamed of; their only dissatisfaction came from their exile to the back of the booth. She listened to them talk and, for the first time in her life, felt like a foreigner, as if her Deshinivi blood lacked some vital element that made the Euskalans immune to the dark glamour she could feel all around her.

COLD HILLSIDE

At last, Dareh and Hazlet stepped in through the curtains. "That's that for another year," Hazlet said.

"It's over?" Toyve asked. "So soon."

"There has been quite enough drama for one day, so we should be grateful for that. Pack up the boxes and we'll go. The tents will wait until the morning."

The packs were gratifyingly lighter than then they had been on the first trip and the wind in the crevasse seemed to have calmed for the night. On the other side, their burdens stowed, wrapped in their furs and blankets, Lilit heard Toyve swear she could not be expected to sleep after such excitement, then heard her snore, and then heard nothing at all.

She woke up at the edge of the cliff.

She came awake with no knowledge of having been asleep; as if one moment she had not existed and the next she did.

She was crouched at the start of the bridge, the stones cold against her flesh, the ropes rough beneath her hands. For a moment, she stayed still, disbelieving, wondering if she was still asleep. It was dark, after all, save for the bright disk of the moon and the river of stars that flowed over the mountains. By their light, she could see the bridge stretched out before her, still and waiting. On the far side, the bulks of the booths, empty and abandoned, were dimly visible. Her eyes were drawn inexorably to where the great pavilion of the Queen had stood but it was gone; there was nothing there now but the night.

I was dreaming, she thought numbly. *I was dreaming and I walked in my sleep.* She had never done such a thing before but here . . . who knew what she might do? She tried to remember her dreams but they came back to her only in flashes; the sky and mountains broken and reassembled like an elaborate mosaic, her hair across her eyes, in her mouth, a feeling of flying and falling, a long rise and a sudden inevitable plunge that was exhilarating and terrifying at once. And in that tangle of confusion and fear—something that felt strangely like desire.

She shivered violently in the chilly air but did not dare to move. What if she tried and could not? What if she tried and her body, no longer trustworthy, sent her spinning down the hungry mouth of the gorge waiting before her. Lilit put her hands over her face and closed her eyes. When she opened them again, the night was still cold, her feet still bare, and her body was still shaking on the icy stones.

This is real, she told herself. *I am not dreaming this.*

She tried to stand but her knees, cramped and complaining, would not allow it. Instead, she crawled backwards off the foot of the bridge and onto the solid ground. She huddled there for a moment or two, her palms pressed against the dirt, then managed to push herself ungracefully to her feet. The wind caught her robe and opened it, slithering cold fingers inside her underrobe. She pulled her robe tight, her teeth beginning to chatter, and started towards the Auster tent. She went the longer way, around the circle of tents, for fear someone would see her. It would not matter, she told herself, she would claim to be relieving herself, that was all, though why she would do it on the opposite side of the camp might be a harder question to answer.

Still, she was grateful she saw no one on her stumbling progress through the outskirts of the camp. At last she reached the tent and slipped inside. Toyve shifted beneath her blankets but did not wake. Lilit found her own heap of bedding and slid beneath it, shivering.

What would have happened if she had actually stepped onto the bridge or if she had awoken part way across?

Maybe you did. The thought came like the cold wind from the abyss of the crevasse. *What if you were not about to go across the bridge? What if you had just come back across it?*

In a burst of sudden terror, Lilit pushed aside the blankets and fumbled her way to her pack, searching with numb fingers for the cold metal of her rings and bracelet. She put them on, one by one, and found her lips moving involuntarily in a childhood prayer of protection.

Reassured, she crept back beneath her blankets, tugged them up over her head and closed her eyes.

When she woke, she thought it had all been a dream, until she saw the dark bands of iron on her fingers and wrists.

CHAPTER 11

Teresine

Perhaps the biggest and most surprising lesson I learned in my four years with the Asezati was that faith was not required to join them.

True, for many of our teachers and the monks their worship of Jennon was wholehearted and genuine. Among the students, belief was automatic, the faith of their lives and their families. They might struggle with doubts the same way some of our teachers had, but the faith was always there waiting for them, like the mountain beneath their feet.

I had no such mountain. In my past lay the gods of Deshiniva, who had turned their backs on me before I turned mine on them. If in moments of extremity I still swore by them, or whispered a half-finished prayer, that was only habit.

At first, I hid my failure to believe. The Asezati were a test I meant to pass. Inability to mouth the proper words might be enough to banish me from Sarit, so, if a mask of faith was required of me, I would wear it diligently. The one thing my life in Jayasita had prepared me for was deception.

It had not prepared me for Yeshe.

Yeshe Bukoyan had taught at the Asezati school for almost thirty years by the time I was assigned to attend her classes and her needs equally. In our final year at the school, service to the teachers had been added to our regular duties of cooking and cleaning. A student so assigned was responsible for whatever tasks the teacher chose to assign, from fetching tea and emptying night pails to copying archives and teaching other students.

We had all heard the stories from the older students; which teachers were kind and easy to work for, which were demanding and irrational. Yeshe Bukoyan was reckoned odd but not difficult. Her demands might occasionally be eccentric but rarely involved messy clean-up, which most students counted a blessing.

I presented myself at the start of her afternoon classes. The school was not so large I did not know her by sight. She was full-blooded Newari; her skin was almost as dark as mine, her face was round and almond-eyed. In the spectrum of inhabitants of the school, the golden-haired children of the royal house assumed one extreme—and Yeshe Bukoyan and I were, by default, the other.

We managed well enough together. She was a demanding teacher and more than once I cursed her while redoing some task for the third or fourth time. But I was honest enough to admit my fourth attempt was generally much better than my first. The day she accepted an assignment in the state I submitted it, I was so surprised I dropped a pot of tea and so had to scrub the floor of her chamber for the second time that day.

She was older than she appeared. Her unlined face belied her years, but her fingers had begun to knot into claws and the crack of her knees as she slowly climbed the stairs to her chambers made it impossible for her to take me by surprise. More than once, I arrived in the morning to find her asleep in a cocoon of blankets by the braziers, papers scattered at her feet, and her bed untouched. She claimed she had too much work to do but the truth was that the ache in her bones would only allow her to sleep when she was too exhausted to move.

One morning, near the end of the term, I climbed the stair and entered her chambers. To my surprise, she was in bed, her breathing heavy in the chill, morning air. I moved about my duties as quietly as I could, stoking the fire to life and setting the pot of water over it for her morning tea. I'd brought a basket of warm biscuits from the kitchen, and a little smear of precious honey on a plate.

"Teresine." I turned around to see her sitting up. With her freshly shaved head poking out over the blankets wrapped about her shoulders, she looked so much like a sleepy-eyed turtle I almost laughed. Instead,

I took her a cup of tea. She wrapped her stiff fingers around it and looked at me. "I'm old this morning, Teresine. I was young yesterday and now I am old." She sighed and sipped her steaming tea. "Have you thought what you will do when your final year with us is done?"

Old she might be, but her gaze was clear-eyed and intent, missing nothing. "I hope I will return to the palace," I said carefully. I assumed that the leaders of the Asezati, at least some of them, must know Sarit's intentions—but no one had ever spoken of them aloud.

"Of course, of course. But as what?"

"I do not understand, Zayan Yeshe."

"As Teresine—or as Azi Teresine."

"Azi Teresine?" I echoed involuntarily then regained some semblance of wit. "I had not thought of that, Zayan Yeshe. I have no vocation." To my astonishment, Yeshe snorted.

"Of course you don't, child. Even a blind woman could see that. What has that to do with it?"

"Forgive me, Zayan," I said, baffled. She stared at me for a moment, through the steam that rose from her cup, and then sighed.

"There are many kinds of vocation, child," she said at last. "It is quite clear that you have at least one of them. But never mind an old woman's tongue. Just think on it."

I knew quite well that Yeshe's mind was as sharp as her tongue and when she called herself an old woman was generally the time one had best be paying the most attention. But she said nothing else on the matter, not for a long time, and I put it from my mind. I could guess quite well why the Asezati might want me in their ranks; it was far less clear to me what benefit that would be to me.

It was Yeshe who showed me that, as well.

In her class, she presided over our debates and arguments, attempting to steer us with the crack of her cane on the floor and the sharp rudder of her tongue towards some semblance of wisdom—or at least acuity. One class we discussed the use of power, while outside the shuttered windows nature demonstrated its own in wind and snow and bone-chilling cold.

It came down to an argument between another student and me and for half an hour Hekat and I batted logic, emotion and morality back and forth. Hekat lobbied for mercy and compassion, I countered with justice and the greater good. Yeshe refused to decide and the class split much as we had.

"So Hekat's arguments did not move you," Yeshe said after the class, as I tidied the room and she sat in her chair, leaning on her cane.

"Should they have?" I asked and Yeshe laughed.

"Circumspect as always. Sometimes I cannot tell with you, child, when you are telling the truth and when you are merely telling us what we want to hear."

"I do my best to learn what you teach me."

"Then tell me, did Hekat's arguments sway you?"

"Yes," I admitted reluctantly.

"And if you were called upon for counsel, would they be yours?"

"No," I admitted, equally reluctantly, wondering what test she was setting now and what would constitute passing it. "I would not change my choice."

"Do you know," she said, "when I posed that same choice to your friend Sarit, her decision was the same as yours?" I was not surprised but said nothing, only bowed my head a little and waited. "Do you know what we Asezati are?" I looked up, startled, into the dark solemnity of her gaze. It was clear she expected an answer to this question.

"You are the followers of Jennon," I said carefully and she laughed, though there was very little amusement in the tone.

"You were born for politics, child. Or survival. I do sometimes wonder in what school you learned your lessons. You're not a fool, Teresine. You know what we are. We are the heirs of the Euskalan empire. We hold its history, its wisdom and its folly. We are the right hand of the Sidianas—and sometimes their wits as well—and the foundations of the city. And yes, we are also the followers of Jennon—but Jennon's will can be served in many ways." She knew the irony in her words; by blood she was no heir of Iskenden's but she was Asezati through and through nonetheless. "Sarit will be Sidiana after her mother, barring disaster. *You* will be *her* right hand."

"And through me, you would wish to be as well," I pointed out, matching her bluntness with my own.

"Sarit is no fool, either. She will use what resources she has. She sent you here to learn from us."

"But not to find another master. I swore fealty to her; I have no oath left to give."

"We are sworn to the service of the Sidianas."

"I am sworn to *her*," I countered and she looked at me.

"But who is sworn to you?" she asked softly.

For a moment, we looked at each other, two dark women in a room where the braziers guttered and the wind tugged at the shutters with cold fingers. I knew what she meant, I knew all the things she was not saying. I had known them from my first night in the city, as much as I

82

had chosen to forget them during much of the past years.

"Zayan," I said at last and bent my head, remaining still as she heaved her weakening body to its feet, bones creaking. I felt her hand brush the braids coiled around my head.

"Think on it, child. You need not be foresworn. Necessity is a harsh master—but Jennon's mercy is infinite." Her breath sounded as harsh and laboured as the wind. "Now help me to my room."

I did, in a silence neither of us seemed inclined to break.

The time to choose came quickly, in a rush. The students who faced this final season had a new recklessness. The hidden gate to the outside world saw the passage of students who had long since denounced such risks as juvenile. Gossip hinted at orgies and revelry, a last grasping at flesh and pleasure and irresponsibility, a frantic testing of the promise of a world that might have to be abandoned.

I had never stopped using the gate to accompany Sarit on her midnight adventures or simply to meet to talk. "We can go outside the iron," she teased, more than once that spring. "Half your schoolmates are there, after all."

"No, thank you," I replied, content to sit in the little sheltered courtyard we had found, sipping tea. But two nights later, I went by myself, to walk the crowded streets and pass by the hidden bars Sarit herself had now abandoned. I stood in the shadows outside a tavern and remembered the first night I had gone there, when I had sat against the wall and the foreign captain had kissed me and my mouth had filled with ashes.

I know what the world offers, I thought to myself. I know what the Asezati are. I know my path.

When the ice cracked and melted on the lake below the city, the ritual journeys began. The graduates would spent the required night in seclusion in the meditation hut on the edge of the lake and emerge in the morning, tired and exultant, to take one path or the other; back to their households to resume their places or to the school to take up their new life among the Asezati.

I watched each take their turn with an uneasiness I stubbornly ascribed to impatience. The ritual was merely a formality; I knew where I belonged. None of the Asezati had made any more overtures to me, though I had half-expected them in the wake of Yeshe's cryptic offer.

Perhaps they realized what they asked was impossible for me.

At last, my turn came. I knelt in the chapel, my fingers moving on my iron prayer beads, the chanting that thrummed through the smoky air sounding like the ceaseless rhythm of waves on a shore. It was Yeshe who came at last to take my hand and lift me up, to lead me at the head of the procession down to the lake.

The hut stood alone on its little island of rock and the most reclusive or enlightened of the Asezati would sojourn there in the cold embrace of the ice, searching for wisdom. A line of teachers formed on the path that led to the bridge. I passed down it, bowing to each in turn, touching my forehead to their folded hands. One or two whispered encouragements and blessings. At the end of the row waited Yeshe. I bent my head to her hands and then felt them rest for a moment on my hair. "Remember," she said softly. "Jennon asks only what you can give. The world does not. We all require sanctuary, in the end."

I lifted my eyes and met her gaze. I expected to find calculation there or a conspiratorial persuasion. I saw only sadness and compassion. "I shall meditate upon your words, Zayan," I said and her hands slipped from my hair.

"Go now," she said loudly, the public ritual resuming. "Seek wisdom from Jennon in the darkness, seek counsel from your heart in the water, and seek your path in the winds that touch all worlds: the one now lost, the one in which we live, and the one to come. In the morning, let what will be, be."

The gathered crowd echoed her words and the chants began again. To their murmur, and the click of the iron beads, I walked across the bridge and into the hut.

I had not been honest with Yeshe; I meant to spend the night and emerge unchanged. But in the long hours of that night something *did* change. Perhaps it was simply that, once I had lit the braziers for light and warmth, there was nothing to do in that hut but think. I examined the finely carved interior and the altar to Jennon with its white statue and the tools I would need to declare my intention then I went outside onto the deck. The moon had risen, a bright half-coin above the mountains, and the stars draped around it like a silken scarf. The wind had died and the water lay before me like a second sky, still and star-spangled. If I looked to my left, I could see the torches of the city and the white walls beneath the moonlight.

COLD HILLSIDE

Yeshe's words echoed in my ears: "Seek wisdom in the darkness, seek counsel in the water, seek your path in the winds." But the darkness was silent, the water showed me nothing but the sky, and the wind had vanished. I sat down and found the prayer beads tucked into my sash. This was the last time I would be required to pray, I thought, so perhaps I owed it to the Asezati to try.

Feeling slightly self-conscious, I muttered the words of the mantra, my fingers slipping over the corresponding characters etched into the beads. I recited the prayers I knew by heart, while my thoughts slipped in and out of the words. Memories surfaced: my mother's voice, the yellow boat pulling up to the dock in the village, the twinkle in old Maya's eyes that we took for humour and was really the thought of gold, the long first night in Jayasita, the boards of Sarit's ship beneath my knees as I knelt and swore loyalty to her, the night we had stood on the roof of the palace and felt the city shake for one terrifying, exhilarating moment in an earthquake so brief most thought they had imagined it.

I looked towards the city, where the torches cast back another mirror of the starry sky. Somewhere in that darkness was Sarit, waiting for me. Sarit, to whom I had given my fealty and who would one day take her mother's place on the throne of Lushan.

I remembered her mother's kind, implacable eyes on the night I had knelt at her feet and told her the truth of my past.

I remembered Yeshe's words: *Necessity is a harsh master. . . . We all require sanctuary. Who is sworn to you?*

Who is sworn to you?

I was sworn to Sarit—and Sarit was sworn to the city. She was sworn to all the principles the Asezati had taught us both. She was sworn to always make the hard choice and always pay the hard price. I did not doubt her love for me; I did not doubt her trust. I did not doubt she would make a good and just Sidiana when the day came.

My parents had loved me, as much as they could. It was not enough. For a promise and a piece of gold, for belief or blindness, they made a choice that could have destroyed me.

For her city, Sarit would do the same, because she was worthy of all the oaths I had made to her.

You need not be foresworn.

Was it possible? I wondered. Could I swear to the Asezati, the way that Sarit had sworn to me, an oath to be cherished and believed but one which must always come second to that first, greater oath?

They told us that night would be the longest of our life. (They were wrong, though I did not discover that for many years.) In the cold isolation of the hut, I stared at the thing Yeshe had made me see—or remember—and wondered what I should do.

As the dawn lightened the sky, I took the knife and the soap from their place on the altar and did what was required. It took a long time and left its marks on my skin.

Outside, I heard the prayers begin.

Forgive me, I thought and bent in front of the altar, though I did not know to whom I prayed. *I do not know if this is cowardice or wisdom or madness. Forgive me for it all.*

Then I rose and walked out into the dawn, my shaven skull still bleeding slowly, and prostrated myself at the feet of Yeshe Bukoyan.

CHAPTER 12

Lilit

Lilit returned to Kerias the day after the fair, tired and bleary-eyed from the Auster celebrations the night before, to a casual greeting from one of her cousins and reminder from one of her aunts that her mother wanted to see her.

Of course she does, Lilit thought wearily as she climbed the stairs to her little room. She hoped none of the Kerias party had heard about her fainting spell or her midnight walk through the camp.

Dareh Auster herself had pronounced herself moderately pleased with the performance of all her apprentices. The House had had a successful fair and, as was customary, there were tokens for each of them. Toyve's was a length of silk, for her Auster artistry ran to needlework instead of jewellery. Colum received a little lump of gold, enough for the ring he had talked of designing. For Lilit, there was the small brocade bag. She had only had to open it a little to recognize the rough shapes inside: uncut lumps of vitisara. It was a semi-precious stone, common enough to use for luck charms and children's rings among the richest Houses. But it was hers, to make what she wished of its bright, bitter-apple green.

In her room, Lilit shed her travel-stained clothing and, shivering, changed into clean garments. She wanted nothing more than to spend an hour in the steamy luxury of the Kerias House baths but knew it would be much more politic to visit her mother first. She tucked the bag of geodes into the carved ashwood box at the foot of her bed and went to do her duty.

Amaris was in her office, ledgers spread out on her desk. Counting the gains from the fair and already planning how the House would earn both the next year's tribute and a reasonable profit, Lilit guessed.

"Good morning, Mother," she said from the doorway. Amaris looked up, dark eyes sharp and searching. Lilit had to fight the urge to check that her hair had not escaped its braid or that her sash was straight. Yet there was an odd quality to her mother's scrutiny, as if she was searching for something altogether different than a flaw in dressing or deportment. Just when Lilit felt as if she could not bear the weight of that examination a moment longer, her mother's mouth moved into a smile and she beckoned her into the room.

"I hear the Austers did well at the fair," Amaris said.

"I believe Dareh Auster was satisfied," Lilit replied, her back stiffening. That was Auster business and her mother knew it.

"And was she satisfied with you?"

"She said so."

Silence lingered as her mother leaned back in her chair and looked at her. "Was it worth it, the Fair? Was it everything you dreamed?"

"It was worth seeing," Lilit acknowledged carefully. "I had to go. But," she watched her mother's face carefully, "it was different than the stories."

"Oh?" Amaris touched one of the books on her desk carelessly, rearranging its position by an inch or two. "How?"

"It was stranger. And darker. I cannot quite see how anyone *enjoys* it, but some seem to."

"And the fey? Were they different as well?"

"No," Lilit said. "They were just like the stories. It's only that I don't think we always truly listened to the stories when we were young. Someone said *with them, there are no happy endings.* I think she was right."

Amaris nodded but her eyes were on the spread of ledgers in front of her, so Lilit could not see her expression. "She was." Her mother looked up and smiled. "Next year, if you want to go, talk to me. We'll see what is possible."

"Thank you," Lilit said in astonishment. Her mother's sudden acquiescence was so surprising it was not until she was in the hallway that she stopped to wonder whether she did want to go to the fair the next year. Maybe it gets easier, she thought as she headed towards the kitchen to see if the cooks would spare some tea and toasted bread to settle her still queasy stomach. Maybe next time, it would only be a grand adventure, as it was for Toyve and her cousins. But she remembered the itch beneath her skin, the cold touch of the fey lord's finger against her cheek and the dizzying depths of the chasm as she crouched beside it and thought she would be quite happy never to go to the fair again.

COLD HILLSIDE

Just like Mother, she thought with sudden wry amusement. Who would have suspected it? But then it came to her to wonder exactly why her mother had chosen not to go to the fair, when the weight of tradition and expectation and her own ambitions should have set her at the head of the Kerias delegation. What had happened on her one journey that outweighed that?

The next day she was on her way up the mountain to see her Great-Aunt Teresine.

Until that year and her defection to the Austers, Lilit had spent almost every summer of the last decade at Teresine's mountain home. Her mother's motives for the arrangement had always eluded her, given her own, uneasy relationship with her aunt. Lilit suspected it had begun as a way for Amaris to avoid making her own visits while keeping peace between them. The presence of visitors such as the Sidiana herself was no doubt another incentive. Lilit made a show of protesting, once or twice, but she always went. In her heart, she was not sorry, for summer on the high mountain was beautiful and a not unwelcome break from the bustle of Kerias House. If she chose to spend the day lying on the sun-warmed stones of the patio reading, her great-aunt might ask her pointed questions about the book but would not demand that she do something useful, like peel the potatoes, instead.

She loved the mountain, the brief bloom of flowers among the rocks, the days that seemed to last forever beneath the bright sky.

She loved the house, with its cool, silent rooms, its warm kitchen presided over by Filiat, the bowls of subtly coloured tiles that lined the shelves in the room where her great-aunt worked on her strange, never-finished mosaics.

She loved her great-aunt as well. Despite her quick tongue and bitter humour, she was intelligent, thoughtful and well-educated and she, of all the adults Lilit knew, expected her to be the same. More than any of the tutors in House Kerias, Teresine taught Lilit to think and question, as she herself had once been taught by the Asezati. She had left the order many years before but she still wore her hair cropped close to her skull, out of habit or, Lilit suspected, because it flattered the spare, elegant curves of her head.

That her great-aunt was sad dawned on her slowly. The stern façade she presented to the world was old and practiced. Without those summers she might have thought it was her real face. Once, she had innocently dared to suggest such a thing to her mother. "Your great-aunt does exactly what she wants and is precisely what she chooses to be," Amaris had snapped. "If she is unhappy she has no one to blame but herself."

For years, she had felt like a cord stretched between her mother and her great-aunt; a tie that both chafed against but neither could bear to break.

Lilit stopped on the track, shifted her pack from her back and found a comfortable rock on which to perch and eat the food she'd scavenged from the Kerias kitchens before she left. The sun was still high, warming her skin as she tilted her face towards the sky and breathed in the thin, cool air. Soon the snows would begin and the path would turn treacherous but for now the solitary half-day walk up the mountain was as much a lure as the prospect of a visit with her great-aunt.

The year was moving towards its close, when the nights would lengthen and she would have to leave and return to the Kerias compound in darkness. In a few weeks would be the Soul Moon festival, when the dead would be grieved and celebrated and remembered. In the city, the people would troop down to line the lake and from there launch the little paper boats that bore their candles, blessed with wishes and memories and sorrow, out into the night.

Once, when she was twelve, illness at Kerias had kept her at Teresine's for the ceremony.

That night, the household had assembled in the courtyard to make their way to the small mountain stream. She had spent the afternoon with Urmit, Teresine's housekeeper, making paper boats for the ceremony. She'd asked whether they needed to make some for her great-aunt but Urmit had replied that the lady usually made her own. As the household gathered, Lilit noticed Teresine carried only a small box but the stable boy had shouldered a larger one.

The priestess puffed her way up the hill from the nearest village, having conducted their ceremony first, so it was full evening by the time their procession wound its hazardous, lantern-lit way to the stream. Urmit muttered something about hoping none of them broke their necks and required boats of their own the following year but other than that they went in silence.

COLD HILLSIDE

At last they reached the proper place. The stream levelled and widened a little here, forming a pool whose chilly waters Lilit would sometimes briefly brave in the summer heat. As the priestess began her prayers, Urmit lit long twigs from the lanterns and passed them around, so that each of them could light the candles nestled in their little boats. Then, to the drone of the prayers, each went to the edge of the pool and knelt to place their boats into the water. Lilit whispered the name of her father's parents, her cousin who had died of pneumonia the previous winter, and, sacrilegiously, her favourite, much-mourned cat, then released each of the fragile little craft. They joined the others there, bobbing inexorably towards the lip of the rapids that led down the hill.

The last to release her boats was Teresine. Lilit could not hear the names she whispered as she placed boat after boat into the water. She was mildly curious but her great-aunt was old, after all, and no doubt knew many people who had died. At last, Teresine took three boats from the little box she had carried and lit their candles slowly. Lilit saw her eyes close as she bent over them, lips moving on names she could not hear, and then Teresine set the boats into the river with a tenderness she had not shown the others.

She rose and watched them go, following the others towards the curve in the rock that hid their final destination. The prayers ended and the mountain seemed very still. The silence lingered, but Teresine did not move. Lilit heard the rustle of cloth from behind her and the faint sound of someone coughing but no one spoke. At last, the final boat vanished and Teresine turned away.

The priestess began to apologize for being so late but Teresine waved the words away. "It's better in the dark," she said shortly. "Then you can't see them break on the rocks on the other side." Lilit could not see her face as she passed her to lead the procession back to the house, but in her voice she heard a pain that was more potent than tears.

In the morning, Lilit had clambered down the hillside to look for the broken boats and candles but the rocks were empty.

Lilit opened her eyes and looked back down the valley, towards the city and the wink of the gilded roofs in the sun. With a sigh, she slid from the boulder, shouldered her pack and resumed her journey up the mountain.

It was Urmit who greeted her when she arrived in the courtyard. She had kept house since Teresine had returned from Deshiniva with her sister Keshini and her sister's child in tow. She was older even than her employer but the latter's lean figure and smooth, shaved head always made the gap between them seem larger. Urmit was all wrinkles and pillowy flesh. That softness concealed a tongue sharper than expected—she'd been honing it on Teresine's own hard edges for years.

"Not a word of warning from you first," Urmit scolded her, once she had hugged her fiercely.

"You sound like Filiat," Lilit said. Her great-aunt's cook was famous for her grumbling at Teresine's tendency to attract unexpected guests, and for her ability to conjure an astonishing meal out of two potatoes, a handful of barley and an old chicken. "And I know quite well there's a bed and more food than I could ever eat waiting somewhere in the house."

"Yes, well, we'll manage," Urmit admitted and Lilit noticed for the first time how drawn the old woman's face looked.

"How is she?"

"As ever, as ever. Expect the mountains to change before that one," Urmit assured her as she led the way into the house. "She's in her workroom. Go on." Urmit waved her towards the back of the house. "I'll be talking to Filiat about lunch and some tea."

Lilit followed the dim hallway toward her great-aunt's workroom. She found Teresine there, hunched over the spread of coloured tiles, clicking two between her fingers in a familiar sound. For a moment, Lilit paused in the doorway, watching. The shutters had been opened wide and the afternoon sun filled the room along with the cool air. Teresine sat before the window, the light gleaming on the bronze of her shaved skull, laying highlights and shadows across the fine bones of her face. From Lilit's vantage point by the door, the unfinished mosaic before her was only a sweep of colour, ranging from iridescent green in one corner to somber indigo in the other with a splash of red in the centre.

In all the years she had been coming to the house, Lilit had never seen her great-aunt paste down a single shard or leave a single mosaic complete for more than one night.

Teresine placed one of the tiles in her hand into the centre of the mosaic and then looked over towards the doorway. "Someday you'll scare me to death creeping up on me like that," she said and Lilit laughed.

"I didn't think anything scared you." Teresine rose from her chair and came to embrace her. Beneath the layers of robes, her great-aunt's body felt thin and brittle in her arms. When they parted, Lilit looked at her in concern. She had always thought that Teresine was made of iron, unbreakable and unyielding. Now she felt as if her aunt's robes and flesh lay like a frail shell over one of the strange metal devices she had seen at the fair, fragile and irreparable. "May I see your mosaic?"

"It's all wrong, of course," Teresine said. "It always is. But look if you want."

Lilit stepped over to the table. The design was almost completed, which meant the tiles were destined to return to their bowls in a day or two. The green turned out to be a profusion of plants studded with pearly flowers. It faded into a pyramid of black topped with white. On the other side of the stylized mountain was a night sky of deep blue. It held no moon and only the faintest of stars slid like a thin mountain stream across the top. In the centre was a flower, shockingly red, almost carnal. Petals fell from it like drops of blood.

"It's beautiful," Lilit said aloud but did not add that it was disturbing as well. She was used to the fact that Teresine's mosaics looked nothing like any art she had ever seen. She had always assumed that it was the art of Deshiniva, that the strange plants and symbols that sometimes appeared in the work were her great-aunt's memory of her long-left homeland. She put one finger out to touch the centre of the flower, a black shard at the heart of the red bloom."It's a lie," Teresine replied bluntly. "They're all lies." It was the most her aunt had said on the subject of her mosaics in the long time.

"Why?"

"Because there are some things you can never put back together."

CHAPTER 13

Teresine

My choice to join the Asezati caused my first and only serious disagreement with Sarit. She did not understand my decision and I could not explain it to her in any way that would not insult her. She was angry for a dozen reasons; I had not told her, I did not trust her, I had made her doubt me, I had changed the plans she—and her mother—had carefully laid.

I in turn was miserably aware that she had cause for anger—and that her anger only reinforced all the reasons that I had made the choice in the first place.

We had one shouting match in the dubious privacy of her suite at the palace and two months of utter silence. I retreated to the school and went about my new duties with stiff precision, as if to convince myself of my devotion to them. I told no one of our estrangement but no doubt everyone who mattered knew. In the past three years Sarit and I had barely gone a week without seeing each other.

I broke first, of course. I was the one who had traded her friendship against an unknown future. I saw her by the simple expedient of walking to the palace one day and going to her rooms. No one refused me entry.

Sarit arrived just before the evening meal. Someone had told her I was there; she entered the room already stony-faced and regal, as remote as the blank-eyed temple statues of Jayasita. I went down on my knees and put my forehead to the floor at her feet. "Do not do that," she said coldly. "That is only due to Jennon."

"It is due the one to whom I owe my true allegiance," I said as I sat back onto my heels. "I swore that to you on the ship and I have made no oath greater than it since."

"Only to the Asezati. Only to Jennon."

"I do not believe in Jennon. And my oath to the Asezati is explicit; it has power only as long it does not cross my true loyalty."

"They allowed that?" For the first time, something other than anger and betrayal creased the place between her eyes.

"I have what they want. Or, I had it."

"Which is?"

"Your trust."

To my astonishment, she squatted down and looked at me, our eyes level. "Why did you trade it away, then? And for what? For a goddess you say you do not believe in?"

"For sanctuary," I said honestly. "For a place to go if I do not die at the same moment you do. For a place to go if you ever require that I leave."

She stared at me for a long time, so long I almost put my head back to the floor to avoid her gaze. "Why didn't you tell me this before?"

"I did not know how."

"Give me your hand." I held it out to her and watched as she unfastened one of the pins on her sash. The tip of it pierced my finger and drew a quick, sharp pain and a line of bright blood. She did the same with her own flesh and then brought our hands together, blood mingling with blood. "I bind you to the oath you gave me," she said, her voice fierce. "Beyond all oaths and all promises and all vows you ever make, swear you will be true to this one or lose your soul to the winds and the darkness forever."

"I swear to hold that oath above all other, or lose my soul to the winds and the darkness," I repeated without hesitation. "As long as the river runs, as long as the fish rise, as long as the sea waits," I added, the old words of the land of my birth. "May the river swallow me if I speak false."

"I accept your oath," she said and, taking my face in her hands, kissed me once, her mouth hard and cold against mine.

And so we were reconciled. I did not officially move back to the palace but spent much of my time there nonetheless. I taught at the Asezati school and was appointed as aide to one of the teachers who served on Kelci's council. Much of the business was tedious but at least Sarit was there as well. In the worst moments, when one of the representatives of the Houses had droned on too long for endurance, we could at least look at each other across the room and try not to laugh. I was better at it than she; but she suffered much less scolding for getting caught than I did.

I do not know if she ever truly forgot that other, lesser oath I'd made. We never spoke of it again and when the test of my loyalty finally came, it was not Sarit who had to bear it.

For the next year, I was as happy as I have ever been. I discovered I enjoyed both teaching and my work for the council. Even the slippery game of palace politics was interesting, in its own fashion. There were no great issues to divide the city and the lobbying for the succession was muted and half-hearted; Sarit was clearly her mother's heir, by both blood and skill. Because it did not matter, we could play the game of alliance and stratagem and have it be nothing but a game, a test of our wit and skill and wisdom. Sarit had an instinct for it, tempered by an innate sense of justice and balance that made the losers regard her as highly as the winners did.

When she was twenty-three, Sarit followed the accepted path for a future Sidiana—she bore her first child. Though she had an easy pregnancy, growing more golden and glowing with each month, the birth was hard and bloody. It left her ill and weak for weeks after and the healers who attended her shook their smooth heads and told her a second child might kill her.

If her pregnancy was approved, her refusal to name the father was not accepted so sanguinely. She and Kelci argued over it, the members of the council all made their way into private conference to try to persuade her to be explicit, and the palace buzzed with gossip but she waved them all away with a beatific smile.

The baby girl was darker than her mother but otherwise looked like any other human baby, red-faced and wrinkly. *Their babies look just like ours*, I remembered Sarit saying but did not for a moment believe Ayriet was anything but mortal. Neither would anyone else who had heard her cry, I thought, but there the very air in the palace seemed cleaner after the day of her welcoming ceremony. The iron symbols laid on her brow and heart had left no mark.

Ayriet's birth changed little about our routines. Sarit carried her to council meetings, where the assembled delegates fussed over her for the opening moments and then ignored her, unless she cried. She became a part of everything we did. Somewhat to my own surprise, I did not resent this; she was, after all, the closest I would ever come to having a child of my own. The Asezati had no children but their students and took vows of celibacy, though these were rumoured to be honoured as much in the breach as the observance. I took those vows without regret and with some relief, wanting neither lovers nor children. I never envied Sarit her lovers but I think I envied her Ayriet.

Three months after the first anniversary of Ayriet's birth, the storm sickness came to Lushan. No one knew how it came; perhaps with returning troops or engineers, perhaps with traders, perhaps it simply blew in on the wind. It had swept the city before and both the Sidiana and the Asezati knew what to do. The quarantine rules were set, the healers worked long hours in the makeshift infirmaries in the school, and in the end the toll was lower than it might have been.

But among the two hundred who died of the plague were three members of the council, ten of the Sidiana's cousins, six of Sarit's generation—and Kelci.

It was a subdued council that affirmed Sarit as Sidiana. They wasted no time about it, for the sickness took Kelci on the third night of the plague, and there was too much to be done for the city to be without a leader. Sarit did what was required of her with grim, dry-eyed efficiency. I only saw her weep once. We were on our way back from the lower city, where she had gone to inspect one of the infirmaries. Despite the bone-chilling cold, she had insisted we walk, she and I alone, while the guards the worried councillors had insisted upon walked well ahead and behind us. We talked in a desultory fashion about relentlessly practical matters; the threat to the spring planting if the plague took the countryside, the reserves the palace could call upon if we had to buy the tribute through middlemen, if word of the storm sickness made our merchants unwelcome.

The streets were empty save for us. On a normal night at this hour, they would have been nearly deserted but there would still have been life about; apprentices hurrying home, a drunk or two staggering along the cobbles, lines of light that framed the shuttered windows. Now it was all stillness, except for our low voices and the faint echo of the soldier's steps. There was no light but the moon and it seemed almost possible to believe that we were all that was still breathing, still living in Lushan.

I don't remember what I said, something inconsequential about the lateness of the thaw on the lake or the state of the grain reserves within the storage rooms of the palace. Sarit stopped suddenly, her face turned away. When I said her name, she looked at me and I saw the tears bright in her eyes. "I cannot do it, Tera," she whispered. "I cannot fix the grain and the lake and the tribute and all of it. I cannot even care about it. I—" She lost the words in a sudden sob.

I looked back at the captain of the guard, who had paused a dozen paces behind us, his hand going automatically to his sword. I sent a plea along my look and after a moment, he nodded and held the little troop at their distance. It was a requirement of the palace guard to see more than they said—but there were some things they did not need to see at all.

I caught Sarit's arm and pulled her into the narrow alley a pace or two ahead of us. Even in the winter's deep, it smelled of rotting waste but it was quiet and safe from the eyes of everything except perhaps a brave or foolish rat. "She's dead, Tera," Sarit said brokenly. "She's dead and they will not even leave me alone long enough to weep for her."

"They are not here," I assured her. "And I do not care how much you weep."

She laughed at that, a sound that slid into a choking sob and then we were both crying, holding each other in the dark quiet of the alley, mourning a mother and a queen and a time that would never come again. At last, she whispered, "I do not know if I can do this, Tera."

"Yes, you do," I said and drew back to look at her tear-streaked face in the faint light of the distant moon.

"Am I allowed no doubt?"

"Doubt if you must—but I have none."

This time her laughter was cleaner, touched only lightly with sorrow. "Then your faith will have to suffice for both of us for now. And your handkerchief, if you had the wit to bring one." I retrieved one from the depths of my robe and we cleaned away the tracings of our grieving. The Sarit who stepped back into the street was once again the Sidiana. She nodded faintly in acknowledgement of the captain's discretion then we continued on our way back to the palace as if nothing had happened.

During the the crisis, there had been no time for anything but the battle against the plague. Once the danger had passed, the formalities of the burial of one Sidiana and the investiture of the other were required. Sarit insisted that the former proceed the latter by a month, despite the voices on council that wanted both resolved as quickly as possible. "Why not have them the same day, then?" she'd asked. "That way the people could line the streets to say goodbye to my mother in the morning and wait in place to welcome me in the afternoon? It would save on rations for the feasts as well. If the treasury is so empty, better tell me now and I'll make sure to economize more prudently than I had planned." The council, recognizing the tone, wisely agreed with her.

For all Sarit's insistence, the funerary rites for Kelci could never be the normal rituals that would attend the passing of a Sidiana. For safety, the bodies of the plague victims had been burned, consuming precious wood that normally would not be wasted on the dead. It was not a body the procession bore through the streets of Lushan but a small iron box of ashes. One faction of the counsel had advised that the box be full-sized, to give the people the illusion it was Kelci's body that passed. Sarit's response had been "If you would have me begin my stewardship of this city with a lie, at least make it one the people will believe." And so it was only Kelci's ashes that passed through the streets.

I understood their discomfort but I could not share it. I had grown up watching bodies burn on the banks of the river. To me, the Euskalan practice of immuring their dead in the cliffside caverns was as soul-shivering as they found those ashes. They feared Kelci's spirit would be lost without her body to guide Jennon to it; I feared her soul would be trapped without the freeing balm of flames.

After passing through the city, the procession made its way to the valley and then Sarit and her company climbed the trail up the mountain to the caves, where the box was placed beside the twisted shapes that lay beneath their own fading shrouds. Sarit had told me once that the graves had never been robbed; the Sidianas were buried only with their simple clothing and their iron amulets. Still, there were fireside tales of unquiet souls and the curse that lay on the changeling babies whose bodies lay somewhere within the labyrinth.

If the fey had no souls, as was said, then those babies left only bones behind them. But I could not help but wonder what rituals the fey used to honour their dead and quiet their ghosts. What happened to the offspring they abandoned? A shiver that had nothing to do with the cold went down my spine.

It is nothing to do with you, I told myself sternly. *Your duty is to Sarit and her grief. You should be thinking of Kelci's soul, not those of inhuman babies dead a hundred years ago. Say your prayers for those who require them.*

But I said a prayer for those lost babies, just the same, if only to keep their ghosts at bay.

A month later, another procession rode the streets of the city in the opposite direction. This time, each tradition of the Euskalans was upheld. Sarit wore a thin white gown and rode a horse of the same colour. She went bareheaded and unadorned, the iron stripped from her fingers and her earlobes, a symbol of the Euskalans coming into their mountain sanctuary with only the burden of their past and their hope for the future to sustain them.

Today the crowd was jubilant and noisy. After the long winter, with its coda of death and sickness, they were eager for a reason to celebrate.

I rode in the throng behind her; councillors and cousins and guards intermingled. Ayriet was strapped to the accommodating chest of her nurse and seemed content to sleep her way through her mother's ascension. It took an hour to travel the switchback streets up the hill, to pass beneath the great iron gate, and climb the last distance to the palace. The crowd massed behind us, trailing along the narrow roads to get as close the palace as they could. I could hear the cries of entrepreneurs hawking tea and sweets and silk scarves in honour of the new Sidiana.

At last, we reached the plaza in front of the palace. The investiture took place in the central courtyard where I had first set foot in the city. I watched as Sarit ascended the dais they had built to kneel before those assembled there; the High Priestess of Jennon, the General of the army, the Master of the Builders Guild, the chosen representative of the great mercantile families, an elder of the villages in the valley.

The ceremony was simple and, in recognition of the crowds clogging the courtyard, the plaza and the roads, short. The High Priestess went first, placing the iron rings back onto Sarit's outstretched hands, tucking the earrings back into the naked holes in her lobes. Shoes were brought forth, their heels crossed with iron and Sarit stepped out of her slippers and into them. A sigh, like the faint whisper of wind, slipped through the crowd, an exhalation of breath they had not realized they were holding. Their Sidiana was once again safe from the dangerous magics of the fey, and undoubtedly, incontrovertibly human.

The Newari elder, his face almost invisible beneath his elaborately embroidered hat, brought her a black robe and helped her don it, a visible symbol of the help and protection the Newaris had granted the refugees upon their arrival in the mountains.

COLD HILLSIDE

Sarit rose then and went to the box that sat on one side of the dais. From it, she drew each of the gifts that represented the pact between the Sidiana and her people. To General Roshan, cheerful and bull-shouldered, she gave an iron sword, which he kissed once and then laid across his lap. To the Priestess, an ivory statue of Jennon, as simple as a child's doll but one of the treasured relics of the Euskalan's lost world. To the Master of Builder's Guild went a key, heavy with gold and tasselled in silk. To the Newari, a wooden box, containing seeds, a symbol of what the Euskalans brought with them to their new home. For the clan representative, there was a single opal, borne on a velvet tray.

When each gift had been given, she gathered the long black robe around her and went to sit on the great throne inlaid with iron that had been laboriously carried from the audience room for the occasion. It was not a comfortable seat—indeed, I had only seen Kelci sit in it a handful of times since my arrival in the city—but I suppose that was part of its purpose as well. Sarit sat still as each of the symbolic gifts was placed at her feet, under her protection and at her command.

The crowd watched it all in silence, though I could hear the murmurs from the throngs waiting in the plaza above the sound of the banners fluttering in the wind above us. As the last gift was set down, the wail of a hungry infant rose, startlingly loud. For a moment, we all looked about in automatic consternation but I had already guessed the culprit. Ayriet's nurse shushed her frantically but she was adamant and large-lunged. From the dais, Sarit laughed and rose. "Even the Sidiana has a master," she said loudly and the assembled crowd laughed and parted to let the woman come forward to hand the squalling child to her mother.

So, while the Priestess recited the final prayers, the crowd echoing her in the click of prayer beads and the mutter of voices, the Sidiana of Lushan nursed her daughter beneath the bright blue banner of the sky.

CHAPTER 14

Lilit

"I went to the fair this year," Lilit said at last. They were in her great-aunt's small study, the night's cold kept at bay by shutters and heavy felt hangings. Oil lamps leaked light in carefully inscribed patterns: stars and crescent moons, lotus flowers, a fanciful city created by the images pricked into the metal, turning absence into presence. As a child, Lilit had loved these strange, impractical lanterns.

Teresine finished refilling their cups with smoky tea and sat back into her chair, her fingers wrapped around the tiny porcelain cup. "So Amaris finally relented, did she?"

"Not entirely," Lilit admitted. "I went with the Austers. She had no choice but to allow it. She was't happy about it, though."

Teresine laughed. "I imagine not. And so what did you think of the fair?"

"It was strange, though not in any fashion I'd expected. I think about all the things I've heard my aunts and cousins say about the fair, and it's as if they all just describe one tiny portion of it and leave all the rest unsaid. Or as if the words they say bear no resemblance to the thing they are trying to describe."

"Kerias has never been noted for imagination," Teresine said dryly. "Your mother is quite at home there. But I am not interested in what your esteemed Kerias aunts and cousins say or don't say. What do *you* say?"

"I hated the bridge," Lilit began and Teresine laughed.

"So did I. What else?"

Lilit told her as best she could, describing the alternating mad scramble of preparation and long hours of waiting, the way the last hours of it passed with the vivid unreality of a dream. "Was it like that when you went to the fair?" she asked curiously and Teresine nodded. "But Dareh Auster and the others, it seems none of it touches them. To them, it's just . . ." She cast about for the word. ". . . business."

"It is never just business," her great-aunt replied. "Not to the ones with any sense. Not to Raziel." At the mention of the Sidiana's name, Lilit remembered the moment at the bridge, the strange look that might have been dismay. She wondered suddenly whether the announcement of her journey had been a surprise to her great-aunt at all.

"How many times did *you* go?" she asked.

"Ten, twelve," Teresine said with a dismissive flick of her fingers. "It was a long time ago. And the fey? What did you think of them?"

"It hurt to look at them. It hurt more to have them look at you. They . . ." Lilit stopped, the memory of the fey lord Bastien suddenly vivid in her mind. "It was hard to breathe around them. I fainted," she admitted reluctantly. "After the procession, when the Queen came out of her tent."

"You fainted." Teresine set down her cup and the porcelain rang with a dull chime against the little bronze table.

"I must have been in the sun too long," Lilit added hastily. "I didn't tell Mother this."

"Of course not."

"I'm fine. It was just . . . too much sun." She thought again of waking at the foot of the bridge, with her mind full of strange dreams and her body shivering. Remembered the panicked speculations she had forced from her mind with prayers and iron. "Too much sun," she repeated and took a sip of her own tea to cover her sudden confusion. She had begun this conversation in hopes of discovering some of Teresine's experiences at the fair, not with the intention of revealing all her own. She was aware of her great-aunt's suddenly watchful gaze. "One of them spoke to me," she said at last.

"One of the fey?"

Lilit nodded. "He said his name was Bastien. He said . . . I should tell you that he visits your mosaics, that he remembers you. He said I should tell you that others remember what the Queen forgets. *Chooses* to forget," she corrected herself automatically, as the quiet, compelling voice echoed in her ears.

"Bastien." The name was a whisper, as if her great-aunt did not realize she'd spoken it aloud.

"What did he mean?"

"Nothing," Teresine said. The look she turned on Lilit was fierce.

"They meddle, the fey. They throw stones to see what will break. They cannot be trusted. Oh child, never forget that. It is said they cannot lie but that does not mean they cannot turn the truth against you. They destroy whatever they touch. " Her voice had the sharp, stinging quiver of a line strung tight in the wind.

Lilit sat still, unable to think of a way to ask the questions that savage certainty tried to contain. In the sudden silence, Teresine gripped the arms of her chair and pushed herself to her feet. "I am going to bed," she announced and stamped her way towards the door. Lilit rose to help her but she waved her away. "Don't fuss, child. Urmit fusses enough for a dozen. We'll talk in the morning."

Abandoned, Lilit stood in the quiet room. It seemed colder now, empty of the weight of her great-aunt's presence. After a moment, she blew out all the lamps save one, the city with its strangely shaped roofs, which she carried with her out into the dark corridor. In her room, huddled beneath the blankets, she looked at the flickering outline and wondered if the city it depicted was real or as illusory as the rumoured cities of the fey.

She could well believe her great-aunt's words. She imagined the fey could deceive mortals without compunction. But, she asked silently of one star-like window in that mysterious city, what exactly was it that Bastien could not be trusted about?

In the morning, she woke to the cackle of the late-lingering sparrows, grown fat and lazy on the charity of Filiat. When she pulled aside the curtains and opened the shutters, she discovered the sun already lying across the stone terrace. Teresine would have been up for hours, she thought, and would tease her about her sluggishness.

But it was only Filiat she found in the kitchen. "She's still abed," the cook said, in response to her question. "She's feeling poorly this morning. Urmit's taken her tea." Filiat set a cup in front of her and poked at a pot over the fire. "You may as well have your tea and porridge now. She's an old bear on mornings like this. Wait till she's had a scratch or two at Urmit before you brave her lair."

"Does she have many mornings like this?" Lilit asked, accepting the bowl of barley porridge and the pot of honey that Filiat set before her.

"A few," Filiat admitted, with a sharp look. "We're none of us as young as we were. No need to be worrying." She meant the words for more than comfort Lilit realized, and was careful to contemplate her porridge more seriously than the meal required. They were a warning as well, or a plea, not to admit her great-aunt's weakness to the world. Or perhaps only to Amaris?

Lilit was just finishing her second cup of tea when Urmit returned to the kitchen, carrying an empty tray. "How is she?" she asked and Urmit sighed, shifting her bulk onto the bench that lined one side of the table.

"Her hip pains her sometimes, where she fell on it last year. She does not sleep much of late, just goes and jumbles those stones of hers around and around. But," she gave the empty tray a glance, "she eats enough, once she gets through grumbling about it. Don't you be worrying, Lily-child. She's iron through and through, your great-aunt is."

I would worry less, Lilit thought, *if you were both not so eager to urge me not to.* She had never thought of Teresine as young, could barely imagine that her fierce, iron-boned great-aunt could once have been her own age, but she had never thought of her as old either. But it was no longer possible to pretend that she was as ageless and eternal as the mountains above them; her bones were only bones, not iron.

She downed the last cool dregs of the bitter tea and rose. "I'd best go say good morning then," she announced and did not miss the glance that slid between the two women.

"See what she wants for midday," was all Filiat said.

Lilit knocked on the door of Teresine's room, heard an unintelligible response and entered. Her great-aunt was hunched at the edge of her bed, struggling to find the arm of her loose black robe.

When she looked up, Lilit saw a flash of angry humiliation cross her face. "Well, don't just stand there. Help me if you're going to come in without an invitation," Teresine snapped and Lilit hastened to her side. Urmit had opened the shutters and the cold air followed the sunlight into the room. Lilit could see the goosebumps on her great-aunt's arms. Beneath the white underrobe, worn and patched, her body seemed less like iron than one of the rare, stubborn trees that clung to the rocks beside the path up the mountain; thin, withered, surviving on the memory and promise of water.

As she sorted out the tangle of the black overrobe and began to draw it up Teresine's arms, Lilit saw the dark mark on her shoulder blade. Curious, she paused and twisted her head to see it more clearly.

It was, astonishingly, a tattoo. She thought it must once have been green but now was an ashy smear against the coppery skin. It was a stylized leaf, pointing downwards as if it were falling down her back. "What?" Teresine asked sharply. "What's wrong?"

"Nothing," Lilit replied and pulled the fabric up over her shoulders. "I never knew you had a tattoo." The Euskalans disdained such bodily alterations, though the old Newari families still sometimes pricked the hereditary patterns on their wrists and once in a while a vogue for these would flourish among the more rebellious city daughters and sons. Several of Lilit's older cousins still bore such marks from the last time they had been fashionable.

"Oh. That." Teresine shrugged and busied herself with fastening her sash. "I forget it is there."

"When did you have it done?"

"A long time ago. In Deshiniva."

"What does it mean?"

"Nothing that matters anymore."

"Then why won't you tell me?" Lilit persisted and Teresine looked at her for a long moment, her expression unreadable.

"They put it on me to show who owned me," she said at last. "In Jayasita, before I escaped onto Sarit's ship." Lilit had known about that; it was part of the colourful tale of her great-aunt's past, a tale that persisted despite Teresine's general refusal to discuss it. Urmit had told her parts of it, and Amaris, and Filiat, and even one or two of her aunts in Kerias, who were of an age to remember the arrival of the young refugee. "At least they put it where I did not have to look at it."

"Or where it would show."

"In Deshiniva it would." Lilit remembered her aunt's stories of the heat of that land, the moist air thick with perfume, the nights barely cooler than the days. She could hardly imagine such a place, such a heat. "Now, help me to my workroom," Teresine said shortly and allowed Lilit to put her hand under her arm and trail her down the hallways.

Lilit opened the shutters and stoked the braziers, while Teresine settled into her chair in front of her worktable. Duties done, Lilit found a seat by the window and waited to see if her great-aunt would actually ask her to leave. For a while, it seemed as if Teresine would pay no attention to her at all, then she finally said, "If you insist on staying, come and help me."

COLD HILLSIDE

She joined her at the table, finding a stool to sit on as she helped pick the tiles from the previous day's work and set them back into their bowls. When they were done, a constellation of colour surrounded the empty space where the mosaic had been. Teresine lapsed into stillness then, staring at that blank canvas, curling and uncurling her thin fingers.

At last, she took the bowl of blue tiles and spilled them into the empty frame. Her fingers moved among them, selecting and discarding. There was an odd rhythm to it, to the click of the tiles as they took their place on the table or fell back into the bowl. Lilit leaned her chin on her hand and watched silently, trying to guess which shapes and shades Teresine would choose and which she would reject. Slowly, inevitably, an indigo sky filled the top of the frame.

"Where did you learn to do this?" Lilit asked at last.

"Jayasita." Teresine studied a bright blue tile, the hue of poppies under the fierce, brief summer sun, and set it aside. "The house that—that I lived in there—was old. The mosaics needed to be repaired. They sent me to serve the artisans who did the work, to fetch and carry and bring them tea." She grimaced and tossed another rejected tile into the bowl with sudden force. "One of them asked my opinion on the work and liked my answer. So he taught me." Her laugh was a cough. "The house deducted the cost of my service from his fee. He was furious."

There were a dozen questions Lilit wanted to ask. She could not think of a way to ask any of them that would not cause Teresine's unexpected openness to vanish back behind the armour of her cryptic sarcasm. "What was the mosaic of?" she ventured at last. "The one in Jayasita."

"The goddess Erzulie, dancing on the back of a dolphin as it crested the waves. There were flowers in her hands and in her long black hair and a chain of rubies around her waist. It took Viram days to find the right red for those rubies, so that they would glow just so when the lamplight struck them."

"And the one Bastien spoke of? What was it?"

For a moment, Lilit thought she would not answer, that she was iron-boned and iron-armoured once again. "I do not know," Teresine said at last. "The Aygaresh made it, or so the fey said. When I saw it for the first time, there was nothing left but a shape that swirled like mist from the mountains and a pattern like a knot of lines repeated over and over. Whether an Aygaresh would know what it was when I was done with it, well, that's anyone's guess."

"When you were done . . ." Lilit repeated. "What did you do to it?"

"Fixed it, child. Or ruined it, as may be. I made it whole again, at any rate."

"But why?"

"Because the fey asked it—and we were in no position that year to refuse them whatever price they named."

"Couldn't the fey make it whole again themselves?"

Teresine made a disdainful snort. "The fey can make nothing whole. And even if they had a mind to, they could not have done it. The Aygaresh knots were made of iron."

"But then why did the fey want it remade in the first place?" Lilit asked in bewilderment.

"Who can say?" Teresine replied. "I never knew." She gathered up the blue tiles and poured them contemptuously back into their bowl. Lilit watched her collect a handful of black ones instead and begin to lay them out on the table. Each answer Teresine gave spurred a thousand questions she desperately wanted to ask and feared to bungle.

"Where was it?" she dared at last.

"The Border Court," Teresine replied and her mouth twisted at the astonishment Lilit could not hide. "The year Raziel became Sidiana, the year that Sarit died, I spent a winter at the Border Court, remaking the mosaics."

For a moment, Lilit was too stunned to speak. No one had ever been to the Border Court. Everyone knew that. The fey permitted no approach closer than the far side of the crevasse. "You did? What was it like?" she asked carefully, as if her merest breath could break whatever spell had loosened her great-aunt's tongue.

"I cannot say." At her look of protest, Teresine shook her head. "Cannot, not will not, child. I was bound to silence on that, by more power than one." The black tiles clicked and turned beneath her fingers, shaping themselves into a looping knot of darkness. She made a sound to herself and traced the pattern delicately with her finger.

"But you remember it?"

"Oh yes, I remember it. I remember it all." Her voice was soft, with just a hint of bitterness, like a trace of spice that lingered on the tongue. "I remember Bastien. He was considerate to me, in his way." Her glance at

Lilit was sharp again, the drift into memory corrected. "All this I say in the confidence that you know how to hold your tongue, Lily-child. There were only a handful of people who knew what happened then and there are fewer left alive to remember it now. And the only person you should speak to about what happened to you at the fair is the Sidiana, if she should ever ask.

"I meant what I said last night. You cannot trust the fey. The Queen's magic can stop my tongue on what their world was like, but it cannot change that truth. I know better than to order you, even if your mother does not. But Lily-child, stay away from them. Let someone else go and dance attendance on them at the fair next year."

The tiles scattered beneath her fingers, the knots of darkness tumbling into randomness. Lilit looked at Teresine's profile, bent over the broken pattern. The last words had been as close to a plea as she could ever imagine coming from her great-aunt's lips. "What does the Queen choose to forget?" she asked at last and saw Teresine's eyes close for moment as if in pain.

"That she ever had so mortal a thing as a heart, one assumes." The bitterness was clear this time, dry and sharp-edged. "I told you, child. What they touch, they break. Even Bastien. He should have held his tongue."

Lilit thought of the bridge, the one thing she had not told Teresine. It was not a lie, she had never managed to lie well to her great aunt, but she had not truly told the truth either.

Just like the fey, she thought. But there was one thing she could say, with no trace of lie about it.

"You don't have to worry. I would be quite happy never to go to the fair again."

CHAPTER 15

Teresine

After the grief and loss of the plague and the hard year that followed, the next year seemed like the sun after the storm. The harvests were bountiful and the traders returned with riches and wonders enough to pay the tribute and tempt the fey into their own extravagant payments that went back into the world in the cities to the south.

Sarit grew increasingly comfortable in her role and her power. The politicking of the council and the Houses did not stop but there was a comfortable, reflexive nature to it. No one truly wanted to risk the gift of peace and prosperity, whether it was luck or Sarit or Jennon that had granted it to them. The Asezati gave me leave from the school to resume my place in the palace.

Ayriet grew into a curious, bright-eyed toddler; the delight of the palace and the bane of her caretakers at the same time. She assumed any adult was there to please or care for her and she was, in general, correct. Of course, no matter whose lap she toddled towards or whose hand she clung to, her appointed minders were never far away. For all their casual openness, the Euskalans were no fools, to trust blindly in either the good nature of men or the mercy of their dark landlords, the fey.

One day, Sarit and I took advantage of the high summer sun and found our favourite private spot, a secluded roof, sheltered from the wind, on which we could sprawl on borrowed blankets, shed as many robes as we dared, and let the light and warmth touch as much skin as we could.

I lifted my face to the sun and sighed. "Now this is how one should live," I said. "Not bundled in a dozen robes in the gloom, in case your skin should freeze."

"Go on then," Sarit replied drowsily. This was an old argument between us and had long since assumed the air of ritual. "One breath of that air in Jayasita will drown you and you'll be whining for a mountain breeze."

"Flowers all year long, scenting the night air," I continued, made blissful by the sun's hand on my skin. "Spices and water warm enough to swim in and trees. I miss trees so tall they are like a great roof above you."

"Floods and bugs and rain for days."

"Soft breeze from the water."

"Snakes," she countered and I laughed. She knew well enough there was nowhere in the world I would rather be. She sighed and shifted, spreading her hair into a golden web around her head.

"What am I to do about Raziel?" she asked at last.

"What can you do? She is at that awkward age."

"Were you such a trial at that age?"

"You would have to ask my mother that," I replied, as if such a thing might be possible. I did not think of her much, but sometimes, in the night, I woke with the memory of a voice singing a song that had never been heard in the high stone walls of Lushan. I did not even know if she was still alive. "Were you?" I countered and then remembered that she knew quite well where her mother's ashes lay.

"Never," she said but laughed. "Perhaps a little." She rolled onto her stomach and propped her chin on her crossed forearms. "She broods and snaps and, when I ask her what is wrong, she either stares at me stone-faced or bursts into tears. Her teachers say she barely speaks during classes now, though she has always been a good student."

"She lost her mother too. And she had no work in which to lose her grief."

"She has work to do," Sarit replied. "Study, service. She is the child of a Sidiana of Lushan. She knows what that means."

"It means," I began carefully, "that she is the younger sister of the Sidiana Sarit. Yours is not the easiest of shadows in which to stand."

"Bah. She knows better than that."

"She might know it but she does not feel it."

"Perhaps I should send her to the Asezati school," Sarit mused after a moment. "Perhaps she would be happier there."

Though I had learned a great deal at the school, found a place there, I did not think Raziel's situation was the same as mine.

"She would be no happier for being banished," I said carefully and

Sarit shot me a sharp glance. "She would take it so."

"So what shall I do then?"

"I do not know," I admitted and she laughed and sat up.

"I do," she said with a smile. "I will give her a tutor. One from the school. One who will understand her."

"And how will you find such a paragon of patience and wisdom?"

"I already have," she replied imperturbably and I knew quite suddenly what she would say. "You."

Sarit would not define exactly what duties this newly created position required, replying to my questions with a wave of her hand and the cheerful instruction that it was entirely up to me. She also left it up to me to inform Raziel, who I feared would take the decision with less grace than I had mustered.

I put the business off for a handful of days, until Sarit observed one evening that, while she had given me free rein in the matter, she did think being tutor perhaps required informing the tutored and spending time with them. Thus chastised, I hunted down Raziel in the stables and asked her if she would see me in the porcelain room when she was done her assigned tasks there.

The porcelain room was at the top of the palace. In the relative warmth of the summer, the shutters on this level were thrown open, the curtains drawn aside and the sun and wind allowed free entry. The rooms around it were claimed in summer by the palace artists, who treasured the light while they could find it, before the winter would drive them back to creating with mittened fingers or by candlelight.

It had taken me some time to grow accustomed to the bright, gaudy extravagance of Euskalan art. The Deshinivi loved vibrant colours, it was true, and I could remember the gilded wonder of the great houses of Jayasita, but they paled in comparison to the intense hues and complex designs favoured by the Euskalans. In their statues and tiny painted images, the colours were subtle and simple, the lines pure and clean. I could not see how one thing grew into the other until I lived through a winter or two.

In the dark halls and chapels, with the candles and oil lamps smoking, all the elegant sophistication of the old art would have been invisible. Outside, in the wide sweep of the valley, the only bright colours amid the ashen hues of the stone, were the flowers that bloomed in brief summer splendour. The Euskalans adopted the vivid pigments of the local artists out of sheer self-defence, to give themselves something to see in the half-light of the winter-bound city.

The porcelain room was one of my favourite places in the palace. The porcelain-makers and potters fired their creations in the ovens across the courtyard, but brought them here to paint and finish. When their own rooms grew too crowded, the artists used it for storage. The tables were scattered with pots and plates, goblets and vases, statues of Jennon and the other gods. At one end of the room was a low table and a heap of pillows, faded and slightly dusty. Sometimes artisans would retreat here, but much of the time the room was empty. I liked it for that, for the great arches of the windows with their slices of sky and for the colours that glowed briefly in the sun. It reminded me of Jayasita; one of the few memories of that city that did not hurt.

I was looking out the window of the porcelain room, down at the busy courtyard below when Raziel entered. She'd pulled her robe on over her working clothes but left it open, revealing the grubby trousers and worn shirt. She did not have Sarit's height nor her older sister's sureness. Sarit had only been four years older than Raziel was now when she had journeyed to Deshinivi, I realized, but could not imagine that the Sidiana had ever been as young as this. There was a confidence in Sarit, a certainty, that seemed as much a part of her as her bones and her flesh. I could see none of it in Raziel, though I supposed it might merely be buried beneath grief and confusion and the remnants of childhood.

Raziel looked around curiously but only stepped far enough into the room to allow the door to close behind her. "You wished to see me, Azi Teresine?"

"Have you ever been here before?" I asked. I was stalling; I admit to it.

Raziel shook her head, then changed her mind and nodded. I did not believe there was anywhere in the palace she had not been. "Once, I think. A long time ago." She gave me a guarded glance, as if she suspected I had some chore in store for her.

"Come in. I'm not going to make you sweep anything." She had the grace to look embarrassed but edged farther into the room, her eye caught by the creations on display around the room. "Your sister is worried about you."

"My sister never thinks about me."

"She does." Her look was caustic this time but she said nothing, just drifted over to look at a row of bowls in varying shades of red with gilded rims. "She thinks you are unhappy."

"Why should I be unhappy?"

"I can think of a few things that might make me unhappy, were I you."

"You are not me. You are not—" she stopped, her lips compressed. I knew well enough what she meant to say. *You are not even Euskalan.*

"No. Though all that means is that I have had more cause to be unhappy than you know."

She made a brief sound, like a snort, and fingered a blue bowl, tipping it up to display an interior of muddy orange. She wrinkled her nose and set it back. "Because she is worried and believes you to be unhappy," I continued, "your sister has made a decision."

"Of course. She always does."

"She thinks you need a tutor."

"I don't want a tutor."

"She did not mention what you want," I said and realized, quite suddenly, that I sounded somewhat like Yeshe Bukoyan.

"Of course she didn't. Why should what I want matter to her?" Her voice rose a little but she caught it before she looked at me again. "It's to be you, I suppose."

"She did not mention what I want, either," I said and gave her a smile which was not returned.

"What are you supposed to teach me? How to be her? That's all I am, after all. A substitute for her, if the city needs one." This time, her voice betrayed her, all raw hurt and longing. I knew that hurt, heard the echoes of that longing in the memory of my own tears.

"I will teach you," I said honestly, "anything you want to learn. I will also try to teach you some things you might not want, although I cannot make you learn them."

"And what *can* you teach me? What do you know except how to pray and how to follow my sister's orders?" She turned to face me, her look as contemptuous as only the young could manage. She had picked up a small plate the colour of the sky and now held it between her hands as if she did not know it was there at all.

"I know how to survive in a place that would break me. I know how to live in a place that does not love me. I know how to choose what I want to be, when that choice is offered." I knew what Sarit wanted of me, what the burden of her responsibility demanded she want of me. I saw Raziel's own fear and longing for the weight that shaped her mother and her sister. My heart went out to her. "You are not Sarit. You can never be Sarit. But I would teach you what I know, so you may choose the Raziel that you become."

I did not know if that was wrong, if I could serve both Sarit's responsibilities and Raziel's need. I did not know if I would betray both by trying to stand between them, to teach Raziel what she needed to know and yet let her learn to be what she desired. I was so caught in my own confusion that I did not see my pupil's until the plate shattered on the floor.

I think her action startled even her. We were both still, staring at the scatter of broken porcelain lying like shards of sky against the dark wood of the floor.

Raziel drew a slow, shaking breath. "Can you teach me how to put that back together again?" she asked, in both challenge and despair.

"No," I answered and looked at the shattered porcelain while the memories moved inside me. "But I can teach you how to make something new from what is left."

"I suppose that will have to do."

CHAPTER 16

Lilit

After three days with her great-aunt, Lilit went home. Teresine had said nothing more on the subject of mosaics or the fey and her temper—or her constitution—remained uncertain. Still, she insisted on stumping down the steps to bid Lilit farewell.

"Give my regards to Amaris," she said. "That will annoy her."

"I will," Lilit replied, laughing. "Though I'm not sure it will annoy her. She's much too busy these days to be annoyed."

"Huh. What keeps her so busy then?"

"Well, I'm not supposed to know this, of course, but she has been asked to stand for the House Council."

"And she has not decided whether being my niece is an advantage or a liability. It were better she'd be satisfied with running Kerias when old Ursul is gone."

"She would do well on the Council," Lilit said, because it was true.

"Well enough. She has the head for it," Teresine agreed but there was something in the gruff cheerfulness Lilit mistrusted. She wondered if her great-aunt's hip was paining her again and decided it would be best not to let her stand much longer.

She said her farewells quickly and then was surprised to find herself caught in a brief, fierce embrace. "Be well, Lily-child," Teresine whispered, her voice seeming to catch on the old childhood name she now rarely used. "Be careful." There was something in the words and in her voice, something that made Lilit return the embrace for a moment longer, till the brittle feel of her great-aunt's body was too much for her to bear.

She went down the path quickly, pausing once to turn back and wave at the dark figures still arrayed in front of the house. She would have to come back soon, before the snows came, she told herself. Before—but she would not finish that thought.

COLD HILLSIDE

She was an hour down the switchback path when she heard voices, the muffled thump of plodding hooves and the faint jingle of harnesses. She rounded a curve and saw three horses labouring up the trail beneath her. From where she stood, she could see nothing of the riders but black coats and black hats. She watched them for a moment, the horses' hooves lost in the dry dust they stirred, and then continued down the path.

Her downward passage met their upward one ten minutes later, though she knew they saw her coming well before that. As she approached, the riders resolved into two women and a man. The man and one of the women were armed, swords strapped across their backs. Flaps of armour hung below the felt brims of their hats. They rode with casual alertness; their hands did not leave the reins but Lilit was sure their swords could be out of their sheaths before she could blink.

She stepped respectfully from the path and waited until they reached her, then bowed her head to the woman who rode between them, awaiting her acknowledgement.

"Lilit." Raziel's voice was warm. "How is your great-aunt?"

"She is well, Sidiana."

"Lilit," Raziel said again and Lilit was forced to look at her. Beneath the shadow of her hat, her face was pure Euskalan; pale skin darkened only a little by the sun, spare, refined features, line-cradled eyes of startling blue. Lilit saw what she had not at the fair; the etching of strain around her mouth, the too-taut arch of the skin across her jaw and cheekbones.

"Her hip hurts her, Urmit says," Lilit admitted. *She is getting old*, she almost said, then remembered Raziel was only twelve years younger than Teresine.

"I see." There was a trace of amusement in her voice. "I suppose Teresine says nothing on the matter."

"No. She just complains that Urmit worries too much," Lilit replied and Raziel smiled. Lilit saw it linger on her lips for a moment after it had left the blue eyes.

"What did you think of the fair?"

"It was interesting." She coloured a little as she said the words, knowing they were meaningless but unable to think of what else to say.

"Ah. And do you want to go again next year?"

"I had not thought about it, Sidiana. It will be up to the Austers, I suppose."

"Of course." The horse huffed and sidled sideways suddenly. Lilit saw one of the guards glance at Raziel, her face full of curious concern. "Give my greetings to Ursul Kerias," the Sidiana said. "And to your mother."

"Yes. Thank you." Lilit ducked her head and waited while the Sidiana's party moved on. She looked once at their retreating backs and then set off down the trail.

Soon after Lilit began to spend her summers at her great-aunt's home, Teresine officially retired from the court. She might have been nothing more than a daunting old Asezat, living in seclusion in the mountains. Yet always there would be something to remind her that there was much more to her great-aunt than that.

Often it was simply a messenger, arriving on foot and left to wait in the kitchen, downing a bowl of Filiat's soup, while Teresine frowned over her scrawled reply. But sometimes it was Raziel herself, journeying up the mountain as Lilit had seen her today. She would stay for a day or two, once for a week. She and Teresine would argue and tease each other and talk long into the night. Lilit found herself drawn into the warmth of their old friendship and she came to think of their guest as simply Raziel, rather than the woman who ruled Lushan.

But for all that, she knew that only at Teresine's could the truth be ignored. In the city, Raziel became the Sidiana once again. Lilit had no more business with her than any other minor daughter of any clan did. If Amaris had hoped for more, if those summers had been meant as something more than the one thread of trust between her and her aunt, she was destined for disappointment.

Lilit met no one else on the path down to the city. Back in the Kerias clanhouse, she found a note from her mother, requesting her attendance upon her return. Lilit paused long enough to unpack her belongings, wash her face in the cold water in the bowl in her room and detour through the kitchen in search of something simple and portable to eat. The cousins on duty preparing the noon meal let her take a savoury pastry—in return for future favours, of course—and, wiping the last guilty grease from her lips, she presented herself at the door of her mother's office.

Amaris looked up from her ledgers and smiled. "How was your visit?"

"It was good. Teresine sends her regards."

"That is kind of her. Is she well?"

"Well enough." The fey themselves would not coerce the truth of

Teresine's health from her, Lilit decided, and gave her mother a bland smile. "I met the Sidiana on the road. She was going to see her."

"Was she?" Her mother's expression did not change but Lilit saw the sudden interest that shaped itself around the slightly narrowed eyes. "Did she say why?"

"No. But they are old friends." Which Amaris knew quite well, which made reminding her mere spite on Lilit's part. She could not quite bring herself to regret it.

Amaris nodded and seemed to set the subject aside with no great reluctance. "Do you know Tristel Auster." Lilit shook her head. "He is the son of Dareh's sister-in-house Kyanis. He is a serving as a clerk at the palace. I wondered if you had met him."

"No," Lilit said, mistrusting the casual interest in her mother's voice. Surely Amaris was not already plotting matches for her, though she knew her mother considered the Auster connection worth cultivating.

"A pity. Could you, I wonder? Or keep your ears open and let me know what they say of him."

"I'll not spy on the Austers for you, mother," Lilit managed to say, trying to be amused rather than outraged and failing.

"Not for me, "Amaris replied, without offense. "For your cousin Sitran." She caught her daughter's annoyed glance and shrugged. "I thought they might suit. If he's an unpleasant, useless creature, I'd rather know it now."

"Would it make a difference?"

"Or course it would. An Auster boy with his wits intact would be much better."

"But an Auster boy by any means?"

"Your apprenticeship is useful. Dareh likes you. But something more . . . solid . . . would never hurt."

"Hurt Kerias or your chances on the Council?" Lilit asked.

"A place on the council would be good for Kerias. We have not served there in a generation." Amaris's voice was patient, as if explaining the fact of the sun rising to a child.

Lilit yawned, suddenly tired, and equally suddenly bored by her mother's ambition. "I'll ask about Tristel. But only because I like Sitran. As for the rest, leave me out of it, mother"

"This House is your home, Lilit. This House is your future, no matter what you do at the Austers. Don't forget that."

Which was true, Lilit thought as she returned to her room, though she did not care to have it pointed out so bluntly. It would serve her mother right if she did as Teresine had done, and joined the Asezati. But just the thought of it made her smile to herself; she was an even more unlikely member of that order than her great-aunt. Kerias *was* her home, but she would serve it as she chose, not as her mother did.

Her life resumed, much as it had been, and stayed that way for another month. Then, on the same day, two things happened that would change it completely.

First, she woke early in the morning (astonishing enough in itself) and was promptly and fiercely sick.

Second, Urmit came down the mountain on her old pony.

When she arrived at the gates of the clanhouse, Amaris was away and so the cousin on duty summoned Lilit from the bed she had taken to after her violent awakening. She was feeling considerably better by this point but had decided that a day off without her mother in residence was exactly what she required.

Byasa had shown Urmit to one of the little receiving rooms by the main hall and, properly polite, provided tea and rice cakes. Lilit knew why she had come the moment she saw the old woman, sitting stiff and miserable in her chair, both food and drink untouched. "Child," Urmit said and then her face crumpled for a moment. "Oh, Lily-child."

"She's dead." She wanted it to be a question, so that it could be denied, but it came out as a statement. The nausea returned abruptly, and with it a queer dizziness, so that she sat down as quickly as she could.

"She was well enough last night," Urmit said, her hands twisted in her lap, as if her knotted fingers could hold her intact. "Better than she had been. She was in her work room all day, fiddling with her colours and her shapes. She's not been sleeping well, I know that, but we old women, we don't sleep much. I made her go to bed last night, I did. She was just sitting there, staring at that mosaic, all the lanterns out, as if she could see it in the dark. I told her she could fix it tomorrow. What could a day matter? I said. Seeing as she'd been working on the fool thing for years now anyway. What's another day? I said. But then this morning, she was gone."

She stopped talking, the flow of words dammed abruptly, and they sat in the silence for a moment. Lilit put her hand over her stomach and swallowed hard. "I'll come with you," she said at last. "Back to the house. We'll leave a note for my mother." She rose and was relieved the room did not revolve. "Give me a few moments to prepare and we'll go together. I want—I'd like to see her."

There were things that had to be done, she thought, as she scrawled a note to Amaris. The priestess to be called, the funerary arrangements made, the Sidiana to—

Lilit stopped, staring at the paper, the words turned to unintelligible scratchings. Someone had to tell Raziel but it did not have to be her. Her mother was quite competent to deal with all of it. Nothing would satisfy her more than to rise to the occasion of her famous aunt's death, especially under the grieving eye of the Sidiana. Jennon knew, Lilit herself had no notion what to do and less interest in doing it. But Amaris had not loved Teresine and she had. She did.

She felt the first ache of tears behind her eyes, in the back of her throat. She wanted to put her head down on the table and weep. She wanted to go back to surrender it to someone, anyone else who would bear the burden. She remembered Raziel's face on the path to Teresine's house, the sharp, sad bones of it shadowed from the sun. She remembered the long nights when she had lain in front of the fire and listened to the soft voices rise and fall. Lilit took a deep breath, folded the note to Amaris and went back to the parlour. "We must go to the palace first," she said and saw Urmit's face turn pale. "I am going to tell the Sidiana."

CHAPTER 17

Teresine

Inspired by my conversation with Raziel in the storeroom, I began to toy with the idea of creating mosaics again. I collected broken glass and crockery, ignoring the bewilderment of servants and cooks and artists. I found a little room in which to work. My first attempts were so awkward I did not bother to affix them and then I ruined the next several attempts with my inability to remember exactly how to mix the paste that would bind the broken pieces together. Gradually the trick of it returned, my eye improved and I was making little things—frames, tiles and the like—that satisfied me.

Emboldened, I decided to teach Raziel. She consented to try, as much to escape my other teachings I suspected, but after several sessions of twitching fingers and bouts of frustrated temper whose source eluded me, it was clear it was not one of my more successful ideas. When I finally told her I supposed there was no need for two practitioners of a foreign art in the palace she admitted the truth. "I would like to do it, truly," she said, her fingers tracing a curve of embedded crimson in one of my works in progress. "But it's too much like making a mourning flag."

When she said it, I understood immediately, though it had never occurred to me, the mosaics being so much a part of my past that I never thought of them in the context of Euskalan mourning. But she was right; for all that mosaics were permanent and the cloth flags lasted only until the wind and sun and rain scoured them away, the process of creation was essentially the same. She would have done this for Kelci, chosen traditional colours and patterns, painted them on a silken banner, and strung the banner on the line with the others, out on the stone monuments that crowned the hill just beyond the palace. When the colours were gone, bleached from the silk, the grief was gone as well, washed away by life and time and Jennon's grace.

COLD HILLSIDE

By tradition, the banners were to be painted and given to the elements before the first anniversary of a death. There were stories of women who had waited decades to paint one, mourning a lover or a child. There were stories of women who never painted one at all, mourning becoming their lover, their child.

I made one for Sarit, all those years ago but it did not ease my grief and I have never painted another.

And so two years passed. The harvests were good, the weather as reasonable as this impossible place allowed, no illnesses ravaged the people. A war somewhere in the east provided steady employment—and income—for the mercenary troops. Sarit remarked, somewhat cynically, that we would prosper when the war was over as well: our engineers would be required to build monuments for the victors. Whatever its source, each year the tithe was paid and the fair was as uneventful as such a thing could be.

Raziel took her place in the council. My mosaics grew larger, cluttering up first my room at the palace, then my room at the school and finally the rooms of my friends. Ayriet blossomed into a child with a quick mind and a surprisingly raucous laugh for so delicate a creature.

And Sarit, Sarit smiled over it all, and took the inevitable machinations of the city's powers with amusement, and kept the iron in her sheathed in velvet. And then she fell in love.

Sidianas did, of course, some more often than others, according to the histories. Some wed the men who fathered their children, some did not. Some wed for politics, some for love, some never at all. Sarit had certainly had her share of lovers in the years since I had snuck out of the school to accompany her outside the iron, but I do not think she had loved any of them.

She met Perin at Spring Festival, at the breaking of the ice. That year, there was certainly enough ice to break, though in some years the thaw came so early the Guild representative's pick shattered nothing but the wind-driven waves on the lake. The Euskalans did not care; the breaking of the ice was only symbolic, after all. I thought it symbolic mostly of the Euskalans' peculiar, lingering belief that they could control the harsh home they had claimed but I kept the thought to myself. The Spring festival was a time of joy, a release from the long cold winter and a welcome to the brief blossom of summer to come.

Perin was one of the engineers, high in the guild, and recently returned from overseeing the construction of the fourth palace of the Fezas Guteras on the far side of the mountains. He was a few years our senior, with the crinkle-cornered eyes of a man who had spent a good deal of time squinting along a level and the callused hands of a man who had worked as hard as the crews he commanded. Somewhere during the long ritual that preceded the Engineers advance onto the ice with picks and flags, he had looked at Sarit with those sun-lined eyes and she had looked back. That evening, at the great feast in the palace, he was at her side. That night, as the Euskalans celebrated the promise of the season, he was in her bed.

To the surprise of all of us, at her side and in her bed he stayed. She bloomed with the coming summer, her eyes as bright as the sun on her golden hair, her joy as expansive as the wide sky above us. He was not the safest choice she could have made—the Engineers' Guild lobbied for influence in the palace as much as any mercantile house—but eventually even the grumpiest of the councillors accepted his presence. Neith had been a soldier and Kelci's uncle had been the son of a bureaucrat so it was generally agreed that an Engineer as the Sidiana-consort was overdue. Sarit, being Sarit, was scrupulous in her treatment of her lover's guild and did her best to grant them no more than their due.

One summer afternoon found us on the roof again, stretched beneath the sun, sheltered from the wind that flared the banners above our heads. Sarit had commandeered a tray of tea and cakes; only crumbs remained and the tea was nicely cool in the thin porcelain cups. "Do you like him?" she asked me and I turned to look at her, where she sprawled on the warm stones of the roof.

"Does it matter?"

"It might."

"If I said no, would you give him up?"

She laughed and opened her eyes briefly, giving me the half-lidded gaze of a sleepy cat. "No. But you will not say no."

"True enough. Well then, I like him. He's thoughtful and intelligent and does not presume too much." She laughed again and closed her eyes, satisfied. I swirled the tea around in the cup and watched the leaves float and settle. "Do *you* like him?" I asked at last.

"Of course not. I make it my habit to sleep with men I do not like."

"No, do you *like* him?" I would not be the first one to say the word *love*. There were places that bore careful treading, even between us. We never spoke of Jayasita, or what I did there. I suspected she believed it had motivated, in some part, my decision to join the Asezati. In truth, I suspected it myself, though it was a thing I was content to leave alone, a shadow I was willing to leave undisturbed somewhere in the depths of my heart.

"Yes," she said, her smile turning lazily sensual. "I like him." She shifted to sit up and rest her back against the parapet. "Was there someone you liked, back in your village?" I shook my head. My parents had talked of wedding me to a second cousin up the river but I had two older sisters whose placement took precedence over mine and I had never even seen the boy in question. "And here? In all the years, has there ever been anyone . . . ?"

"I'm a priestess of Jennon."

"Which has seemed to matter remarkably little to remarkably many women," Sarit pointed out. It was true enough; the Asezati vow of celibacy was surprisingly elastic. No one in Lushan seemed to care, instead making tragic or ribald tales of their loves and passions. I had never thought about whether it mattered to me—it was merely the vow I assumed would be easiest for me to uphold.

"There has never been anyone," I told her firmly, which was also true. There had been offers, of course. There had been men in the court who found me exotic—or thought I might be useful—but no man had touched me since that night outside the inn, when the Isbayan soldier had kissed my mouth and found it as cold as the mountain air. I could not remember his face anymore but the smell of cinquegrass could sometimes conjure his voice and the brief, lonely touch of his lips. To my own uneasy surprise, there were times when I did not find the memory altogether unpleasant, when it stirred an odd, queasy excitement I supposed was as close as I could come to desire.

"Well, you do not know what you are missing," Sarit said, tilting her face to the sun.

There was enough lightness in her voice that I could laugh at her words, and find only the faintest taste of bitterness in it. "Oh, I do," I assured her.

"No." She looked at me squarely then and stepped into the quagmire of the unspoken, confident our friendship would bear it, as it had borne all else. "You don't," she said gently.

And what could I say to that, which she in her love and compassion believed, which all her faith and pity could not make true?

So I said nothing and she let it be and we went on as before.

Then, as the summer waned, she announced she was pregnant once again.

I never asked her if she intended it—though certainly others on the council did. There were those who thought the risks too great, given her age and her illness after Ayriet's birth. Kelci's death was still sharp in many minds and there were those who felt she should not endanger the comfortable peace the city had found. There was still a chance the pregnancy could be ended and there were those who felt her duty to the city demanded that course. ˙

I supported her in the council—and in private—as I had always done. Sarit was twenty-eight; not young but certainly Euskalan women bore children at her age with no difficulty. Ayriet's birth had been hard, it was true, but she was strong and healthy and the greatest healers in the city would be in attendance. And, whatever her intentions had been, this was a thing she wanted, this child of her body and Perin's. Still, I was relieved when the time in which she could change her mind had passed, for now that there was nothing that could be done, I hoped the grim thread of doubt in my heart would unravel and vanish.

All through the winter, the child grew. Sarit seemed herself; as hardworking and sensible as ever, though she wearied sooner than was her wont. She ate what the healers ordered and drank their fortifying potions and prayed diligently to the kind face of Jennon.

When the birth began, I sat beside her, holding her hand as I had done before. Raziel was there and Ayriet tried to be, slithering into the room whenever a door opened only to be scooped outside once again by a sharp-eyed healer or attendant. Perin paced outside the door, seeming as tempted as Ayriet but wisely refraining. It seemed an easier birth than Ayriet's had been, shorter, less painful. But when the child at last slipped wetly from her body on its flood of blood, the flood did not abate.

I sat there by her side, numb, disbelieving, as the healers tried to stem the tide. But there was no dam that would hold it, no moon strong enough to call it back, and, in the end, it bore us all away into the darkness.

CHAPTER 18

Lilit

Three days later, the funerary rites were held.

Lilit had heard the tales of the mourning that had attended the death of Sarit, though mostly from Urmit, for Teresine herself rarely spoke of it. Urmit had told her of the procession through the silent streets of the city, of the white-shrouded body, of the grim, red-eyed palace contingent that had ridden through the gates and up into the Valley of the Dead. "That was the first time I ever saw your great-aunt," she'd said one day, when Teresine had snapped at the young Lilit and sent her scurrying for the shelter of the kitchen and Urmit's warm presence. "That day, watching on the road. We'd walked a day down the valley, from our village, to pay our respects. We were crying, all of us, and putting the dust on our cheeks, like is proper. Half the procession was weeping too, and just as dusty from the road. Not your great-aunt, though. She just rode along, looking straight ahead, as if she were a thousand miles away. But her heart was broken, Lily-child, never you doubt it. It broke and she could no more put it back together than she could one of those plates she breaks up for her mosaics. Sometimes the memories plague her. Live long enough child, and yours'll plague you, too."

As she rode along a different road, Lilit wondered if this would be one of those memories. She could understand her great-aunt's still features and her thousand-mile stare. She was certain the same look had been on her face more than once over the last three days. One moment, the loss would be like a stone inside her, a cold weight in her chest all the weeping in the world would not dislodge. The next, she would find herself in a place where it was nothing but a sad story happening to someone else. She felt like a hawk coasting in the thin blue air, riding untouched and untouchable above the dark plain of her grief. Then someone would speak or a memory would rise inside her and she would plunge back down again into the moment and the world and the knowledge that this was indeed all happening.

There was no one on this road, as there had been no one on the streets of Lushan, save those whose own business had brought them there and who paused, curious and respectful, to watch the procession pass. Raziel had insisted the ceremony take place in the city so she sent a troop of the palace guard up to the mountain house to bring the body back to a place that, living, Teresine had not set foot in for ten years. That decision had surprised more than Lilit, or so she had gathered from gossip overheard in both the Kerias and Auster houses. Dareh Auster, riding now somewhere behind her, had given her a long look when Lilit arrived as always on the day after her great-aunt's death but had said merely "Do what you must. Things are always quiet after the fair."

In truth, Lilit knew she was good for little more than sweeping the floor and sorting supplies. But it was better to be dully engaged in labour at the Austers than idle at Kerias, where her mother had taken over what mechanics of grieving Raziel was willing to surrender.

Lilit lifted her gaze from the back of her horse's head and looked ahead, to her mother's stiff back and, beyond her, the upright figure of the Sidiana. She remembered walking with Urmit up the steep path to the palace, remembered waiting in the great main chamber, watching the light from the high windows shift across the heavy weavings on the walls, starting at every step of every passerby. Urmit had stared determinedly at her hands, as if afraid to look too closely around her. At last, an older woman, whose grave face Lilit was certain she'd seen at the fair, arrived to take them to the Sidiana.

After the dim splendour of the hall, the Sidiana's office was surprisingly plain, decorated more with papers and books than gold and riches. Raziel stepped from behind the desk as they entered and Lilit heard her catch her breath as she looked at them. Lilit knew then that the Sidiana knew, that she had known—or guessed—from the moment she had been told who was waiting to see her, just as she herself had known when she saw Urmit.

"I'm sorry—I thought we should tell you—" Lilit began and then her own breath caught and stuck and no more words would come.

"Thank you," Raziel said with formal, habitual grace. Then her hands were on Lilit's shoulders and Lilit felt the soft press of the Sidiana's cheek against her own. "I'm sorry, Lilit." The words were a breath of sound but then Raziel moved on to take Urmit's hands in hers as the other woman began to bow. "Oh Urmit, how will we do without her? What will we do?"

But Urmit had had no answer to that. No one did, Lilit thought as the procession turned onto a trail that led to the mouth of the river that flowed south from the lake. Invisible from the city across the lake, hidden by a rise of land and a stand of rhododendrons, the site was another reason Lilit had been happy to escape to the shelter of the Austers' brisk sympathy. When Raziel announced her decision, Lilit, drawn into the planning of the funerary rites, saw her mother's moment of blank surprise. "Burn her body?" Amaris had said at last, in something close to a gasp. "You wish to burn her body?"

"She hated the caves," Raziel replied. "Burning is the Deshinivi way."

"She left Deshiniva. She chose to be Euskalan. She was an Asezati. To burn her body would be sacrilege."

"I do not care. She certainly did not. I will give her soul whatever freedom it can find."

"Sidiana, please," Amaris began. "Please reconsider. My aunt was a loyal friend of Lushan. She should rest in honour in the Valley. She should find her soul's freedom there, with—" For a moment, Lilit thought her mother would continue and utter the name of the late Sidiana. But the look Raziel gave her was as cold as the winter sky and the words died, from either wisdom or ambition. "Raziel." The word was a last plea, one Lilit had not expected.

"I am sorry, Amaris. I will give her a pyre. I will give her this one last gift and hope it pays for what I have taken from her all these years."

Lilit had watched her mother nod as if her neck was made of iron and wondered why it mattered so much to her. Amaris was not noticeably devout and the state of her aunt's soul had never seemed of much concern to her before, except perhaps when she seemed to wish it in hell rather than at peace.

But now, Lilit could not help the sense of disquiet that filled her. Souls found their way to Jennon through the Valley of the Dead. Their bones remained, symbols of their passage through life—a last, welcome tie with the mortal world. She knew in her heart that Raziel was right, that Teresine would wish to be immolated in the practice of the land of her birth, but she could not help but feel the deep wrongness of it.

The thought of flames charring bone and flesh, reducing her great-aunt's body to ash, made her queasy. Caught in the smoke and heat, what would happen to Teresine's soul? Would it find its way onward despite that or would the wind catch and tatter it like an ancient mourning flag?

Trust you, she thought, pressing her hand against her stomach to ease the sudden nausea she felt. *Trust you not to make it simple. Nothing with you was ever simple.*

The thought sent her diving back into grief again, catching at memories: the peace of a long summer afternoon on the terrace of the mountain house, the sharp, brief glory of her great-aunt's smiles, the feel of the fragile old-woman's body in her arms, the voice, faintly accented still, softening on her name.

The procession rounded the last corner and Lilit saw the pyre for the first time. She had imagined a mound of dried wood, heaped like straw, but this was a careful construction, square and tidy, the weathered old wood wound with rich, glossy-leaved branches cut from the rhododendron bushes. There were soldiers waiting, the builders of the pyre, she supposed.

There were a few moments of muted chaos as the procession filled the clearing and dismounted, seemingly grateful for the distraction of tethering horses and finding a place behind the stiff-backed Sidiana. There was no protocol for this ritual and Lilit heard whispers rise in worried query and then fade away again. For once she was grateful for her mother's seeming certainty; she simply stayed at her shoulder and trusted that Amaris' sense of propriety would win through, no matter what she might feel about the ceremony about to be enacted.

The soldiers lifted the body from the wagon, bore it on its narrow bier to the pyre and laid it in the centre. The shape beneath the white silk was so thin Lilit could imagine there was nothing there at all, merely cloth draped to suggest a body. The soldiers stepped back and three of their number disappeared behind the bushes.

The wind died. Lilit heard the sound of stone shifting underfoot as someone behind her moved. In the silence, it sounded like an avalanche approaching.

After a moment, the soldiers re-emerged, bearing torches. The flames flickered weakly, as hazy as the sky overhead. Not enough to light a candle, let alone the square of wood, the line of white silk before her.

Raziel stepped forward and turned to face the assembled mourners.

COLD HILLSIDE

"We are here to bid goodbye to Teresine, who was once of Deshiniva but whose heart and soul were Euskalan. We asked much from her—I most of all—but she gave all she was and all she had to serve this city, to serve my sister and myself. She was my teacher, my wise counsellor and my friend and I shall miss her every day of my life."

She extended her hand and one of the soldiers moved to place a torch in it. She held it up and Lilit could not tell if the flicker in the flame was from the wind or the tremor in the Sidiana's hand. "This is not our way—but it was hers. I honour it as I honour her. I set her free, finally, and pray her soul finds what it has been seeking."

She turned and thrust the torch into the pyre, finding the space created in its heart. On the other side, the soldiers set their torches against the wood. Lilit heard it catch, heard the hungry snap and crack as the fire took hold. Behind her, someone caught their breath, someone sobbed. She glanced at her mother's face and saw, as the firelight touched it, something raw and anguished there. Lilit saw her father lay his hand on her mother's arm gently. Her vision dissolved behind sudden tears and by the time she'd wiped them away, Amaris's face was as still and empty as a statue and Hendren had withdrawn his hand.

The dried wood blazed but the new wood seemed only to smoulder, throwing resentful smoke into the air. The wind lifted and for a moment it was hot against her face, the smoke burning her eyes, horror shuddering through her at the thought of the ashes in it. But the smoke smelt of flowers and spice; the burning leaves, she realized. The sickness in her stomach settled and, mercifully, the wind shifted.

Then there was nothing to do but wait. She had never thought—at least until the last few days—how long it took for a body to be cremated. Even now, she was not sure. She had ventured to ask her mother, who had snapped "Much too long. Hours. We will be there for hours, because the Sidiana will be. And because the Sidiana will be, those of the court who choose to come will be as well. It will be," she said bitterly, "a mockery of a funeral and a mockery of a picnic on the same day."

At the time, Lilit had taken her mother's words for exaggeration. Now, in the awkward silence, they seemed painfully true. She did not find the funeral a mockery, despite the deep strangeness of it; Raziel's grief and intentions were too painfully clear for that. But now, the brief formality done, there was nothing for the assembled mourners to do and no familiar ritual to follow. At the caves, the prayers were brief, the true ceremony having taken place in the temple. When they were done, the mourners were happy to leave the long shadows of the valley and return to the city, to finish the day of burial in the comfort of family and friends.

The soldiers had erected open canopies just beyond a little rise, out of sight of the pyre. Beneath that shelter, the rugs and cushions seemed startlingly bright, the hues burning garishly against the dun-coloured ground. They gave the little encampment a festive air that seemed both pathetic and heartbreaking. She remembered how Teresine would take her unending mosaic out onto the terrace on a bright summer day and work there. "The Euskalans look at everything in darkness," she had said. "In Jayasita, they were the same. Sometimes, I just want to see. It is rare to simply see." Her voice had trailed off then, whatever else she would have said scattered by the motion of her hands and the force of her memories.

As with all else since the funeral itself, there was a moment of disconcerted confusion while the assembled mourners found places beneath the canopies. Lilit, who had blindly followed her mother's unerring steps to one of the tents, found herself choking on unwelcome laughter as she watched the swirl of figures move in an awkward, halting dance through the tents. Faces flashed as covert glances darted around the encampment, desperate to find a place, the *right* place. The safe place.

Lilit smothered a giggle and Amaris glanced at her in rebuke. "I'm sorry," she managed. "But she would have found it funny."

"So she would," her father agreed smoothly. The arrival of servants, with hot tea and plain fare, forestalled any further conversation. "Did I ever tell you, Lilit, about the first time I met your great-aunt?" Hendren continued. Lilit shook her head, refusing to notice the angry set of her mother's mouth. "I met your mother at the house of the Vachos; she was a friend of Anil Vachos and had left your great-aunt's house to live there, in the city. She would have been no older than you are now."

Lilit saw him look at Amaris for a moment but her mother was watching the thin line of smoke over the rise and did not glance back. "Six months I kept going to the Vachos to see her. She came to Kerias, once or twice, though I think in truth it was to see Jihan, who was House Head then." Amaris took a sip of her tea and gave no sign she was listening. "So things proceeded and Jihan went up the mountain to see your great-aunt and came back down to say that Teresine had no objection to Hendren Kerias marrying her niece at any time that seemed convenient."

Hendren smiled and Lilit echoed it, hearing the cadence of her great-aunt's voice in his tone. "Well, sooner was convenient for me," another smile, this time aimed at Amaris, "so the next week we were at the temple to wed. Anil Vachos and her mother and sisters came, to stand with your mother, and most of Kerias were there. We were all there, waiting for your great-aunt. The temple was not empty, of course, but Kerias made enough clamour, even in the temple, to make any other group seem subdued. All of this waiting—and my cousins jabbering—made me nervous enough to wander off to a little shrine, just for a moment of peace. I was not alone, for there was a nun there, already bent in her prayers, which reminded me perhaps a prayer of my own might be auspicious. I knelt and put my forehead to the floor and made my prayer. When I sat up the nun was back on her heels, looking at me.

"'Well, Hendren Kerias sa Chesel,' she said, 'if you're not praying for Jennon to deliver you from this business, you'd best go and marry my niece.'

"'And if I am?' I asked her and she looked at me, full in the face. I remember my own surprise at how beautiful she was, with her shaven head and her fine bones and those great dark eyes.

"'Then you'd best pray her heart isn't broken,' she said fiercely and I saw the iron beneath that beauty. For a moment, we knelt there, looking at each other, then she stood up and walked out into the temple."

He stopped abruptly and stared down into the fragile teacup balanced in his long fingers. Amaris moved, pushing with unexpected awkwardness from the cushions to stalk away among the tents. "I've not told that story in a long time," Hendren said after a moment. "I liked her. From that moment on, I liked her."

They lapsed into silence. Lilit watched Raziel moving between the canopies, pausing to speak to each group of mourners. There was nothing to do but sip tea and wait. Her mother returned but would not speak, leaving Lilit and her father to pass awkward conversation back and forth across her rigid presence.

At last, Lilit could not bear it. She rose, muttering apologies, and fled through the tents to find some privacy beyond a stand of rhododendrons.

There were tears in her eyes and she wiped them away as she walked towards the drift of smoke rising in the air.

This is what she wanted, Lilit told herself. The least you can do is honour that. She passed the edge of the little rise and went to stand beside the pyre. There were soldiers there, to stoke the flames she supposed, and they nodded briefly to her.

Lilit made herself watch as the flames embraced the bier and the anonymous white shape. After a while, deep in the pyre something cracked and broke and then bier and shape alike vanished into its heart. A sharp surge of relief swept her. With the body gone from view, she could think of the fire as purifying, almost holy, instead of simply destructive. She turned away, grateful that she had seen that last moment, that she had been given a final image that did not fill her with revulsion.

Lilit let out a long breath. It was time she too returned to the rest of the mourners; she could hear the faint sounds of activity from beyond the rise. She had barely taken a step towards the path when another figure emerged around the screen of rhododendrons.

Lilit bent her head automatically. "Sidiana."

Raziel came to stand beside her. "It is almost done," she said, considering the pyre. "It seems such a strange thing to do. Who knew so many people in this world would wish such a thing?"

"She told me a story once," Lilit began hesitantly. "Her mother told it to her, she said. It was about how a man buried his wife when she died and her soul returned in a tree behind his house. His new wife ate the fruit from the tree and it killed her. Only fire would set a soul free to find the heavenly garden." Lilit swallowed but the ache in her throat would not go away. "I think I would be happy to sit under a tree with her soul in it."

"So would I," Raziel said softly and they stood in silence for a moment, watching the flames. "It is time for me to let them go home, your mother and the rest," Raziel said at last.

Lilit followed her into the little camp. She felt the weight of gazes turned to the Sidiana and tried to find a way to slide discreetly back to her mother and father. Raziel's words caught her before she could take more than a few steps and she was forced to stop and stand, exposed, while the Sidiana spoke.

"Thank you," Raziel said, her voice lifting to carry across the camp.

"I know it was not an easy thing I asked of you today. But, as Teresine would have reminded us all, I am not in the habit of asking easy things of those around me. For whatever reasons you have, I thank you for doing this difficult task with me. Now it is done and home awaits us all. Go with my thanks and my blessings. Jennon's grace upon all our houses and our grief."

Heads dipped in respect and relief that the strange business of the cremation was done and ritual could now safely be resumed. Under the canopies, people began to rise, to gather hats and shawls, to look to where the horses had been tethered. Lilit hurried to join Amaris and Hendren. Her father patted her shoulder with awkward tenderness and, somewhat to her surprise, her mother's glance was more curious than disapproving.

"It was not so bad," Hendren said and Lilit nodded. Amaris shifted uneasily, as if to move towards the horses, and Hendren put his hand on her arm. "Wait. Let the others go first."

Her mother nodded agreeably. *She wants to be gone*, Lilit thought, but it would be unseemly to go first. It might look as if she could not wait to leave the last remnants of her aunt behind. It might look as if she did not care. And as long as the Sidiana was praising Teresine, Lilit knew Amaris would not have it said her niece did not love her.

At last, propriety observed, they found their horses and joined the small procession on the road back to the city, while the last thin plumes of smoke rose skyward from the pyre.

CHAPTER 19

Teresine

There was little enough time for weeping, after the first flood. In the space of three years, I had witnessed the death of two Sidianas, and I knew the business of it well enough. This time the funeral was completely traditional, truly Euskalan; it was Sarit's body and not merely her ashes that were borne out of the city to the Valley of the Dead. Beside her was the body of her son, who had not survived her by more than an hour. I rode in the procession and climbed the trail to the caves. I prayed in their cold, dry depths and tried not to think of Sarit's body decaying, withering away to bones and dust. I willed myself to imagine her soul rising, bright and free, across the blue sky.

The funerary rituals done, the mourners left the cave. This too was one last ritual, and tradition demanded I keep my place among the ranks of the Asezati. We trailed Raziel and Ayriet and their complex web of cousins and aunts, councillors and companions, coming out into the bright sunlight and the bitter chill of the wind that filled the valley. I was grateful for the hat covering my freshly shaven skull and the multiple layers of saffron funeral shawls. I was grateful even for my momentary anonymity among the other hatted and shawled Asezati. I knew I did not truly belong among them but the illusion of community was sufficient for the moment. I knew that when the funeral was done, the future of the city would be in dispute and that illusion would vanish.

Finally, having filed down the path from the caves, the procession was free to spread and regroup on the narrow base of the valley. A young woman materialized at my side. I did not know her but her funeral shawl and long hair, looped in braids, made it clear she was a student of the Asezati. "Azi Teresine, Zayan Bukoyan would speak to you."

I followed her to the donkey cart waiting by a ridge of rock, sheltered from the worst of the wind. Yeshe Bukoyan's joints would no longer allow her to climb the path to the caves but she had ridden at the head of the Asezati column, perched beside the driver on the cart seat. She had abandoned that spot for the cushioned comfort of the cart's bed and sat there now, steam rising from the cup of tea balanced in her awkward fingers.

"Ah, there you are," she said. "Come here then and pour me another cup of tea. Vires, you needn't wait. Teresine knows how I like it."

Her voice had lost none of its command: I was pouring the tea from the swaddled pot and Vires was retreating to a respectful distance before either of us had ventured to think about it. "I am sorry, Teresine," Yeshe said after she had taken a sip of her tea. I nodded, afraid suddenly to trust the tightness in my throat. "When things are settled, come back to the school if you wish. Or go into retreat at our House in Kekit."

"When things are settled," I said, because I knew I was not leaving the city or the palace. I let it sound like a question and she smiled, her eyes vanishing into the lines the last few years had finally laid on her skin.

"When Raziel is Sidiana."

"It is not certain she will be." Kelci had died with a clear and indisputable heir, but Sarit had not.

Yeshe snorted. "It is certain enough, if everyone behaves properly."

Which was a close to an order as the Asezati had ever given me, in all the years since I had prostrated myself at her feet. I was not surprised by it, though my resentment of it caught me somewhat by surprise. I suppose I had begun to think I would never have to pay the price for the promise of sanctuary.

"Then I suppose it is certain," I replied and she nodded. I saw her sharp-eyed gaze go past me to the place where Raziel stood, her face marked with dust and old tears she did not bother to wipe away. At that moment, I saw nothing of Sarit in her, though I knew quite well her face bore the same legacy of Kelci, had the same curve of cheek and angle of eyes. I saw only a girl barely grown into woman. "She is so young," I said, then remembered I had been two years her junior when my own world had been shattered and recreated in darkness. "It is a pity that she has no time to grieve for her sister."

"Grief does not require time," Yeshe said. "Grief is. It happens just as the hours happen, as breath happens. There is no point in wishing otherwise."

She was not talking about Raziel, I knew that well enough. But there was just enough gentleness in her voice to make me wonder how many hours she must have grieved, how many people she must have lost in her long life.

I held out my hands to her and she took them between hers, her palms pressing mine together. I could feel the warmth of the teacup on her skin. I bent my head to touch my forehead to her twisted fingers. "Be careful," she said softly. "And remember your way back to us."

I left her with that warning like a fading echo in my ears. For the first time in a long time, I remembered the reasons I had given Sarit for joining the Asezati. *For a place to go if I do not die at the same moment you do.* And now she was dead and I was not, and I had forgotten, in my grief, that I was not Euskalan. And that if Raziel lost whatever political struggle was about to ensue, I would lose it as well.

At least the struggle was left till the next day, though I had no doubt that more than one opinion was carefully solicited, one alliance carefully sought during the subdued conversation of the funeral supper. It was clear, soon enough, that a good portion of the court thought the Gifts should pass to Raziel. But there were enough who believed otherwise and, naturally, their choice of candidates was quite different. So the council and the court split in three and the jostle for power began.

No one questioned where I stood.

Free from the burden of politics, I discovered I envied those who at least had that distraction from grief. All the things that I could do, that I should do, were things that only added to it. I forced myself to go see Ayriet, who I found curled in a ball in the corner of her room, tear-streaked and miserable, despite the best efforts of her guardians to ease her sorrow. She allowed me to sit beside her for a while and at last put her head in my lap and let me stroke her hair but would accept no other comfort. Neither of us spoke; Ayriet because she had no words for her grief and I because I could not think of anything that would not be a lie.

Some time later during that long day, I remembered Perin. I had seen him at the funeral, of course. There was a place in the ritual for the Sidiana-Consort and he had occupied it with precise solemnity but I saw how many eyes averted from him, how many words of sympathy expressed to him seemed to be as much ritual as the words of the priestesses. In the crowd of mourners, he had seemed as out of place as I had felt, without even the shelter of the Asezati in which to hide.

That memory moved me into the dark hallways, darker now with the shadowed lamps of mourning, and to the rooms that had once been Sarit's. When I knocked on the door, a woman opened it. She had Perin's height and eyes and her belly curved into the taut bow of a soon-due pregnancy. The sight of it went through me like an arrow.

"Azi Teresine," she said and stepped back to let the door fall open. "I am Crisfan sa Alladis, Perin's sister."

"Sidi sa Alladis," I acknowledged. "Is your brother here?" She nodded and moved away, her hand moving automatically to the small of her back. I remembered Sarit doing the same thing, near the end, and wondered how Perin could bear it. He emerged from the second room, a small stack of old books in his hands. His face looked drawn, skin stretched from bruised eyes to unshaven jaw. His sister glanced between the two of us for a moment and then vanished into the other room.

"Azi Teresine," he said, after a moment.

"Are you leaving?" I asked, more abruptly than I had intended, noticing the scattering of wooden boxes open about the room.

The look he gave me was something between amusement and contempt and I felt a momentarily flare of heat across my skin. Of course he was leaving. These were the rooms of the Sidiana—and he had no more place in them. At last, he simply nodded.

"The Guild has a contract in Rajapura. To rebuild the aqueduct. The corps leaves in two days."

It went on, of course, the business of the city. I had forgotten that. The unending, necessary business of the city that the Sidianas were sworn to protect.

"That is fortunate," I said, to say something, because I no longer knew what I had come to say in the first place. The look came again and flickered away before I could tell whether this time there was only contempt in it. Perin turned from me to set the books into one of the crates and then tipped the lip up. I thought he would let it fall with a crash but he caught it before it could and eased it closed. For a moment we both stood wordlessly, looking at the box.

"I thank you for your consideration, Azi Teresine, but why have you come?"

"I don't know. We have not been friends. . . ."

"No," he agreed.

"But we have not been enemies, either," I qualified and he laughed.

"No. Rivals with a permanent truce, I suppose."

There was truth in that but I did not want to look too closely at it. I was not going away to Rajapura.

"She loved you," I said stiffly, my eyes still on the closed box. "You made her happy. Thank you for that."

He was silent for a moment. "Thank you." He looked at me and smiled, a strained echo of the smile that had changed everything. "I do not suppose we shall see each other for quite some time."

"No."

"Then farewell, Azi Teresine. Jennon's grace go with you."

I knew dismissal when I heard it. I bowed my head. "And with you."

And where was there to go then but away, out of the city, beyond the reach of all promises and plots, all love and grief and loss? It was irresponsible of me but I went anyway, with only enough foresight to wrap an extra robe about myself before I passed through the streets and then beyond them. There was a road Sarit and I used to ride, when the day would permit it, up the flank of Mother Mountain, to a ridge not holy enough to reject the footsteps of the local herdsmen and an errant Sidiana and her companion. The path wound up, switchback after switchback. I had no business out at this hour, with the sun already on its downward tumble towards the mountains. When it fell, it would take the last of the warmth with it and I would be alone in the cold darkness, on a path where a misstep might leave me at the bottom of a gully, broken forever. I knew all this but it did not seem to matter. At least at the bottom of the gully, I would have no choices to make.

And I knew that at the end of the trail there was a shelter; I was not so far beyond self-preservation after all, it seemed. So I walked, on and on, while the sun slid away and the moon came up, fortuitously bright, fortuitously early. My breath was steam in the silver light. Two hours later, the trail found its end on a little plateau and an empty building. It had been built as a retreat for the Asezati, Sarit had told me, but they had abandoned it some years earlier, though she did not know why. Perhaps they meant to return, for they had left the doors and windows shuttered against the snows and the walls and roof still stood, solid and sheltering.

COLD HILLSIDE

In the lee of the building, on the stone terrace that spread to the edge of the mountain, I found a little wall of stacked stones and a heap of charred wood, evidence that I was not the only person who had rested there. Beneath the wide eaves, a little cache of wood and dung remained.

But I did not touch that hidden store, some unknown traveller or herdsman's surety against a cold night. I went to the stone balustrades that surrounded the terrace and leaned there for a moment. Darkness filled the narrow valley below me. The moonlight did not touch the depths there and I might have been poised on the edge of a quiet, unmoving lake. But I felt it nonetheless, that precipice, that waiting emptiness spread beneath me. I swung my legs over the edge and sat there, as Sarit and I had done one summer's day, to the despair of the guards who had waited on the terrace behind us.

I could see my duty clearly. I had sworn an oath to the Asezati. I had sworn an oath to Sarit. Before the next days were done, I would be required to swear an oath to the new Sidiana. I was, by most counts, foresworn a dozen times by now. All the promises I had made, from love, from fear, from self-preservation, wrapped me in a web sticky with obligation and betrayal.

The Asezati had taught me morality—or tried to. Kelci had taught me the ruthlessness of power. Sarit had taught me the single-mindedness of responsibility and the perversity of love.

The simplest thing to do would be use whatever power I had to make Raziel Sidiana. It was what the Asezati required. It was what Sarit had planned. If it came to pass, I had no need of sanctuary, no need to lose the place I had found for myself. If Lushan cast me out, out of the palace, out of the temple, then where would I go, having been sold from one home and fled another already?

So why could I not simply do the thing that reason and oath and self-preservation demanded?

I could not because I remembered a certain afternoon in the artisans' gallery, and the bitter words of a grieving young woman. I heard them still, in the back of my mind, a whisper that would not be silenced. *What are you supposed to teach me?* she had asked me. *How to be her? That's all I am, after all. A substitute for her, if the city needs one.*

I had thought perhaps I could find a way to train both the heir that Sarit needed and the woman that Raziel could be. And now, before any of us had imagined it would be necessary, the time had come for both of us to decide if those two things could be the same person.

And if they were not, what oath was I prepared to break? To the Asezati, who expected I would do the one thing they had ever asked of me? To Sarit, who had put the city above all other things—except for the one choice that had killed her? To Raziel, who had come to trust me? And if I broke the ones that held me safe, what did I do then?

Of all the things I chose to do over that next terrible year, the one I never regretted was what I did the next morning.

After a cold night huddled in the empty house, I started back down the mountain when the first edge of sunlight touched the sky. I reached the city just past full dawn. The palace was stirring, servants bustling through the halls with messages and trays of tea. The council would assemble again in an hour or less to hold the vote.

I did not go to my rooms but made my way to see Raziel. She was in the same suite she had inhabited since Kelci's death; two little, high-ceilinged rooms with shuttered and felt-draped windows that overlooked the courtyard. All seemed the same, but there was a guard outside her door now and it was one of those who had once shadowed her sister. "Good morning, Azi," she said, with a polite incline of her head, a gesture all the Sidiana's guard managed without actually lowering their eyes.

"Good morning. Is Sidi Raziel within?"

"Is she expecting you?"

"No," I admitted. She looked at me for a moment then shifted sideways to knock on the door. Raziel opened it a moment later. She was already dressed in her black robes, her hair caught neatly back in two braids, but her eyes were red from weariness or tears.

"Teresine," she said and I bowed slightly.

"May I speak with you?"

She seemed faintly baffled by my formality but opened the door wider to let me in. "Did you hear?" Raziel asked. "Or has something changed?"

"I do not know. What happened?"

She looked faintly surprised. "Sidi Lakshi came to see me. She is prepared to declare her support for me in the meeting this morning." Which would make Raziel Sidiana, for Lakshi and her allies would carry any vote in council. Raziel looked at me carefully. For a moment, I saw Sarit in that quizzical, probing glance and my heart was a lead weight in my chest. "Teresine, is there something wrong? Should I doubt her?"

"No. She will expect some favour, no doubt, but—" I stopped. "Raziel, you do not have to do this."

"What?"

"I know what Sarit wished. I know what tradition and training and duty expect of you. But I tell you, you do not have to do it. Not if you do not wish it. Lakshi would be a good Sidiana."

For a moment, she was silent, looking at me. "As good as I would be?"

I did not consider lying to her. I thought of our lessons, eccentric as they might have been. I thought of the moment on the ride to the Valley the day before, a thing I had seen and, behind the dark veil of my grief, had not truly understood. The Newaris had assembled along the road we travelled, come from their villages and fields, and from the high places where they grazed their sheep. They did not wail, as my own people would have done, but each face was marked with dust and more than one was streaked with tears. And as we passed the first group, Raziel had halted her horse and dismounted. She stooped to the ground for a moment and when she rose, her face was as dusty as theirs.

"No," I said at last.

"Then I have to do it."

She was right—but she was also lying, if only by omission. She wanted to be Sidiana. Not from ambition or hunger for power, but because that was what she had been born to be. She wanted to be Sidiana the way a dancer wanted to dance. She was meant for it the way a hawk was meant to fly. Her gesture on the road had been genuine and her grief unchallengeable, but it had also been the brilliant unconscious calculation of a born leader.

I almost knelt to her then, put my head to the floor as I had once done before Sarit. But I did not, because she would not have understood it. Instead, I bowed my head. "Sidiana."

She laughed then, an awkward sound, struggling between nervousness and elation. "Don't do that. I'm not the Sidiana yet."

But by the end of the day, she was.

CHAPTER 20

Lilit

Lilit found it a relief to return to the routine of her life; the Auster studio, the meals amid the clatter and conversation of clan Kerias, the quiet of her little room. While the requirements of daily duty occupied her mind and body, the grief and strangeness of the last days could find less purchase in her heart. It would still come on her sometimes, the ache of loss swamping her in a wave.

She could feel the careful condolence of others around her, soft cloth wrapping her as if she were porcelain protected for shipment. Even Jerel Auster's sharp-edged tongue found other targets. Lilit both welcomed and chafed at the sympathy but was more discomfited by the rapid unravelling of the cloth and the restored aim of Jerel's temper than she wanted to admit. Still, she managed not to cry in the studio or fail to pay attention to too many of her cousins' stories and tried to consider that progress. It was, she reminded herself, the least that Teresine would have expected of her.

Lilit had told no one of what had happened at the fair—her faint and how that night she had woken at the base of the bridge, lost in a swirl of dreams. There had been no recurrence of sleepwalking, so she had decided the event belonged with her fainting spell, a consequence of the heat and the sun and the strangeness of the fey.

A few days after Teresine's funeral, her mother approached her at dinner and asked to talk to her. Despite herself, she felt like a child again, trailing Amaris through the dim hallways to her office. Being summoned by her mother rarely led to good news. Inside, Amaris lit the oil lamp on the desk and gestured for Lilit to sit. She opened the carved box set by one corner and retrieved an envelope. "This came for you today," she said as she held it out.

Lilit took it wordlessly. The paper was fine and heavy and the seal that closed it was the Sidiana's. The seal was also unbroken and she felt a moment's guilt for having been uncharitable enough to notice the fact. The wax cracked beneath her fingers and she unfolded the letter. The language was official and remote, ending with Raziel's signature and her seal, this time in ink. She read it twice and then looked up to meet her mother's curious gaze.

"It's the deed to the mountain house. Teresine asked that it be left to me."

Something flickered around her mother's eyes, the corners of her mouth. Lilit could not tell what it was: disappointment or pain or anger. The lines of it smoothed and Amaris held out her hand for the letter, as if she did not trust Lilit to have read it properly. There was nothing to be gained by withholding it, so Lilit surrendered it without a word.

"That was generous of her," Amaris said at last, her voice neutral. "But hardly practical. What use is it to you, after all?"

"It is a place to live," Lilit said dryly, aware her mother's calm tone was intended to lull her into doing what Amaris thought was best.

"You have a place to live. And it would be a long walk down the mountain to the Austers each day."

Which was no less than the truth, though Lilit was in no mood to admit it. She knew her mother was right, that she had no reason to own a house so far away from the city and the legacy was as much a burden as a gift. Still, she held out her hand and after a moment Amaris handed back the deed.

"The pension to Urmit and the others is generous," Amaris said after a moment. "The Sidiana could have considered that our responsibility."

"It would have been," Lilit said, stung. "Urmit was your nurse. You grew up in that house."

"There is no reason to argue about this, Lilit. It was kind of your great-aunt to leave you the house and kind of the Sidiana to honour that wish. I know you were happy there. But there can be no question of accepting it, you must see that. It is not possible to maintain it."

"It might be," Lilit said, though even as she did, she knew it was a slim possibility at best. The Sidiana's pensions held whether Urmit, Filiat and the others stayed in the house or not, but her meager pay from the Austers would not be enough to feed them and keep the house in order. "You could give it back to the Sidiana, as a gift. Or donate it to the Asezati. It was theirs first, after all. Then you would be free of the burden and know it would be properly tended," Amaris suggested.

"And such generosity would reflect well on you, as well."

"Lilit—"

"Come on, Mother. You cannot tell me you had not thought of it."

"It would do no discredit to this House, that's true. But that does not change the facts. You cannot keep it."

"I suppose that is why she left it to me and not to you. Because I would try," Lilit said sharply and rose hastily, aware she had taken the conversation in the very direction she had vowed to avoid. "Good night, Mother."

"Lilit—"

Lilit shook her head, knowing if she spoke, she'd be drawn back into the argument and her mother's patient, persuasive logic. She closed the door on her way out, to put its wood and weight between them. Amaris was likely right, of course, but she could not bear to think too closely on that tonight.

Teresine had loved the mountain house and had taught Lilit to love it. She had given it to her for that love, to keep the tie between them alive. She would not let her mother's logic kill that connection until she must. If she had to surrender the house, it would be how and when she chose to do it, not when it was most expedient for her mother's ambition.

As she climbed the stairs to her room, she felt a surge of anger: at the Austers, at her mother, at her lost great-aunt. A month ago, she had been on the edge of fulfilling her dream of going to the fair. Now, that dream had been realized but she had found the reality of it more disturbing than the imagining, and Teresine's death had brought her grief and memories and a gift she wanted but could not think of how to keep.

The next morning, she woke with nausea churning inside her, driving her to the empty chamber bowl to retch weakly. As she sat back and fumbled for a cloth to wipe her mouth, she counted the times she had awoken this way in the last two weeks and came out with a number too large to be denied.

She had no other symptoms of illness beyond the morning nausea and a certain tenderness in her breasts. Her courses were a week late but she had put that down to no more than her body's response to the excitement of the fair and the grief of her great-aunt's death. Now there was no pretending she did not know the truth.

She was pregnant.

CHAPTER 21

Teresine

When I look back on it now, the day Famar Kelinas hauled her withered bones to the palace was the day that dark autumn began, for all the sun was high and heat hung like a memory of Deshinivi in the air. Of course, that is when I look back on it now. At the time, the news she brought was simply unfortunate. The loss of one of her caravans and its little trove of opals would mean the hopes of "some to spare" had been too optimistic, but the yearly tribute to the fey would still be met, and that was all that mattered.

Everything else went according to plan and even the weather held as well as could be expected as the day of the fair approached. I found my wool shawls to wrap over my robes, dug knitted mitts and hat from their winter storage, and prepared to endure the trip through the passes.

Raziel laughed as Sarit had done and I did my best not to hear it as a pale echo of the ritual of exaggerated criticism her sister and I had shared. One night, just before we were to leave, she invited me to join her for a quiet evening meal in her rooms. It had been a day of last-minute crises and I was late, rushing in after the appointed hour with a hasty apology that died on my lips as the scents struck me.

For the moment, Lushan faded, its grey and cold and bustling life replaced by the slow heat of a Deshiniva evening, the long sunset, the lap of the river against the stilts of the house, the lilt of my mother's voice as she called us home. The air was full of spice and my mouth went wet with the hunger for it, for those old tastes of the world I had left behind.

I blinked and was suspended for a heartbeat between both worlds, seeing Lushan and Raziel, tasting Deshiniva and childhood. There was a cloth on the low table, bright green and gilt, and I could see steam escaping from a clutch of covered dishes. There was a stoppered flask, etched in black, which I knew must hold rice wine, because that was what those flasks were meant to do. In a blue bowl, white flowers floated and for a moment I smelt jessamine, though I knew quite well they were mountain bellflowers.

How many years had it been since I had inhaled the heavy aroma of jessamine or tasted the heat of green chilies? I had been twelve years gone from Deshiniva and at least three from the last time Sarit had secretly bargained with the Mersas for a little box of tastes from my abandoned homeland.

Raziel was still standing there, beside the table, the corners of her smile slipping a little. "Do not tell me I paid Ashen Mersa for spices, cloth and recipes from someplace you have never seen," she said, shoring the smile back up with the self-mocking words.

I shook my head. "It is perfect," I managed, through a throat gone suddenly tight. "It is just . . . unexpected."

"You should reserve judgement on the perfection of it until you taste it," Raziel said and this time the smile was genuine.

"Have you? Tasted it?"

"I confess to having pestered Jovah so much during the process she banished me from the kitchen," Raziel admitted. "I quite liked what's in the green bowl, and the red one. The contents of the gold one might be an acquired taste."

I stooped to lift the cover of the golden bowl and the sharp tang of fish paste rose in a swirl of steam. "Definitely an acquired taste," I assured her, inhaling the scent and heat rapturously.

"Well then, if it doesn't smell like anything has gone bad on the journey, is it polite to simply sit down and eat?"

"It depends on whether you are in a river village or the palace. In the palace, several prayers, rapturous comments on the table setting, and a discreet jockeying for the best seat would be required."

"Then I vote for the river village. Rapturous comments can be made with mouths full, Raziel decided and sank into a graceful cross-legged position on one side of the table. "And do not make that tutor face at me. I know quite well how to behave in polite company.

"What does one do with these?" She unwrapped a square of blue linen to unveil a stack of soft flatbreads.

"One uses them to scoop up the acquired taste," I told her and demonstrated. She dutifully followed my lead, seemingly hungry enough to do so with a mere wrinkling of her nose to indicate she might be less than enthusiastic. The chowder would no doubt have embarrassed the poorest wife in a Deshiniva river village, being somewhat too runny and definitely too generously flavoured with fish paste, but at that moment it was the best I had ever tasted.

I ate my way through each of the assembled dishes, Raziel sampling them after me, and for a few moments we were both too preoccupied to speak. The balance of spicing was off, there was mutton instead of lamb in the stew and white-fleshed lake fish in place of the deliciously oily river trout, but it did not matter to me in the least. I went back to each dish a second time, savouring each flavour with intense concentration. "Well?" Raziel demanded at last.

"Next time, I'll help Jovah in the kitchen. For tonight, this is the most wonderful meal I have ever had."

She pinked with pleasure and covered it with a too-large scoop of stew, which made her eyes water until I showed her how to cut the heat with a mouthful of sweetened rice. At last, when we had scraped clean most of the bowls, I poured more jasmine-flavoured rice wine into the delicate cups and we leaned back against the heaped cushions. "Did you eat like this all the time in Deshiniva?" Raziel asked. "If so, I could grow used to it."

"Hardly. If my family ate so well once, it was a good year. We made do with rice and steamed vegetables and fish. Feast days there might be a chicken sacrificed for the pot, or a cow barbecued for the village. In the city, I went to feasts to serve at them. It would have been a great scandal actually to eat at one." And more than one night, I ate no more than a handful of rice with bite or two of vegetables. Madam Amipuri, who ran the House of Falling Leaves, was convinced our breath—and our digestion—was sweeter if we ate only enough to keep our stomachs from rumbling while we worked. In the morning, there might be left-over rice fried with eggs and peppers. Only for a few girls, the Roses, were there meat and sugar-dusted treats. Of course, they had no more choice in it than the rest of us did. The Roses generally were chosen from girls who were already full-fleshed and round, but there were one or two Amipuri had simply decided would look better that way.

"Do you miss it?'

It was an unusually personal question from her. We had known each other twelve years, and I had been her tutor for three, so it could be said we knew each other well but it would not be entirely true. Our positions had always required a certain formality of us, and the difference in our ages had increased that distance.

And, I acknowledged, there had always been Sarit, who knew us each so well it seemed as if neither of us needed one another to do so.

I took another sip of wine, to wash down the sorrow rising in my throat at the thought of what we both had lost.

"Yes. No. Sometimes."

Raziel laughed and the sound had an edge of looseness to it I had never heard before. Rice wine, I remembered belatedly, was rather strong.

"That is a typical Teresine answer. Concise and confusing."

"It is not confusing. And I believe I usually answer your questions with honesty and reasonableness."

"Or you tell me to find the answer myself."

"That depends on whether you are asking me as my Sidiana or my pupil."

"And you are only honest and reasonable about questions that have nothing to do with *you*," Raziel continued doggedly. I did not know if it was the wine or something deeper that moved her but it was clear she would require a better answer of me.

"I miss the heat and the sun and the green," I began, because those were the easy answers. "I always know Euskalan is not my own language and Lushan is not the home of my birth. But I cannot go back, so missing it makes no difference."

"There, that was not so hard. You would have told Sarit that, if she asked."

But Sarit would not have had to ask. The uncharitable thought slipped unbidden through my mind before I could catch it, slippery as a fish in the dark depths of the lake. I sat very still, the wine haze burning away like fog. I caught some glimpse of what moved Raziel; grief and loneliness and fear, fuelled by the wine and the knowledge she went to face the trial that was the fair. Or perhaps, I thought in the next moment, that was only what I was feeling, reflecting back to me from the troubled face I could not quite read, like a fractured reflection from unquiet water.

"I would have liked to see it," Raziel said softly after a moment.

"Sarit told me about Jayasita. And Shimla and Karakul and the ocean. I will never see the ocean. I will never see anything but Lushan and the mountains."

There was nothing I could say to that, for it was true. Travel might come to her someday, years from now, when her successor held the city, but for all the future she could see she was bound to Lushan as closely as any prisoner. It was a loss I had not thought to count, another thing Sarit's death had taken from her.

"There is the fair, I suppose." She set her empty cup on the table and lay back on the cushions. Her face slipped into the shadows, beyond the glow of the lamps. "Perhaps I should consider myself fortunate we Euskalans have the privilege of seeing what most of the world knows only as stories. What is an ocean to the fey, after all?

"They are not so different. Cold and untrustworthy and what shows on the surface is but a fraction of what lies below it."

"Sarit said the ocean was beautiful." Her voice sounded faintly dreamy. "But then, so are the fey."

"So you Euskalans always say."

"Do you not find them so?"

I shrugged. "I suppose I do. They are beautiful. They are also dangerous and unknowable. But so are most people, so it does not matter."

I had long thought my foreign birth gave me one advantage over the inhabitants of the city; I took the fey as I found them. Without the weight of the Euskalans' strange history, I could see them clearly, or so I believed. They were like the snakes of my homeland; shining-scaled beauty and poisoned-fang danger and part of the world as it was. One did not cross them but neither did one worship them. Of course, snakes at least killed vermin. I had yet to determine exactly what use the fey had.

I saw the candlelit gleam of Raziel's eyes as she moved her head to look at me but I could not read her expression. I could not tell which of the various things troubling her she might choose to pursue—or let pass. "Is that what you truly believe? That we are no better than the fey?"

"I said *most people*. I do exempt present company from that."

"But is it what you believe?"

"Does it matter?" I offered but knew that answer insulted her, so made myself continue. "I trust the fey less, if that makes it easier for you. With people, I can at least guess what mischief they might be capable of.

Though I suppose even the fey might have their good points, if one knew how to look for them."

"Sarit used to say that looking into the Queen's eyes was the hardest thing she had to do all year."

"I know." I remembered her coming from the Queen's pavilion, her face as composed as a statue's, wearing her authority as if it were armour, as if it were all that kept her standing. I had stood at Sarit's back a dozen times over the years during the presentation of the tribute but the Queen had never spared me a single glance, for which I was grateful.

"What does she see, when she looks in our eyes?"

"Who can know? Whatever she saw in Sarit's, it was always enough. Whatever she sees in yours will be as well."

"Will it? What if it is not? What if she sees—" she stopped abruptly, her hand jerking gracelessly to cover her mouth.

"She will see the Sidiana of Lushan. Who is bringing her the required tribute, which is all that should concern her," I finished briskly and was rewarded by a brief snort of laughter from behind the hand that still rested over her mouth.

"What do they do with it anyway? Surely they could conjure any riches they required."

"Greater minds than ours have pondered that—"

"More sober ones, at any rate," Raziel interjected.

"Greater minds," I repeated, in my best tutor voice.

"I am afraid of her," Raziel said, sobering again. "Am I allowed to confess that?"

"Why not? Everyone sensible fears her. Sarit feared her." Raziel looked at me fully for the first time, as if the admission had eased her fear that her eyes might betray her. "I will tell you something I have never told anyone. The first time Sarit delivered the tribute, she went through all the rituals flawlessly—and then she went back to her tent and threw up. Twice."

"Truly?"

"Truly," I assured her. She smiled suddenly and sat up to tip the last drops of the rice wine into our abandoned cups.

"To the Faerie Queen," she said and drained her cup. The wine burned in my mouth, my chest, but the warmth was as welcome as Raziel's sudden resolution.

"To the Faerie Queen," I echoed.

We talked no more of the fair or of her fears but as I returned to my room, walking with exaggerated care, it did come to me to wonder what she feared the Queen might see in her eyes.

And to wonder what the Queen might see in mine, if she was ever minded to look.

CHAPTER 22

Lilit

It did no good to tell herself it was not possible, that she could *not* be pregnant. She had certainly been drunk on the night in the inn outside the iron, but she had not been drunk enough to forget the precautions required to prevent such a thing. But Lilit had trusted to the sheaths supplied by her partner and such things had been known to fail.

As they had clearly done, and brought her to her current state, pregnant by a man whose name she did not even remember.

Of course, she was hardly the first woman in Lushan to find herself in such a situation. She was not even the first in House Kerias. Her two-years junior cousin Vinesh had borne a child a few months ago and never named the father. The year before, another cousin had quietly ended her pregnancy, a fact most of the House knew but never mentioned.

The choice was simple—have the child or not. She had only to decide which choice she wanted to make.

It was not a decision she could face crouched on the floor of her room, with her gut churning with morning nausea.

Lilit forced herself to go about the business of the day, to keep the clamour of her thoughts at bay. There was too much to think on: her mother's politics, her great-aunt's legacy, the life taking shape inside her. Each problem seemed intertwined with all the others, so that each time she sought to make some small step towards puzzling her way through one, she found herself caught in a thorny forest of "buts" and "ifs" and "on the other hands." So she did her best not to think at all, submerging herself in work so ferociously that Jerel Auster was moved to comment suspiciously on her sudden enthusiasm.

"I don't mind cleaning the kiln," Lilit was forced to lie politely, with a secret sense of disgust that the sudden muddle of her life would likely now result in her being permanently assigned the one task she disliked most.

"Huh," was all Jerel said but left her to it.

So work kept her occupied at the Austers and at Kerias the aunts had decreed it was time to ready the house for winter, which meant her nights were full of cleaning, washing, setting away and setting out. If she approached the tasks with more willingness than was her wont, the aunts were inclined to act as Jerel had done and simply take advantage of it with no questions asked.

All the time, she knew all her diligence would not make the problem disappear and yet she could not bring herself to face it squarely. It was too much, after everything else, she told herself—and the echo of her great-aunt's voice in her head. *Tomorrow I will think about it.*

A week of tomorrows came and went before she could no longer hide behind a screen of distraction. At last, it was her day of rest from the studio and House Kerias was so spotless even the aunts were unable to find another corner to be swept. To stay in her room would invite comment, so Lilit donned her newly aired winter robe against the chilly morning, begged some freshly baked bread and a flask of tea from the cousins on kitchen duty, and set off into the city.

Her destination was another decision to be worried at; the mountain house was too full of memories and the city too full of distractions. Eventually she wound her way through the streets and down to the edge of the lake. As she walked along the stony shore, she felt as if the wind might clear the fog from her mind, blow away the clutter of worry, and turn the tangle of her contradictory thoughts into choices as pure and discrete as the mourning flags snapping on the lines on the little rise ahead of her. Then she could consider each choice, could count them out like the flags, up one line and down another, until the answer became clear.

Lilit found a jumble of sloping boulders sheltered in a little hollow below the rise, hitched herself up onto the flat plane of one of them and settled into a cross-legged position. She closed her eyes and lifted her face to the sun.

"So," she said aloud because there was no one to hear her but the wind and the memories of the dead fluttering above her. Behind her closed lids, light sparked, reminding her of the darkened temple of Jennon, the oil lamps laying gold across the serene face of the goddess. "Tell me what to do."

She waited, eyes closed, willing herself to stillness, to the opening of the soul the Asezati spoke of, but if the goddess was listening she was not moved to answer.

Her great-aunt was, however, in the memory of a sharp-voiced response to her own doubt. *"A bit of quiet thought in a dark room improves most people,"* Teresine had said. *"If it suits them to call it prayer, I have no quarrel with it. Just remember, even if it is the goddess who gives you the answer, it is you who must follow it."*

Lilit sighed and opened her eyes.

Teresine would have laughed at her for thinking the solution would be so easy. She would have to count up the consequences like prayer flags, after all.

By Jennon's grace, she had realized her condition early. Changing it would be simple enough. All she had to do was go to Aunt Alder, the House Healer. There would be unpleasant potions to swallow and a day or two of cramped misery in her bed but then it would be done. The unsouled life inside her would return to Jennon's embrace until the time came for it to be properly brought into the world. Neither Lilit's soul nor her body would be the worse for the choice.

If she chose the other way, there would be different potions, to give her and the baby strength. When the time came, Alder would bring the child into the world. She could keep her place at the Austers, for there were always cousins designated to care for the children of the busy women of Kerias. The child would grow up as she had, in a house of boisterous cousins. Its unnamed, unknown father would not matter—the child would be Kerias, just as she was.

Unless, of course, the handsome lover of her drunken night outside the iron had not been lying about his own parentage.

Something colder than the wind touched her spine. She had assumed his hints about his origins had been nothing but his part in the game they had both willingly played. She had not truly believed it, except as a faint shiver of apprehension that had added spice to her desire.

But what if it had not been a lie? What if her dismissive assumptions about him had been her own rationalization in the morning light?

If she were prepared to end the pregnancy now, who and what the father was did not matter. She could consider the matter done, a lesson learned about too much arrack and too much trust in sheaths. It was the most sensible solution, she thought, the flags of her reasons bright and confident in the sun.

And yet . . .

She had always assumed she would have a child. It was general wisdom that a woman should bear her first child before her twenty-fifth summer, while she was young and strong, though of course many chose to wait. She still had years ahead of her.

But it would be a different child, the wind-voice whispered. Yet why should that matter to her? Jennon would give her child, if it was born, the soul it was meant to have. What difference would it make if the soul that would soon enter the seed inside her waited a year or two or more to join the world?

All her reason told her it made no difference whatsoever. But the memory of the smoke rising up from her great-aunt's pyre would not leave her and wind seemed suddenly full of the scent of burning leaves. She remembered her own unease, her fears for Teresine's soul, borne aloft on that thin swirl of ash.

It was sheer superstition to believe one thing had anything to do with the other. No one knew what design lay behind the melding of soul and flesh, but for the soul of one generation to find haven in the body of the next so quickly was the stuff of stories.

Lilit knew that, considered rationally, her pregnancy and her great-aunt's death were unconnected. Perhaps it was not the soul she was trying to preserve but the blood, the Deshinivi blood had bound the three of them—Teresine, Amaris and herself—and now bound only two. The only other trace of that land, a place she had never seen, was now part of the life inside her. It might be a part no one would ever see, a part that could not be separated from the other heritages inside her—Euskalan, Newari—but it was still there, a symbol that her great-aunt had once left a hot, green land a thousand miles away and made her mark in Lushan.

That was no reason to bear a child, Lilit knew. She should only have this child if she truly wanted to, if she were prepared to raise it.

And the truth was, for all her counting of consequences, she still did not know. She was no surer she was prepared to accept the responsibility for another soul—or surer she was ready to accept the responsibility of denying it a chance to be born into the moment now offered.

All that was clear to her, the only flag that flew atop the lines of her calculations and conclusions, was that she had to know the truth about its father before she could make any choice at all.

Unfortunately, there was only one way to accomplish that. She would have to go to the inn and hope she could find him or someone who knew him. She could all too vividly imagine what he—or anyone she asked about him—might think. The thought that she might not be the only woman who had come looking for him did not make it any easier to contemplate.

That night, she eluded her cousins, who were intent on dragging her back to their continuing game of cards, and hurried through the streets and passed the gate. She missed her turning twice in the jumble of streets and old, whitewashed houses, but at last found herself outside the tavern. She waited in the little courtyard for a few moments, rocking on her heels on the cobblestones, and rehearsed her casual questions. They sounded just as false and awkward as they had all the way down the hill.

The door opened, spilling light and a cluster of exuberant guests into the courtyard. As they staggered happily away, Lilit slipped forward to catch the door before it closed and gave her an excuse to delay.

The White Bird was as she remembered it; crowded, hazy with smoke, and sharp with the smell of warm bodies, arrack and the pungent liquor that the tables of apprentices, labourers, clerks and students consumed without complaint. There was no place for her to sit and quietly scan the crowd so she settled for making a circuit of the room, just another apprentice on the hunt for errant friends. Thankfully, she met no one she knew—but neither did she find the man she was seeking.

Defeated, she worked her way towards the bar, found an open space at the far end and pushed herself into it. As much as she wanted to ask her question and be gone, she knew that, on as busy a night as this, it would not be so easy. She would need to order a drink (not arrack, she thought with an edge of humour) and wait until the barkeeper or one of the servers had enough time to spare that they would not simply dismiss her question out of hand.

At last, the barkeeper—a tall woman with a broad, cheerful face that did not match her sharp, sarcastic voice—made her way to Lilit's end of the bar during a temporary lull. As the woman wiped at invisible stains on the wooden counter, Lilit took a breath and leaned forward.

"May I ask you a question?"

The woman's gaze lifted to hers but her hand did not stop moving on the bar. "I don't promise an answer, unless you're asking for another cider."

"I'm looking for someone and hoped you might know him. He's tall, handsome, blond and . . . a bit different." Lilit knew quite well how ridiculous it sounded but she did not want to say the word "fey" in such a place, no matter how the man himself might have hinted at it.

"I might know a dozen men like that. What did he do?" the woman asked, the lift of her brow suggesting she knew quite well what he might have done. Lilit felt her face heat suddenly and blundered on.

"He's in no trouble, if he's a friend of yours. But I do need to talk to him."

"If you mean who I think, he's always in trouble. And he's no friend of mine, as he managed to leave town without settling his tab."

"He's gone?"

The woman's hand stilled and she leaned on the counter for a moment, her sharp eyes searching Lilit's face. "I'm thinking you mean Feris Kijhold. Tall, handsome, blond and likes to put it about there's a reason he does his drinking outside the iron." Lilit nodded. "I heard his aunts finally decided they'd had enough of picking up after his spills and sent him off with an uncle to work on the aqueducts in Madranas."

"His aunts?" Lilit asked in surprise and the woman laughed.

"You think he sprang from the rocks? The Kijholds mostly live in the lower city but there's no reason they need to." *Are you certain?* Lilit wanted to ask but could think of no way to do so that would not make it clear why she wanted to know. Someone called from the other end of the bar and the woman straightened, giving her a sudden grin sharp with mocking humour. "Don't worry, girl. That boy is no more one of them than you are. That's just a pretty story he tells to impress silly girls down slumming from the clanhouses. It usually works—but then you'd likely know that better than I."

She left on those words and sauntered back to the other end of the bar, leaving Lilit to swallow down the last of her drink and walk with as much dignity as she could muster out into the night, mortified and relieved in equal measure.

That is the end of it, she thought as she trudged up the streets towards the gate. The barkeeper's contemptuous certainty, humiliating as it was to hear it, meant she could make her choice without any fear for the nature of the child's unknowing father. She even had a family name to put to that half-remembered face and if she had any lingering doubts, she could likely put them easily to rest with a few careful questions at Kerias or Auster.

Lilit went to bed that night and fell asleep easily for the first time since she had acknowledged the pregnancy.

And dreamed of clinging naked to a narrow bridge swinging over a black crack in the earth, while the wind tore at her hair and froze her skin. When the moon came out, bright and blinding, she saw the river far below her, red as blood. Then the bridge bucked like an angry horse and pitched her downward. As she fell, she heard a laugh: high, androgynous, and as cold and clear as a mountain stream.

She woke, trembling, her mouth sour with fear and sickness. The darkness of the little room was absolute but comforting; no bright moon could find her and there was nowhere to fall. She put her hand beneath the blankets, half-expecting to find blood between her legs, and did not know whether she felt relief or disappointment when she touched nothing but her own warm flesh and rough patch of hair.

Only a dream, she thought dazedly, *it was only a dream*. But the words echoed in her mind and rang off memories of finding herself crouched at the foot of the bridge in the moonlight. She rolled over and curled up, cocooning herself in a nest of covers which smelled of smoke and home and safety. It was possible, she thought, just possible, that the barkeeper of *The White Bird* was wrong.

CHAPTER 23

Teresine

The morning we left for the fair was glorious: the sky bright blue, the air crisp and the sun warm enough to make that crispness merely invigorating, though the sun was altogether too bright for my head after the previous night and my definition of the point between "crisp" and "cold" was still somewhat different than the Euskalans. I could tell by the way Raziel kept her hat carefully tilted to shadow her face her head was in no better state than mine. Rice wine was stronger than one might suspect—and its effects were almost as bad as the strongest arrack served in the city's less savoury bars.

Despite the inevitable delays, the caravan made a good start and by mid-afternoon we had begun the journey up the switchbacks that led to the first pass through the mountains. By the time we reached the top of the pass, the sky had lowered to meet it and air had long since turned from crisp to a damp chill that passed with ease through cloth and flesh to wrap cold fingers around bone.

On the other side of the pass, it began to rain, turning the trail to mud. The guides slowed the pace and the horses splayed their legs and swayed precariously as the water ran over the rocks beneath their feet to vanish over the edge of the long drop to the valley floor.

I heard a shout from the front of the line and dared to lift my head enough to look past the brim of my hat. We were almost clear of the cloud line and below us the valley shone muted green beneath shafts of watery sunlight. At the sight, even the air seemed a little warmer and, around me, voices rose in relieved conversation and a thread of laughter echoed along the hillside.

The hunch left my shoulders in anticipation of some semblance of warmth and I was wondering whether the rain was easing when I heard a cry from the back of the line. This one was panicky and its echoes were not laughter but the clatter of falling scree and the terrified whinny of horses. I twisted in my saddle as far as I dared, fearing to unbalance my own plodding beast, and peered through the thinning veil of rain and mist.

I could see little clearly, just the line of people behind me doing the same as I, and at the tail of the train, a clot of dark shapes leaning ominously over the edge of the steep scree slope. Tattered scraps of shouting reached me, curses and prayers and exhortations to hold on. For a moment, it seemed as if the cries had worked, then there was one last despairing sound and one of the silhouettes resolved into a horse, tumbling down the scree and over the sharp lip of a crevasse.

There was no room to pass side by side on the trail, so the news made its way up the line, told by one person to the next. One of the pack horses of the royal party had fallen. The guards had managed to cut it free of its traces, saving the rest of the pack line. "The horsemaster says it was a bay, with one white foot and Jennon's thumbprint between its eyes," the palace guard who rode behind me said. I dutifully passed it on to the rider in front. None of us dared to ask the question we were all wondering: what burden had that horse been carrying?

Long ago, in the early days of the tribute, there had been a similar accident on the journey to the fair. That time, more than one horse had fallen, taking the better part of the tribute with them. The price they had paid for the failure to deliver the tribute had been high: four daughters and sons of the great Houses were to be sent to the fey or the truce that kept all the city's children safe was forfeit. The Sidiana Vinesse had wept but she had done what she had to do—she ordered her own cousins to go with the fey when they rode away from the fair. Each year, she asked the Faerie Queen to return them and each year the Queen refused. Each year, their mothers and sisters and daughters dared to ask the fey about their lost ones. "They are well," was all the answer they ever received and, eventually, the generation passed and the question was no longer asked. If, once in a while, there was a fey whose eyes held the blue of Silvas, or the line of whose cheek recalled Erraz, those who saw such ghosts did not speak of it and the stories stayed nothing but rumours.

But the Euskalans had learned the lesson and now the tribute was spread among the members of the royal party and the great Houses, so any disaster might be lessened.

We had no choice but to ride on and hope the horse that had fallen carried nothing more vital than folded tents or food. For even if it had, there was nothing we could do from here. If a rescue of the fallen beast's pack was even possible, it would have to be attempted from the floor of the valley, up the narrow defile cut by the icy river that ran beneath the trail we now followed. I watched for riders to set out ahead of the slow-moving procession, but I saw none and dared to hope this meant the bay with the white foot and Jennon's thumbprint blaze between its eyes carried nothing that would cost us more than a cold or hungry night.

Several hours later the trail widened, the mountain melting into plateau valley, and I made my way to Raziel's side. One look at her face told me it was more than a cold night we faced. "We lost a bag—twenty-five stones. They say there is no way to retrieve it, not and reach the fair in time."

"The reserve?"

"There should be enough. Diamet will do the count, when we camp." There was nothing else we could do until then, though I do not think that stopped either of us from worry. The lines of it were already between Raziel's brows and I suspected that if the business of riding had not kept her hands occupied, and the cold kept them gloved, she would have bitten her fingernails to the quick. It was a habit no number of reminders could break.

"The tribute should be carried by ridden mounts tomorrow," I suggested.

"So I've already been advised. Though the thought of losing a rider as well as stones does not make me feel any more cheerful."

Better than losing someone to the fey, I thought, but caught myself before I said it. She did not need to be reminded of it.

At the camp, we waited by the fire outside the Sidiana's tent for the outcome of Diamet's count, Raziel barely touching the tea or barley soup. The Auster House Head arrived at last and we left the warmth of the fire for the privacy of the tent.

"We're short ten stones."

Raziel closed her eyes for a moment. "What can we do?" she asked at last.

"We ask," I replied, swallowing the last of the cold tea in my cup. "I wager there is more than one spare stone in the camp."

"It was all counted. And accounted."

"Was it?"

"That is an unworthy thought. No Euskalan would . . ." She stopped and sighed. "Of course they would, once their tally had been met. I would, if it were my children I might have to surrender." She looked at Diamet and the other councillors. "I'll go and ask them."

"We can," Diamet began but Raziel shook her head.

"They won't want to admit it to you. I'll go."

So she went, alone, to each of them. I didn't ask what it cost her to ask for what no one acknowledged might exist, especially of those who had not supported her ascension, but she came back with ten stones. Diamet took possession of them and left to arrange the next day's transportation.

Then it was only Raziel and I in the lantern-lit dimness of the tent. We sat in silence for a moment, as the wind carried the faint sound of singing and then snatched it away again. "The Fowler's Reel," Raziel said.

"If you say so."

"I ought to know. I got drunk and sang three verses of it by myself the first time I came to the fair." The lantern flickered and a shadow moved across her face. "Back when I was an apprentice and therefore allowed to sing and be merry on this night."

"You could sing," I said. "I would not stop you."

"I think I will pass on that. I sing better drunk anyway."

"*You cannot worry anything into existence—or out of it.*"

"*So worry not and let desire be borne away, like a leaf upon the river, until what passes, passes,*" Raziel finished. "Azi Bevan had a good deal more detachment than I do."

"Azi Bevan was sixty-five and had been meditating for forty years. If she did not, then that was forty years wasted. It would be better not to compare yourself to her."

Her laughter was a faint breath of sound, like a sigh. "It would be better if no horses fell, it would be better if I could sing and get drunk, it would be better if I did not worry so. I suppose if I can get some sleep, I shall have to consider that enough."

I took that as my cue and left her to whatever rest she could find. My tent was near hers but I walked the long way to it, circling around the camp. . It was Kerias's turn to host the apprentices and a bonfire burned there, turning the gathering into dark shapes that swayed and shifted against the bright glow. Someone was singing, a pure, clear masculine voice that sounded very loud in the still air.

I had been one of those surrounding the fire once, sitting at Sarit's side as she sang and laughed and got carefully drunk along with the rest. I paused to listen for a moment and the singing resolved into a song of doomed love from a world already centuries gone. It made me feel old to hear it; old and dry and dusty as the high, sere plateaus where no rain fell.

As I walked away, back towards my tent, I thought perhaps that was not such a bad way to feel. It was a change from the heat of grief that I still woke to sometimes, the loss that crushed breath from body and tore at the throat with a silent scream.

In the morning, the clouds had gone. We began the climb over the pass in good time, no horses fell, and the early afternoon found us on the plain beside the crevasse. The bridge was laid and, on the far side, the pavilions went up as the tents were raised on the near.

The next morning, the Queen's tent was there, golden beneath the rising sun. The day stretched on and I envied the House representatives and apprentices who hurried back and forth across the swaying bridge. I had nothing to do beyond what assistance I might give Raziel and she seemed to have no need of either aid or distraction.

In the end, I sat at the door of my tent and made patterns with the shards of a set of china cups broken in the journey, provided by Arian Nessi, who was happy to accept my promise of future payment to cover her cost. I did not envy the cousin who had packed them so poorly.

At last, in the hour before twilight, it was time to cross the bridge. I shed the iron from my earlobes and fingers. Raziel and the councillors chosen to accompany her were required to don their court finery but my religious vows exempted me from anything beyond a clean robe and a finely embroidered sash. I had shaved my head before we left the city, so all the proprieties were safely observed—though I doubted the Faerie Queen either noticed or cared for the requirements of Jennon's worship.

I left my hat in the tent and set out bareheaded to find Raziel. She was emerging from her own tent, clad in indigo robes banded in silk, with gold in her ears in place of iron, and a necklace of coral and turquoise beads around her throat. Her eyelids were painted in black and red; the Newari charm against the evil eye. I wondered if the Faerie Queen knew *that* custom—or would care if she did.

"I know," Raziel said, before I could comment. "I know what I am doing."

"Which would be . . . ?"

"Chadrena Rumah is standing at my right shoulder."

It made sense, in its own fashion. Rumah was the only great House headed by a Newari. Chadrena had married into Rumah a dozen years earlier and she was sister to Nelay Koirenda, whose lands held the forts that guarded the passes from the lands to the east. The Newaris had never explicitly aligned themselves with the tribute; they considered it Euskalan business and quite apart from their own policy with the fey, which seemed to involve both sides pretending the other did not exist.

To stand at the Sidiana's right shoulder was an honour, but a fearsome one. That Raziel had asked Chadrena was one signal—that Chadrena accepted was another. I could see the sense—and the risk— in it, but Raziel's instincts in such matters had so far proven good. I still hoped the Queen would consider the eyes no more than some strange mortal fashion.

"And who is standing at your left?" I asked, as we walked towards the bridge. I thought it was likely to be Diamet Auster, but Chadrena had been a surprise, and I preferred no more of them.

"Diamet," Raziel confirmed and the black and red paint flickered as she looked my way. "And you are at my back, so do not think you have escaped the business this year."

The positions were symbolic, harkening back to the stories of the founding of the city. The Faerie Queen would not speak to the men and in the end it was four women who had gone to negotiate for the city's future. By tradition, the honour of standing at the Sidianas' shoulders went to members of the great Houses and the post at the Sidiana's back went to the Priestess of Jennon. I was not the highest-ranking Asezati in attendance—the Priestess Cserin was technically my superior—but I was the one who had stood there for the last six ceremonies.

On the far side of the swaying bridge, two soldiers were waiting with the tribute, their faces anonymous beneath the shadows of their helms, the two boxes at their feet. There was a restless quiet and, though I could see people darting to and fro down the long alley of pavilions, I could hear nothing but the wind and the flutter of the banners.

The Euskalans had tried for years to determine the exact moment of the fey's coming. *When the sun reaches the mountains* was all the instruction they had ever been given and they had learned to interpret it liberally. Some years, the Sidiana was left standing at the end of the long corridor for almost an hour. Other years, she had barely taken her place when the horns sounded in the sharp air.

Raziel and I were nearly the last to arrive. The representatives of the council had assembled. Diamet Auster was there, her lined face betraying no trace of tension. Chadrena Rumah had dressed with perfect Euskalan propriety, but her fingers were lost from joint to knuckle beneath coral and turquoise rings. When she tucked them into to the sleeves of her robes, I saw the flash of a braided silver bracelet there. It was another Newari charm against ill-luck, though her eyelids were painted only in shadow.

Raziel nodded to them both and I caught the twitch of Diamet's eyebrow at the sight of the Sidiana's chosen jewellery and cosmetics. Chadrena's face betrayed even less than Diamet's, but her bow was more than courtesy required.

Raziel took her place before the boxes of tribute and I slipped into mine behind her. When just enough time had passed for feet to begin shuffling, weight to begin shifting and careful comments to be whispered, the horns sounded.

It was believed that the fey rode from the border court, all save the Queen. Yet it always seemed to those at the far end of the camp that they simply materialized from the air, shimmering into life in the distance. Most likely, they merely passed over the rise that had concealed their approach, I thought, choosing the place that would be most likely to make their appearance seem magical.

No matter how they accomplished it, even I could not deny the dramatic glamour of their entrance. Their horses were so graceful that they seemed another form of creature altogether from our shaggy, rugged horses. The fey dressed with no concern for the weather: I had seen some wrapped in furs on a rare warm afternoon and others in nothing but thin silk on a night of bitter cold.

There were some I recognized over the years, though I did not know their names. Others would seem new, until some tilt of the head would recall a different fey, and I would realize it was one I had seen before in some new guise.

This year, amid the jumble of silks and furs, hues of skin and hair, I could see a subtle change. While some were merely impossibly beautiful, others seemed impossibility itself. Wings shimmered over shoulders, horns curved back from brows, scales shone across slender limbs. I had seen such alienness before but this year it seemed more plentiful. I wondered if it were simply fashion or some dark, unknowable current of fey politics. I had no doubt that such existed—they had a Court, after all. I did not think it would be any more virtuous than mortal ones.

At last, they were assembled outside the golden tent. The horns sounded again, all around us, as if the sound was made of the air itself, and the flaps of the great tent were drawn back.

The fey horses went to one knee, as graceful as the riders who bowed beside them. The Euskalans bent their heads and bowed as well, the careful tipping of squared shoulders and straight backs. They would give the Faerie Queen her due and not one inch more. I might have found it amusing, if I did not understand it so well. Once I had calculated my own obeisances that finely, that I might hang on to some slim thread of self that would not break.

The Queen stepped from the darkness at the mouth of the tent and it seemed as if the world held its breath.

In the years I gone with Sarit to the Fair, the Queen had not changed, no matter how many among her entourage had. For all those years, she had been black-skinned and golden-eyed, with ebony hair that fell in amber-seeded ropes to the ground. Her dress was always gold silk, wrapped with gilt ribbons in a complex fashion that seemed to have no beginning and no end. Whatever the fey did with the opals the Euskalans laid at her feet, they did not wear them. The Queen's long neck and elegant arms were always bare of anything but the black sheen of her velvet skin.

All that was utterly changed.

Her skin was white, as white as the face of Jennon. Her hair was white as well, the length of it now braided and knotted into a fantastical headdress across her brow. Crystals sparkled in it, flashing blue and green and red in the fading sunlight. More jewels hung from her ears: clustered, glittering fruit. Her dress was encrusted with them, beaded crystals covering heavy silk the colour of pearl, outlining the lift of pale breasts, the extravagant narrowness of her waist, and the flare of her skirts.

Against all that white bedazzlement, her eyes were black.

The silence hung in the air, sharp and crystalline, as if the world might shatter if any dared to break it.

COLD HILLSIDE

It was Raziel's duty to break it, to say the ritual words that would begin the tribute. She stood as still and silent as the rest of us and I could not even see her shoulders move with her breath. There was nothing I could do but watch her back, the arrangement of golden braids across her head, and hold my own breath.

"Great Queen." Her voice wavered a little and I saw her shoulders hitch and stiffen. "We have come to fulfill the promise our ancestors made to you."

"You are new, Little Queen."

"I am the heir of my sister, whose loss we grieved at winter's end." For a moment, I thought she might say more, but she did not. There was no point in giving the Queen her name; the Queen had never called the Sidianas by name anyway.

The Faerie Queen said nothing to that, simply turned away, the movement sending a kaleidoscope of sparks flaring from her jewels, and walked back into the dark heart of her pavilion.

Behind us, I could hear the soldiers lifting the burden of the boxes. With Chadrena and Diamet a pace behind her, me at their heels, and the soldiers at mine, Raziel followed the Queen into the shadows.

I had been in the Queen's pavilion a dozen times but this time I had no idea if the transformation that had taken place in her person would also be echoed in the pavilion.

It was just as thorough, just as extreme. Where torches had lit the darkness in the years before, now four great silver candelabras held a dozen white candles. The ground had once been covered by heavy furs but now there was a solid platform beneath my feet. I did not know what it was made of, but it was as dark as a moonless night, a heavy, liquid black that was vaguely disorienting, as if one might look down and discover oneself suspended over some endless abyss. I resolved not to look down.

The throne at one end of the room was no longer gold-banded ebony, but opalescent and crowned with a spiky halo of crystals. On either side of the throne and down the circle of the walls, there were great mirrors hanging, seemingly suspended in the air. Reflected back and forth between them, an infinite number of White Queens walked towards the throne, infinite black-clad mortals following her with hesitant steps.

I could feel the presence of the other fey and caught glimpses of them from the corners of my eyes. They filled the spaces between the mirrors and were reflected back from a dozen more, bright shapes and dark, though none, I thought, in white.

The Queen reached the throne and turned to face us once again. She did not sit, but stood with her ringed hands folded at her waist, perfectly still.

Raziel bowed again and stepped to one side, our cue to move. She and Chadrena stood on the right, Diamet and I on the left, as the soldiers carried the boxes between us to set them before the Queen. They opened each one and then retreated. The gossamer curtains shifted as they left the tent but no sunlight seemed to reach us in the circle of mirrors. I kept my eyes on Raziel, to keep them from the temptation to watch the reflections of the shadowy fey behind me.

She stepped back to her place and we to ours, to wait while two fey emerged from behind the throne. They were plainly garbed, as the fey went, swathed in heavy robes of black silk. Veils edged in silver covered their faces, concealing gender, age or hue. I had always wondered how they could see from beneath those obscuring veils, but they moved with easy grace to stand over the open boxes. From beneath their robes, their hands emerged, startling white and graceful, like night-blooming flowers against the black cloth. They did not crouch to touch either boxes or contents but merely moved those hands across them, fingers moving gently, like reeds in the water.

After a moment or two, they stepped back and bowed to the Queen, then vanished into the shadows once again. The Queen's black eyes blinked once and the corners of her eyelids glittered. "There is one stone short." Her voice was expressionless, softly implacable. "The price has not been met."

A dozen things flashed through my mind: that she lied, that someone had, that it was simply a test, that Raziel must challenge her, that she must not. I heard Diamet's indrawn breath and saw Chadrena's shoulders stiffen.

"Great Queen," Raziel began, her voice shaking, "that is not possible. The tribute was complete."

"Five hundred stones was the agreement. Four hundred and ninety-nine stones only are there here. The price is not met."

"Great Queen, there is some mistake on our part then. Give us leave to find that last stone and deliver it to you. It will only—"

"The price is met now or not at all."

There was silence for a moment. I saw Raziel's head bow briefly, caught her quick, convulsive swallow. My heart ached for her even as my mind dreaded what might now happen. She could not seek counsel, dared not ask grace to think, and must not let the Queen believe her weak or fearful.

"If there is no stone, how might that be done, Great Queen?"

In the Queen's faint sigh of breath, I heard the doom of another hand of the city's children. But she did not answer, simply looked at us each in turn and this time we could not refuse to meet her gaze. Her eyes were like the floor beneath us, an unfathomable abyss in which one could fall forever in darkness. Her look scoured me, and I felt as if every hot secret of my heart had been ripped from me and held up to reflect, raw and naked, in the infinite mirrors.

When her gaze moved on, it was all I could do not to shudder in relief. She looked at Raziel longest of all.

"There is a thing of the Aygaresh in the place we choose to bide," the Queen said at last. The words were so unexpected it took me a moment to understand them. "It is broken. We would see it as it was."

"Great Queen, we are not the Aygaresh."

"Nothing that breathes is. But mortal hands could serve to place stone with stone. Do this thing and the price will be considered paid."

"Great Queen, the price is our debt and we will pay it. But I will need to consult with my people. I do not know if there is one among us who can do what you require."

"Little Queen," For the first time, the Queen's voice held some colour, a thread of amusement that chilled me more than her usual emptiness could. "You need do nothing but turn around."

Place stone with stone, she had said and, though I had heard it, I had not understood it until that moment. Raziel turned around sharply. Our gazes met and I saw her face pale, her eyes widen against the black and red paint surrounding them.

"Teresine—"

I shook my head slightly, hoping she understood the signal for silence. We could not debate this before the Queen. No debate would change what must come next.

"If that is the price, Great Queen," I said and it took all my will to keep my voice steady. "We will pay it. But until I see this thing, I can only promise to pay it with the attempt and not the achievement."

The coal-dark eyes turned to me. For a moment, I thought she might refuse but then she nodded in brief, contemptuous acceptance.

"Great Queen," Raziel said, into the silence, and the Queen looked at her again. "So that we might be certain we have met the price truly and fairly, I must ask how long this duty might require?"

"How can we know this?" The Queen inquired. "Say that at next year's fair, we will bring your companion with us."

A year, I thought dizzily. How would I survive a year with such creatures?

"Is this thing such a great undertaking as that?" Raziel asked. This time, she did not lower her eyes before the Queen's gaze.

"Say then that when the passes next clear, we will send your companion—or word."

Raziel looked as if she wished to cut that time in half, for which I was grateful, but willed her to hold her tongue and take what the Queen had given. A thousand old tales of the perils of bargaining with the fey flickered like whispered warnings in the back of my mind. It was best to leave no condition unstated, no loophole unguarded but, for all that, Raziel dared not bargain with the Faerie Queen like a vegetable vendor in a market.

After a moment, the Sidiana bowed. "Thank you, Great Queen. We would not lose her counsel for longer than we must. I trust she will come back to us in all ways as we have sent her to you."

The Queen's eyes flickered and there was no shadow of amusement in her voice at all. "She will be my guest, Little Queen."

"Then we consent to give you this service, which shall be done to the extent that mortals may, and will last until the passes clear after this coming winter."

If the Queen was offended at Raziel's precision, this time it did not show. "We shall send for her at the end of the fair."

"Great Queen, we would beg for two nights' grace before this service begins, enough time to pass back over the mountains and make preparations," Raziel said, to my surprise. I had been too stunned by the request to realize what the impact of it might be on the rest of the party— or what I might feel on being publicly surrendered to the Queen.

COLD HILLSIDE

The Queen's gaze shifted from Raziel to me. The corners of her lips moved, the ghost of a shadow of a smile. I suspected she knew quite well the reason for Raziel's request. I wondered if it would amuse her more to grant or deny it.

"At the hour of the fair's end, on the second night, we will find you," she said at last. "The price is met, Little Queen."

With those ritual words, we were dismissed.

"Say nothing of this," Raziel ordered softly before we stepped into the twilight and the waiting throng of mortals and fey and the horns sounded once more, to signal that all was well and the fair could begin.

She did not need to fear, for what was there to say? I had consigned myself to the world of the fey and, for the first time in fifteen years, I was terrified beyond words.

CHAPTER 24

Lilit

Lilit had thought her conversation with the bartender would resolve everything and leave her free to make her choice with a clear mind and an unclouded heart. She was disappointed to discover it did no such thing. Her recitations of the reasons for and against bearing the child growing inside her continued to be precisely balanced, and neither heart nor mind could settle on an answer that would bring her peace.

She counted the days each morning, a mantra flicked off on her fingers, as if somehow that would help her to decide. She had time yet, she reminded herself. If she left it long enough, of course, the choice would be made for her but that seemed like the coward's way. She owed it to the soul waiting to blossom into the world to choose to bring it forth, no matter what happened after that.

She missed her great-aunt with a fierceness that took her breath away. She did not imagine it would have been easy to admit her foolishness— or that Teresine would let it pass unremarked. But Teresine's clear-eyed, unsentimental good sense would have been able to cut through the tangle of conflicting impulses that led her first one way then the other, leaving her stranded hopelessly at the crossroads of her choices.

And every night, she dreamed of the bridge at the fair.

At last, after a week of fruitless thought, she went to her father.

She found her moment one evening, when she had returned home from the Austers early enough to join a group of Kerias going to the main temple. There was a chapel in the house, of course, but most of the household tried to attend the evening services at the great temple up the hill at least once a week.

The ever-shortening twilight had faded into night when the knot of her family emerged into the courtyard of the temple. Lilit found Hendren amid the jostle of temple-goers taking the opportunity to chat with friends. "So tell me, daughter," he said with a smile, "what were you praying for this evening?"

"Only the usual things: good fortune to the family, that Jerel Auster does not yell at me, that Mother does not yell me at me."

"I am afraid Jennon might be inclined to view Jerel and your mother's remonstrances as necessary for gaining wisdom."

"But Jennon also has mercy on the oppressed," Lilit pointed out, tucking her hand into the crook of her father's arm and letting him steer her towards the great gateway to the street.

"Such a hard life you have, child. Jennon might grant your prayers, after all, seeing how you suffer."

"I know, I know. I should be grateful for the easiness of my existence. When you were my age, I would have been required to work from dawn until midnight and walk to the temple in my bare feet in midwinter. Carrying my elders on my back, as is proper, of course."

"Just wait, daughter, just wait. I can only imagine what hardships you will claim to your own child." It was a jest, and an old one, but near enough the mark that Lilit found it hard to laugh. She managed a smile and leaned her head against his shoulder for a moment. "And what did you pray for?"

"For a grateful child who would carry me to temple on her back," Hendren said. "For my daughter's grief to grow less with each day."

The sympathy was so unexpected it summoned a wave of the grief it sought to comfort, and Lilit felt tears burn at the back of her eyes. She swallowed around the hard stone of loss in her throat. "I cannot believe she is gone. I thought she would be the like the rocks—or her house. I thought she would be there forever."

Her father patted her hand in wordless comfort and said nothing, for which she was grateful. For a moment, the image of her great-aunt filled her mind, blotting out even her nervousness over the questions she must find a way to ask. And then, tangled in the grief, she saw how it might be done.

"Did Great-Aunt Teresine know the Kijholds, do you know?"

"The Kijholds?"

"They live in the lower city."

"The weavers?"

"Perhaps. I know they have an uncle among the engineers." Which was no help at all, she reflected, as most Houses had men among the engineers, as they did among the soldiers.

"I know little of the family. Kerias buys cloth from them on occasion. But your mother would know that better than I. Why?"

"I met one of them one night," Lilit said, awkward in the lie. "He offered the family's condolences on my great-aunt's death. So I wondered how he would know of her."

"Your great-aunt knew a number of surprising people. Though," she saw his eyebrows lift, "even I would be surprised she knew a young Kijhold son. I assume he's young." Lilit nodded, aware that her cheeks were flushing, and hoping the night would hide them. "Ah. And handsome, I wager." She acknowledged that, too, and was grateful her father had the kindness not to laugh.

"But someone said, that is, someone suggested that they were not quite—that they had dealings with—" She could not say the word out loud, not from fear, but because here, on the busy street, her father's arm warm beneath her hand, it sounded ridiculous.

"Such has been said of every family in the city, at one time or another."

"Then you have never heard so?"

"I did not say that. Lilit—" She did not want to look at him but he waited until she turned her gaze back to his before he continued. "If you want me to say a Kijhold son has no taint, I cannot do it. No more than I could say he did bear such a curse. But if you met him in the city, he is as safe as one can assume any to be." He patted her hand, where it rested in the crook of his elbow. "It is not like to you listen to gossip—or to worry over it. Did something happen to make to believe it?"

"No, of course not," she assured him, shaking her head. "Likely it is just all that has happened—the fair, Teresine, the funeral and the rest. It is making me weepy and worrisome."

"Not that, believe me, daughter. Now your Aunt Virat—she is weepy and worrisome. And badgering me about talking to my friend Goden Herrell about whether Fanell Herrell means to give your cousin a horse as a marriage gift or whether she should try to persuade Iselt Ardari to do so."

"And what will you do?" Lilit asked, accepting the change of topic gratefully.

"Talk to Goden, I suppose. It seems a small price to pay to be able to dine in the common room in peace." They talked of inconsequential House business the rest of the way home but, when they parted in the courtyard, her father gave her an uncharacteristic kiss on the forehead. Though nothing he had said either confirmed or denied her lingering fears, his confidence and the parting kiss bestowed a sense of safety that let her drift off to sleep easily for the first time in a week.

She did not dream of the bridge, but of her great-aunt's house. The hallway in which she stood was dark and cold and Lilit knew the house was empty. She walked slowly down the hall, towards a patch of shadow she knew was a door, despite the fact no door stood there in the waking world. As she drew near, she heard a sound, a faint wail she told herself must be the wind. If she opened the door, she would let it in, which seemed a foolish thing to do, given all the shutters and hangings and doorways designed to keep it out. But her hand moved, as if another will controlled it, and reached for the door. Then the doorway vanished and she was in a room filled with nothing but the sound. Which was not the wind, she realized in despair, but a baby's lost and lonely wailing. At that realization, the room resolved around her; shadowy grey stone and a window full of dull light that illuminated a waiting cradle. The baby's cries tore at her heart and set her dream feet in motion, her dream arms reaching out to find the little form in the shadowed cradle and bring it out into the light.

For a moment, the child was heavy in her arms and its milky smell surrounded her. She looked down and saw, for a moment, a round pink face and wide, blue eyes. Then it changed, its face narrowing into a livid, wrinkled triangle, its eyes flaring green, its body turning as light as a bundle of twigs. It opened its mouth—to speak, to cry, to curse— and she saw rows of teeth in a hinged jaw.

She dropped the thing and ran, her hands over her ears, blundering back into the hallway that now seemed to stretch forever away from her. Behind her, the wind caught the sound of laughter and flung it her way, two voices twining around each other with malicious delight. Then the hallway was gone and she was on the bridge again, clinging to the ropes as it moved beneath her. The laughter was now in her ear, deeper, more intimate, and she felt warm breath against her skin.

The hammering of her heart flung her into wakefulness, breathless and dizzy. She lay huddled beneath the covers, pinned there by the palpable sense of *presence* that filled the room. The old childhood remedies to fear thrummed through her mind: do not breathe and it cannot find you, do not open your eyes and it cannot see you. It took an endless moment and a fierce thrust of will to fling back the blankets and sit up to strike a flint to a lamp.

By its flickering light, she pushed her hands through her tangled hair. Her gaze slipped down to her lap, hidden in the white fall of her cotton night robe, and her hands followed, touching the faint swell of her belly. "Who are you?" she whispered to whatever was forming itself into life beneath her fingers. "What do you want me to do about you?"

CHAPTER 25

Teresine

When I had left the city two days earlier, it was with a mind that I'd be back within the week. I had brought with me little but the clothes upon my back; my trouser and robes, the soft chemise, worn now to transparency, which was all that remained of the clothes in which I'd fled Jayasita, a sash stripped of amulets and iron. My one saddlebag held a spare shawl, cap and mittens to fend off the cold, a change of underrobes, and a copy of the *Meditations of Auralian*, which Sarit had long urged me to read. I did so now, as penance, wishing with every sentence she had not left me before we could argue on it. I did not even have the razor for my freshly-shaved head.

How was I to survive for at least six months in the court of the Faerie Queen with one robe, one pair of trousers, a shawl and a book?

But then, how would I survive one day in her court with the finest silks in Lushan on my back and the collected wisdom of the Asezati in my saddlebag?

There must be ways to wash one's clothes, even in the Faerie Court. Unless they simply conjured up a new set when the old set was dirty. Still, I imagined even the fey must require water. Though no one had ever seen them drink or eat.

That thought sent me scrabbling through the other bags beside my sleeping mat. Though the Sidiana's party contained a cook whose duty it was to see to the provisions, most of the household carried their own store as well—a bag of tea and of barley, a skin of water, a wrapped cheese. These served if one rose early or lingered late and were a sensible, if mainly superstitious, precaution against the dangers of travel in the mountains.

As dangerous as making bargains with the fey might be in the old tales, so too was eating and drinking with them. One bite of a Faerie delicacy might doom one to a lifetime in their world, or so the old stories said.

And yet what choice did I have? I calculated the number of days and the bags of rice required. It was not possible for me to carry so much, even if the Queen would allow me to scorn their fare.

I tugged open the bag of barley and tilted it to the lamplight, slipping one hand inside to bring out a palm full of seeds. If I ate one or two a day, would that be enough?

The absurdity of it made me laugh aloud, though I did my best not to notice how the sound slid into the choked semblance of a sob. To place my fragile faith in the dubious sympathetic magic of a handful of barley seemed ludicrous—but I tucked the bag away into my pack just the same.

With the true perversity mortal minds were capable of, I wished Raziel had bargained for more time and yet thought it would have been easier if the Queen had spirited me away in the moment the decision had been made. Then I would not have had time to be afraid or time to wonder if barley would keep my soul safe. Then I would not have to spend so many precious hours acting as if nothing was wrong.

I was grateful, at least, that we dared not discuss it except in careful, whispered asides. There was nothing either of us could say that would change the choices we had made, even Diamet's despairing apologies and self-recriminations. So after we left the Queen's tent, we had done what the Sidiana and her companions always did during the fair: visited each of the booths, smiled and made polite conversation with the fey who chose to acknowledge us, and rested in the Sidiana's open tent, drinking tea and doing our best to pretend all was well with the world.

The little brass bell that hung at the doorway of the tent chimed, a sound with too much intention to be the wind. When I called "come in," expecting Raziel, the flap lifted to reveal Chadrena Rumah, still in her tribute splendour.

"The Sidiana asks if you will be returning to the fair," she said.

"If she needs me, I will come."

"It might be best. She is afraid," Chadrena said, "but she hides it well. The paint was a wise choice, it seems, for everyone prefers to pretend they do not notice it, and so they do not look too closely in her eyes." Her bluntness surprised me; we served together on the council but we were not friends, and only sometimes allies.

"I had my doubts of her. Lakshi seemed the safer choice." She looked at me, her eyes as dark as my own, a darkness still rare among the blue-eyed women who ran the city. "But do not fear you leave her undefended."

"She does not require defending," I replied then repented my own lack of grace. Raziel might not require it, but it was not my place to scorn any support offered to her. "But thank you," I added and managed a slight bow.

I saw amusement in the deepening lines of the corners of her eyes as she rose from returning the gesture, but that was all. "Jennon protect you," she said. "And the Mother Mountain be the rock beneath you." As I thanked her, she held out a small felt purse, bound by purple and scarlet ribbon.

"For what it might be worth, accept this with House Rumah's good wishes," she said with a trace of a smile. "If we do not have the chance to speak privately again, I will see you when the passes clear, Azi Teresine."

"Thank you."

She bowed again and disappeared through the tent flap, the brass bell shivering as she passed. I looked at the purse in my hands for a moment, then undid the ribbons and unwrapped the cloth to reveal a silver bracelet inlaid with coral and turquoise and two small silver boxes, their lids fastened with silk cords. Inside one I found a cache of red cosmetic, the fat and oil that bound the red powder gleaming in the lamplight. I did not need to open the other to know it held the mate in black.

I could not imagine I could paint my skin with such things—or if I did it would make any difference to the fey—but I put them in my bags just the same. The bracelet I fastened about my wrist, which welcomed its weight in the place of the iron one I had shed the day before.

Then there was nothing left to do but cross the treacherous bridge back to the fair and Raziel.

When I reached the other side, I could see that the throngs of fey had thinned, the glitter of their presence no longer so prevalent in the long alley between the booths. I walked the length of the fair looking for Raziel. I found her with Hyanith Vineret, passing the Kelinas booth with a stride that looked rather more like pacing than browsing.

When she left the other woman, I slipped across the alleyway to catch her on the way back towards the Queen's tent. I could see what Chadrena Rumah had meant; the dramatic cosmetic was so distracting against her pale skin that one could almost miss the worried frown between her brows and the tight line of her mouth

"There you are. I was worried."

"I'm sorry, Sidiana. I needed a few moments alone."

"To meditate?"

I laughed. "To pack."

"Perhaps they will not come. Perhaps she will forget," she said softly, almost to herself, a child's wish I pretended not to hear. We reached the pavilion and two servants emerged from the shadows, with tea and the hard little almond cookies of which she was fond, and a shawl against the cold. She accepted them all with distracted gratitude but would not settle into the pile of pillows provided. We stood, sipping tea, and watched the flow of fey and Euskalans through the fair.

"The cosmetics, the jewellery was well done," I said quietly at last. "You can rely on Chadrena. The dispute between the Sangam village and the farmers you will need to settle before the snows come, so planting can be done where the irrigation has been agreed. General Forent wants that new barracks built by spring and the engineers would prefer to spend the winter repairing the eastern walls, so both of them will start sending deputations when you return. You should—"

"I know this, Teresine, I know it. Don't speak of it."

"What should we speak of, then? Nothing we say will change anything that has happened. And we may not have another chance."

"I said I wanted this, didn't I? That morning you came to tell me I could choose, I chose this." She spoke without looking at me, her shadowed eyes on the torchlit corridor that led out into the darkness and, out of human sight, to the Border Court of the fey. "I even said I would be good at it."

"You are."

"No. If I was good at it, I would have found another way. If I was good at it, I would not be sending you into service to that . . . creature."

"There was no other way," I told her, as I had told her a dozen times already. "Raziel." The sound of her name, not her title, drew her to look at me. "If it had been Sarit in your place, I would still be going. I am afraid to go; I will not pretend I am not. But do me one parting grace: let me be afraid *of* them and not *for* you."

"Do good Sidianas not doubt themselves, then?" she asked, after a moment, her voice tight.

"Of course they do. But they do what must be done. I learned that from your mother and your sister."

She managed a laugh at that, though I did not miss the sharp edge it held. "I hope they managed to show you a few things more pleasant than that."

"The best place to sit in the sun on the roof on the summer afternoon, how to get from the west wing to the east without being seen, the bar with the best arrack outside the iron, how to ride a horse and a sled, how to make a butterfly in the snow," I said promptly and this time her laugh was bright and unshadowed.

When I glanced at the fair, I could see it was truly ending. I could see no fey wandering between the booths and the small knot of dark shapes passing by resolved into the Kamakaris, on their way back to the bridge, their House Head nodding respectfully to Raziel as they passed.

"We have two more days," I said. "I can leave the party after the pass and claim I'm going to the monastery at Kekit on retreat. Such can last as long as we need it to. Go to Yeshe Bukoyan when you get home and she can ensure whatever support you need in such a tale."

"Teresine." She sounded outraged. "I cannot ask an Asezati to lie for me."

"Of course you can. Of all people, she understands that. Trust me on this." It might be another debt that the Asezati could lay at my door but that was a problem for the future. "Come. Let's go back across a bridge and consider our duties done for the day."

If the journey to the fairhad seemed full of evil omens, the next two days would have been taken as a promise of good fortune. The sun shone, the wind was mild, and the night clear and cloudless. Raziel and I wore masks of cheerful relief and were grateful the long narrow paths over the passes freed us from conversation. Raziel brought Chadrena and Diamet into our plan and it was agreed that, at the bottom of the final pass, the Sidiana and I would take the road that led to the monastery and they would wait at the crossroad for Raziel's return.

And so the tale was given out, the turning reached, and on the afternoon of the second day, Raziel, her guards and I began the ride along the valley road.

The Queen's words had been imprecise, as was her wont, but I assumed she would find me wherever we chose to go. What form that finding might take, I could not guess. I kept my precious horde of shawls, meditations and barley in a bag on my back, in case she might simply wave her hand and I would vanish from the saddle and reappear in her court.

In the end, the process was not nearly so quick but almost as strange.

When it became too dark to ride, we set up camp in the shelter of a rise. The soldiers lit a fire. There was food and tea, of which I managed a mouthful each, and then there was nothing to do but wait. I don't imagine Raziel listened to much of my last-minute advice, wisely recognizing it was born of my own nervousness and thus was likely utterly unreliable.

Neither of us said aloud what both of us could not help but think: maybe the Queen had indeed forgotten.

Then one of the soldiers was on her feet, sword half-drawn, head turned to stare down the road. I heard it then, the beat of hooves on hard ground, the huff of equine breath, the creak of a leather saddle. We all came to our feet as, beyond the fire's radius, the night shaped itself into something solid.

I thought the fey courtier's horses impossible creatures, with their slender legs and dancing steps. The animal that emerged from the darkness seemed equally impossible but as unrelated to those delicate animals as they were to our own sturdy horses. It was as black as iron with shoulders that topped my head and a chest like a wall. I remembered the stories the soldiers told of far-off armies with horses that were mount and weapon and warrior in one. Surely this beast must be kin to those.

It seemed a mount for a giant. The rider on its back was not that, but big enough just the same. He wore leather armour over heavy cloth, black on black, and a helm shadowed his face. The fur of some grey beast lay across his shoulders, the wind stirring the long hairs to life. He drew the greathorse to a halt before us and held it while it tossed its head and pawed at the ground, impatient for battle.

And we could do nothing but tilt back our heads and stare at the darkness where his eyes should be.

The helm dipped a little. "Sidiana." His voice was a quiet rumble, like distant thunder.

"Lord," she said, after a moment's pause. He was the only fey who had ever used her correct title.

"The Queen has sent me to collect the last of the price."

Raziel turned to me and I saw her eyes widen at whatever she read in my face. "Teresine . . ."

"I am ready. Let us have done with it."

She hugged me then and, though I knew I should have counselled discretion, I hugged her back. I could feel her trembling. "Be careful," she whispered. "Oh, Tera—" and my heart broke on Sarit's old name for me "—be careful. Come back."

"I will. I will," I promised. When she let me go, I saw the tears in her eyes, and turned away before the hot threat of my own could overwhelm me.

I shouldered my bag and forced myself to walk to the warhorse's shoulder. When it turned its head I found myself staring into one great amber eye. I thought I saw amusement there, then the light refracted off it, turning it as green as a cat's eye in the darkness, and I looked away and up to the horse's rider. I could see nothing behind the helm but the line of a bearded jaw and the faint gleam of his eyes.

"Well." My voice sounded dry and broken. "I am ready."

For a moment, no one moved. *He did not know. She sent him here and he did not know.* The thought was so surprising that for a moment I even forgot to be afraid.

Then he slid his booted foot out of the stirrup and leaned down to offer me his gloved hand.

I cannot do this, I thought, helplessly, hopelessly. But as with all the other times I had thought it, there was no rescue, no escape. And I did what had to be done.

I put my hand in his.

I heard Raziel's sharp whisper and then one of the guards appeared at my side. He bent and cupped his hands, for there was no way I could have raised my foot into stirrup the fey lord had left empty for me. I put my foot into the guard's hands. He lifted and the rider pulled and then somehow I was in the saddle.

The horse danced sideways, surprisingly light-footed for a thing with such great hooves, and I clutched the back of the saddle. My thighs were against the rider's, my chest against his broad, armoured back, but if I had a choice over where to put my hands, I would not touch him. When the beast settled, I shifted the bag from my shoulder, stuffed it down into my lap and tucked the ties into my sash.

The rider turned his head a little. "Are you ready, Sidi?" I nodded, not trusting my voice, and he turned the horse back towards the road.

I almost twisted in the saddle to look back, but thought better of it. Instead, I dared to lean sideways a little, to see beyond the rider. I did not know how the horse could travel in that blackness, without even the moon for light; then I remembered the flare of its eye and supposed it could see in the dark.

"You will have to hold on now, Sidi."

"I am holding on."

"No." He reached back with one hand, caught my own, and dragged it around to place it on the unyielding armour across his ribs. "Hold on."

Self-preservation seemed more sensible than pride. I put my other arm around him tentatively and felt him take a breath beneath my hands.

He leaned forward then, drawing me with him. He cried out once in a strange language, kicked his heels into the horse's sides and then the world blurred and my breath was snatched away.

The horse ran like a dark wind across a landscape I could no longer see. I held on to the rider without urging, fearing to fall more than I feared him. I put my head down against his back, my cheek against the dead fur. The wind stung my eyes and I let it, to have something beyond myself to blame for the tears in them.

CHAPTER 26

Lilit

There was one demand she had procrastinated on nearly as well as she had been avoiding her pregnancy. Teresine's house in the mountains belonged to her now and Lilit would have to decide if her refusal to agree to her mother's plans had been nothing but childish, automatic defiance.

She was not required at the Austers for a day or two, so, after telling the nearest cousin where she was going, she set off up the long, switchback trail. She was grateful for the work of it; it kept her warm in the brisk air and distracted her from the memories of the last time she had taken this path.

She reached the house as the sun reached its zenith and paused for a moment at the edge of the little plateau. It looked the same as it always had; solid, weathered, almost indistinguishable from the rocks that rose behind it. In the summer, Urmit planted flowers in pots at the door and Filiat set out containers of herbs at one side of the house. They were gone now, brought into to the warmth of the house or cut, their seeds hoarded against the next spring.

It looked the same—but Lilit knew it was not. That knowledge knotted her throat with sudden, strangling grief and the view blurred behind tears. She swore in Deshinivi—words Teresine had taught her once long ago, to Amaris's disdain—then took a breath and followed the widening path down to the door.

She half expected to find it barred, but it yielded as if nothing had changed. In the cool dimness of the entrance, she paused, listening. After a moment, she heard the faint whisper of voices. The kitchen, she decided, and followed the sound, moving quickly before memory and grief could catch her again.

Memory found her anyway, a rush of warmth as she recognized the voices. This was coming home, as much as passing the doorway of Kerias was.

"It was Silveran's daughter, the one that went South with that soldier," Urmit was saying.

"Bah," Filiat replied in disgust. "It was not. It was Kiji Forness. And she ran off with a musician up from Rajapura. Waste of a good worker, though I suppose she'd end up working enough to support that tone-deaf lout." Lilit heard the thwack of a knife on the table for emphasis and smiled, lingering just outside the door for a moment. From there it was possible to pretend for one last moment that nothing had changed.

She realized it was unfair to eavesdrop on Urmit and Filiat, no matter how many times she had done so as a child. She was not a child anymore; she was now, whether she wished it or not, their employer.

Lilit stepped into the doorway as Urmit looked up from of black cloth curled like a sleeping cat in her lap. "Lily-child!" The mending was dumped unceremoniously on the bench as she rose and held out her arms. They were warm and solid and Lilit was content just to rest in them for a moment, as if she were still the child Urmit named her.

At last, she pulled herself away, accepted a scrawnier, if no less heartfelt, hug from Filiat and allowed herself to be given the most comfortable chair and a cup of tea. She had not seen either of them since the grim, strange day of the funeral, when they and the other household staff had formed an uneasy group of mourners at the farthest edge of the gathering.

"You should have told us you were coming," Filiat scolded her. "There's naught but a bit of old chicken made for dinner. And some onion and fennel. And a bit of dried apple that might soak out nicely, if yon dragon will let me touch some of the wine."

"I only decided this morning I'd come, so would have arrived on the heels of the messenger and you'd have had two mouths to fill with old chicken and onion," Lilit said with a laugh. "Which I am quite certain is delicious, no matter what you say. And by all means, we should have wine with apple."

"As if I could keep her from wine when she wished it," Urmit said. "But it would be nice if it would hold us the winter."

"Are you staying the winter?" Lilit asked and then was ashamed at her own utter lack of grace. She knew she should have come earlier, or sent word. She had only the confusion of her pregnancy as an excuse; she could imagine her great-aunt's disdain if she should have offered it.

"I am sorry," she added hastily, "I meant to come earlier. And you may stay as long as you wish. I only wondered if you wished to. I would understand if you did not."

"Have we anything to stay for?" Filiat asked bluntly and, at Urmit's distressed glance, pointed her knife. "Don't give me that look, old woman. Lilit is used to plain talk. If I have to spend the winter here with only you for company, I've a mind to take the Sidiana's pension and go back to Lushan. My old bones would be warmer."

"You'd have more than me to gripe to, that's your real reason," Urmit countered. "And there's a difference between plain talk and rudeness. Not that you ever knew it before, mind."

"Peace." Lilit held up her hands. "I wish I knew, Filiat. I wish I knew the answer to so many things," she admitted. "But I hope you will tell me honestly what you want. She would have wanted you both to be happy."

She saw a glance flicker between the two women and then Urmit pushed herself up from her chair. "I'll make up your room, Lily-Child," she said. "And get some wine." Filiat kept her smile decently hidden as she returned to her chopping. At the door, Urmit paused. "Unless you'd prefer another," she said awkwardly. "Your great-aunt's room is larger."

"No, thank you, Urmit," Lilit replied, repressing a shudder at the thought of sleeping in the bed in which Teresine had died. "My old room will be perfect." She finished her own tea and stood up, glancing from Urmit at the door to Filiat at her table. "I think . . . I think I will look around a little. If you need me."

The old women nodded and took refuge in work, setting Lilit loose in the dim, cold hallway. She supposed it was as odd for them as for her; she had been their child and their charge and now her choices shaped their futures. They had lived here for forty years, they and her great-aunt, and that life must have seemed as unchanging to them as it had to her.

She crossed the hallway and climbed the narrow stairs to the second floor.

At their top, she felt a shiver that had nothing to do with the cold. It had been this hallway in her dream, though attenuated with the strange texture of dreams, and ending in a door rather than a blank, whitewashed wall decorated with a red and gold hanging.

Behind her, around the railed walkway that ran beside the stairs, she could hear Urmit moving around in the little room that had always been hers. To her left were the two spare rooms, used for guests and storage. To her right was the carved wooden door that led to Teresine's workroom and, beyond it, beside her own, her great-aunt's bedroom.

The thought of that room laid a chill down her spine again but the workroom was safe enough.

Here, the hangings had been drawn aside, the shutters opened. Weak sunlight lay on the wood floor and touched the edge of the abandoned work table. Lilit went to it, to stand where the sun could warm her shoulders, and looked at the last mosaic her great-aunt had created.

There was a dark sky and mountains, with bright clear stones to stand for stars. Shapes of lapis lazuli and pale blue became a moon-washed city set behind a lake that reflected the sky. In the middle of the lake, a blaze of red bewildered her for a moment then, when she squinted, became something burning. A boat, she thought, and wondered why her aunt would shape such a thing, then the memory leapt to life like a flame. The torch descending, the wooden pyre catching the fire and flaring up, the smoke and scent of burning leaves.

Lilit closed her eyes for a moment, fighting the familiar nausea that seemed entwined with both her pregnancy and her memories of that long strange afternoon.

Had she known? she wondered. After all those years of making and remaking the symbols of her own mysterious unhappiness, had her great-aunt finally known that her soul was leaving? Had she made this one last mosaic as the pattern of the last moments of her betraying body in the world?

Lilit's fingers touched the stones, slid across the crimson, the indigo. She traced the edge of the lake absently and then her fingers seemed to catch on a rough set of smaller tiles. They were tiny, nothing but chips of colour and she had to squint again to make sense of them. A figure stood on the edge of the lake, a shape whose face held the only brown tones in the mosaic. Its robes were black, picked out from the surrounding darkness by a thin gap. It was anonymous, nearly invisible, but Lilit knew who it was meant to be.

If it were not her own funeral she witnessed, who then was her great-aunt watching burn?

Lilit lingered there for a moment, tracing the mysterious lines as if the answer lay in a language only touch could read. *I will never know,* she thought. Whatever Teresine had not been able to find the words to say would stay unspoken and unknown forever.

The sting of that thought drove her from the table, propelled her to the line of shelves and boxes along the wall, seeking distraction. Her great-aunt's collection of coloured tiles did not hold her but there was a chest set into the corner that promised mysteries that might be easier to solve. She crouched down and lifted the metal-bound lid.

It seemed to contain nothing but woven blankets but when she slid her hands down beneath them, her fingers found the lumpy mystery of wooden shapes. As she was unpacking the blankets, she heard a step in the doorway and turned to see Urmit watching her.

She felt the heat of automatic guilt in her cheeks. "I wondered what was in here," she said awkwardly, a child caught prying into her elders' business.

"Naught but cloth," Urmit began but the words died as Lilit lifted the wooden curiosity into the light. The jumble of shapes and colour clattered, rearranging itself into a child's toy.

"I remember this," Lilit breathed, turning the carved doll in her hands. The joints were held with metal pins and the arms and legs fell loosely around the painted torso.

"Oh yes," Urmit said with a chuckle, the floor creaking as she moved into the room. "You loved that one. So did your mother, when she was a little bit of a thing."

Lilit looked at the face, nothing more than angles in the wood and the remnants of paint at lips and eyes. The painted hair had almost rubbed off, but black remained in the seams of the wood. There were metal hooks at wrists and elbows, knees and ankles. The one set into the top of the head had been missing as long as she could remember. It was a not really a doll, but a puppet, though she had preferred to act out her childish dramas without strings or rods, the puppet's gold-painted limbs dangling with spidery fragility.

"It came with her from Deshiniva, when she and her mother came here with your great-aunt. Barely bigger than it, she seemed, just a toddler. But she slept with it every night."

"Was she happy here?" Lilit asked, half to herself, as she looked at the austere face with its enigmatic smile.

"Yes, I think she was. Not when she first came maybe. I think it took her a while to realize they were staying here and it wasn't just another place they stopped while your great-aunt came home from so far away. But after that, I think she was happy. She was always a quiet child—not like you, always running and getting into things and arguing with your elders—but she had the sweetest smile I'd ever seen. But then her mother died. She never forgave us for that."

"I've never understood that. It wasn't Teresine's fault. It was nobody's fault."

"I suppose she thought your great-aunt should have saved her. She thought she could. She thought Teresine could do anything, back then. You should have seen her pretty black eyes light up when your great-aunt would come back from the city. She'd run right up to her and just stand there, holding on to her sash or the corner of her robe. Teresine would let her and that seemed to be enough, though sometimes she'd put her hand on the little one's head. They'd just stand there, your great-aunt talking to your grandmother, or to us, with your mother holding onto her robe and Teresine's hand stroking her hair." Urmit sighed, shaking her head. "But after her mother died, she never did it again."

Lilit set the puppet to one side and drew out the cloth on which it had rested. Beneath her careful hands, it unfolded into a length of sheer green, thin with age, patched and faintly tattered. The edges had been trimmed in white, embroidered with patterns now yellowed with age. "That was hers, your grandmother's," Urmit said. "It's what they wear down there in Deshiniva, I suppose." Lilit lifted the cloth carefully to her face but she could smell nothing but dust. It had been too long in the mountains, she thought, and held none of the scents her great-aunt used to speak of: spices, flowers, sun-baked skin.

"What was she like?"

"Keshini? She was quiet. I forget her sometimes, truth be told. She never learned to speak Euskalan very well. I suppose we could have been kinder to her but she—she never seemed to *need* anything. She'd follow the sun around the house; wherever it was, you'd find her. She'd sew or mind Amaris or just sleep there, her face up to the light." She moved and Lilit glanced over to find her brushing at the dust on one of the shelves. Automatically, she drew a cloth from her robe and began to run it over the wood, the boxes it held. "She'd been sick after the birth, Teresine said. She was just a young thing, no more than twenty, when she died."

Satisfied, Urmit tucked the cloth away again. "She was never happy here. She was like a plant you take from one corner of the garden to the other and it withers."

Lilit looked at the gauzy stuff her in hands, imagining a young woman draping it over her black hair, veiling her shadowed face. She wondered what had happened in Deshiniva that had forced her to tear up her fragile roots and follow her sister up into the mountains, where she could find no nourishment among the rocks. Yet if she had not, Lilit herself would not exist. Her soul would have found life in another family and, in the heat of another country, some other child would have been born to her mother.

She swaddled the puppet in the green veil, aware of Urmit watching her as she set it back in the chest and closed the lid.

"Tis a shame to bury toys away," Urmit said. "Likely there's a child down in Kerias who would like to dream on it."

For a moment, Lilit saw it clearly; saw herself sitting in the sun on the terrace as she had seen her great-aunt do, watching a little girl dance the puppet across the stones, as she herself had done.

"Who knows?" she said. "Maybe there'll be someone to play it with, someday."

CHAPTER 27

Teresine

Even now, I am not certain how long that blind, whirlwind ride back through the pass lasted. Long enough for the tears in my eyes to be only from the cold wind, short enough that my fear of the journey itself left no space for fear of the destination.

With my eyes closed, my face against the fur, my fingers turning numb in their grip on leather armour, I missed the moment the magic ended and the greathorse's gait turned from impossible to merely fast. One moment there was nothing but wind in my ears, then I heard the rhythm of hooves on earth. I opened my eyes and saw that the moon had come out. There were mountains cutting darker profiles against the sky but I could not tell if they were the ones I expected to see, for I had never seen them from this end of the plateau. I might be able to find a horizon I recognized if I could see the ridge behind me but I did not dare to look back.

The horse slowed, shifting from a canter to a bumpy trot but I did not move until the fey lord's stance shifted, his body straightening. I saw the turn of his head as he glanced back. There was nothing to be read in the expressionless profile of his helm but I imagined amusement, or contempt, and sat back with as much aloof dignity as I could manage, resuming my grip on the back of the saddle.

I heard him mutter something to the horse, his gloved hand patting the heavy neck. The beast snorted and shook its head but did not slow its pace. Like the mountain horses, I thought, on the last stretch of the track to the stables, eager for their dinner. I leaned sideways to peer past the armoured shoulder in front of me. I do not know what I expected to see: the pavilion of the Queen, a palace, a door in a hillside that led to another world. The half-shrouded moonlight showed nothing but the dark bulk of an unlit building, low and unprepossessing. When the clouds unveiled the moon, I could see that it was a ruin, with walls half-tumbled and no sign of a roof.

The horse huffed and stopped. I looked up at an archway, its centre fallen away. I could hear nothing but the wind and the horse's breathing and the creak of the saddle. "We are here, Sidi," the fey lord said at last and this time I did not imagine the amusement. "You will have to get down now."

I did not manage it very gracefully but when it was accomplished I was grateful to be on the ground, which seemed solid and real enough beneath my feet. I untied my pack and shouldered it once again, while the fey lord dismounted with considerably more competence than I had demonstrated. He whispered something in the horse's ear and stroked its shoulder. I saw the moonlight spark green from its eyes as it looked back at me. It shook its mane, gave a whinny that sounded like laughter, and then trotted off into the darkness with purposeful confidence.

The fey lord watched it go; I did my best to watch him and study the ruins at the same time. I could see no sign of life there, no trace of light or sound or any suggestion that the place was not as dead as the Aygaresh who had built it. I wondered for the first time if there was in truth no Border Court, or at least not one that mortal eyes could bear, and that the fey, ever careless of mortal lives, expected I could survive the winter in these ruins. *There is a thing of the Aygaresh where we choose to bide*, the Queen had said, which had seemed clear enough at the time, but I should have remembered that nothing the fey said was clear.

I heard the snap of a buckle and looked at my escort, who was in the process of removing his helm. He pulled it off with what seemed relief, ran his gloved hand over his hair and looked around, as if expecting someone to materialize to take the helmet from him. When no such service appeared, he muttered something I could not quite understand but which, from the tone, seemed likely to be an expletive, and made a complicated gesture with his hand.

Torches flared into sudden flame on either side of the arch and their light touched a heavy wooden door where before there had been only emptiness. The arch itself was whole once again, with no sign it had ever been broken.

"Welcome to the Border Court," the fey lord said. Though I said nothing, some trace of my doubt at the reality of that sight must have shown on my face for there was a trace of mocking amusement in his voice as he said, "Please come in, Sidi," then stepped forward to push open the great doors and take a servant's stance against the light that spilled out.

My one great gift for survival had been knowing when to hold my tongue, how to school my face to show not one flicker of my true thoughts and I knew I would not survive this if I had let my years at the side of the Sidianas, who valued my honesty, dull that instinct.

I stepped beneath the arch. The doors fell closed behind me without a sound and I had to glance back to see they were still there.

In this new space, high-ceilinged, lit by racks of candles, I saw the fey lord clearly for the first time. His hair was brown, sweat-darkened at the base of the heavy waves crushed against his forehead. His beard was the same colour, paling to amber at the corners of his mouth and down his throat. He was round-faced and dark-browed and there were lines at the corners of his eyes.

I had seen many fey in the years I had attended the fair at Sarit's side; dark and fair, tall and short, dressed in silk and armour and fur. As I had told Raziel, I supposed that they were beautiful, though that beauty had no power to touch me. But I had never seen one who looked so prosaically mortal and I found it hard not to stare.

He looked back. This time I remembered caution and was the first to look away. From the room in which we stood three dark doorways opened into three darker corridors. There were no candles there and I wondered if the fey could see in the dark, like their horses.

"Well, Sidi," the fey lord said at last, into a silence that had stretched well past comfort, "what does the Queen want with you?"

"The Queen mentioned an Aygaresh mosaic," I said. Though, I suppose, to be truthful, she had not precisely said *mosaic*. "I believe she wishes me to repair it."

"Repair it?" he echoed. "Why would she want you to do that?"

"I've no idea," I replied, startled by the odd lack of respect in his voice. That he was surprised also suggested this was not some well-known interest of the Queen's and *that* thought was less than reassuring.

I caught his half-covert glance down the corridor to his left. *He does not know what is supposed to happen next*, I thought and had a vision of us standing there all night, the Queen's whim forgotten as quickly as it had been conceived. Under other circumstances I might have laughed.

The fey lord shifted his helmet from one arm to the other and I could see the threat of waning patience in the set of his shoulders beneath the grey pelt. I did not think I cared to see him angry.

"What is your name?" he asked at last.

"Teresine."

He repeated it and it sounded different than it did in either Deshinivi or Euskali; shorter, sharper. As if it was not my name, but a stranger's. "And yours?" I asked, because at least courtesy lent some semblance of normality to the business.

"Daen."

I nodded and we stood in silence once again. He made a sound at last, that half-heard expletive muttered beneath his breath. "Well, Sidi Teresine, if the Queen has not the grace to send a guide, we shall have to seek one."

"Perhaps—" I began, reluctant to either argue with him or follow him into the mysterious corridors.

"My Lord Daen." The voice materialized out of the darkness to the right and then the corridor there was ablaze with torches, silhouetting the tall, slender figure in the doorway.

"Ferrell." The fey lord's greeting was as cold as his smile had been. "It's about time. Is this how you demonstrate the Queen's hospitality?"

"The Queen's guest was in your hands, my lord. Why should there be any doubt of the kind care she would receive?" Ferrell replied, stepping into the chamber.

I was torn between fascination and the profound wish to be elsewhere. There was nothing prosaic or mortal about Ferrell; he had the fey beauty and impossible grace, the fey arrogance. Set against him, Daen seemed less fey, but less mortal as well. He was like the greathorse; solid, straightforward, immovable. Both of them were likely equally dangerous.

For a moment, the two bristled at each other like great cats, then, like cats, each feigned complete disinterest in the other.

The unfortunate consequence of this was that each took a sudden interest in me. Ferrell looked at me for a long moment, contempt eloquent in the tilt of his head and the frosty blue stare. "So this is the mortal," he said at last and the disdain in his voice matched the stare for chill.

I had found my old armour again and was confident my face showed nothing at all, though I was still grateful for the little concealment offered by the scarf wrapped around my bare head and throat.

"Why, Ferrell, one might think you didn't like mortals. And I thought you shared every fascination of the Queen's."

"All of the Queen's interests are of interest to me," Ferrell replied. "You need not doubt that, oh Queen's Champion, oh Queen's Best Beloved, oh Queen's—" He paused, smiling over the last word he did not say, as if it were a delicacy too precious to relinquish just yet.

Before he could open his mouth again, Daen gave him a look that would have seared stone, as sharp as the blade that had not been drawn. The elegant fey lord did not flinch, but the ice in his eyes cracked for one almost imperceptible moment. Whatever he might have said, he kept it swallowed.

Daen's smile was almost as ferocious as his glance had been but he merely said "Good. I assume you were sent here with a message."

"The Queen has had rooms prepared in the East Corridor for the mortal, if you would be so good as to escort it there." Ferrell's arrogance was back in place and he managed to make the message sound like a command. "And our Queen bids you attend her when your duties are done." Feeling safely ignored, I could marvel at the fey gift for making malice of politeness.

"With all haste," Daen agreed. There was a moment of silence then as they looked at each other. The air crackled with aggression again and I realized that each was waiting for the other to move, as if movement would be retreat. With some astonishment, it came to me that perhaps fey males were not so different from mortals of the same sex after all.

In the end, it was Ferrell who conceded, with a tilt of his head that was barely a nod. Daen waited until the other fey lord had vanished back down the corridor before he looked at me again. "He's an ass, but he has the Queen's ear. And he doesn't like mortals. You'd be best to stay away from him."

I nodded automatically, baffled at his confidences and also at how I would possibly arrange to avoid anyone. Daen turned to consider the three doorways for a moment and then went to stand at the mouth of one, rubbing his jaw thoughtfully. My sense of direction was never very good and I had no idea which way east might be or even if to the fey it was reasonable that the East Corridor would lie in such a direction. The fact that even Daen did not seem entirely certain was not reassuring.

Eventually, either by sight or sound or some other sense, he decided the choice was acceptable and set off with a long stride. I stared at his disappearing back, the black of his armour blending with the darkness. Then my wits returned and I ran after him, catching up just as the lamps flared to life around him.

"The torches won't light for you," he said, "And the corridors change. So don't go wandering the hallways by yourself, even if you think you know where you're going." I nodded, stretching my stride to try to match his, knowing I could not sustain it for long but willing myself not to do anything as unseemly and mortal as pant or fall behind. For whatever reason he gave it, I would likely need the information he was sharing, and I did not wish to miss any of it.

"This is the South Corridor, at least right now. It is not much used, nor is the East, which is no doubt why the Queen chose it for you.

"Don't open doors you don't recognise. In truth, you should be careful with the ones you do recognize. Neither necessarily lead where you think you're going." It would be helpful if he would explain to me how I was supposed to get anywhere if I could neither walk in the hallway nor open a door, but I hesitated to ask him, for fear he would take it as impertinence and stop talking. "If you find a door that leads outside, don't go past the threshold. Whatever it might be in here, it will be winter soon out there."

He slowed his stride and glanced at me. "You don't talk much, do you?"

"I am required to, Lord?" I asked and was pleased my voice had remembered the old supple submission, the soft tone that deflected both interest and anger.

He only laughed. "We'll see."

We reached the junction of the South Corridor with another. Both looked identical, with dark stone walls punctuated by darker doorways. The stone floors were uncarpeted and the only decorations were the lamps; their unnatural flames cast wavering shadows on the bare walls. I glanced back the way we had come and saw that the light was gone, the lamps extinguishing behind us as we moved. The cold simplicity of it was so utterly unlike the gaudy brilliance of the fey at the fair that it seemed impossible they could inhabit such a place.

"This is the East Corridor," he said, gesturing to his right then striding into the darkness.

"Does it go east?" I asked and he paused for a moment, which allowed me to catch up to him once more, as the candles blossomed in the lamps.

"You know, I have no idea," he replied thoughtfully and was silent for a while. I wondered if he was puzzling the geography of the Court in his head. "I suppose you could find a window at the end of the corridor and see if you could see the sun rise," he said at last. "But even that wouldn't necessarily mean anything."

"Why not?"

"Time here is different than in the mortal world. Here, it is whatever time the Queen wishes it to be. At least where she is."

"And where she is not?"

"Does not matter," he said and in his voice was something as dark as what had lain beneath Ferrell's frosty courtesy. "Where she is not, time does as it pleases."

Far down the corridor, light bloomed, illuminating a stretch of hallway. "This must be it," Daen said, as the lanterns snuffed themselves out around us and we walked towards the light in a dim twilight glow.

On the last steps through the shadows, the world around me changed. There was carpet beneath my feet and hangings on the whitewashed walls. The lamps were no longer shaped to a foreign aesthetic, but the homey and familiar ones of the hallways of Lushan. Along the row of anonymous doorways, there was one that was anything but. The wide lintels were painted bright blue and red and there were luck amulets hammered at the corners. To my astonishment, even the iron wards were there, on the doorknob and on the doorstep but when I reached out to touch them, I realized that what I had taken for iron was nothing but painted wood.

"Fucking hells," Daen swore and I looked up to see him staring at the door, a look of disgust on his face. "Might as well put up a sign—*Here be mortals.*"

"They would know where I was anyway," I said tentatively, because I could not help the comfort the decoration of the door gave me. I knew that comfort was a lie, but I was exhausted in body and soul and could not bring myself to reject it.

"True." He looked down at me as I put my hand on the doorknob. His words of warning echoed in my ears but I could not see I had any choice but to open the door. "You might as well," he said and I turned the handle then pushed the door open. I got a glimpse of a canopied bed in the alcove of one wall and the banked glow of a brazier. It might have been any room in the palace of Lushan. I wondered how the Queen knew what one looked like, to recreate it with her magics.

I was aware of Daen looking curiously over my head and I turned in the doorway, pulling the door half-closed against my back, reluctant to let him see the room, as if it revealed some part of me I would prefer remain hidden. "Do you know what the Queen will expect of me tomorrow morning?"

He shook his head. "She will make her requirements clear. Let us hope they don't include conversation."

"Thank you, Lord Daen," I said politely. "You have been most kind."

"No, I haven't. I've done my Queen's bidding and amused myself in the process. Don't confuse that with kindness."

"All those things you told me, were they true?"

"They're true enough."

"Was that part of the Queen's command?"

"No, Sidi, that was part of my amusement," he replied with a grin, though I did not understand why he should consider it so. "Now, I must attend my Queen. Good night, Sidi Teresine. I wish you pleasant dreams."

I smiled blandly and wished him good night in return. When he turned away and headed down the corridor with his purposeful stride, I slid into that deceptively comforting room and shut the door behind me. If it had borne a lock, I would have locked it, but the Queen had allowed me no such grace.

I stood there for a moment, my back against the door and looked around. Nothing changed, nothing wavered. The illusion that I was in the palace of Lushan held. I stepped warily around the room, my fingers drifting over the bed hangings, the chests, the rough walls. It all felt real; the hangings had the rough texture of felt beneath my fingers, the wood was grained and seamed, indistinguishable from reality. And yet, there was a subtle falseness to it, an elusive unreality that eluded my fingers, my eyes.

It was not cold, I realized, nor hot. The palace in Lushan always seemed to be too much of one or, rarely, when a room was full, the other. And it smelt of nothing. There was no lingering scent of dung smoke and sweat, no faint stuffiness of rooms closed against the winter, no perfume of incense from the temple or spice from the kitchen. No mortal but I had ever touched those hanging and those chests, I thought, either in making or using. I was certain the bed would be as virginal, untainted with another's weight, another's heat.

This newness, this false familiarity, disturbed me more than anything else I had seen on this long strange night.

I did not put my belongings in the drawers, but tucked my bag at the corner of the bed, by the untouched pillow. I let the brazier burn, for fear I would have no way to light it again if the magic that made it allowed it to fail. I knew I would need all my wits when the morning came (whenever that might be, I thought, remembering Daen's words) but I shed only my outer robe and crawled beneath the uncomfortably comfortable blankets in my tunic and pants.

I worried I would lie awake, too aware of all the strangeness around me to sleep, fearing what fey-haunted dreams might seep into my mind, born from the magic that must be in the very air of the place. In the end, I slid into sleep between one breath and the next and dreamt not of the fey, or of Lushan, but of Deshiniva.

CHAPTER 28

Teresine

I woke in the Border Court of the Faerie Queen, my drowsy mind full of Jayasita, night-blooming jessamine, and the whisper of fans moving in the humid air. The memory of the mosaic at the House of Falling Leaves filled my closed eyes; Erzulie's jewelled girdle burning red in the lamplight, the blue sea that cradled her glowing as if lit from within. Viram had painted the backs of the blue glass with electrum so that the faintest light would fire that blue to life. He had let me paint the last row of them myself and I remembered hunching over the glass stones, labouring as if one imperfection would cost my life.

I had no electrum, no glass, no paste. I had no idea what the mosaic of the Aygaresh might look like. I had no idea at all how I would repair it.

With those thoughts, I was truly awake, no longer able to pretend that the bed was the one I had left behind in Lushan. I opened my eyes and rolled up, wrapping the blankets over my shoulders as I pushed aside the bed hangings.

For a moment, I thought my awakening was another part of my dream. The room in which I had gone to sleep had changed. The walls were still whitewashed but now the hangings that covered them were not the bright felt of Lushan but the gold-threaded silk of Jayasita. The carpet had been replaced by woven grasses bound in linen. The bed curtains I held in one hand were no longer heavy but gossamer, meant to keep out only night-flying insects. There was a window at one end of the room now, covered in a carved wooden screen, filtering a fall of light softer than any that had ever touched the mountains. There was the faint scent of flowers in the air. On one of the chests, now low and lacquered, a large bowl of water steamed.

I had dreamed of Jayasita and woken in the room that might have been there. I dreaded that thought as soon as it slid into my mind, fearful that whatever power had read my dreams could read my thoughts and make them come true. I wanted the room from Lushan, with all its falseness and deception, back again. At least it was the simulacrum of a place I loved. I wondered what would happen if I said that thought aloud. Would I close my eyes and wake to find the room changed once again?

But if I did, I would betray that the memory of Jayasita held any power to hurt me, if my thoughts had not already done so. I felt a rush of despair; I had learned once to control every word, every expression, but I had made them a mask that left me free to think whatever I chose, clinging to that one last freedom. If I lost that, which had kept me whole in the place that wanted me broken, I did not know if I could endure it.

Whether my dreams or my thoughts could betray me, I could not simply sit on the bed forever. I shrugged off the blankets and slid my bare feet down to touch the floor. I stood still, wondering what to do next.

I did not want to go to the window; I did not want to know what fey magic might have created behind those screens. At last, I took the few steps to the chest and laid one hand carefully on the surface of the water. It was deliciously warm and the steam carried the scent of the petals strewn across the surface.

There was another smell in the room; something sharp and bitter. It was me, I realized. Unwashed flesh, sweat, horses, dung fires, incense. All the aromas that were as much a part of Lushan as the scent of rotting fruit, sea, and salt on skin had been part of Jayasita.

The fey had no smell, I thought, remembering the night before. The hallways had held no scents, not even staleness. Even the greathorse had smelled only faintly of horse and the saddle—and Daen's armour—had borne the scent of well-used leather. In the pavilion of the Queen, there had been nothing but the hint of candle smoke.

The water, by the grace of fey magic no doubt, was as warm as when I had first touched it. I shed my robes and washed myself with the cloth folded by the bowl I found my old, soft chemise and put it on, then wrapped my robe over it and my sturdy trousers. My fingers and earlobes felt naked without their iron adornments, but I kept Chadrena's bracelet around my wrist.

Though I was washed and dressed, I did not dare to leave the room. Even without Daen's warnings, I would not have wandered the corridors of the Border Court on my own. I had no choice but to remain where I was until the Queen chose to remember me.

There was little enough to do there. I overcame my unease enough to open all the drawers and store my meagre belongings. I was still wary enough of the window to stay away, but everything else I examined seemed absolutely ordinary. Just as it had the night before, I thought.

My stomach growled, reminding me I had not eaten anything since the previous day. I found the little bag of barley I had carried with me and held it in my hand. I did not quite believe in its power but there was comfort in its weight. Here, I suspected, neither doubt nor belief made any difference. The fey world was what it was and there was nothing I could do but try to survive.

I took a single grain of barley from the bag and swallowed it.

That choice made, I had nothing to distract myself with but the *Meditations of Aurelian* and meditation itself. It seemed wiser to preserve the *Meditations* against future inactivity, so I settled cross-legged on the floor and began the ritual chants. To give weight to the saying that trouble made believers of us all, for once my whispered pleas for grace and mercy were not rote words. If there was a possibility that Jennon might protect me, I was willing to ask for such protection.

I am not sure how long I sat there. Long enough to reach the state of suspension that sometimes came upon me in prayer, in which thoughts were of no more weight than the breath moving in and out of my chest. In which the sound of a knock on the door was like the toll of a distant bell, summoning someone else.

The echoes of that bell finally reached my mind and I realized what had created them in the same moment the door opened. I sat still and looked up at the fey lord Daen, who looked down at me. For a moment, his expression was purely fey; impenetrable and unknowable.

Then he laughed, a sound woven of rueful amusement and something much darker.

I did not move, holding on to my own armoured silence. I tried to let his laughter follow the sound of the bell, to let it pass without speculation or injury, to betray nothing.

"Forgive me, Sidi," he said, though for his laugher or his intrusion I could not tell.

"There is no need to apologize, Lord. I was inattentive," I replied as I slid the bracelet back onto my wrist and rose.

"You were praying. We do not pray here so it was somewhat unexpected." It might have been an oblique explanation of his laughter. It was not true but I did not correct him.

"Do you have no gods then?"

"Only her," he replied. "I did not realize your vocation, Sidi. Or shall I call you Azi?"

"Whatever you wish." I was accustomed to both but preferred Sidi: Azi had always seemed a lie. But I was not about to tell him that.

"Sidi then," he said without explanation, leaving me with yet more fearful suspicions of the fey ability to read my thoughts. How had he known those titles, when the Queen and most of the fey disdained to learned them? He looked around the room for a moment but, to my relief, forebore comment on the changes, though I had no doubt he had noted them. "Well, Sidi, are you ready? The Queen requests the honour of your presence."

"That is gracious of her," I replied, quite certain the Queen had not phrased it so politely and somewhat surprised Daen had bothered to add that gloss of courtesy. "I am ready to do her bidding." Which was my own unnecessary addition to the business, but in truth I was not entirely reluctant, my trepidation at meeting the Queen balanced against the thought of remaining trapped in my room.

I half expected to find the corridor altered as well but all remained as it had been, down to the painted iron on the door. Beyond that strange simulacrum of Lushan, the corridor was as anonymous as it had been the night before.

Daen set off down it without ceremony, leaving me once again to trot to catch up to him. "The Queen is holding a moon-viewing party," he said.

I remembered the sunlight streaming through the screened window I had not dared to open. I had thought it at least reflected the true time, if not precisely the true light, and now doubted even that conclusion. "Is it day or night?"

"Does it matter? Time is her servant here. You become accustomed to it in the end. Though," he gave me a sideways, sharp-edged grin. "I'm much more in the mood for pastries than boar, so my stomach considers it morning. It has always been as good a guide as any."

At the mention of food, my own stomach reminded me one symbolic grain of barley would not be enough to sustain me. I wondered if his words meant that pastries might be on offer and how long I might go before risking my mortal soul by eating one. I would not even scorn a bit of boar.

The world beyond the corridors seemed to consider it day as well, for through the windows that now seemed to line it, sunlight made the gossamer curtains glow red and gold and copper as we passed. I risked a glance or two as I stretched my stride to keep pace with Daen but could see nothing beyond the thin silk but a haze of light.

We turned one last corner and, to my astonishment, walked straight into a crowd of fey. After the long empty corridors we had walked last night and this morning, I had almost forgotten there were other fey in the Court. For a moment, I was lost in a sea of bright colour, perfume and a sound like birds singing. My head spun and, from a great distance, I could feel my knees begin to bend, my limbs go limp.

A hard grip on my arm pulled me up sharply and I heard a distant sound, like a lightning crack and then a voice like resounding thunder. "Enough! Not one more spell out of any of you."

"Our apologies, Lord Daen," a silky voice said. The dazzle in my eyes faded and I saw a fey woman bow with delicate contempt. The great gossamer wings that rose from her shoulders shimmered like opals in the light. "It is our nature. How can we help it? How can any of us help it?"

"And I thought there was nothing you fey could not do," Daen replied, his hand still holding my upper arm, iron-fingered, bruising. "If you deigned to try, of course. So I advise you to try."

With that, he pulled me with him through the crowd of fey and down the hall, around another corner into a hallway once more empty and anonymous. "My apologies, Sidi," he said, releasing my arm. "You should try to stay away from them, as well."

"Who are they?"

"That was Madelon. Lady Madelon," he corrected himself with private irony. "She is the Queen's cousin."

I knew what that might mean. I had spent fifteen years in the court of the Euskalans, after all. There were a dozen questions crowding my mind but I thought it wiser to ask none of them. It seemed that Daen told me what he wished to tell me, whether I asked him or not.

We rounded another corner, less precipitously this time, and arrived in a corridor that blossomed candelabras and lamps glowing with coloured glass. A great door rose before us, guarded by two matched soldiers in armour that seemed as delicate as the lamps, etched silver and jewelled edges. The pikes they held did not seem meant for battle for the metal on them looked like lace and the shafts were made of gold.

The soldiers moved, each gesture in perfect unison, and I wondered if there were even living creatures behind the elaborate helms. Perhaps they were nothing but empty suits of armour, animated by fey magic. Daen spared them not a glance as they opened the doors and bowed us through.

I was dazzled again, this time by the beauty and impossibility of what lay before me. It was a vast garden of smooth lawns and sculpted stands of trees, lit by the glow of a round, silver-white moon. I could hear the trickle of water in rocky fountains echoed by soft laughter. The fountains spilled down into a decorative river, arched over by wooden bridges. On the river bank, I could see a crowd gathered, surrounded by a constellation of paper lanterns, their lights touching an uplifted face, sparking a jewel to life, vanishing behind the sweep of the robe.

"I hate moon-viewing parties," Daen said casually and set off down the path with his usual briskness. I caught up to him as the path slipped into a great stand of trees and the moon vanished

"Why?"

"Fucking boring. Poetry contests and singing. The rice wine is not bad though."

"It's a little early for rice wine," I said as we emerged into the fierce light of the moon again.

"Or a little late for pastries. You take what you can get."

"Is this real? Or an illusion?"

"It is best to assume all things here are real, Sidi," he replied. "Especially the illusions." There was a distance in his voice I recognized: I might have sounded that way speaking of Lushan. *You fey*, he had said. Not *we fey*.

I had no more time to wonder at that, for we had reached the edge of the groomed lawn and the gathering of fey assembled there. They lounged on cushions heaped on plush carpets, each anchored by delicate lanterns. The moonlight drained everything of colour, rendering it in black and grey, white and pearl. I saw flower-faces turn towards us, was aware of ebony eyes lingering as we passed. Whispers rose and shredded in the scented breeze. There seemed the usual multiplicity of dress and skin, but I dared not look at any of them long enough to tell, or guess if I might have seen them at the fair.

Near the river's edge, there was a low dais. Beside it, servants, nearly invisible against the dark river, the dark lawn, held poles bearing lamps, elaborate confections of paper and filigree and candles that burned as if there were no breeze at all.

On the dais sat the Queen. I lowered my eyes but the image of her remained there, as if burned into my lids: the white hair, like a cascade of moonlight that fell past her knees, spilling over the dais to pool on the ground. Her robes, layer upon layer of silk held by a jewelled girdle, were more shades of white than I would have dreamed possible.

We stopped. I saw Daen's shadow bow slightly, followed by my own. "Daen." Her voice was softer than I remembered. "Mortal."

"Great Queen." The words sounded as dry as dust.

"Welcome." That courtesy surprised me into risking another glance. She was not smiling. I was not even certain she was looking at me, speaking to me. There was a nest of pillows to the right of the dais, a tray of mysterious delicacies and an exquisite flask arranged with artistic precision beside it. From the corner of my eye, I saw Daen settle down with vigorous grace. He surveyed the selection of offerings and popped one inelegantly into his mouth, then washed it down by drinking directly from the flask.

"I trust your lodgings are sufficient," the Queen said and this time there was no doubt she was speaking to me. I felt the weight of the gaze I did not quite dare to meet.

"Yes, thank you, Great Queen."

There was a ripple of laughter, like trees moving in a breeze, and then it was gone.

"Your Little Queen wants you back by Spring. Best you begin your work." Her white hand moved, a drift of smoke in the air. "Daen will show you. What you require, he will bring."

"I just arrived. I haven't even had breakfast," Daen protested, to my astonishment. Even more astonishing, the Queen laughed.

"Give me a poem and you may stay. I will send Ferrell to deal with the mortal."

"The Queen commands the sun and moon. Who am I then not to move?" he recited, with courtly extravagance and she laughed again and held out the white wisp of her hand. He shifted to his knees and bent his head to kiss her offered palm, then rose, pausing to scoop up the tray, flask and all.

"Come on, Sidi. We are dismissed," he said. Baffled and relieved, I followed him back through the field of fey to the safety, such as it was, of the path. "There, that wasn't so hard, was it? We got off with only one bad poem and a tray of food. And some rice wine."

"For which it is still too early."

"Take what you get, Sidi. Remember that."

Some mysterious cue set the doors in motion and I saw the guards silhouetted against the torches as they ushered us back into the stone corridors once again. Daen stood still for a moment, contemplating each direction with a look of momentary distraction, then set off towards the left. As he walked, he contemplated the tray of food. "No pastries, but these round things have honey and nuts. The fish rolls are rather nice, though perhaps not really for breakfast. I don't care for the pickled beets myself but you might like them." He held the tray out for my inspection, as if expecting me to choose something and devour it there.

"I'm not hungry at the moment," I managed to say, though my stomach was protesting that fish rolls, pickled beets and honey and nut things seemed like a perfectly good breakfast.

"You might as well eat, Sidi. What are you planning to do? Eat one grain of rice each day for six months?" That was so near the truth that I could feel the betraying heat in my skin, though I did not look at him. "You'll starve," Daen said bluntly. "And it won't make any difference. The food is safe enough. Eating it won't doom you to eternity in the Border Court. Well," his grin came again, edged this time with malice, "unless she wants it to."

"How will I know if she wants it to?"

"You won't. So you may as well enjoy the food." He pushed the tray my way again. I took one of the nut and honey things. It was sweet and chewy and delicious. I wondered if I had lost my soul for a sugary trifle but decided there was little enough I could do about it if I had. I took another one and followed Daen down the hallway.

Another turned corner and the corridor changed once again. There was stone beneath my feet now and the walls were rough and unadorned. The roof seemed higher, the lamps farther apart. I tucked my hands beneath my sleeves and watched my breath turn to mist in the cooling air.

It seemed impossible that the warm night of the moon-viewing and this forbidding space could be part of the same building. After a quick swallow of rice wine, Daen held the flask out to me. "Consider it protection from the cold," he suggested. "Until I can sort out who is responsible for making sure you don't freeze to death."

The logic was dubious but I had already yielded on the subject of breakfast. And it was cold. I took the flask and sampled a careful sip. It tasted almost like Deshiniva rice wine, though with a sharper bite. I took another mouthful and handed him back the flask.

"Ah, here we are." He stopped before a heavy wooden door. I found the tray thrust into my keeping and then Daen put his hands on the door. He muttered something I could not decipher and the air turned colder around us. I felt my skin crawl even as I waited for some magical wonder, for the doors to swing open and reveal whatever waited beyond them. Instead, Daen swore fiercely and then took hold of the door and hauled it open. It creaked, protesting, but it yielded. I hoped that I would never be expected to open it on my own, or I would never get past it, let alone complete the mosaic.

Through the open door, there was a courtyard, very like the ones in Lushan. The Aygaresh had built both the palace and this place, unnumbered years ago, so I should not have been surprised to find it so heartbreakingly familiar. I stepped into the open air and looked around. The walls were just higher than the height of a man, though columns of ragged stone rose above them to support the roof that must have long-since fallen. Beyond the walls, I could see the mountains, and the bright sun in a cloudless sky.

I glanced at Daen, half-expecting him to stride off across the courtyard without looking to see if I followed. He was lingering by the great doors, the tray he had taken back balanced in one hand. He took another swallow of wine from the flask absently, his gaze going beyond me to the mountains and the sky.

I looked around again, for there were no mosaics that I could see. Then the dull grey on the walls shaped itself into a long, curving wave and yielded a glint of reflection. I walked towards the far wall, the grey becoming lichen rather than stone. There were patterns beyond nature there, though my eyes could make no sense of them. When I scraped my nail across one of the stones, black fire flared beneath it. I did the same to the lichen and the grey turned emerald.

To my relief, the adjoining walls were nothing but honest stone. I looked along the length of the wall, some twenty paces, trying to ignore the despair in the pit of my stomach. I remembered a tale from Deshiniva of a clever boy set impossible tasks: to pick up all the sand from a beach, to fell a forest that grew again each morning, to climb a stair that never ended. He accomplished them all, with the help of magical creatures repaying his earlier kindness.

It might be easier to repair this mosaic than pick up all the sand from a beach, but not much, and no enchanted beasts owed me for past charity. It seemed unlikely I would find any suffering mice in the corridors of the Border Court in order to establish such a debt.

How many weeks would it take to clean the lichen and dirt away just to see what the wall might be? I could see the rough shape of broken tiles and hoped the Queen knew that I could not make glass, that such things would need to be conjured by her magic.

I looked over at Daen. "Do you have a knife I might borrow?"

"Is it that bad?" he asked, making no move, and I laughed.

"Not for my throat. Not yet. I'd like to dig out a stone or two."

"With my knife? Forgive me, Sidi, but I'm rather fond of its edge. Perhaps a chisel might be better."

"Do you have a chisel?"

"No. But," he plucked a silver pick from the tray and held it up for my inspection, "would this do?"

"It is not as sharp as your knife," I pointed out, attempting to imagine myself gouging at the wall with the delicate wand of silver.

"True. But I won't be obliged to try to stab anyone with it, so that hardly matters."

I wondered if that was an obscure threat, delivered as a jest, but could see no danger other than the obvious: that he was big and armed and fey. "Then thank you, Lord. The pick will do."

He took a step or two forward, then stopped, holding it out to me. Baffled, I waited for a moment, but when it became apparent he did not intend to move again, I crossed the distance to take it from his outstretched hand.

For all its delicacy, the pick proved an efficient chisel and I had three sample stones in my hand in a few moments. I scrubbed at the lichen with my thumb and found amber glass. The black, brittle film of another stone turned to dust and yielded a circle of black-backed blue.

"I do not understand," I said at last, looking at the shrouded mosaic and thinking of that strange moonlit garden. "If she can stop time, if she can conjure a moon in daylight, why can she not simply make this into whatever she wishes it to be?"

"Because it contains the one thing in all the world she cannot change," Daen said. I glanced back at him and saw his wry smile. "The Aygaresh made it with iron."

CHAPTER 29

Lilit

In the end, Lilit left Teresine's house, *her* house, and Filiat and Urmit stayed. They did not talk about it, beyond that first day, but Lilit left a pile of coins on a shelf in the kitchen, and the old women waved her off from the door, looking as much as part of the house as the stone walls.

She remembered the last time she had walked away from there, down the long, switchback path to the city, remembered her great-aunt's fierce embrace, her whispered words: "Be careful, Lily-child." Had Teresine known how close the end was that day? Remembering Raziel's tired, remote face, Lilit wondered if the Sidiana had recognized that her ride up the mountain was the last one she would ever make. She could believe it of both of them, that they could know that Teresine was dying and never speak a word of it.

Flickers of conversations overhead on those long summer evenings surfaced. *Kindness is a luxury you cannot afford*, Teresine had told Raziel once, while they debated some problem the Sidiana faced.

It is always what I cannot do, Raziel had replied despairingly. *Always what I cannot afford. I could not afford to deny the Queen, I could not afford to be merciful, I could not afford to let you be. If I cannot afford kindness for those I love, what power do I have?*

Teresine had laughed then, a sharp, bitter laugh that had made Lilit's child's heart turn cold. *No power at all, except to serve. Were you ever promised anything else?* In the end, Lilit remembered, Raziel had vowed to do what her conscience and not her position required. *Do what you wish*, Teresine had said and even the child-Lilit had recognized the mingled pride and bitterness in her voice. *You should not always listen to me. You know that.*

They had a lifetime of secrets kept between them, Lilit thought. What was one more?

That night, she accepted Teril's invitation to join a gaggle of cousins in a jaunt outside the iron. A night bidding farewell to her cousin Iraf before he left the city for a winter spent rebuilding bridges in far-off Simila was the distraction she needed to keep her from her endless worrying at her dilemma. The Kerias cousins were already boisterously celebrating with arrack by the time she arrived at *The Snow Lion*.

In the doorway the smoke and smells of the tavern hit her and she remembered all too vividly the night that had begun her troubles. And then remembered that, for the sake of the trouble itself, she did not dare to drink enough to banish the memory. She was not sure how she would explain *that* to her cousins and had to plead a headache as her reason for nursing one jug of drink through the whole of the evening. They teased her but let it pass, happily plying Iraf with drink until the tavern closed and the little knot of Kerias cousins began their giddy, staggering trek home.

They were making their way along one of the narrow streets that led to the main road when Teril stopped short and peered down the little alleyway to their left. "Ha!" she said triumphantly, as Lilit almost ran into her heels. The other cousins continued their way up the street, oblivious to the stragglers. "I knew it was here somewhere."

"What?"

"The faerie tester's house."

"The faerie tester's house?" Lilit repeated in bewilderment, looking down the alley; a short stub of a street with four whitewashed buildings on each side and another at the end. The moonlight did not touch the houses on the south but she could see that the ones on the north looked just like all the other houses in the area; whitewash peeling, windows shuttered and dark, the painted lintels fading. "Why would you be looking for a faerie tester's house?"

"I'm not, idiot. I just heard it was here and always wondered where." Teril looked around furtively and lowered her voice. "I know someone who went."

"There are no faerie testers anymore," Lilit said but there was no conviction in her voice.

"Oh yes there are. If you know where to look."

"And who would you know who would go to a faerie tester?"

"Can't tell, can I? I promised. But she had a lover outside the iron and came up pregnant. There were rumours about his family and he urged her not to have the child. So she went to the faerie tester."

"What happened?" Lilit asked, grateful that staring down the alley gave her an excuse to keep her face turned away, that her cousin was too dizzy with arrack to hear what she could not make her voice conceal.

"She paid her fee and got her answer. She would not tell me what it was—but," Teril's voice dropped to a whisper, "she didn't bear the child."

"There are a thousand reasons for not bearing a child."

"Of course." Her cousin sounded vaguely insulted to have the dramatic ending to her tale dismissed. "I'm just saying she didn't have it. But that's the faerie tester's house there, the one with the blue door. A house with a blue door, in an alley off the street that goes from the Chanjit road to the spice market."

"She might have been lying," Lilit said, her eyes drawn to the door at the end of the alley. Even in the moonlight, she could tell it had been painted bright blue.

"Fine," Teril huffed, as they heard their names called by the cousins who had finally realized their absence. "Last time I tell you something interesting."

"I just—" Lilit began but it was too late. Teril turned away and stomped up the dusty street, leaving her no choice but to follow. Halfway up the hill, Teril looked back over her shoulder, though her gaze would not meet Lilit's.

"Forget what I said. Too much arrack. It's just a story I once heard."

Lilit nodded automatically, willing to ease her cousin's attack of conscience and as willing as her to have the conversation forgotten. But she knew she wouldn't forget it.

A house with a blue door, in an alley off the street that goes from the Chanjit road to the spice market.

Across from the mouth of the street, there was a small, stepped entrance to a gated garden. It provided barely enough room to sit and no concealment at all but Lilit hunkered there for a long time. She could see the bright blue door of the faerie tester's house. It did not open; no one went in or out. With the darkening twilight, it faded until it was discernable only as a patch of shadow against the whitewashed walls. Light slipped through the shutters of the window and striped the cobbled street.

People passed, some glancing curiously at her, others were too intent on their own business to bother. When they looked, Lilit self-consciously pretended to inspect her boot, as if it there were a hole in it. It seemed a pathetic ruse but it kept her from having to meet their eyes. Dogs barked, a baby cried, voices rose and fell, and the door vanished into the night.

It was a week after the night at *The Snow Lion* and Teril's drunken revelation. During that long week, Lilit had gone about her days as always, but her cousin's voice was always there, a whisper in the back of her mind. *A house with a blue door, in an alley off the street that goes from the Chanjit road to the spice market.*

It was foolish, she told herself. It was superstition, nothing more. More, it was unnecessary. Feris Kijhold was not fey. It had just been a disguise he donned to lure a giddy Auster apprentice into bed. It was her own foolish imagination that made her dream of the bridge and woke her in the middle of the night, cold with sweat, her hands clasped across her burgeoning belly.

On the third day, she walked down the street in daylight, to see if the house with the blue door was really there.

On the fourth day, she passed by it at twilight, as the lights flickered into life behind the shutters.

On the seventh evening, she sat on the stoop, pretending she had a broken boot. Lilit wished she had asked Teril questions that night, before her scruples overcame her drink-fuelled confession. She had slipped surreptitiously into her father's room one afternoon and hunted among his books on the fey. In the early days of the city, when there were dozens of changelings a year, faerie testers had been common. The testing was both serious and symbolic, the testers healers and fortune-tellers. But as the years passed, there were fewer and fewer changelings, and testing was no longer part of the rituals of pregnancy, replaced by the laying on of the iron after birth. There were faerie testers still, her father's books had said, but women went to them in the dead of night and they were likely to be unscrupulous charlatans, preying on customers' fears.

She should leave, Lilit told herself. She should stand up and walk back to Kerias and save her silvers for something that would matter. She should make up her mind and go on with her life.

She sat for a moment more, then rose and walked slowly down the street to knock on the blue door.

After the second knock, it opened. The woman who answered the door was Newari, the only betraying trace of Euskalan blood the blue eyes that flickered over Lilit with neither surprise nor interest. Her hair was bound back in a long greying braid; her face was younger than her hair but her eyes were older. The woman stepped back to let her enter.

Lilit stepped inside, grateful when the door fell closed behind her. "I hope this is the right time," she began. "I wasn't sure—"

"There's day work and night work," the woman said. Her face was impassive, as if the necessity to be impervious to her clients' pain had turned her to stone. "The night work costs more."

The woman's bluntness made it easier. This was a business transaction, nothing more. Neither names nor sympathy were required. "How much?"

"Five silvers."

It was outrageous, but Lilit had brought twice that. She did could not imagine haggling over this, so she simply nodded.

"Put them there," the tester said, gesturing to the table, and sat down in the only comfortable-looking chair in the room. There was nothing luxurious in the room, nothing to ease either the mind or body of a customer, or to suggest the tester made more than the barest wage at her work. Lilit wondered what lay behind the curtain that covered the doorway behind her. Did she have a family, a husband and children, waiting for her to finish her work so they could have their dinner? Over the fire, something in a pot steamed, scenting the air with the pungent aroma of spices. Lilit felt simultaneously nauseous and ravenous. She set the coins on the scarred table and the woman beckoned to her to come and stand beside her. "Undo your robe. It needs to be skin on skin."

Lilit opened her robe and loosened her trousers. Without ceremony, the woman laid her hand against the faint swell of her stomach. Her narrow eyes closed for a moment. "Too early," she said at last.

"Is that it?" Lilit asked. "Isn't there something else you can do? Use iron or—"

"I touch, I know. You want a hedge-witch with her charms, go find one in the marketplace. I tell you it's too early to tell if the babe is fey or not."

"When?"

"Three months, four."

"But—" She stopped. The woman knew well enough that four months was too late. And she had known well enough that the small curve of Lilit's belly was not enough but had not bothered to say so.

"Sometimes, if the blood is strong, I can tell earlier," the woman admitted. Lilit wondered if it were an elaborate game, the woman's reluctance a ruse to raise the price of an answer.

"I'll come back. When?"

"Two months. If the fey be strong in it, I'll be able to tell then. Now," she shrugged, "all the fey I feel is you."

"I'm not fey," Lilit said automatically.

The woman shrugged again. "You would know." There was a whisper of empty scorn in the words.

"Yes. I would. I passed the iron tests." Lilit held out her hands, to show the bands of iron on her fingers, darker than her skin. The woman's eyes showed a flicker of something that might have been contempt. "My mother is foreign." She had almost said Deshinivi, but caught herself in time. The woman was a charlatan after all and Lilit remembered what a risk she had taken in coming there. The thought of what Amaris would do if she knew was enough to turn her cold with dread.

"Iron is false comfort. And fathers count," the woman said and Lilit almost laughed. Hendren of Kerias could not be fey. It was unimaginable.

The smell of the food was making her ill, she thought. That was why her head was spinning, why she could taste her own last meal in the back of her throat.

"I'll come back," she managed to say, to say something, and reached for the coins scattered on the table. The tester's hand closed on her wrist.

"Leave the money."

"You never read the child!"

"I read you."

Lilit knew then that she wasn't a fraud or a fool. She took your coin and gave an answer and never cared whether the answer ruined your life or redeemed it.

She let the coins fall and stumbled out into the cold embrace of the night.

CHAPTER 30

Teresine

In the courtyard, it was always summer. I could not imagine the power required to make that so, but I was nonetheless grateful. The heat in the surrounding hallways was less predictable, though it always improved after Daen grumbled about it. On the mornings I could see my breath there, I took some pleasure in the thought of his temper inflicted on the hapless—or malicious—fey responsible for such things.

I would pass the great doors (always open now) and emerge into the bright sunlight with a sense of relief. It was always midday, the light slanting at the perfect angle to illuminate the mosaics and lie warm across my shoulders.

But it was still a Lushan summer, for all that, and I rarely shed my robe. I was tempted to ask if perhaps it was a Deshiniva summer the Queen's magic could summon but did not want to ask favours in this place, and so took what was offered and enjoyed it more than I showed.

More than once I wished, guiltily, that fey magic could simply scour the mosaic of grit and lichen and be done with it.

But it could not, so I spent those first days with an array of tools Daen procured to replace the silver pick, scraping at the wall. The work required enough concentration that I could not do it mindlessly but was repetitive enough that it grew tedious. Which made me grateful, if guiltily again, that Daen had acquired the habit of spending a fair part of his time in the courtyard.

It had been two weeks since my first morning in the Border Court. I marked the days in the back of the *Meditations of Aurelian* so that I would not lose track of even the Court's dubious passage of time. In truth, for all the bewildering wonder of the Court, my days had assumed a routine that was notable mostly for the ordinariness of it.

When I woke in the morning, the sun was shining through the

screened window I had still not looked through. For the first morning or two, the basin of steaming water was waiting for me. Then on the third morning a full-blown bath lay behind a new set of gauze curtains, complete with soap, oils and a razor that never needed sharpening. Perhaps I should have spurned it, but I did not have the will for that either; even forty years later, I can remember the luxury of that heat on my skin. And the luxury of donning robes that, while my own, were always cleaner and fresher than was natural.

I never saw where the water came from; it was simply *there*, like the food in the covered tray that sat on the cabinet. It was usually traditional Lushan fare, though there were always one or two of the nut and honey confections I had eaten on my first morning. I supposed I had Daen to thank for that. I had no idea where the food came from, if it was cooked in some mortal fashion or conjured out of the air, but it was warm and filling and I did not seem to be wasting away, so I decided not to consider the question too closely.

Despite what Daen had said that first morning, I began the day with one grain of barley from my little cache.

After I had bathed and eaten, I did my best to meditate. I was not always successful, but the habit kept the worst of my fears at bay.

Some days I would be finished by the time I heard the knock on the door but on others, it would summon me back from whatever labyrinth of thought or no-thought I had lost myself in. If the door opened before I could reach it, I knew my escort that morning was Daen. Only the silent and anonymous guards who occasionally replaced him respected the closed door enough to leave it that way. From them, however, I knew what to expect; a silent escort through the deserted corridors to the courtyard, where they would take up posts out of my sight, beyond the doorway.

If it was Daen at my door, it was quite another story. He might be cheerful and talkative, surly and withdrawn, or, as on one or two occasions, bitterly the worse for drink. On the days he was out of temper, I was careful to keep up with his steady stride, to ask no questions, and to ignore him if he chose to linger in the courtyard. He was rarely directly rude to me and, ignored, his ill humour would pass, if not without a spate of inventive invective and a certain amount of stamping about the courtyard to exorcise the last of his corrosive fury.

On the days he was cheerful, he would slow his step, share whatever delicacy he had plundered from wherever he had been, and try to make me laugh at least once before we walked into the perpetual mid-summer of the courtyard. I grew used to him succeeding at the last task, which made the next success easier.

After the first week, I grew curious about the fey reaction to the mosaic. The guards were reluctant to enter the courtyard, though they hid it well. If I asked them to acquire a tool or materials, they would nod once and turn away. Sometime later, I would hear the thump of a box being deposited on the doorstep of the courtyard.

Daen, on the other hand, would freely enter and wander about, though I noticed he maintained a certain distance from the mosaic wall. Supplies acquired by him would be left a foot or two beyond the spot that would have been convenient. During one tedious stretch of cleaning lichen from stone, I tested where that invisible border lay, though it was half-consciously done. "Hand me that chisel, the smallest one," I had said absently, thinking only of the tool I had left in the box a few feet behind me. When no chisel appeared, I turned around, to see him standing just beyond the box, the tool in his hand.

"It would do you good to stretch, Sidi," he said, voice and face impassive. I sat back on my heels but did not rise; curious, made safe by the iron at my back. I saw his eyes narrow a little. He took one deliberate step forward, just beyond the line I had imagined he avoided, and then, so quickly I had no time to flinch, he threw the chisel. It buried itself in the scrubby grass by my knees. At that distance, the edge would have not have hurt me, bundled as I was in my robes, but the sudden violence of it took my breath away. "Your chisel, Sidi."

"Thank you," I said carefully. His smile was sharp and sudden and did not reach the lines around his eyes.

"Don't play games, Sidi. Not even here. There is no way for a mortal to win in this place."

I bowed slightly and picked up the chisel. "Then thank you, Lord, for your kind advice. And for the chisel."

He bowed in return, then went to lounge on the tumbled remains of one interior wall, procuring a cinquegrass cigarette and flame by unknown means. He tilted his face up to the false sun and closed his eyes. I watched him blow the smoke up to catch in the breeze and then turned back to my work. I chipped at the wall once or twice with enough force to damage then forced myself to stop and breathe. I knew he was right and it was foolish to play games with both fey power and his temper. But there were things I needed to know, and both the effect of iron and the limits of his self-control might one day matter.

In the two weeks that had passed, I had not seen the Queen. In fact, I had not seen any fey at all save Daen and the faceless guards. Were it not for Daen's occasional reference to events—great feasts, hunts, balls— that happened when he was not required to wait upon me, I might have believed that the fey had quit the Border Court and returned to whatever kingdom they inhabited when they were not here.

Then, one evening, their world was there again, bright, dangerous and dizzying. The guards were escorting me back to my room, where I fully expected to spend the evening as I always did: a quick meal and an exhausted collapse into my bed. My fear that I would have to parcel out chapters of Aurelian had proved groundless so far; my days working on the wall were so tiring that I would manage only a page or two before I fell asleep.

We turned the corner of one of the blank corridors and I felt a sudden charge of magic in the air. There was a sharp prickle in my skin, and then a momentary blackness behind my eyes, while below my feet the world seemed to shift sickeningly sideways.

When my vision cleared, the corridor was no longer empty and anonymous.

Candelabras hung from ceilings so high their colours were lost in shadows. There was carpet beneath my feet, thick and brightly woven in a tangle of leaves and flowers and shadowy shapes of beasts. Music filled the air and I realized how long it had been since I heard anything but two voices and wind.

There was a knot of fey before me. These were the fey as I had seen them at the fair, with a dizzying multiplicity of colours and garb. But there were also things I had never seen before: a woman with the high-boned face of a cat, a man as thin as a collection of twigs, a sweep of glittering, translucent wings curving above a fantastical horned headdress of feathers and fur.

No, those wings I had seen before. The headdress turned and I saw the pale, perfect face of the Queen's cousin.

She lifted a hand and the chatter and music died.

From the corner of my eye, I saw the guard to my left shift, his hand raise as if he meant to take my arm and drag me around the corner, much as Daen had done that first morning. But he did not touch me, though the gilt ceremonial spears came down to cross before me, as if to keep me from moving forward.

They need not have feared that. I would have welcomed being dragged away but, if they would not do it, I would not retreat. I had faced the Queen; I could face her cousin.

"Why, it is the little mortal," Madelon said. "I did wonder where she had been hiding."

There was scattered laughter in the crowd but when she stepped forward, no one followed her. She came to stand before the crossed spears. Her robe was fur as well, the smoky pelts sewn into a gown that left her shoulders bare. Her wings moved idly, like the absent twitch of a cat's tail. I felt a faint breeze, scented with honey and blossoms.

She lifted a slender hand to touch the tip of one of the spears. "I am no threat to the mortal, good soldiers," she said with a smile surprisingly mischievous. "And I am sure there is no reason for me to fear her."

The spears held and her look sharpened. The air grew heavy, a hand pressing down. At last the tips lifted, though the guards did not retreat. Madelon looked at me, tilting her head as if the elaborate headdress weighed nothing at all. "Such good care they take of you. What poor hosts you must think us that you should be kept so well-hidden and well-guarded. But perhaps my cousin is wise. There are some of us who do not care for mortals."

I could not tell if that was a warning, a threat or mere observation, but she seemed to expect some response. "Just as there are mortals who do not care for fey," I said at last. Her brow lifted and the silence lingered but I was well versed in that game and held my tongue.

"Tell me, little mortal," she continued after a moment, "how goes your work for my cousin?"

"Well enough, Lady." I looked back as blandly as I could, offering neither challenge nor submission.

"A strange thing, this obsession with the Aygaresh creation. Is it beautiful? Is it precious?"

"I cannot say if it is precious, Lady, except that little remains of what the Aygaresh made. It is beautiful, in its own way."

"Is it? But mortals are easily dazzled and their eyes see but dimly. Perhaps I should ask Daen what he sees." The corner of her mouth curved up again. "I trust he is taking good care of you."

"Lord Daen has been most kind."

Her laughter rippled.

"Little mortal, be careful. Daen does as he is told, for the moment. And what amuses him. But his amusements rarely last. He has his father's look and bright, fierce hunger for life. That is why my cousin lets him go, to keep that hunger alive. And that is why she brings him back, like a hawk to her hand, so that she may feed upon his fire. But now perhaps she has brought the feast to him, a tasty dish to consume without all the trouble and travel."

She leaned forward, her voice conspiratorial, her face a mask of concern that did not conceal the wicked glee beneath it. I felt a brief, distant contempt that she thought me so dull as to be fooled by it.

"Do not trust him, little mortal. He has his father's look—but he has his mother's cold heart."

She drew back, seeming to expect no response, inclined her head in a mocking salute, and glided back to her coterie, who resumed their laughter as if it had never been interrupted.

The spears dipped again. I took the hint and let them guide me back into the cold corridor once again.

Her warning raised more questions than it answered and I could not help but wonder why she had given it. She had no love of mortals, that was clear, and, based on their earlier encounter, no love for Daen, either.

I did not trust Madelon, did not for one moment believe she meant me anything but ill.

But that did not mean everything she said was a lie.

CHAPTER 31

Teresine

As if my encounter with Madelon in the corridor had breached some barrier that lay between me and the fey, it suddenly seemed impossible to avoid them. The next morning, the halls that had been cold and empty for two weeks now contained a steady stream of fey who drifted by with curious glances and the occasional elegant bow.

After the fourth encounter, Daen made a sound of disgust at the retreating velvet-clad back. "So they have finally decided a mortal presence does not pollute the halls so much they dare not set foot in them. How brave of them."

I did not confess that I found the new life in the hallways a relief after the weeks of feeling as if I and my escort were the only living creatures in the court. "Are there fey who dislike mortals so much they would alter their steps to avoid one?"

"There are some who would have quit the court the night you arrived, had not the thought of the Queen's whims having such power stuck in their throats. There are those who would prefer the Queen had no dealings with mortals at all. But that, Sidi, is politics," he added, "which I find tedious. Though I gather you do not."

"Why do you say that?"

"You are the Sidiana's former tutor, the confidante of the previous Sidiana, a member of the Council, and one of the Asezati. One assumes you either enjoy politics or belong to a sect that likes suffering."

I was astonished—and not a little disturbed—to discover that they knew so much. I had always assumed that to the Queen we were a series of indistinguishable, insignificant individuals whose identities meant nothing. "You are well informed," I observed and he laughed.

"I know who is, in any case, Sidi. I guessed you were precious to the Sidiana, from that farewell, but I admit I had no idea you were so important.

Perhaps it's because you never talk."

"I was not aware you required me to," I replied, rather more acerbically than usual, but he only gave me a sideways grin.

"You're not required to, Sidi, but even I get tired of the sound of my voice."

Do you? I thought, but, thank Jennon, had the wit not to say. Though I feared, based on the sudden wicked edge to his grin, that he knew exactly what I was trying to conceal.

"What would you like to know?" I asked. It was a dangerous question, but I could lie—or refuse to answer—easily enough.

"What did Madelon say to you yesterday?"

"Nothing of consequence. That some fey do not care for mortals. That she does not understand the Queen's interest in the mosaic." She had said a good deal more than that, but little of it made any sense and I was not certain his parentage was a subject that would sustain his current cheerful mood. What she had said at the end, however, I had no qualms about sharing. "That I should not trust you."

"You should not trust *her*, Sidi. She has no love for mortals or the Queen. Or me, for that matter."

"Do not fear, Lord," I assured him and could not help my own cold smile. "I do not trust any of you."

Which was true, though I was uncomfortably aware that, were I drowning and they both extended their hands to me, I knew without question whose I would take.

"Wise of you, Sidi," he replied, unruffled. "Where are you from?"

"Lushan."

"Before that. You're not Euskalan—or Newari, for that matter."

"I was born in Deshiniva," I admitted, disconcerted once again that the fey could tell Euskalan or Newari from any other race of mortals. There were fey who seemed fascinated by mortals, just as some Euskalans made a study of the fey, but if he were one of them, he had been discreet about it. His name was not known and I could not remember having seen him before. But then, the fair had been happening for hundreds of years, and I had only stood at the Sidiana's shoulder for a handful of them. To the fey, that would have been the merest blink of an eye.

"I was in Jayasita once," he said, to my continuing astonishment. "I remember the golden temple, the houseboats on the river, the bars along the Parang way." The corner of his mouth lifted. "The brothels on the Lotus Island."

"When were you there?" I asked, pleased my voice did not tremble around the sudden taste of ash in my mouth.

"A long time ago, Sidi."

And how long was that? Ten years? Fifteen? A hundred?

"It was beautiful," he said quietly. "Dirty, crowded, full of perfume and stink and life. Did you ever see it, Sidi?"

"Some of it," I admitted. "I lived there for six months, before I left with the Sidiana Sarit."

"Now there's a tale, I imagine."

"You may imagine what you wish. The reality would likely disappoint you."

"You brought it up, Sidi. Now you have to tell me."

"Do I?"

"Oh yes. You might as well, you know. I'll just badger you until you do. I usually get what I want in the end." His smile was a flash that did not quite touch his eyes, as if somewhere between them he doubted the truth of that statement. I did not doubt the veracity of at least part of it; it was certain he would indeed badger me.

I was careful what I said, of course. I gave him the bare bones of the story as we arrived at the mosaic and I set to work. He propped himself again one of the unadorned walls and began the business of preparing to smoke and asking me questions. Before I realized it, an hour had passed and I had told him far more than I ever meant to reveal. Not everything, not the things I had kept locked away for almost fifteen years, but enough to make me feel vulnerable and unsettled.

"I was there, I think, when you were," he said suddenly. "To think we might have passed each other in the street."

It was possible, I supposed, though it made a shiver run up my spine to think so. Jayasita was a port and merchants and travellers from a dozen races walked the streets. He would have seemed no stranger than the rest and I would only have been another poor Deshinivi girl passing by. When I was outside the House, I did my best to be nothing but that.

"I did not realize the fey travelled to mortal lands," I said, to change the subject.

"*They* don't. At least not often. I'm the only one who makes a habit of it."

COLD HILLSIDE

"Where have you been?"

"Deshiniva, Bharuch, Alamaneya, Parzie, Isbayan, Sahvaaini, Tkysland. Places that had no names but "here." As far as I can go," his voice turned self-mocking. "Which is never quite far enough."

I heard Madelon's voice: *That is why my cousin lets him go . . . and that is why she brings him back.*

"Will you tell me about them, these places you've been?"

"Do you want me to? Or do you just want me to stop asking you questions?"

"Perhaps I have not *quite* grown tired of the sound of your voice yet."

I meant it for distraction, to avoid answering his questions, and he allowed it with a laugh. He scratched his bearded jaw contemplatively. "Say we trade tale for tale then?"

"I have to work. It does require concentration."

"Whereas my conversation does not, Sidi? Thank you indeed."

"It is easier to listen and work than to talk and work," I qualified. "At least, I find it so."

"Tale for tale . . . but you may tell me yours later. Distract *me* while I work. I *do* have duties, Sidi, appearances to the contrary."

"I have always assumed so," I said, as I scrubbed at a newly cleaned section of wall with a rough cloth, removing the last of the grit and lichen. Milky-pink stones, the hue of dawn-touched snow, curved into a shape like a snake. "I imagine it would be tedious to have no tasks but escorting me and acquiring chisels."

"Well, in truth, that is my main task at the moment. But I am not finding it tedious, Sidi."

The words were politeness only, or born of his own boredom. I scrubbed harder at the stone, finding a line of darkness that shadowed the snake. I regretted that I told him anything, that I had asked for anything.

But I listened, just the same, as he told me of the lands he had travelled, how he had journeyed through the jungles of Bharuch on the back an elephant, sailed with spice traders through the Alamaneyan archipelago, competed in the great tournaments of martial prowess in the flower fields of Isbayan. Some of the tales seemed so strange I doubted the truth of them but I said nothing. What could be stranger, more alien than the place I now was, after all?

Of the other places of the fey, of the rumoured palaces and gardens and shores they inhabited when they were not at the Border Court, he said nothing at all. Indeed, I had begun to wonder if such places existed at all, or if all of the Queen's kingdom was contained within the changing walls of the Border Court. One simply opened a door and was *elsewhere*, an elsewhere no more fixed in place and time than the stone corridors seemed to be.

As always, there was no way to tell the passing of time in the courtyard. Only the hungry rumble of my stomach betrayed it was midday and, as if cued by that thought, the silent guards appeared. They left my meal and took Daen away, to attend upon some wish of the Queen's. I worked the rest of the day in silence and, if the afternoon seemed to stretch longer than the morning had, I made more progress on the mosaic that way, and so could not complain. In another day, I would have finished cleaning it and could then begin the infinitely harder task of trying to determine exactly what I should do next.

When the guards left me at my door, with its falsely familiar lintels and falsely fashioned wards, I was quite ready to eat, loll in the miracle of the hot bath for a while and then take myself to bed. I had only to open the door to discover I would not be allowed such leisure.

Hovering above my bed was a flower of light, petalled in pink and lavender. As I stepped into the room, a voice with the tone of bells said: "The Queen requests your presence. Prepare and you will be summoned." At the last word, the flower burst into a thousand shards of brightness, which rose and then fell away, like the fireworks I had once seen bursting into the sky over the palace in Jayasita.

When they reached the bedcovers, the scraps of light reassembled themselves and spread, turning to rose and gold, shaping into a silken confection of a dress.

I stood where I was as the last light faded and the lamps flickered into life on the walls around me. At last, I went and carefully lifted the dress from the bed.

Prepare and you will be summoned.

There were things the Faerie Queen could ask of me. There were things I suppose she could force upon me, though I did not wish to think too much on that.

This dress, this foolish, frivolous bit of stiffened silk and beads would require forcing.

I made my preparations as I chose and when the knock on my door came, I was bathed, my skull freshly shaven, dressed in the best of my robes, a red and purple sash around my waist, and Chadrena's bracelet on my wrist. I had not dared Raziel's band of warding cosmetics, but there were black and red shadows across my eyelids.

It was Daen at the door. He had gone through his own transformation; beard trimmed, unruly hair tamed, usual attire of dark trousers, perpetually untucked shirt and dusty coat replaced with sumptuous cinnamon-coloured velvet and a fur-trimmed robe that swept the floor. I saw his glance take in my newly shorn head, the cosmetics on my eyes. "You look quite severe, Sidi."

"Do you know why the Queen wishes to see me?" I asked, ignoring his comment.

"It's the Midwinter Eve Ball." I almost pointed out that it was not Midwinter Eve and then stopped, remembering that here it was whatever season the Queen wished it to be. Daen looked at the dress lying abandoned on the bed and lifted his eyebrow. "The Queen generally prefers her gifts to be accepted."

"I regret I cannot, then. My vows forbid vanity." Which was not quite true, I admitted to myself, nor was I quite immune to it. I had rejected the dress for reasons of politics and power, it was true, but that task was made easier because it would ill become me.

"Well, this should be an interesting evening. And that is an ugly dress, isn't it?"

"It is not to my taste," I admitted and he laughed.

"Tell me, Sidi, do you ever simply tell the truth? Or has politics turned you into too much of a diplomat to say anything straightforward at all?"

That stung my pride a little. Sarit had trusted me because I told her the truth as I saw it. Raziel did the same. If the dark side of that was that the truth was heard in part because I was not Euskalan, I had long ago accepted it.

But the truth was also that almost every word I had said in faerie had been hedged with careful calculation of the consequences and the knowledge that more ears than his might hear it.

I had nothing to prove, I told myself. I owed him nothing, despite whatever confidences and kindness he had chosen to bestow on me.

"It is an ugly dress," I said at last.

"Allow me to escort you to the ballroom, Sidi," he said with a smile.

"Thank you, Lord."

And so I went to the Midwinter Eve Ball, armouring myself for my second meeting with the Queen, not realizing that the first crack in my world had already appeared.

CHAPTER 32

Teresine

I believed that I could no longer be awed by the Border Court, now that the cold corridors had shown me the truth behind the magic and so robbed the façade of power. When the guards opened the golden doors that night, I realized I was wrong.

Where there had been a moonlit garden, there was now a great hall, two stories high, dominated by a staircase that swept towards a broad terrace in a flow of white marble. Columns rose to the ceiling, as wide as ancient trees, but made of glass; cerulean, crimson, and carnelian. I stared like a peasant girl on her first day in Jayasita, my eyes dazzled despite my mind's knowledge that all this was not real. Not illusion, perhaps, for I had no doubt that the glass would shatter if I had the weapons and strength to wield them, but *not real*.

"Fucking hells," Daen breathed.

I could only nod, realizing that the ceiling so far above me was covered in huge flowers of the same vivid glass. While my eyes marvelled at the artistry involved, whether mortal or magic, the sensible part of me noted that if Daen were moved to swear, clearly this display must surpass the Court's normal extravagance. Which begged the question of why the Queen chose it. She could have awed me with a good deal less so she must have some other purpose.

The sound of the doors opening behind me brought me back to myself. I was willing to be dazzled before Daen, but I would not let the other fey find me gape-mouthed and staring. I took a breath and looked up the stairs to the torchlit terrace. Flowers grew there, a mix of glittering glass and what seemed to be true petals. Music drifted down, and laughter, and there was the scent of perfume in the air.

"Come on then, Sidi. We may as well go see what other wonders the Queen has conjured," Daen said.

We walked up the stairs, a tide of chatter rising behind us from the fey entering the hall. At the top were three wide doorways draped in gauzy curtains and beads that dripped from the lintels like suspended rain. I could hear them ring as the breeze touched them into motion.

Beyond the central doorway, a fey in elaborate livery waited. Daen ignored him but as we stepped forward, the servant's voice boomed out: "Lord Daen Sigur's-son, Queen's Champion. Teresine of Lushan, Mortal."

Every eye fell upon us and I felt them all, scouring me with contempt or curiosity. For a moment I could not breathe. Then I remembered who I was, who I served. I had weathered withering looks before. I had learned to bear the weight of both scorn and desire, to let those looks possess only my surface and not my soul.

I kept my back straight, my chin lifted, my hands tucked into the sleeves of my robe. My fingers touched Chadrena's bracelet and rested there as I followed Daen onto the open floor before the dais that held the Queen and her companions. I caught nothing but the briefest impressions of the room around me: a press of tables and couches and fey as brittle and bright as the false flowers over our heads.

The Queen's throne was crowned with glass garlands. There were sharp blossoms in her white hair, glittering with jewels, and the dress that bared her shoulders held the faintest hint of green. I did not dare look along the table but I was aware that the seat to her left was empty.

"Daen." Her voice was silvery, a fall of water over steel. From the corner of my eye, I saw him bow, much more formal and respectful than he had been at the moon-viewing party.

"Majesty."

"Little mortal." I echoed the bow and risked one flickering glance at her. Her eyes narrowed a little. "Did our gift displease you?" I was aware of the silence at our backs; the fey no longer even bothered to pretend not to watch.

"It was generous beyond words, Great Queen. Too generous for one of my order. We are forbidden vanity."

"But not pride, little mortal?" They laughed at that, glass breaking and falling all around me. I bowed my head and stayed silent. "Tell me how your work progresses."

"Well, Great Queen. I am about to begin the restoration in earnest. I will require materials."

She waved her white hand. "Daen will see to it."

"Lord Daen is most kind."

She laughed then, though which of us she mocked I was not sure. "You are to be Lord Bastien's for the evening, little mortal. Daen will see it done."

Then she looked away, over our heads, to the next group of fey come to offer obeisance, leaving me with her words echoing in my mind, reverberating with other, older voices and a sudden sickness rose in my throat. *You are to be Lord Bastien's. . . .*

I barely felt Daen's hand on my arm, steering me away from the throne towards a long table set beneath a great hanging sculpture of glass, lit by candles set amidst the twisting shapes. "Bastien is one of those fey who harbour a strange fascination with mortals. Though I warn you, Sidi, he will expect you to talk. . . ." His voice trailed off. "Sidi, are you well?"

"Yes," I managed, as his words penetrated the fog of memories, and I realized he was watching me with speculative curiosity. "You know how little I care for talking, that is all."

"The trick, Sidi, is to distract you. Making you laugh or making you angry always seems to work."

"Pray do not tell Lord Bastien that, then."

"Of course not. Why should the old bastard have it any easier than I do?"

Lord Bastien was darkness given mortal shape, as black of skin as the Queen had been before her new incarnation in pearl and alabaster. He was dressed in sombre robes whose style was unfamiliar and a heavy gold earring, weighted with a ruby the size of a songbird's egg, hung from one ear. His voice was dark as well, with a strange echo in it, as if it came from someplace deeper than a mere cave of bones and flesh.

There was no mistaking him for mortal but he displayed none of the ostentatious otherness of Madelon and her companions. No wings sprouted from his shoulders, no horns from his brow and his eyes, though green-tinged ice, were round-pupilled and set as if in a mortal skull, not a beast's.

I knew him from the palace archives and from the fair; he was one of the few fey who troubled to give his name to mortals. He had a reputation for a magpie curiosity that had enriched many a House's fair and a manner reported by one House Head as "courtly but daunting."

There were worse fey whose company I might have been required to endure, I thought as Daen presented me to my host and the empty chair at his side slid magically away from the table. Madelon, for one. Or Ferrell. Or the Queen, though that fate was reserved for Daen, who had returned to the dais and assumed the empty seat to her left.

After a brief exchange of introductions, awkward silence ruled the table. The other fey feigned disinterest but seemed unwilling to engage in conversation either for fear of missing my mortal words or scandalized at the thought of a mortal hearing theirs. I was happy to let the silence linger; I had found safety in it more than once in my life. I took a careful sip of the garnet-coloured wine that appeared in the goblet at my place.

"We are pleased you can join us," Lord Bastien said at last.

"Oh, indeed," agreed the fey lady at his side. Ileane, her name was. She was amber to Bastien's black, even to the mesh gloves that covered her hands and turned her nails to golden claws. "We had begun to believe you were nothing but a tale to annoy the purists."

"I am quite real, though I have no wish that my presence cause anyone annoyance. I do the Queen's bidding."

"And how does it fare, this bidding you do?" Bastien asked.

"Well enough, I believe."

"But what exactly do you *do*?" Ileane asked.

"To this point, it has been mostly scraping and cleaning."

"How tedious."

"True, Lady, though it is necessary."

"It is good that you mortals are so used to drudgery. I could not bear it." There was laughter from the others and Ileane looked vaguely offended. "And tell me you would spend one moment 'scraping and cleaning,' any of you."

"It might be amusing," one fey lord said lazily, "for a moment or two."

"But that is what gives human art its poignancy, its beauty," Bastien observed. "That such brief lives spend so much time in the messy, tedious work of it. Do you not agree, Sidi?"

I sensed this was an old argument, with Bastien the established defender of humanity's quaint ways. "There are more tedious tasks than cleaning mosaics, Lord Bastien. And I am not the artist, merely the restorer."

"Yet you must have learned the art through study and practice. Was it in Deshiniva or Lushan?"

"You are well-informed, Lord," I said, hearing the echo of my own words and realizing who Daen must have consulted to acquire his own knowledge.

"One looks, one listens, one pays attention. There are so few chances to observe the mortal world so closely."

"For which the rest of us are profoundly grateful," said the pale fey lord (Lindel, I recalled). "Though Bastien is almost as tedious on the subject of mortals as mortals are themselves."

Bastien ignored the insult with imperturbable dignity. "It was in Deshiniva," I said, as if the other lord had not spoken.

"How interesting," Bastien said and Lindel groaned in exaggerated disgust and turned away, the line of his silk-draped shoulder conveying contempt with admirable eloquence.

"I have seen you at the fair," Bastien continued, ignoring his companion. "But we have never had the opportunity to speak."

"I remember you as well, Lord Bastien. And you, Lord Lindel. Though perhaps I have seen you all each year and cannot tell it, if you have changed as the Queen did." It seemed a reasonable assumption that the Queen's alteration might send a wave of change through the court, the outgoing ripple of her own magic cast like a stone into the obedient water.

"Does that make Bastien and Lindel the honest ones among us, that mortals remember the shape they do not change? Or are they simply unimaginative?" Ileane asked with a laugh.

"This shape suits me well enough," Bastien replied. "There is enough frivolous shapeshifting in the court without my contribution to it."

"There is a difference, dear Ileane, between style and fashion," Lindel said, with a flicker of barbed amusement. "And politics is the worst fashion of all."

He was being disingenuous, I thought; the fey breathed politics with the perfumed air. But it gave me an excuse to ask: "And the Lady Madelon? Does she attend the fair in another guise?"

Lindel laughed. "Madelon would not change her shape to suit a mortal—unless it were to frighten one to death."

"Why should any of us change to suit what mortals wish to see?" Hilare turned away from his conversation to ask and, in the silence after the question, I saw Lindel and Ileane cross glances.

"Why indeed?" Lindel agreed. "Especially when mortals are dazzled enough by us as we are? I have always found them singularly easy to bewitch."

"So are beasts, but I do not bother to bewitch them," Hilare retorted and I caught the current of old enmity, ancient bitterness.

"There, Sidi, you are safe from one of us, at least," Ileane said, but the dart seemed equally aimed at both of us. "Hilare will forebear seducing you. And you, Lindel?"

"I make no such promises, Sidi, so be warned. I've never seduced an Asezati."

"Rumours suggest it is no great feat, Lord," I said lightly. "But the vow of celibacy is one I had no regrets in taking and have had no difficulty in keeping. I would not have you waste your time."

He laughed but there was a measuring speculation in his look that made me regret my words. "The mortal has claws, after all. You should be careful in issuing challenges, Sidi."

"I meant no challenge, Lord. If I issued one, I withdraw it." I folded my hands at my heart and bowed a little, waiting until I heard the ripple of laughter from the fey before I looked up again.

"Don't fear, Sidi. You're safe from all of us. Save perhaps Bastien, who will ask you questions until you wish you were scraping and cleaning again."

Whatever Bastien might have asked was forestalled by the arrival of a servant bearing a small glass bowl shaped like the flowers at the entrance. He presented it to Ilene. "Ah, I was wondering when the Queen would deem it time," she said and dipped her golden claws into the bowl and then held what she withdrew up to the candlelight. "Lovely," she breathed.

What she sighed over was an opal, its white sheen running with blue and green fire. We had never known what the fey did with the opals we so dutifully consigned to them every year and I found myself eager to discover the secret at last. To my astonishment, she dropped it into her wine, swirled the glass with deliberate theatricality for a moment and took a slow swallow, eyes closed. "Perfect," she announced.

Lindel selected his own stone and followed her example, as did Bastien. I was not surprised when Hilare declined with cold contempt. The servant paused for a moment, uncertain, and then held the bowl towards me. I almost accepted, from curiosity alone, but then thought the better of it and declined.

"What do you fear?" Ilene asked. "You cannot claim your order's rules on this—I have seen you drinking the wine."

"It is a custom foreign to us, Lady, and to be honest I am not so certain I should be drinking a wine strong enough to dissolve such a stone."

She laughed and Bastien assured me that the wine, with or without an opal in it, was perfectly safe. "It but enhances the flavour," he said.

"And the evening," Lindel added, which suggested that an altered taste was of less interest to them than an altered perception. Which I supposed was the point of alcohol, with or without opals, but the fey's desire for it was still a surprise. One would suppose there was enough wonder in their world without it.

I glanced towards the Queen's table but saw no bowl-bearing servant there and so could not tell if the Queen—or her champion—chose to indulge. I suspected from Hilare's reaction that Madelon and her fellow purists would definitely and ostentatiously abstain. Their contempt for mortals would surely extend to any pleasure procured from the mortal world.

The fey seemed to forget my presence and resumed their cryptic conversations full of gossip and gaps, giving me a store of names and incidents but very little idea how they related to one another.

My gaze drifted around the room, across the faces lit by the flames of the candles suspended from the strange chandeliers. As the voices murmured around me, the world reshaped itself into a mosaic, details becoming broken colour. With the dazzle flattened into fragments, it was as if I could see the splinters in the court, the fantastical glamour of the fey turning into stones whose pattern I could almost comprehend.

On the dais, the Queen was opal and moonstone. The ranks of fey with her were smooth and ancient as river rocks, jewels whose facets had been worn away but whose glow remained. I felt the image beneath my fingers, the coolness of the stones, the softness of fur, the gaps where the divisions were made concrete. Bewitched eye, imaginary finger snagged on one sharp, rough rock, one piece that did not quite fit.

I blinked and the strange vision faded, leaving me looking at Daen, ordinary and familiar. He was listening to the Queen, whose white, elegant face was turned to his. I watched him lift his glass of wine and down it with an efficiency that suggested a practiced journey into drunkenness.

"I have heard, Sidi, that there are mortals who keep the remains of their dead in jars in their houses. Is that true?" Bastien's voice drew me back though for a moment his question was nothing but meaningless words.

"Bastien, please," Ileane sighed. "Not now."

"They must be very large jars," Lindel remarked, without glancing away from his other conversation. "Or very small mortals."

"I have never heard of such a thing, Lord. But the world is larger than I know and it is possible that such things happen."

"Your own people, then? What do they do with the dead?"

"Bastien," Ileane protested more vehemently. "Please save such shocking questions for another time."

"The Sidi is not shocked, are you, Sidi?"

"I do not shock easily, Lord Bastien. But I have no wish to offend the other guests. Perhaps we could discuss this later."

Bastien looked disgruntled but Ileane's half-smile to me was marginally warmer and the talk drifted to topics the fey deemed less distressing. Questions tended to centre on some aspect of mortal life the fey found incomprehensible and my answers, when I had them, seemed to confirm their belief in their own superiority. It was a game I played with distant amusement, if only because it spared me having to reveal— or conceal—anything remotely personal.

The evening slipped by, borne on the half-heard music, the scented air, the delicate wine I drank more of than I had intended, the rituals of question and answer, the finely gauged attack and disinterested retreat. I was wondering how I could excuse myself and find an escort back to my room when the air filled with a sudden flourish of sound.

I followed the gaze of my tablemates towards the dais and saw the Queen rising, Daen at her side. She put her white hand on his arm; they walked down the length of the room in a sudden stilling of voices, a wave of bending heads. The jewels dripping from the lintels chimed as they vanished through the curtains.

"Are you shocked now, Sidi?" Ileane's voice asked into the heartbeat of silence before the room filled with sound once again.

"Should I be?" I asked with automatic ease, to cover the fact that for a moment I had no idea what I was presumed to find shocking.

Then I knew her meaning and understood her expectation. The fey knew enough of mortal mores for that, but could not know that life in Jayasita and Lushan had made me proof against such things. It was hardly shocking to me that the Faerie Queen should have a lover; it was no more shocking that it should be Daen. There had been clues enough; Ferrell's words and Madelon's, the Queen's indulgence, her white hand lifted to his lips.

"The court of Lushan must be more interesting than I assumed," Lindel said with lazy lasciviousness. "I always thought mortals were so . . . moral."

"I am the servant of queens, Lord," I replied. "Queens do as they please." Which was not precisely true, not in Lushan, but if it served to change the topic I felt no qualm at the lie. I had no interest in a salacious discussion of the tastes of either mortals or fey.

"True enough. Though I had no idea that the mortal Queens made a habit of—"

"Lindel." Bastien's voice was dark and heavy as a thundercloud. "Enough. This is not the place."

"Dead bodies but not live ones, is that it, Bastien? Or are there things you think might so shock even this unflappable little Asezati that she'd forget all the answers to your questions?"

"I think there are things that are beneath discussion, Lord Lindel. Unless you would care to discuss them while the Queen is in the room."

"I do not care at all. It is all tedium. Old tedium, at that." Lindel turned away, though beyond him, I saw Hilare open his month as if to add something to the argument, before he appeared to think better of it.

I was torn between my desire to be gone, now that Queen's exit would allow it, and my sense that there was some secret in the words they would not say, something darker than the simple fact that the Queen took her champion to her bed. Such a secret might be worth knowing but I could not bring myself to give them the satisfaction of prying into it.

"Lord Bastien," I said, before someone could begin the conversation again, "I wonder if you would be kind enough to escort me back to my room?"

He agreed, with a speed that suggested that he too was grateful for a reason to leave. Polite farewells were exchanged. As we left the table, there was a burst of bright, vicious laughter, and the vulnerable spot between my shoulder blades itched until we were on the long stairway down into the forest of glass columns.

To my relief, Bastien seemed happy to chat pleasantly about

inconsequentialities—not quite the weather, there seeming to be none in the Border Court, but close enough. It was only at my door, before the brightly painted lintels with their false protections, that he grew sombre. "This is not the mortal world, Sidi. There are things you should not judge by that standard."

"Thank you for the advice, Lord. Believe that I never forget where I am."

"No, I suppose you cannot. Still," he paused. It was strange to see a fey, especially one with his sombre gravity, disconcerted. "As you said, Queens do as they please."

He left me with a bow, with those words echoing in the dim, cold hallway. I wondered again why the fey found it shocking—and why they were so eager to have me find it so. I slipped into my room and the lanterns flared around me, a little magic, like the steaming bath, I could not quite regret.

I was not shocked. It was only fey wine and fey food that caused the strange queasiness in my stomach, only the strain of the long night in fey company that caused restless disquiet in my mind. Only that.

CHAPTER 33

Lilit

Her feet knew the way home; that was all that allowed her to reach it. Safe in the chilly safety of her room, Lilit barely remembered her passage up the dark streets or which cousin had greeted her at the Kerias door.

Numb fingers tucked beneath her armpits, she rocked on her heels and waited to stop shivering.

The only fey I feel is you.

But she could not be fey. There was iron on her fingers, in her ears, around her wrist. She had passed through the iron-bound door to Kerias every day and felt nothing at all. None of the rumoured signs of fey blood had ever manifested around her. Nothing strange had ever happened to her at all.

Except once.

Could such a thing be buried so deep that only being at the fair could call it forth? Perhaps it was possible to have fey blood so thinned by generations that it only emerged when the air itself seemed charged with fey magic. But if that was so, how had the faerie tester known?

It was a lie. It must be. The faerie tester had lied to cover her failure with the unborn child and keep the silvers Lilit had so foolishly given her in advance. But then why hadn't she simply lied about the baby? Such a lie could not be refuted, could only be believed or disbelieved. The woman must have seen her iron rings, the amulets that hung from her sash. Why tell such a blatant lie when all the evidence would deny it?

Lilit spread her hands before the brazier and looked at her fingers. The rings lay against her skin as they always had. They did not brand her flesh; she barely even felt them. Was it possible the old stories were not true, or so exaggerated that very little truth remained? Was all the iron in the city nothing more than ornament that fended off nothing but fear?

If she were sensible, she would consider the faerie tester's words a lie and forget them. She would make her decision about the child as if this night had never happened.

But if she were sensible, it never *would* have happened.

Lilit looked at her fingers again. They were the same fingers she had always had. There was no fey elegance about them; there was a scar across her knuckle from childhood clumsiness around a stove, and the beds of the nails were dirtier than her mother would have countenanced were she still that child.

Even if it were true (though it could not be true, of course), what difference did it make? She wore iron and walked under the iron gates without consequence. What did it matter if there was a ghostly trace of fey blood in her veins? If even half the rumours were true, she would hardly be the only one in the city with that secret.

Some equanimity restored, she crawled into bed and, to her own surprise, fell straight to sleep. If she dreamt of the bridge or the unreal hallways of Teresine's house or cries of babies that might or might not be human, she did not remember it.

The next day, she went to talk to her father. It might not be sensible, it might have nothing to do with the child, it might lead her down paths she did not want to tread, but she had to know. It was as simple as that.

After her day at the Austers, and the evening meal in the crowded Kerias hall, she tracked Hendren to his room beside the archives. She had feared he might be engaged in yet another long-running game of chess with one of her uncles but he was alone, studying a book by a brace of candles.

He welcomed her, setting aside his book, and for a moment, there was nothing but casual conversation about her day and his, and the state of Aunt Virat's wedding gift negotiations. When she had almost exhausted her store of comments on that topic, her father gave her a look of patient sympathy and said, "And why did you really come to talk to me? I assume it is too much too hope you've developed an interest in chess?"

"Am I so transparent?"

He shook his head with a smile. "Very nearly as opaque as your mother, when you choose to be. But I've twenty years practice at reading her signs, so I have an advantage. You've been troubled since the fair."

That topic seemed safe enough, a way into the careful almost-truth she'd decided upon, so she took a breath and began. "Why don't you go to the fair anymore?"

"Me? I went for twenty years. My old bones don't care for the damp, my old knees dislike horseback, and it was time to let someone else do the work. I've more than enough information on them in my notes and records to keep me occupied."

"Did you like them? The fey?"

"Like them?" he repeated, baffled. "Well, liking is not a word I would use in relation to them. I find them interesting. There were some I met I suppose it might have been possible to like—or at least to like the aspect they chose to show me. But I was never foolish enough to make that mistake. They are not mortal; it would be dangerous to assign anything resembling mortal feeling to them." The look he gave her then showed the beginnings of alarm and Lilit realized what he suspected.

"No, oh no," she said hastily. "Not that. Nothing like that." She felt a moment of guilty relief that at least that one reassurance was not a lie. "I cannot even imagine that." She saw the lines of suspicion around her father's eyes fade a little. "I met someone there, at the fair. She said something that suggested I should be careful around them, because I . . . because House Kerias . . . has some taint of fey blood."

The lines reshaped themselves into worry, even while her father's voice was calm. "Who said such a thing?"

"Someone at the apprentice fire. It was just a passing remark. I might have misinterpreted it. . . ." Lilit's voice trailed off. She had managed the lie but she could not embroider it. "And then, the night of the fair, I fainted."

"You would not be the first," Hendren said but his voice was as opaque as he claimed her to be.

"I know. And likely it was just too much sun. That is what Hazlet Auster said. But—" She shrugged and let her silence do her deception for her.

"Likely Hazlet Auster was right. As for the rest, I ought to make you do your own study and tell me the answer."

"Would it be written down?"

"Somewhere *everything* is written down. We come from a long line of scholars. But do not fear. I'll spare you the time and trouble, this once. There were changelings in the Kerias household, in those first years. There were changelings in every great House of Lushan. In the centuries since then, four children of the House have failed the iron tests. The last of those was a hundred years ago."

"What happened to them?"

"You know the answer to that." His voice was gentle, gently chiding. She did know; they all knew. If a baby did not pass the tests, whether it was a changeling or had been conceived through a forbidden union, there was only one solution. The cautionary histories and whispered ghost stories of her childhood were full of tales of women who tried to hide their fey babies and the consequences. All the stories ended the same way: a dead child, a weeping mother. The only difference was who else suffered on the journey to that end.

"Do the tests always work?"

"If they did not, how would we know?" Hendren asked, with the habit of long instruction. Or taking refuge in it. "In other Houses, not this one, there are old records of sons and daughters who passed the baptisms and failed their coming of age, or fled before it."

"And what happened to them?"

"If they fled and did not return to take the test, they were banished."

"And if they failed it?"

"You know the answer to that as well. There is no place in the city for anyone who cannot pass the test. Those were not stories we adults made up to frighten you, truly. They were the truth. Come now, my Lily-girl," his voice softened as he looked at her face, "what is wrong? What difference does some fireside malice make? You were baptised, you came of age, and here you are, a Euskalan daughter of Kerias." He held out his hand and she slipped to her knees beside his chair, to hide her betraying face against his knees. His hand stroked her hair. "I know it has been hard for you, Lily-girl. I know you miss her. But you mustn't let grief conjure empty ghosts and foolish fears. Whatever was said, forget it. It means nothing."

Lilit nodded beneath his hand, wanting to surrender to his comforting words, the reasonable and confident tone in his voice. What was the faerie tester's bland, uncaring pronouncement against that logic and certainty? She should do as her father said, forget it, and let it go as only the frantic worry of her grieving heart.

You were baptised, you came of age, you are a Euskalan daughter of Kerias. The only fey I feel is you.

Certainty against certainty and she did not know which one she believed.

CHAPTER 34

Teresine

In the morning, it was the anonymous guards who arrived to escort me to the mosaics. To my own annoyance, I was relieved at that; I had not known what I would say to Daen. Which annoyed me even more, as there was no reason that the confirmation of that half-suspected truth about his relationship with the Queen should make any difference to what I said or did not say.

The courtyard seemed as out of kilter as my mood. It was hotter than it had been for the weeks I had been working, the sun a hard, bright coin that made the shadows sharp and distracting. After an hour of work I had shed my overrobe and was sweating beneath the shelter of my wide-brimmed hat.

It should not have surprised me that the work went badly. I chipped a stone or two I had intended to reuse, my fingers bore the evidence of my clumsiness with my tools, and too soon my temper seemed as fragile as the ancient tiles.

Daen arrived soon after the midday meal, bearing supplies for my work and his own burden of bad temper. He looked tired, with shadows under his eyes and lines between them that seemed chiseled there. "Did you enjoy the Midwinter Ball, Sidi?" he asked, after he had deposited my goods and taken a step back to survey my progress, or lack of it.

"It was very informative."

"No doubt. Bastien's decent enough but the rest of them are rats, all pointy noses and sharp claws." That made me laugh, which did not seem to improve his mood. "Don't tell me you found them charming dinner companions."

"I do not think charming me was on their agenda. Insulting me, scandalizing me, and threatening me seemed more interesting to them."

"Who threatened you?"

"It was nothing," I said, deciding I preferred not to discuss Lindel's flirtation. "And recanted. It was not as bad as it might have been."

"How did you get back to your room?"

"Lord Bastien was kind enough to escort me."

"Did they manage to scandalize you?"

I stooped to collect my supplies, shaking my head. "I do not shock easily, Lord. It was a great disappointment to them."

"And did—?" He stopped abruptly and I looked up, frozen by the frowning gaze that searched my face. "Curse them all anyway." He backed away and looked up at the sky for a moment, as if puzzling at the difference. "Balls are almost as boring as moon-viewing parties, but the wine's better."

"And the opals?" I suggested.

"They offered you one, I suppose. Did you try it?"

"I decided it would be better if I didn't. Did you?"

"Wine is sufficient for my purposes, Sidi, and opal wine just makes my head hurt more the next day."

"It seems we go through a great deal of trouble for something of so little consequence."

"Come now, Sidi, narcotics are never of little consequence."

"But couldn't the Queen just wave her hand and there would be opals?"

"Ah, but what would be the pleasure in that? It's so much more entertaining to know that mortals suffer and die for them. Would it make you happier if she wore them or simply heaped them in a room like a dragon's hoard?"

"No," I admitted, though in truth the frivolous use of what we struggled for was galling. "Though I think I was happier knowing nothing at all."

"Remember that then, Sidi. There are things here it is definitely better you don't know."

I thought that he would leave or settle onto the ruin in the corner and let the sun and smoke drain away his morning mood, but he seemed as restless and discontented as I was. I took myself back to my work with a will, trying to pay no attention to his presence as he paced behind me. I succeeded, if only a little, until he coerced one of the guards into sparring practice with him. It took an order that was equal parts instruction and obscenity, but the fey soldier shed his helm, drew his sword and joined Daen on the far side of the courtyard.

I pretended to pay no attention, but could not help my covert glance, for I had never seen the soldiers unhelmed. This one was fair, hair caught back in a long golden braid, eyes as blue as the cloudless sky beneath his slanting brows, his expression as unreadable as a statue.

I went back to my tiles and paste until curiosity got the better of me again. Whether from boredom or resentment, they had gone at the practice with considerable intensity and had shed layers of clothing in the heat. The guard's sharp cheekbones gleamed and Daen's shirt was damp with sweat. My experience of combat arts was limited to having accompanied Sarit when she went to observe the soldiers, either officially in her duties as Sidiana or unofficially when one of their number had caught her eye, but it seemed clear that Daen's title was not mere courtesy. The guard, for all his grace and quickness, was outmatched.

A stray thought flickered: if they had done this on the practice yard in Lushan, Sarit would have stayed to watch.

I turned my back to them and poked at the wall with my chisel. Behind me, I could hear the clash of their swords, the huff of breath, the stamp of feet on the hard ground. My chisel slipped and another tile cracked and broke.

"For mercy's sake, go do that somewhere else!"

I'd said the words without thinking, and then found myself on my feet, as two puzzled faces turned towards me.

"What did you say?"

"Please go do that somewhere else."

I saw the guard slip his sword back into its sheath, retrieve his abandoned helm and armour and retreat into the shadows of the doorway.

"We're required to be here on your behalf, Sidi. The least you can do is let us break the boredom the best way we can." The words were reasonable but beneath them I could hear the edge of anger, the first distant thundering rumble of a storm about to break.

"We are both here on the Queen's behalf," I reminded him. "Shall I tell her I cannot work because you are distracting me?"

He laughed at that, a hard, sharp sound that seemed worse than the temper I had waited for. He caught up his coat and walked toward me, sword still out. He crossed the line I believed the iron cast without the slightest indication he noticed it existed. "You do that, Sidi. It would make my life much easier. I can find better ways to spend the day."

He turned and stalked away. The guards, helmed and anonymous once more, did not acknowledge his passage.

I sat back down on the ground and picked up my chisel but it was several minutes before my hands stopped shaking enough to let me wield it without doing either the wall or myself more damage.

After that, the day slowly became as other days. The courtyard cooled, though the sun did not move. My fingers remembered their skill and my temper its former equanimity. I worked steadily in the silence, finding myself peacefully absorbed by my task. It was not until my stomach rumbled for the third or fourth time that I realized how long I had been lost in the mosaic.

As I began to pack away my tools for the next day's work (a habit Daen found amusing, as clearly nothing would happen to them in the spellbound courtyard), I glanced towards the doorway to see if my silent guards were ready to resume their escort duties. They must have retreated to the cold corridor, as I saw no sign of them. Silent they might be, but they were remorseless in their duty, and it did not occur to me to wonder at the absence until I had finished my tasks and confronted a corridor as empty as the doorway.

I walked down the hall and called out tentatively but there was no reply. They were gone, and I realized I was unaccompanied and unguarded outside the confines of my room for the first time.

At first, I was merely annoyed. I was hungry and tired and wanted a meal and my bed. I went back into the sunny courtyard and sat down on the jumbled ruins in the corner to await their return. One thing my time among the Asezati had taught me was patience, or at least the ability to wait without fretting, but that lesson deserted me sooner than I might have hoped.

As an escort was required for me to return to my rooms, based on Daen's warnings and their own clear reluctance to have a mortal loose in their hallways, then one must appear eventually. The guards had evidently been called away, though by whom and why I could not guess. Perhaps it was simply a misunderstanding—they had left their post expecting Daen to resume it, and he had assumed the duty was theirs.

Or he was angry enough to ignore it and childish enough to consider a few extra hours spent in the courtyard only what I deserved.

My own choices were clear: wait in the courtyard, where I would be safe, if hungry, or venture into the corridors and trust I could find my way back to my room.

I retrieved my sharpest chisel from among my tools, tucked it into my sash and walked down the corridor.

I admit now to being somewhat angry and childish myself, and not entirely unmoved by the vision of Daen returning to an empty courtyard. At the time, I told myself it was sometimes prudent to be bold.

During my travels to and from the courtyard, I had counted turns and doorways, passages and junctions. They changed, but not so much that I did not have a general idea where I was going: two rights turns, a left, down the corridor with the jade-green carpet, past the ominously and heavily chained door, another left and on.

Somewhere past the chained door and the hallway with ivy-covered windows, I knew I was lost.

I had seen no fey, nor even heard a voice or a footstep but my own. There was nothing I recognized—or rather it all looked somewhat familiar but completely unplaceable. Each anonymous door might have been a hundred other doors I had passed, each hallway might have been one I walked before but none of them yielded any clue to where my hallway, my door might lie.

After a while, I stopped at the crossing of two equally empty passages and allowed myself to acknowledge I was lost and I was afraid. I stood there for a few moments and then took the turning to my right, on the theory that moving made my growing fear more manageable.

I suppose it was the belief that doing something was better than doing nothing—and recklessness fuelled by the last remnants of my anger—that made me open the first door.

There was nothing to separate it from any of the other doors I had seen, it was simply the door that was there when I decided that having broken one rule I might as well break the other.

I was cautious, that first time, easing the door open by inches, ready to slam it shut if there should be some terrible beast behind it. There was no beast, only the sound of wind-tossed leaves and pearly light and then, when the door stood fully open, the sight of a forest spreading out before me. I looked around, gripping the edges of the doorway.

The trees were widely spaced, so that I could see the ranks of their slender ashen trunks marching into the distance. Their leaves were silver-grey as well, moving in a steady rustling that sounded like conversation in a language even fey magic could not translate. Those leaves filled the space above me as far as I could see, blotting out even the faintest hint of sky. Mist clung to the leaf-clogged ground, glowing in the dim light and drifting in an oddly purposeful fashion. Something white moved among the trees in the depths of the forest, something in which my eye could almost find a shape I recognized, and I spent several moments staring into the trees, waiting for it to reappear. When I shifted my gaze again, I saw the mist had drifted nearer and a long tendril of it was almost at the doorstep.

I watched it for a long, bemused moment, as it swirled and gathered itself into a shimmer of pearly light.

There was the stench of something rotting then a blur of white bone and teeth flared in front of me. I slammed the door and heard the scrape of claws on the other side.

I stopped running two turns away and leaned against the wall, waiting for my heart to remember its old rhythm and my knees to stop shaking.

After that, it would have been sensible to open no more doors. But I was not sensible, not anymore. I was frightened and angry and I thought if I breached enough of the fey's strange gates sooner or later someone would come to stop me.

Behind the doors, I found forests and meadows, a quiet, richly adorned corridor that smelled of spices and sounded of moans, an alleyway that opened onto a street full of mud and rain and strange, closed carts drawn by wet, miserable horses. I found empty rooms that seemed no different than empty rooms anywhere and once, I found a darkness so deep I could not tell if there was anything on the other side of the doorstep at all.

At last, when my mind was reeling and I was opening and closing doors with numb efficiency, I turned a corner and almost walked in Daen. He had brought the lights with him, the torches flaring, and I could see quite clearly that he was still angry.

"Didn't I warn you about wandering in the hallways and opening doors?" The words might have held humour, if he had said them with a smile. As it was, they scraped along my stretched nerves and found my own frightened fury.

"So you did. But among all that advice you so kindly and copiously gave me, you neglected to tell me what I should do if my drunken, bad-tempered, selfish escort went off for a sulk and failed to remember his duty. Since I had no idea if you would ever return, the hallways seemed a safer choice."

"Did they? And look how well you've done. Your rooms are," he glanced around with corrosive theatricality, "nowhere to be seen. Yet here you are. Did none of the worlds suit you?"

"They seem more suitable by the moment," I snapped back.

"How long do you suppose you would survive in those worlds, Sidi," he asked softly, "without your goddess and your Sidiana to protect you? A lovely little thing like you?"

His stance did not change, his hand did not move toward his sword, but suddenly the corridor seemed too small for his bulk and the air crackled with male threat. I knew, as the protected cousins in Lushan did not, that it was more than bluster. There were some equations that could never be changed, that in the end, will and wit were no match for muscle and mass. Even the chisel in my sash would not protect me, if he truly meant to do me harm.

It was perversity and bravado that stiffened my spine. "I lived half my life with protection from no one. I survived that. I would manage."

"Then choose a door, Sidi."

It would be folly to take that dare, to let his temper drive me into risk or his contempt dictate a single step I took.

I turned around and flung open the door at my back. Through it, I saw a wide expanse of grey sky mirroring grey sea and heard the distant cry of birds. There was the salty tang of ocean in the breeze that rushed through the open door.

"It would be that one, wouldn't it?" Daen said behind me, but his voice was flat and empty, the anger drained away. "You bitch." Even those hard words seemed only half-hearted and I knew that they were not meant for me.

There were bare trees stretching away from either side of the door and rough grasses bent in waves beneath the wind in front of me. Beyond them, the land seemed to fall away into a long, stony beach that ended in the white foam of waves. Across the water, I could see another shore that seemed to mirror this one; beach, grass, trees. But farther away, I saw the flicker of firelight and the distant lines of walls and roofs.

"Go on then, Sidi. Don't you want to see the world you've chosen?"

Daen's voice was in my ear and his hand was on my arm, pushing me through the doorway before him. The ground beneath my feet felt real and when I put my hand out to touch the grass that moved around me, the sharp edges of the blades scored my skin. I looked back but the door was gone; there were only trees behind us. I reminded myself that Daen must know how to return to the Court and the thought steadied me a little.

"Where is this place?"

"It's called Varansheld. I don't know where it is from Lushan, I've never been able to find it, except through these doors. Down there, where the lights are, is Hilerev, where the Firebeards rule. At least they used to."

He released my arm and walked to the edge of the dune, where the ground fell away to the beach. I followed and looked down the bay to the town. "Not the best choice you could have made, Sidi. The Varanshelders live by raiding the softer, greener lands to the south. There's no place for an outsider woman here, except as a slave. But," he gave me a mocking glance, "perhaps your beauty would outweigh your age, and you'd be given to the Lord for his household."

"How do you know this?"

"Haven't you guessed, Sidi? This is where I was raised. If things had been different, the Lord you'd have been given to would have been me."

In forty-six years, I have told no one what Daen told me that day. Not even Raziel, who had every right to know, though that betrayal was still to come. All these years later, it seems I remember every word, though I know it cannot be. He told it haltingly, with interruptions and revisions, curses and pauses. He had never told it before, I realized; there was no one to tell. The fey knew what they needed to know; the rest was the one thing he kept secret, the one truth he held inside, despite all the other truths he scattered about without regret.

Life in Varansheld was as harsh and elemental as the landscape. The men were warriors and sailors, taking their beast-prowed ships to plunder the shores of the nearby lands in summer and fighting amongst themselves in the long, ice-bound winters. His father was a lord among them. Daen remembered him as something larger than life; big-bellied, bronze-bearded, brawny-armed. He had a fierce appetite for wine and women and battle and his men would have followed him to the edge of the world and over it.

COLD HILLSIDE

Daen was his only son. He grew up as a prince in that rough, passionate world. He had his father's look and his father's love and no touch of his golden-haired mother but her hazel eyes. At sixteen summers he had the promise of his father's height and breath of shoulder, he had gone on a raiding party against the Sealey islanders, and more than one local maiden met his glance with a smile and a flick of her hair.

If sometimes he knew a thing a moment before it happened, if sometimes, late of a winter's night, he looked around the hall and felt as if he were a thousand cold miles away from the people who crowded into the warmth—well, as long as he pretended well enough that no one else ever knew, he could deceive himself as well.

Though the Varanshelders lived their lives facing the sea, there was a world inland that also belonged to them. Farms were carved out of the forest and woodsmen harvested the logs that built the coastal towns and great ships. Deep in the woods and up in the hills lived the skrimdryks, primitive barbarians to Varansheld eyes, and each side raided the other when harvests were bad and winters long.

That autumn, his father's household made a passage through those inland domains to collect tribute and ensure that the farmers and herdsmen, woodcutters and hunters remembered their lord during the snowbound winter. They moved slowly, their pace dictated by the jolting progress of the carts laden with goods. Sigur Firebeard Njal's-son, his son and his finest soldiers rode the valuable horses, still rare on these shores. Everyone else walked.

Sigur was no fool; scouts travelled the rutted road ahead of them and his men rode with their hands on their heavy swords. It made no difference.

Daen had time to see the man in front of him fall, a skrimdryk arrow in his throat, then his horse reared in terror. He heard shouts, saw the sky and trees wheel above him, and then there was only darkness.

When he woke, there was more darkness, twilight brushed with the silver of the rising moon, but there was light enough to see what the skrimdryks had left.

He counted all the bodies; they were all there, which was strange, for the skrimdryks took slaves just as the Varanshelders did. His father's body was propped against a tree, pierced with arrows, stained with blood turned black in the waning light. His throat had been cut, the skrimdryks' victory marks carved into his forehead.

What he felt, standing among the dead bodies of his kin, with no mark on him but a lump on the back of his head, Daen would not say.

He made a pyre of the carts and laid his father's body on it and crouched there watching it burn. It should have been a boat that burned, out on the cold grey waters of the bay, with the Firebeard insignia on the sails and treasures heaped around the fallen lord. But it was a day's walk back to the town and he would not leave his father to be eaten by animals.

In the darkest part of the night, as the pyre burned down, he heard the sound of bells and saw a light in the trees. For a moment, he thought it was the skrimdryks returned and felt a fierce savage joy. He would die but at least this time he would fight.

But it was not the skrimdryks who rode out of the forest, it was the fey.

Liosdissar, the Varanshelders called them. The underland folk.

They rode armoured in silver, on horses finer than anything he had ever seen. The Queen rode in front, fearless in her own armour, in her glacial beauty. Daen's knees were on the ground before he had time to think of kneeling.

She gave him a choice. To stay in the mortal world, to summon the men that remained and take vengeance on the skrimdryks, if they could find them. To take his father's place, if he could, against the other lords who might see his youth as their chance to rise. Or to go with her and her host, to learn to use both magic and sword, and then avenge his father's death with certainty.

When he asked her why she would offer such a thing, she told him though his father had been mortal, his mother—his true mother—was fey. *There is a place for you among us*, she told him, *higher than you have ever imagined*. She told him a story then, of how a Faerie lady saw his father and wanted him and had him and then, when the child she bore him was a boy and no use to her, she gave him to his father who, being a lord, needed a son, even a half-fey one.

He did not doubt her words, for though they altered all he had thought he knew about his world, they made it at last make sense. All that had been strange and hidden in him did not make him less, it made it him more, made him strong.

He went with them.

It was not easy in the fey Court but he learned what he had to learn. He had little magic but what he possessed was almost all useful only for fighting. He learned how to use that as well, until he could beat warriors many years his senior.

Time passed in its strange way among the fey. He grew taller, broader, harder, gifted at mortal violence and his own, peculiar fey magic and, after what might have been a year, the Queen gave him permission to exact his vengeance.

Do this, she said, dressed in her own warrior garb in honour of the upcoming battle. *Do this and come back to me for your reward. Then I will tell you your mother's name.*

He knelt to receive her blessing, her cold lips against his forehead, and then led his fey soldiers out of one world and into the other.

They swept down on the skrimdryks like the winter wind, one camp after another. Daen did not know how many men he killed and, after the men were dead, how many women and children. He did not ask if they had killed his father. After a while, he did not care.

I shivered in the cold wind that blew across the water and listened to him tell the story, as the world darkened around us. "Hilerev used to be right across the sound, right there," Daen said suddenly, pointing to a gap in the trees on the other bank. "Sometime after that night, the skrimdryks came down from the hills and burned it. The men were off raiding, so it was the women and children, the old, the slaves who died. When the men came back, they built the new town, then went raiding for new women, new slaves."

There was nothing to say to that, to say to any of it. I stood there, my hands tucked into my sleeves, my shoulders hunched, and waited for him to remember the story he was telling. It was a dark and terrible tale but I could feel a worse darkness waiting.

"I went back to the Court, to the Queen. I laid the head of the skrimdryk chieftain at her feet and felt as if I could rule the fucking world. Then she took me to her bed and gave me my reward." He looked out over the water and the raw wind seemed to touch him for the first time. "And in the morning, she told me my mother's name."

"No," I breathed. "Oh, no."

"Oh yes. My mother. Veradis. The Faerie Queen." He looked at me then and in the waning light I could see his hard, bitter smile. "Are you shocked *now*, Sidi?"

CHAPTER 35

Lilit

Lilit clung to her father's words and, against their comfort, the faerie tester's pronouncement lost some of its weight. Still, more than once she caught herself touching the iron beads in her bracelet, turning the iron band on her finger in absent ritual.

She did not go to her aunt, to either release the child inside her or accept it.

For a week, she slept dreamlessly, then one night she found herself crouched by the bridge again, mocking laughter in her ears. Rest banished, Lilit dressed and went quietly through the darkened house, aiming for the kitchen and a warm drink.

She walked through the garden, turned silver by the bright moon in the cloudless sky, and turned towards the stone path that led along the wall toward the kitchen entrance. In the centre of the garden, the memorial monument rose higher than her head. Into each stone was carved the name of a dead Kerias, from the first to the last, and the dates they had breathed in the world. When it had grown too high, the stones were laid against the house, creating a second wall.

Lilit found her feet on the path that circled the monument without remembering choosing to walk there. The moonlight brought some names into sharp relief, the shadows swallowed others. Her eye caught on the name of a child a hundred years gone, who had lived only four months. Babies died for a thousand reasons, it was true. Did those who cried too loudly at the touch of iron have their names carved there? The babies who were changed or cursed into creatures with mortal looks but fey souls, were their names added? Or did the House pretend they did not exist?

As a child, the memorial had been the object of midnight excursions, delicious with terror of both the dead and the aunts. The older cousins told shivery stories in its shadow, and pointed out the names of those they claimed were changeling babies. She supposed the children of Kerias had been playing some variation of that game for hundreds of years. Though she had not entirely believed the stories, she could still remember some of the names.

She hunted along the rows of rocks until she found one: Elizet Kerias, 176 Barat, three days. She was the rumoured fey baby, born nine months after the fair. The stories had said her mother was banished; you could tell because there was no age listed for Vaneyen Kerias, whose stone lay below hers, which meant she had died somewhere far away, alone and unacknowledged.

Lilit shivered. She had no business standing here frightening herself. She could imagine her great-aunt's caustic voice scolding her and clung to the memory of that exacting, exasperated tone.

But when she was back on the path beside the mourning wall, her gaze went automatically to the line of stones that bore the names of her paternal grandmother and father, and the aunts and uncles who had died over the years. And the name of her brother. No shadow hid it, the black lines clear against the stark grey stone. Neven Kerias sa Amaris. 423 Dasim, two days.

She had been four and had only the dimmest memories of that cold winter; her mother's gaunt face and empty eyes, Hendren's tears, her own fear and bewilderment as she was sent to stay with her cousins in another wing of the house. She was no longer certain if her image of her brother, a quiet, golden-skinned baby with wide hazel eyes, was a true memory or only an imagining.

They had let her come home after a few days, to her mother's brisk busy-ness and her father's retreat into his books. But there had been no more children.

Babies died for a thousand reasons, she thought. Illness and being born too soon and in the night for no reason at all. Babies died and mothers grieved and that was the way of the world.

Babies died and mothers grieved. . . .

CHAPTER 36

Teresine

I remember very little of the walk to my door, though the sensible thing to do would have been to try to determine where I had gone wrong. But there was no place in my thoughts for corridors and corners; it was too full of Daen's story and the last thing he had said, almost casually, as he turned back to the door to the Court now open again behind us.

"I wonder sometimes," he had said, when my silence had answered his question, "whether I ever found my father's killers after all." The implications of that stilled whatever words I might have said.

After a dozen turnings and gloomy hallways frosted with cold light, there was my doorway, bright, garish and welcome. "Thank you for coming to find me," I said, meaning it, meaning more, afraid he had taken my silence for blame, my shock for censure.

He looked at me for a moment and I felt the weight of that gaze through to my bones. "Don't do it again, Sidi. There are worse doors than the ones you opened."

I could not imagine what might be worse than that bleak shoreline he had once called home, at least for him.

"I will not," I promised, not at all certain it was a promise I could keep. I wanted to say something else but could find no words that would not be cold comfort or, worse, patronizing. Who was I, after all, to judge what he had done, what he did? I bid him good night and opened the door to my chamber.

"Pleasant dreams, Sidi," he replied with a trace of bitter humour and a brief bend of his head.

It was a long time before that wish, however he meant it, could be fulfilled. I lay in the darkness, watching the long slats of mysterious moonlight shift across the sheer curtains that hung around the bed.

Daen's story made sense of a dozen things that had puzzled me since my arrival: his reference to *you fey*, Madelon's warning, Bastien's words—*Queens do as they please*—the fey's eagerness to see me appalled by such sins, Daen's stories of his travels—*As far as I can go, which is never quite far enough.* It even made some sense of why the Queen's champion was assigned the duty of guarding a mortal; being half-mortal himself, he presumably found my presence less toxic than did the other fey. Just as, presumably, his loyalty to the Queen (*his mother, his lover*) was unquestioned, despite his casual rudeness, his repeated flights into the world.

What had Madelon said? *But now perhaps she has brought the feast to him, a tasty dish to consume without all the trouble and travel.*

I did not trust Madelon. I did not trust the Queen. I did not dare to trust Daen.

My task was to finish the mosaics and keep myself clear of the reefs of fey politics and plots. What they did in their court or in their beds was no business of mine.

It occurred to me that they were allowing me to see far more of both than I imagined they wished the mortal world to know. I could only hope that it was because they had no fear of us rather than that they knew I would have no chance to share what I had seen.

Not thoughts to inspire pleasant dreams—but the truth was I did not dream at all.

The next morning, it was Daen who arrived to escort me to the courtyard. We walked in silence, for which I was grateful. After the drama of the previous day, this one passed in utter normality (or at least the normality I had come to know in the fey Court). Daen left me to work in peace and reappeared exactly when expected to walk me back to my room. He was polite but distant, barely more communicative than the anonymous guards.

By the third day, I found, somewhat to my surprise, that distance no longer made me feel grateful, merely lonely. I told myself I was accustomed to loneliness, especially in the wake of Sarit's death, but it was no longer true. I missed Raziel and Ayriet, my room in the palace, my life in the palace. I even missed Lushan itself, with a fierceness that frightened me. During my time in Faerie, some of my old armour had regrown, but it felt thin and rusty. The long nights alone in my room had begun to feel less like shelter than imprisonment.

I hid my feelings with silence and work, and bundled myself in one more layer of shawls against a cold that I pretended was nothing but the mirror of the winter that must lie outside the walls and not Daen's failure to ensure the magics that maintained the courtyard were working.

I supposed he regretted having let his temper goad him into telling me the truth. His own silence suggested that would not happen again; he seemed to require neither laughter nor shock nor even an audience from me anymore.

A week later, the Queen summoned me to another grand dinner. The room was different this time: low-ceilinged, heavily carpeted and lit with lamps of stained glass that seemed to colour the dark rather than light it. The guests reclined on banks of velvet cushions beside low tables and ate from trays of barely visible food. I supposed fey night-sight must be better than mine, for the murkiness seemed to bother them not at all. My only consolation was that I had once again been seated with Bastien, who was as curious and courteous as he had been at the Midwinter ball.

There was no dais this time but the Queen was impossible to miss, glowing luminously in the shadows, as if possessing her own light. When the guards brought me before her, she asked me how my work progressed, waved off my answer as before and sent me on my way. Daen was seated beside her but I never saw her look his way and when she left, she left alone.

Bastien once again escorted me to my room.

The next day, I worked until my back began to ache (a daily occurrence that made me even more grateful for the endless supply of hot water in my room, no matter its provenance). I straightened, wincing as my muscles complained, and shifted my shoulders, tilting my head back into the light of the always-noon sun.

Quite suddenly, I hated it, that false sun. I hated the false warmth, for all it kept me comfortable. I hated the endless cold and confusing corridors of the court and the mutable extravagance of the Queen's feasts. I hated the doors that promised escape and delivered only monsters and terrible truths. I hated the mosaic and its thousands of tiny shards that combined into nothing that made sense to mortal eyes.

I wanted to scream or cry or take my chisel to the mosaic and shatter it in a frenzy of destruction.

Instead I put my tools away, just as I did every night, and then sat down beneath the false sun to wait for my escort.

COLD HILLSIDE

It was Daen who appeared, looking tired and mortal. Knowing his heritage explained the ordinariness of his appearance, its incongruity amidst the glamour of the fey. *He has his father's look*, Madelon had said and I had a momentary vision of the man Daen had described, the father overlaid upon the son: handsome, brawny, heavy with presence and power. *Perhaps that is why she wants him.* The thought flickered before I could stop it; it made me feel queasy, uncertain.

"Is it possible to leave the Court?" I asked, to say something that had nothing to do with my thoughts.

"It is winter outside the Court, Sidi."

"Not everywhere," I replied, as the diversionary question sparked a real plan. "There must be a door, a safe door, that opens somewhere warm. Somewhere with a real sun, one that moves."

"Deshiniva?" he asked and I shook my head.

"No, not there. Someplace I've never been. Someplace where I could sit for a few moments and breathe real air, feel a real breeze."

"I know a place," he said, after a moment. "But I can't promise that the door will open."

"I would be grateful if you would be willing to try."

"Well then, Sidi, how can I refuse?" The question, and his bow, balanced on the line between sarcasm and humour. I thanked him politely and followed him from the courtyard.

I don't know how he determined which door it was; he stopped in front of several and put his hand on the knob, then moved on. At last he seemed satisfied and opened the door carefully, peering into the sudden dazzle of sunlight before he stepped aside and allowed me to look.

Beyond the door frame was a world of gold and green. I could smell flowers and earth and there were birds quarrelling in the trees

"Will this do, Sidi?"

"Oh, yes." I stepped through the door.

We were on the side of a hill, in a copse of trees whose leaves whispered in a faint breeze. Through the thin veil of branches, I could see flickers of colour. When I stepped from the trees into their shadow, my breath caught.

Spread out below me was a patchwork of fields: green, gold, the most astonishing purple. Tall narrow trees ran along fences that converged on a farmhouse made of stone, its roof tiled in bright red. On the far side of the valley, hills rolled up to an azure sky. It was mid-afternoon, to judge by the shadows and the sun. It was hot and I felt sweat gathering beneath my robes. "Where are we?"

"The border of Isbayan and Ranska."

I thought of the captain in the alley outside the iron. No wonder he had thought Lushan cold. It was not only Lushan he had found cold, I remembered and felt a strange prickle of discomfort in my skin. I did not want to think of soldiers. Or of kisses.

"What are they growing?"

"Sunflowers and ilvenia, I think. The purple is a kind of lavender."

"Is it safe here?"

"Safe enough. We can see anyone coming up the hill."

"May I sit for a while?"

"Of course, Sidi."

I took off my hat and my shawls, hesitated over my robe and then shed it as well, to stand in the sun in my trousers and thin Deshiniva bodice. There was a flat stretch of ground before the trees; I sat down, letting the rich, foreign, *real* beauty of the scene fill my eyes. The scent of Daen's cinquegrass mingled with the heavy fragrance of the flower fields below us. The sun spread across my skin, sank into my bones. After a while, I felt my eyes begin to droop, the peace of meditative dissociation filling me as it so often failed to in my room at the Court.

I don't know how long I sat there or what drew me back, but suddenly I was present again. The sun had moved and a treetop shadow was aimed at my knee. I looked over my shoulder to find Daen sitting on a stump, his elbows on his knees, seemingly engrossed in watching a faint plume of smoke from the cinquegrass stick between his fingers curl in the still air. "Do you suppose your god can hear us, from the other side of the world?" he asked curiously, without malice.

"I would suppose she could hear a prayer from anywhere," I said, reaching for my robe. "I was not praying."

"What's her name, your goddess?"

"Jennon. Though the Newaris call her Paldensorma. To them, she lives on the mountain over Lushan."

"Are you a good Asezat?"

"No," I said honestly. "Perhaps. I have kept the vows I swore." Which was true enough; though my suggestion to Raziel that she could reject the position of Sidiana had clearly fallen outside those vows; she had not accepted it, so I was not foresworn after all. "But I have no faith. Whatever capacity I had for that died in Deshiniva."

"Whatever capacity I had for it died in a forest in Varansheld," Daen said after a moment. "And in the Queen's bed." He stubbed out the cigarette in the dirt. "But now I'm shocking you again."

"I am not shocked," I said, collecting my hat.

"I am. An Asezat without faith. Is that common in Lushan?"

"More than you might suppose. The Asezati are an intellectual order. And a political one. Faith matters less if you are brilliant. Or well connected."

"Which are you?"

"You know the answer to that," I replied, picking up my shawl. I stood up, brushing the dirt from my robe. "I am the former tutor to the present Sidiana and the confidante of the previous one."

"I thought it was polite to ask," he said mildly, rising to hold the branches back to let me pass into the shelter of the trees.

"Now I *am* shocked."

"That's better. I've missed your sharp tongue, Sidi," he said as the branches fell into place, turning the tiny grove into dappled green.

"You had only to insult me to find it again." I watched as he muttered something and the door shaped itself from the trees. "It has been very quiet in the courtyard these last days." I spoke quickly, before the door opened and the quiet, dreamlike beauty behind me was lost, replaced by the cold reality of the Court.

Listening did not mean trust, I told myself. It just meant a voice to fill the silence of the courtyard. It meant remembering what my own voice sounded like.

"So it has," he agreed. "It's been quite tedious, in fact, hasn't it?"

We walked back down the hallways, silence banished. Still warm from the sun, the sloping fields of flowers lingering bright in my mind, I forgot to be lonely.

CHAPTER 37

Teresine

A week after my trip to the flower fields of Isbayan, two helmed soldiers came to the doorway of the courtyard after my midday meal. I was alone beneath the unmoving sun. "Sidi Teresine," one said.

"The Queen bids you accompany us," the other finished for him.

"As the Queen commands," I agreed. They betrayed no impatience while I set my tools neatly aside and wrapped myself in my robe. I exchanged my hat for one of my lighter shawls and, as presentable as I could make myself, followed them into the corridors. My own guards were nowhere to be seen.

Within moments I lost track of where we were; nothing in the corridors we travelled seemed in the least familiar. At last, I heard a swell of sound from ahead of us, voices and laughter and drums. We turned a corner into the midst of a crowd of fey, all funnelling into two great open doors. I turned back to my escort but they had vanished. Bewildered, I stepped back and then heard a voice I recognized call my name.

Lord Bastien materialized from the crowd. "Why, Sidi, have you come to watch the duel?"

"I was summoned and then abandoned, Lord. I was not told of any duel, but I must assume the Queen wishes me to attend."

"Come with me then, mortal child. Join me in my box. We shall have a good view—but do not fear. I do not expect bloodshed. Well, very little. The Queen will relent and end it once her honour has been satisfied."

Accepting his offer seemed the safest course, keeping me from far less courteous company and giving me a companion who would be willing to explain what was happening without assuming I was either a child or a moron. I followed him up a staircase and then into a small curtained chamber that overlooked a courtyard. It was night here; the courtyard was bright with torches. When I looked up, I could see the moon, palely yellow, set in a garland of stars.

Fey filled tiered benches below us and the other chambers that lined the courtyard, giving it the look of a theatre or an arena. At one end, banners of green and gold proclaimed the Queen's seat. She was dressed in sombre black, the first time I had seen her in that colour, and her white hair was bound into a corona of severe braids. She wore a crown of jet, studded with pearls.

Bastien pulled back one of the curtains to reveal Ileane, Lindel and Hilare settled into the booth next to his. A small table had been set before them, bearing sweets and glasses of wine. There were nods of greeting and grudging, sharp-edged smiles in my direction.

"Some wine?" Ileane offered. "Lindel kindly brought it."

"It's not a picnic, dear lady," Bastien replied, somewhat stuffily, and the fey laughed.

"Come now, Bastien, it's posturing. Garrich is a pup and a foolish one, but he's Lord Moriah's get and the Queen will not forget that. A sound beating and she'll send him off to guard the troll mines for a century or so and it will be forgotten. No reason not to enjoy ourselves." Lindel waved an airy gesture over the refreshments.

"Garrich is a fine swordsman," Hilare said seriously. "A beating is by no means assured."

"We could wager on it," Ileane suggested. "I've no objection to winning a favour from you because you cannot stand Daen."

"Who is a better swordsman," Lindel said. "As the Queen well knows." They laughed at that, even Hilare, even Bastien.

The dark fey lord seemed to remember my presence. "Garrich is one of Lord Moriah's sons. The Lord has favoured the Queen's cousin, Madelon, in some recent controversies. Garrich made several uncomplimentary comments about the Queen and her champion in a place no one could afford to pretend they had not heard. The Queen must make an example of him. So here we are. But don't fear—it is only ritual. And Lord Daen is the finest warrior in the court, so you needn't worry for him."

I was about to protest that I was not worried on any account—what was it to me, after all?—when the doors at either end of the courtyard opened and the opponents stepped into view. There were cheers from the crowd, though I heard no names called. I supposed the fey court knew well enough to keep their allegiances to themselves.

Garrich was dark and tall, armoured in silver mail from throat to thighs. It looked like the scales of a fish and made his movement glitter like water in sunlight. He bowed to someone in the crowd and when I followed the motion I saw the opalescent sheen of Madelon's wings. That gesture completed, the fey lord turned to his squire and accepted his silver-hammered helm.

Theatre came naturally to the fey, it seemed.

At first glance, Daen's entrance held none. He walked into the courtyard, helmet under his arm, armoured in serviceable leather. There was grace there, but it was economical and solid, the confidence of a workman come to do a task without drama. He unhooked the sword across his back and let it fall to his hip then donned his helm, a curved shape of dull metal with no trace of ornamentation.

It was theatre of its own sort, I realized. Every gesture, from stance to walk to armour, was calculated to define itself in opposition to the fey, to turn their grace and glamour into nothing but a showy reflection of his straightforward competence.

The combatants approached the centre of the courtyard and bowed to the Queen. Ferrell rose from her side to stand at the edge of the royal box. "Garrich of Moriah, you stand accused of insult to the Queen and she has claimed the right of defence by her champion. Do you retract your words and submit to her peace?"

"I retract nothing. The Queen knows the worth of my words and I will defend my honour."

"Then the duel begins and ends upon the Queen's pleasure."

The Queen looked for a moment at the two men, anonymous now behind their helms, and then nodded.

It was a little like the sparring match in the mosaic courtyard; a series of exploratory feints and blows, each man judging the other, escalating to a battery of fierce attacks. The courtyard seemed to amplify the sounds, the clang of swords, the stamp of feet, the sharpening breaths seeming to echo around us. As before, the fey was faster but Daen was stronger.

It came to first blood in a matter of moments. The blood was almost invisible against Garrich's skin—it was only when it fell red and bright to the sandy floor that the audience sighed. There was an uneasy ripple of applause.

In the yard, both men paused and looked at the Queen.

"That's it then," Bastien said. "The Queen will stop it now."

But she did not.

The duel resumed, growing harsher and more ragged as the moments passed. There was blood on Daen's arm now, dripping slowly along his bicep. Garrich's smooth movements and perfect form began to falter. The rituals of the duel fell away and it was battle we were watching, savage and serious, with no quarter given. There was no sound from the audience, no cheering or whispering, only the occasional gasp as a particularly hard blow landed.

"She'll stop it," Bastien repeated softly, but he sounded less certain.

"She won't," Lindel said. "She means one of them to die."

I saw the moment the combatants came to that conclusion. Garrich found a reserve of strength and drove forward, the whirling silver of his blade forcing Daen back across the yard. When they parted, there was blood on Daen's other arm and he was breathing hard. The leather armour had withstood the last set of blows but I imagined he had felt them all the way down to his bones.

There was a dull pain in my hands and I looked down, realizing my own fists were clenched, my nails digging into my palms. I unlocked my fingers and thrust my hands into the sleeves of my robe. I had seen many things in my life but I had never seen men kill each other.

Make her end it, I prayed, an automatic action I could neither help nor believe in. *Mother Jennon, have mercy and make her end it.*

In the yard, Daen straightened, shifting his shoulders, settled his grip on his sword, and waited, leaving Garrich no choice but to attack again. The swords clashed and rang and then the edge of the fey's silver blade bit hard along Daen's ribs. For a moment, the two men were frozen, the crowd transfixed.

Then there was movement again, so quick I barely understood what happened. Daen's sword moved; Garrich's blade, snagged in the split leather armour, did not. When it was done, Daen's sword was at Garrich's throat.

The fey's weapon fell soundless to the ground.

Daen looked at the Queen.

Who did nothing.

"She will not dare," someone, Hilare perhaps, whispered. "She will not dare."

Other whispers began, tentative, disbelieving. A man's voice called "My Queen, please—"

The Queen looked at no one but Daen.

He bowed low to the Queen and walked out of the yard as calmly as he had walked into it.

The Queen rose, her white face expressionless, and disappeared through the hangings at the back of the royal box.

It was Ferrell who pronounced her judgement. "Garrich of Moriah, you are hereby banished from the court at the Queen's pleasure. If your foot falls on any land of the Queen's hereafter, your life is forfeit. Leave now." He cast a contemptuous glance around the assembled court. "All of you."

"Well," Bastien said after a moment, "that was unexpected."

"Daen will regret that," Hilare said, with just a trace of pleasure.

"Lover's quarrels are always so interesting," Lindel observed. "It's a pity this one has so much potential for damage to bystanders."

"Well, little mortal," Ileane leaned over to look at me, "was that more exciting than scraping and polishing or whatever it is you're doing now?"

"I would prefer to be scraping and polishing, Lady."

"Surely you mortals would rejoice when one of us dies," Hilare said.

"I rejoice at no being's death, Lord."

"And, after all that, no one died. Not even half a fey," Lindel said, pouring himself another goblet of wine and collecting the tray of sweets. "As there's nothing left to see, I suggest we find somewhere more comfortable to picnic, as Bastien says."

We joined the crush of fey leaving the courtyard. They were subdued, the gossip reduced to quiet malice and whispers. "We will find you an escort, Sidi, and you can return to your work," Bastien promised, but somewhere on the stairs I lost him. When I reached the hallway, I saw no one I recognized, save for Madelon, who noticed me in the same moment. She smiled her catlike smile and shifted against the tide of passing fey to move towards me.

The thought of listening to her elliptical warnings and politely phrased contempt was more than I could bear. I slithered sideways behind a tall fey lord dressed in heavy velvet, found the shadows of the courtyard doors and slipped along the narrow passage that led behind the tiers of seats.

In that shelter, I took a breath; it felt like the first time I had breathed since the fight began. I had thought it did not matter to me what the fey did but I could not lie to myself so much—it did. I was relieved I had not had to watch anyone die or kill. No matter what Hilare believed, I would not have rejoiced in Garrich's death, though he was a complete stranger. As I would not have rejoiced in Daen's, who was not.

I kept moving through the shelter of the passageway until the sounds from the hallway had died away, though I knew it meant I had likely lost Bastien, and thus hope of easy escort. I had to trust there would be guards about, reluctant enough to see me wandering the court that they would take me back to the mosaic courtyard. There were none here, in the depths of the arena, which surprised me a little. I wondered if this was always an arena or if it would revert to something—or perhaps nothing—when the Queen's need for it faded. I wondered what would happen to me if I was there when it did.

That thought spurred me, as did the realization that I was perhaps a little lost. I opened doors and walked through dim, indistinguishable corridors; the arena seemed a smaller Court in that regard. At last, I saw a light and passed through another corridor to emerge into the torchlit courtyard where the duel had been fought.

"So they dragged you out to see this farce, Sidi," said a voice to my left and I turned to see Daen sitting on a bench; I had emerged through the door through which he had left. There was a heap of bloody cloths on the bench beside him and a basin of water, tinted faintly red. "But how did you end up here?"

"I lost Bastien by mistake and Madelon on purpose," I said. "Are you hurt badly? Shouldn't there be someone to attend you?"

"I'll live, thank you, Sidi. I don't like being around people after I fight," he said, returning to the business of smearing something green and faintly luminous on the wounds on his arm.

"I'll leave you then."

"No, Sidi, stay. You'll need an escort back, I assume."

"Yes. Thank you." I stood awkwardly in the doorway, watching him. "Can I help you?"

"Hand me a clean cloth, if you can find one."

I found one only faintly blood-smeared and passed it to him. From here, the torches cast the stands and boxes into darkness. I looked up at the Queen's box for a moment. The air smelled of leather, sweat, blood, and something astringently herbal I assumed must be the ointment in the pot by his side.

"Why did you call it a farce? It seemed serious to me."

"Garrich is a young fool, of which there is no shortage at Court. The Queen needed a message sent, to his father in part, so his indiscretion was suddenly deemed insult."

"She would have had him die for that?"

"Exile serves well enough. His father might even be grateful for it." He stood up and began to unbuckle his armour. I saw the place where Garrich's sword had struck, the leather splitting to show flesh.

"Why didn't you kill him?"

"I might be drunken, bad-tempered and selfish, Sidi, but I'll not kill a man because the Queen wants to teach me a lesson," Daen replied and tugged the armour off with a grunt. There was an oozing cut along his ribs and the promise of bruises from heart to collarbone. Old scars cut faded paths through dark hair across his chest.

I looked away, to the black shadows of the Queen's box.

"What lesson does she want to teach you?"

I heard the splash of water and a muttered oath. "That when she wants a thing done, I'm to do it."

"What does she want you to do?"

From the corner of my eye, I saw the shape of him move, reaching for another cloth, going about the business of wiping away blood and sweat and water. For a moment, I wasn't sure if he would answer.

"She wants me to seduce you."

That almost shocked me into looking at him. I stopped myself and stared at the Queen's box, imagining that white face staring back. It was a moment before I could find anything to say. "Are you required to achieve this goal or merely to attempt it?" The calm distance in my voice astonished me; there were things I still remembered how to do after all. "If only the attempt is necessary, I give you leave to try. I cannot be seduced."

"Anyone can be seduced, Sidi," he replied matter-of-factly. White flared at the edge of my vision and I heard the sound of cloth sliding over skin. "But thank you for the offer. Don't be concerned. It's my business, I'll deal with it."

COLD HILLSIDE

I almost argued that it was my business as well, that being the object of such orders made it as much my concern as his. But it was not a discussion I cared to prolong, and there was nothing I could say that would make any difference. He was paying a price for defiance, and the Queen would have made Garrich pay that price as well. It made me feel angry, a little frightened, and oddly guilty.

I wound my fingers together beneath the shelter of my sleeves and waited for Daen to finish. "I'll take you back," he said at last and I turned my head to watch him shrug on his coat. He smiled and I felt the heat in the back of my neck. I would have preferred he had not noticed where I had kept my gaze.

He left water, bloody cloths, and ruined armour behind him without a glance. Once we were safely beyond the doors, I asked him the questions that had occurred to me in the empty corridors of the arena.

"You choose odd times for philosophy, Sidi. It's there when she requires it. I've never opened that door and found only a void. But I've never seen it in daylight, either. What that means, I leave to better minds than mine."

Back in the mosaic courtyard, the midday sun still ruled, startling after the night-shrouded battlefield. "You'll forgive me if I don't stay, Sidi," Daen said. "I've an appointment with a hot bath and a medicinal dose of wine."

"Of course," I agreed politely. I suspected he might also have an appointment, voluntary or not, with the Queen.

I did very little on the mosaic that afternoon. Eventually, I abandoned any pretence at work and pretended instead to meditation, sitting in a corner of the yard. I went through the rituals of mantras and breathing but neither were any match for the whirl of speculation the afternoon's events had set in motion.

Viewed with a dispassionate, political eye, Daen's revelations were not so surprising. The Queen could have a dozen reasons for desiring the seduction of a mortal guest, from the hope of gaining control over a potential spy to simple malice. Her choice of weapon was somewhat of a gamble. For those dazzled by fey glamour, Daen's mortal ordinariness would be scant temptation. Others might find it comforting and gravitate instinctively to that familiarity. I remembered my conversation with Raziel on the night before we left for the fair, our speculation about what the Queen might see when she looked in our eyes, and wondered uneasily if her choice had been based on what she had seen there. It was true that fey glamour held little allure for me—but then neither did mortal male charm.

Even Daen's admission of the plot made sense; having been forewarned, I was unlikely to be susceptible and there was then no reason for the Queen to insist on his compliance. It was possible that she would make him pay a price for that but I suspected a long history of defiance, struggle and surrender between them.

And if the Queen did not relent?

That was Daen's business, as he had said. My task was to finish the mosaic and leave this cold, treacherous place as soon as possible. What the Queen wanted did not matter to me.

After all, I could not be seduced.

CHAPTER 38

Teresine

A week after the duel, the Faerie Court went hunting.

There were hunts in Deshiniva and Lushan, of course. Among the poor of Deshiniva, hunting was a way to feed your family or deal with dangerous beasts. In Lushan, it was much the same, though there were those at court who took pride in their ability to shoot a grouse from the sky or track one of the small, fierce boars through the forests.

The Faerie Court hunted for sport, for entertainment, for politics, and to find some edge of danger to lend spice to their extravagant revelries.

The summons I received was only a note, not an exploding flower, and this time I accepted the Queen's gift of appropriate attire. The hide trousers, thin red shirt stiff with embroidery, and sleeveless leather coat seemed far more practical than my own clothing for such business, though I wrapped my sash around my waist and took my felt hat.

By the time the guards had led me through the corridors to another anonymous doorway, I had to admit to curiosity about what world lay beyond, what wonders the Queen might summon for such an occasion.

What she conjured was heat and dust and twilight, with an indigo sky painted red by the sun across one horizon and silver by the moon across the other. The courtyard before me was framed by walls of ochre stone. When I looked back, I could see the rise of a palatial building behind me, the walls pierced by high windows covered in carved screens. Something fluttered white in one of them and then was gone. The yard teemed with fey, clad in brighter, more elaborate variations of the clothes I now wore. The elegant fey horses had their own finery; bright tassels dangled from bridles and saddles. Despite the frivolity of it, I noticed that arrayed around the edges of the throng were soldiers and servants, all bearing long, wicked-looking spears.

In the centre of the yard, I saw the Queen, already mounted on a white horse. She was dressed in robes of sand and fire, her white hair hidden by a veil. Amber and gold gleamed on her forehead, wrist and breast. Beyond her, Daen's black horse tossed its head, its heavy mane rippling. Tassels of maroon silk dripped from its bridle, an affectation that looked strange on so massive a beast, but which matched the colour of its rider's coat.

A servant materialized to lead me to a horse and wait patiently while I mounted. It was a pretty thing, chestnut and white-footed, and if it disdained the weight of a mortal—and one that had never cared for horses much—it had the grace not to show it. I was only grateful that it did not throw me off—and that the servant did not also offer me a spear.

She did, however, lead the horse through the crowd towards the Queen. I took the opportunity to put on my hat. Though I did not need it against the waning sun, I felt less vulnerable with its brim shadowing my face. "Little mortal," the Queen said, as the servant bowed herself away. "I see this time my gifts met with your approval."

"My order has no stricture against function, Great Queen. I accept your generosity with gratitude."

"Do you hunt, little mortal? Or does your order forbid that as well?"

"I have ridden with the Sidiana on hunts, Great Queen. I claim no skill at it myself."

"Ride with us then. Ractors are dangerous and we have made oaths upon your safety."

Oaths she had made, but that had not stopped her from ordering her lover, her son, to seduce me. But I had resolved not to think of that.

"I thank you for the honour, Great Queen." I bowed my head and then managed to manoeuvre my horse into position amongst her retinue. Ferrell gave me a disdainful look, Daen an opaque one. I pretended I had seen neither and took great interest in the assembly of the hunt.

The crowd now bristled with spears, looking more army than hunt. I saw that the saddles, mine included, were equipped with brackets, suitably embellished, to hold the weapons.

Daen's black warhorse danced backwards beside me and I realized again how massive it was; my own mount's withers came only halfway up its chest. "Be careful, Sidi. Stay with the Queen's guard and you'll be safe enough."

"What are ractors?"

"Lizards," he replied and grinned at my no doubt baffled expression. "Very big lizards."

A horn sounded and there was a flurry of motion as the hunt assembled. My horse seemed quite content to keep its place behind Daen's warhorse, between two of the Queen's guard. I found it hard to imagine a lizard large enough to require the spears they bore and was torn between curiosity and the hope that there was nothing but mice and grouse in the low hills beyond the walls.

Another horn called and the hunt flowed out through the arch of the open gate. A path had been beaten in the dry earth, leading into the rocky hills. The only vegetation was withered and sere; a twisted tree clinging to the bank of an underground stream, a clump of barren twig blowing across the sand.

The procession began across the empty landscape towards the hills and I noticed that the sky had not changed since that first moment in the courtyard, that the moon and the sun were still precisely balanced in the sky, the light retaining a strange twilight clarity.

As none of the fey around me seemed to fear imminent attack by large lizards, I urged the horse forward to ride beside Daen. "Where is this place?" I asked. "Is it in the mortal world or the fey?"

"Both," he said. "The land is real. You could get to it from Lushan if you knew how. But it might be a thousand years in the past or a thousand years in the future. It's as if you could suspend a moment in the world and move through it. When you're gone, the world goes on as if you had never been there."

"So the sun doesn't set and the moon doesn't rise."

"Exactly. And whoever lives in the palace doesn't wonder why their yard is suddenly full of fey."

"But the ractors move."

He laughed at that. "We're not hunting statues, Sidi, though that would certainly be easier. Less sporting, though." Which was not really an explanation but would have to serve.

He told me about ractors. They were predatory, mortal-sized, quick and fierce. Arrows were not guaranteed to pierce their scaled skins so the fey hunted them with spears. If the terrain permitted, they would hunt from horseback but there was more honour in a kill from the ground. When we reached the canyons, the hunt would separate into smaller parties, with the aim of driving whatever prey they could find into the larger central canyon. "Once in a while one will attack from the rocks. They try to disembowel the horses and then pounce on the downed rider."

"And if one attacks?"

"Hope it gets its claws stuck in the horse and get behind the first spear you can find, Sidi."

"Useful advice, as always. Thank you."

"Don't worry, Sidi. If a ractor attacks your horse, I'll rescue you."

"I suppose it would be easier than explaining to the Queen why you have allowed her to be forsworn," I replied tartly but I found the promise rather comforting, whatever his motives for offering it.

"True, especially as the Queen is already displeased with me." He smiled as he said it but it did not touch his eyes. We had not spoken of the Queen's command since that duel and I was content to leave it unmentioned, if not forgotten.

We passed into the canyons, beyond the reach of either moonlight or setting sun. Cold blue light flared at the top of the fey spears and settled into a glow that lent the stone walls around us an austere beauty. "I gather we do not take them by surprise," I said and this time Daen's grin was genuine.

At the junction of three canyons, dark gashes in the rock, the hunt separated. There were ten in our party, including the Queen's Guard, and we ventured into the centre canyon. It was wide enough to allow four horses to ride abreast. The spear-lights cast shadows on the rocky ground and turned the fey ghostly.

Several minutes down the canyon, my horse snorted and tossed its head. I could hear the creak of leather as the other riders reacted to their mounts' distress. I feared what my own unease might cause the horse to do, and gripped the saddle pommel like a child. Even my slow, careful breaths did not quell the sudden coldness in my belly, the race of my heart. In the front rank of the guard, soldiers lowered their spears.

In the darkness ahead of us, I heard the rattle of stones.

The canyon widened suddenly, opening into a circular vale before closing once again. Given Daen's description of the hunt, I expected to see the blue lights of the other hunting parties, but there was nothing but darkness and silence. The spears flared and light brightened, sending moonlight where the moon could not reach.

COLD HILLSIDE

The ractor waited at the edge of a scree slope. It was a lizard only by courtesy, I thought, looking at the long, ugly jaw edged in teeth, the scaled body hunched over the powerful back legs. It cocked its head like a bird, black eye tracking us as the hunt spread out before it.

"The first kill is yours, Champion," Ferrell said softly and the cold dread inside me uncoiled. This was like the duel, another move in the Queen's game of wills with Daen. But he knows it, I thought. He has killed ractors before. He is the Queen's Champion.

He is her son. She would make him kill but she would not let him die.

Daen swung down from his warhorse, loosed his glowing spear and walked towards the ractor.

It watched him come, seemingly hypnotized by the blue glow, its heavy head dipping to track that light. When it seemed as if he could simply walk up and place the spear in its breast, it moved.

It bounded sideways and drove forwards, great teeth snapping, one taloned foot coming up to rake the spot Daen had vacated one second earlier. It swung its head, too far past to close its teeth over his arm, but enough to knock him sideways.

He regained his balance a heartbeat later, the spear lifting as it turned. It dodged but he was ready, bringing the weapon around to catch it as it darted forward again. The blue light vanished as the point pierced the creature's side. Its scream echoed off the cliffs and ended when Daen's sword cut off its head.

I let out my breath, aware I had been holding it. That was not so bad, I thought.

And then the second ractor came out of the darkness and bore Daen to the ground.

Someone gasped. The guard urged their horses forward, their spears coming down.

The ractor screamed and fell backward, scrabbling on the rocks. Daen staggered to his feet, shaking his head, his sword arm hanging limp.

A guard set his spear and kicked his horse forward.

"Hold." The Queen's voice was cold and clear.

The ractor went in again, great talons flashing in the blue light.

There was stone beneath my feet, though I did not remember dismounting. A spear came down, a bar of metal and light in front of me. "Do not move, mortal," Ferrell's voice said, somewhere above me.

279

I had been wrong, I thought numbly. She would let him die.

I do not know how he evaded the killing blow, but he did, falling back onto the rock as his knee gave way beneath him. He was retreating, half-crawling back towards the dead ractor. Its mate bore down, one clawed foot landing on his leg, its head snaking down to seize flesh and bone.

This time, it was his voice, scream and curse and war cry combined, that echoed off the walls and then his sword flashed in the false moonlight. The ractor's blood fountained black in the silver air and its head rolled across the sand.

No one moved as Daen hauled himself to his feet, methodically cleaned his bloody sword and then restored it to its sheath. He limped over to collect first one head then the other, dragging them behind him across the sand. Half his face was shadowed, painted with the last beat of the ractor's heart.

He passed the guards raising their spears and dropped the heads at the feet of the Queen's white horse. She said nothing, her face still and unreadable in the ghastly blue light. Her mount, less disciplined than she, took a step backwards. Daen did not bow or offer her any other courtesy, simply turned to move slowly towards his waiting mount.

As he drew alongside Ferrell and me, he stopped. "What are you doing off your horse, Sidi?"

"I believe the mortal was planning to rescue you," Ferrell said with amused contempt.

"Get that spear away from her or I'll cut your head off too. And you, Sidi, get back on your horse."

Ferrell obeyed him. I did. If he had looked at the Queen that way I was not surprised she had found no words to say.

Mounted once again, he retrieved his waterskin, dumped its contents over his head, scrubbed at his bloody face with an equally bloody glove, and then tossed the skin away. I wondered what the mortals of this world would think, finding two beheaded ractors and an empty waterskin. It was a foolish thing to wonder but it was safe. There were far more dangerous thoughts circling like vultures, waiting to find words.

One of the soldiers collected the heads and then, at some unseen command, the hunt turned around and left the canyon as silently as we had entered it.

The other two parties found us on the road and they fell in, laughing and gossiping as if their merriment could dispel the grim silence of their Queen. Gradually, the silence caught them too, until only the thud of hooves and the creak of leather accompanied us through the twilight.

In the courtyard, I wondered what it was like to be one of the inhabitants of the castle. Did they notice their world freezing between one step and the next, one word and the next? Did they feel a strange chill, a breeze blown from one world to another, a momentary double vision bright with alien splendour?

A servant materialized to take the horse. I dismounted and looked for Daen. He was standing by his greathorse, head bent against the beast's neck. It turned its head to push his shoulder and I saw its amber eye gleam. The court moved around him, like a bright stream around a boulder.

I went to stand beside the saddle and put my hand on the stirrup to steady myself. He rolled his head to look at me, his own eye white again the blood-smeared skin and hair. "Tell her," I began, looking past him, to the blind screens of the mortal palace. "Tell her she has won. Tell her I consent."

Then I walked out the courtyard, into the cold corridors of the Court, past all chances to change my mind.

The guards took me back to my room. There was no further summons; I supposed that the Queen considered my part in the day's drama done. I was not ungrateful for being ignored, for I could not imagine sitting through whatever elaborate feast the Queen conjured in ironic celebration of her champion's victory.

The only drawback to being abandoned was that it left me little to do but wait for—whatever happened next.

I filled the hours as sensibly as I could. I lay in the always hot water of the bath until my fingers and toes wrinkled, then dressed in my sleeping robe. It made me feel far more vulnerable than my usual attire, but all those layers of cloth seemed unnecessarily impractical for the act to which I had committed myself.

I read Aurelian, though the words swam into nonsense as they reached my eyes. I meditated, striving to reach the point where I could watch my fear and regret float past me. The candles burned down, one by one, until only one lantern was left. I lay on the bed, drowsily watching the flame behind the pierced metal illuminate a golden moon and stars.

The knock on the door startled me from near-sleep. For once, he waited for me to answer it.

"I'm sorry it's so late, Sidi. Did I wake you?" I shook my head and held the door open, mute invitation. He came in and we stood in silence for a moment. The blood had all been washed away and I realized that some of it must have been his, for there was a new cut above his brow. "Did you really get off your horse to try to help me?"

"I don't know," I said. "I don't remember doing it. I was just there, and then Ferrell stopped me. It was for the best, I suppose. I don't know what I could have done. Throw rocks, perhaps."

"You were the only one to try, Sidi. I thank you for that."

"The guards would have done something," I told him, to be fair. "She stopped them." I took a breath and let it out. "Did you tell her?" He shook his head. "Why not?"

"I thought I should give you a chance to change your mind."

Given that unexpected grace, I almost did. Instead, I hugged my shawl tighter and shook my head. "It would come to this in the end."

"What of your vows?"

"Should I be the only Asezat in Lushan to honour them?" It was meant for humour but somehow came nowhere near it. "You know what my faith is worth. And Jennon's compassion would not hold words above lives."

"A fey life," he pointed out.

Your *life*, I thought.

"I am not a virgin," I said abruptly. "I know how the act is done."

"That's good."

We lapsed into silence again and the last candle guttered out, leaving only the patterned moonlight and the shelter of the dark.

I thought—when I had let myself think of it—that I would simply lay on the bed, lift my gown and it would be over in a heartbeat or two. What he might want, or need, had never crossed my mind. When I realized that it was not to be merely a thrust or two, short of rape only by my consent, it was too late; my robe and his clothes were gone and the sheets were cool beneath my skin.

I suppose it should not have surprised me that he talked during it, a steady, soft litany of reassurance. I found it oddly comforting, letting the words wash over me, ignoring their sense—or nonsense—and listening only to the quiet rumble of his voice. Perhaps he needed the comfort as much as I. I had only to endure, after all, but he had to perform.

I panicked only once, when the full weight of him was on me. For a moment, crushed beneath him, I could not breathe, could not think, and I pushed against the heavy strength of his shoulders, whimpering. From far away, I heard his voice, a low croon of reassurance, then he thrust into me. My cry of shock and pain had barely ended when he rolled away, pulling me up over him. Free of his warm weight, the air chill on my bare skin, I could breathe and think again. It was only the illusion of control but I was grateful for it nonetheless, for it made it easier to bear what must be borne.

It hurt, but not as much as I had feared, and, at any rate, it was over soon enough.

When it was done, it seemed churlish to shrink from him and reclaim a distance in the cold bed so I made myself lie in his arms, my head against his shoulder. His fingers touched the back of my neck, curved around the shape of my skull with surprising delicacy. I felt the warmth of lips, the soft brush of beard against my skin. It drew an involuntary shiver and I lifted my head, to protect the flesh that felt suddenly more naked than it had since the dawn I first shaved away my hair.

His mouth touched my forehead, the corner of my eye. I knew what would happen next, though he had not tried to kiss me in all the awkward moments that had gone before. I could have stopped him from doing so now but did not, from weariness or gratitude or curiosity. To my own surprise, my mouth did not fill with ash against his, my blood did not roar in my head with terrified thunder. I pulled away from him, from his careful mouth and careful hands, and wrapped myself in the cold embrace of the abandoned blankets.

We stayed like that a moment, in our separate spaces of the bed, then he rolled to his feet and began to retrieve his clothes. I sat up, pulling the blankets tighter, and stared at the latticed window, the silver light bright in my eyes. "Will she let you be now?"

"I hope so." I felt his weight on the mattress again and looked at his back as he pulled on his boots. "I regret if I hurt you. It seemed necessary to get the business done."

"I know." I understood it, that abrupt penetration that had replaced anticipation of pain with pain itself and thus let it pass. "You were very kind."

"Not the compliment I usually wish to hear in bed," he said with a trace of weary amusement, "but thank you, Sidi." He had called me Sidi during it all, his voice turning the title into a strangely intimate endearment. He rose, a dark shape in the dark room, in a place the lattice-bound moonlight did not reach. "And I owe you thanks for this as well, for suffering it for my sake. I'll see you in the morning, Sidi. Sleep well."

I nodded, waiting in my shroud of blankets until the door had opened and closed on the sliver of torchlit hallway. I knew what I should do next, the practical motions required. The bath, perpetually warm, waited just beyond the curtains. In it, I could wash him away, seed and scent and the skin-memory of touch, weight, warmth. It was simple and necessary, a routine I had once done without either relief or regret.

It was a routine I would do again now, I told myself, shivering beneath the blankets. But it was a long time before I did.

CHAPTER 39

Teresine

I thought that after the hunt, and what had followed it, the Queen would be content to ignore me once again. But the next night, after the silent guards had left me at the door to my room, I discovered another invitation . . . and another dress.

As I touched the gold-embroidered fabric, I knew this was a gift I would not be allowed to decline. No matter how little I wanted to wear the finery of Deshiniva, to refuse to do so would be a defiance I could not risk.

So I dressed: the short chemise, the narrow skirt, the heavy, gilt-encrusted belt that lay low across my hips. My body remembered this, the constricting silk of the skirt, the weight of the ornamented straps of the chemise, the thongs of the sandals between my bare toes. The chemise buttoned up the front, for which I supposed I should be grateful, I thought ruefully. If the Queen had chosen to gift me with the most elaborate of Deshiniva clothing she would have had to supply me with a maid to fasten me into it.

The last item I held in my hands for a long time. It was a golden helmet with its crowning spike and circlet of jewels. In Deshiniva, my hair would have flowed out beneath it, oiled into an inky curtain that fell to my hips. Here, it would hide the bare curve of my skull and erase the years that lay between the girl in Deshiniva and the Asezat in Lushan.

At last, I set it on the dresser and instead painted my eyes with Chadrena's cosmetics, then fastened the silver and coral bracelet around my wrist. Those protections in place, I stepped back to consider my reflection.

I felt a moment of dizzying disjunction, the memories of enacting this same ritual swamping the true image in the mirror. In Lushan, mirrors existed only to determine that my face was clean, my head properly shaved. In Jayasita, my safety had depended on what I saw there;

the perfect creation of Deshinivi femininity, no hair or line of fabric out of place, no trace of self visible beneath the armour of cosmetics and gilt.

I had forgotten what the gold looked like against my skin, forgotten the arch of my collarbones, the shadows between my breasts. I had forgotten I had once been beautiful. With a trace of terrified pride, I realized I still was.

In Deshiniva, beauty had been my curse and my power. In Lushan, it had not mattered, save in the way that a pleasant appearance had its uses. My darkness and my shaved head had defined me more than any beauty could.

I shifted the deep neckline of the chemise and remembered that the back swooped as low, baring spine and shoulder blades. Turning, I peered at my left shoulder in the mirror. Even in the flickering candlelight, I could see the pattern of the tattoo on my skin. It had been placed so that it could be seen, ownership and advertising combined.

I knew there was at least one person in the Court who would know what it meant.

The translucent gold-shot scarf that still lay on the bed would cover, if not conceal, it. I fastened it to the shoulder of the chemise with one of the pins from my sash, and hoped that there would be nothing brighter than candlelight at the Queen's feast.

I had barely finished this hasty camouflage when there was a knock on the door. To my intense relief, it was not Daen, but another anonymous guard come to escort me. I had not seen Daen all day and, like as not, tonight he would be safely tethered by the Queen's side. We would have to speak to each other eventually but I was cowardly enough to hope for some delay.

As soon as I had seen the dress, I knew what the Queen had planned for the evening. I believed that, forewarned, I was prepared for it. But, as with the ballroom of glass flowers, the reality of it was still overwhelming.

It was the palace of Jayasita in all its glittering, perfumed glory. I had walked this dark wooden floor before, I had seen these walls of woven gold, seen the niches with their dazzling god-statues, had gazed up at the high ceilings and the patterns of jewels that created new constellations there. The air held the scent of jessamine and spices I remembered and beyond the open doors I could hear the night birds singing.

Low tables were set around the great room, pillows and fey heaped about them. The aromas arising from the feast already being served made my mouth water. At the end of the room, a raised pavilion of translucent veils of gold and bronze sheltered the Queen's table. The centre curtains were drawn back but the Queen was nothing but a dazzle of gold.

The guard had left me at the doorway and I had to walk the length of the room alone, skirting the long pool in the centre, where lotuses bloomed white and fragrant and golden fish darted in the blue-tiled depths.

A soldier stopped me at the end of the pool but I heard the Queen's voice calling to let me approach. I stepped forward and bowed. When I lifted my head, I saw the Queen standing at the edge of the dais.

In my room I had indulged in the brief vanity of believing myself beautiful. I had long prided myself on my immunity to fey beauty. The Queen ended both notions.

She was dressed as I was, in chemise and skirt and belt. She too had left off the golden crown but there the similarities ended. Her skin was honey and amber, her hair so black it looked like night pouring down her back. She was everything of grace, symmetry and elegance in Deshiniva, refined and perfected, distilled to an essence that left no room for doubt or even breath.

Against that perfection, I was nothing but mud and dust.

"Great Queen," I managed to say through the hollowness in my throat.

"Little Mortal." Her smile was like sunlight on water. "Are you pleased with your gifts this time?"

"Yes, Great Queen."

"And this—is it not your homeland?"

I nodded numbly.

"Good. We thought perhaps you grew homesick for it. Your people have some gift for beauty, it seems."

"It is no match for your own, Great Queen." It was nothing more than the truth.

She laughed and I bowed, grateful to retreat, though I had no idea where I was going. It was not until she had turned away that I glanced at the pavilion again and saw the others there; Ferrell, a fey woman in red, Daen in his dark coat, no trace of Deshiniva about him at all.

I heard my name and saw Lindel waving from his indolent spot in a heap of silken cushions. The faces I knew were there: Ilene, Bastien, Hilare.

I felt a spark of resentful gratitude, then considered what other company I might be forced to endure and went to them. At least we knew each other, in a fashion.

"You look quite lovely, child," Bastien said kindly.

"She's an Asezat. I think there are rules against such compliments, aren't there, Sidi?" Lindel said.

"I accept such compliments in the spirit in which they are given, Lord Lindel. Thank you for your kind words, Lord Bastien."

"You always forget her claws, Lindel." Ileane's laughter rippled.

"I forgive you your claws, Sidi. But I do not forgive you excluding us from the drama yesterday. Are we not your closest companions in the Court? Or," I saw his elaborate glance towards the Queen's pavilion, "nearly so."

"Drama, my Lord?"

"The hunt. Our little group found nothing but stones and dust. Meanwhile you were throwing yourself from your mount to rescue the Queen's Champion from the claws of ractors."

I managed to laugh, only a little shaky with relief. "Whoever told you the tale exaggerated greatly, Lord Lindel. I do assure you I threw myself nowhere and Lord Daen was quite capable of dealing with ractors without any assistance from me."

"Whatever happened, it seems to have served to mend his quarrel with the Queen," Ilene observed. "She seems well-pleased enough with him now."

"No doubt not nearly as pleased as she'll be later," Lindel added with a salacious grin and a glance at me. I looked back at him blandly.

"Your land must be indeed beautiful," Bastien said, with a firm air of someone intent on changing the subject. "And the fare is quite delicious. Will you not taste it and tell us if it is true?"

He was right. The dishes unveiled on the low table made my mouth water with their scent, and burn with their wonderful heat. They were Deshiniva cuisine at the highest level and I could not help but devour them all. But even as they satisfied my body's craving, they did what the recreated palace's glamour could not. They made me homesick, not for Deshiniva, but for Lushan. I remembered the night before the fair and Raziel's gift, a meal not nearly so accurate but a thousand times more precious to me.

COLD HILLSIDE

The conversation at the table turned back to fey gossip, with only the occasional barb thrown my way. No one mentioned the hunt again. I stayed as long as seemed polite, then took the chance to retreat to the open doors, curious as to whether the Queen's magic had created a false Jayasita to match the false palace.

Beyond the veils, the long terraces stepped down to the riverside. Torches burned in patterned glass and metal cages, candles floated on their flower-boats in the still pools that lined the edge of each level. Beneath the moon, the river was silver and black, set with gold where boats passed, their lanterns lit. Across that expanse, the city was another darkness, inlaid with gold.

It all looked real; the air smelled of the river and the gardens and the torches, I could hear the faint brush of waves on the rocks of the dock below me. Yet there was something false about it as well, a sense of suspension, as if with one wrong breath it would dissolve away.

I walked down the steps, passing each empty terrace, until I stood at the edge of the river. On the far side, the city stretched across the horizon from end to end. Unable to resist, I bent down to put my hand into the water. It was water, nothing else.

I heard a footstep behind me and rose. Daen looked past me, across the river. "It's beautiful from here, isn't it?" he said casually and I nodded. "Do you miss it, Sidi?"

I shook my head. "Lushan is my home. Though," I could not help a smile, "please trust I am grateful the Queen did not choose to summon *that* palace for the evening."

"It's all the damn iron," he said with a grin.

"Is it real?" I asked, looking back at the city. "If there was a boat here, could we cross the river and be in Jayasita?"

"No. We'd be able to go so far, far enough that it would seem the city was just a breath away, and then we'd take the last step and be back where we started." I glanced at him, startled by the bitterness in his voice. "Trust me, Sidi. I know."

"But Isbayan and . . . Varansheld. They were real. Why could one have walked into those worlds and not this one?"

"The Queen was not there."

"Is that how you travelled to all those places? Chose a door and passed through it?"

"Sometimes. Others, I did it the hard way. It never made any difference. Eventually, I'd open a door and I'd be back."

"Would you truly leave this place?"

"Why do you suppose I keep trying?"

"Because you know you can always come back."

"Do you think you're the only one who would choose freedom over slavery, Sidi?"

"You might choose being a prince over being a penniless exile."

"I'm not a prince. Do you suppose I'm her heir? A son she bore simply for the sensation and the future sport? I may live longer than a mortal but never long enough to see the end of her. And there are only Faerie Queens. So yes, Sidi, I would truly leave this place if she would let me go."

He was angry, though not at me. I did not know why I pressed, except perhaps that I had once made my own escape.

"Do you know what time of year it is, outside the Court?" I asked, because it seemed a safe question. He shook his head, hunting in his coat for a cinquegrass stick. He lit it from the nearest torch and exhaled smoke towards the sky. "I have tried to keep track of the days," I admitted, "and think it must be close to midwinter."

"Likely enough. Does it matter?"

"My work on the mosaic goes well. If I finish before the passes clear . . ." I did not complete the sentence, finding no way to say it without accusation.

"The Queen won't turn you out in the snow to walk home, Sidi. When you finish, the passes will be clear. It's that simple."

"It is not at all simple," I protested.

"Simple or complicated, do not fear, Sidi. If it comes to it, I'll take you home."

"Thank you, Lord. It would be much easier, I suppose, if there were a door conveniently near—" I stopped. There was a door. Of course there was a door. Not in Lushan, of course, but somewhere nearby, somewhere there was no iron to deter their passage. But neither of us would say that out loud.

For a moment, there was silence, broken only by the water on one side and the faint drift of music from the palace on the other. "There was much talk during the feast," I said at last, "the Queen and her champion are no longer estranged. So it would seem that she is satisfied."

The look he gave me recalled Lindel's jest and I regretted my choice of words and the involuntary heat beneath my skin. "She got what she wanted," he said. "She is always satisfied when the world runs to her command."

"Well. That's good, then," I said, awkward with relief. We could consider the business finished, a whim of the Queen's now indulged and to be forgotten.

I saw Daen's gaze move past me, back up the terraces towards the palace. In the shadows, his expression stilled, unreadable, his eyes in darkness. I turned to follow his look and saw the palace doors spilling a golden flood of fey down the terraces, the Queen in its centre.

"It seems my service is required elsewhere, Sidi." His voice was flat. I nodded, looking for my own escape as he flicked his cinquegrass into the river and walked up the steps to meet the Queen. There was nowhere to go but the corner of the dock behind me, beneath the sweep of an overhanging branch.

Boats materialized on the river; low, lantern-lit barques, gilded and graceful. They swept into the dock as the crowd of the fey descended. None of the assembly glanced my way. I watched Daen take the Queen's hand and help her into the first barque. There seemed more fey than the boats could ever hold but in a blur of gold and rippling laughter, they were gone.

I stood still for a moment, watching the lanterns turn to fireflies and then vanish around the bend in the river. I wondered where they were going, where they could possibly go in the false world.

There was nothing for me to do but to climb the stairs back to the palace and look for some way back to my rooms. As I did, I suddenly understood what the night had meant.

Tonight had been a demonstration of the Queen's power: to recreate a world I had lost, to give me back my awareness of my physical beauty and then reduce it to a faint shadow of her own glory, to play at honouring me and then turn me invisible in the space of a breath, to order her lover into my bed and then take him back to her own.

The only thing I did not understand was why she thought such a demonstration necessary at all.

CHAPTER 40

Teresine

I finished the mosaic some weeks later, when by the marks in Aurelian, midwinter had come and gone.

As if the night of the Deshiniva feast had settled all matters, the Queen had let me be. There were no more summons to banquets, hunts or duels and, if it meant I spent each evening alone, I was grateful for that grace, if lonelier than I was prepared to admit even to myself.

In the perpetual summer of the courtyard, I had less time for loneliness and, after a week of absence, Daen resumed his occasional duties as escort and company. Neither of us mentioned the hunt and its aftermath. I grew accustomed once again to his moods, stories and the smell of cinquegrass in the still sunlit air.

When I finished the mosaic, everything polished and prodded and inspected, I sat down on the tumble of the wall and looked at it. It was beautiful, in its own way, though that way was alien to Deshiniva, Lushan and the Court. The subtle graduations of the dark stones, the winding shapes barely perceptible among the seemingly random tones had a hypnotic power that, crouched close to it, I had never truly seen.

I still had no idea if what I had recreated bore much resemblance to what the Aygaresh had made, or why the Queen had wished it restored.

But if she was satisfied with it, then she must send me home.

And if she was not? I had an uncomfortable vision of having to take the mosaic apart stone by stone and restore it again, for the remainder of my mortal days, because the Queen was displeased. We had hedged the bargain with protections, Raziel and I, but the Queen was older and slyer than either of us could live to become and I had no doubt she could find a way to trap me in the cold limbo of the Border Court if she so chose.

I heard the sound of horns, bright and sudden, and the world around me blurred. When it cleared, the sun was gone, replaced by torches that flared around the courtyard. Beyond their smoke, the moon was a huge silver disc.

The Queen stood in the doorway, silver and mother of pearl, turning even the golden torchlight white where it touched her. I saw faces around her—Ferrell, Bastien, Daen—and the sweep of Madelon's wings.

I rose from my place and bowed my head, waiting.

"Little mortal." I looked up. She had not moved—*dared not? I wondered*—and her black gaze was on me, not on the mosaic on the far side of the courtyard. "Your task is done?"

"As well as I can do it, Great Queen, yes."

"The bargain is fulfilled. Your Little Queen may have you back." I was not certain if I imagined the distant amusement in her voice and wondered again what power she might have to see the thoughts mortals believed they concealed. Though I supposed it would not have taken magic to guess what I might be thinking, I still found it unnerving.

"Thank you, Great Queen."

"We have found your presence among us interesting, little mortal." A breath of laughter stirred in the night air. "We would be pleased to grant you one boon, as reward for such interest and your work."

"I have no need of a reward, Great Queen."

"One boon," she said again, iron beneath the soft voice. "Whatever you might wish—save what might touch upon the old agreements."

Behind her, I saw Ferrell smile, as if anticipating some folly I was about to commit. I could not imagine what it might be; there was nothing I wanted, nothing the Queen could grant me I might wish beyond safe passage home.

"You are generous, Great Queen, but—"

"One boon."

Thoughts flickered of gifts I might request that held no hidden traps: a jewel, a flower, the luxury of my endlessly warm bath. Absurd things all. I saw Daen, standing a pace behind the Queen and almost sent him a look of desperate appeal. No doubt there were a dozen things he could suggest.

No doubt . . .

It *was* folly, of course, but the Queen could refuse. Daen could. It cost me nothing but the contemptuous gossip of the Fey Court to ask.

"Then I would ask that you grant Lord Daen the freedom of the mortal world, if that is what he wants."

I looked at the Queen's white face, the depthless dark eyes. The courtyard seemed utterly silent, as if even the torches held their breath.

"*Is* that what you want?" Her unreadable gaze did not leave mine but I knew she was not speaking to me.

"Yes."

"If you go, there will be no return. No door will open for you."

"I know."

"Her iron world will kill you."

"There are places in the world without iron."

"But none that can be claimed without price. Will you pay it?"

"Yes."

"You must take her to her iron city. What you do then is your choice," she shrugged, eloquent dismissal. "Your boon is granted, little mortal." There was nothing to read in her voice, no shadow to suggest anger or disappointment or satisfaction, no echo of anything that could be considered mortal emotion at all. I might have asked for a flower after all, and not for her champion, her son, her lover.

The horns sounded again. The torches flared, dazzling enough to blot out the moon, and then I was standing alone in the courtyard.

The Queen had taken the magic with her. There was snow on the ground now and heaped on the tumbled blocks, the uneven walls. My breath turned to clouds that the winter wind snatched away before it reached its greedy fingers into my robes for my body's heat as well. Above the walls, the sky was leaden, the mountains shrouded in clouds.

And so it ends, I thought. I was not certain the Queen had ever actually looked at the mosaic.

I heard a creaking sound, like ice breaking in the lake, and realized the great doors were beginning to close.

The bone-chilling air swept the last dazzlement from my mind and I ran, terrified I would be trapped in the courtyard and freeze to death in front of the wall I had remade.

Beyond the doors, the hallways were dark and cold. I knew my way through this part of the court by now, at least well enough that I could find my way back to a corridor the cold did not touch.

I rounded a corner, still shivering, my heart still hammering, and found light, warmth, and Daen.

"It is still winter," I said, an inadequate explanation, and he looked at me blankly. "Outside the court. She took the magic with her and the doors began to close."

"That's the bitch, true enough," he said with a laugh that held no amusement. "She never breaks her word, but she is not above making it impossible for it to be fulfilled. Perhaps she assumed I would not take your corpse back to Lushan."

I shivered, pushing my shaking fingers up under my sleeves in search of warmth. I could almost believe he was right and that the Queen had meant me to die in the cold courtyard.

"More likely she simply let the magic lapse," he amended. "She had what she wanted, after all."

"But what was that? She did not even look at the mosaic."

"Why did you ask her to let me go, Sidi?" he asked, ignoring my question.

"It seemed a shame to waste a wish. Everything I could have asked for myself is in Lushan and it was all I could think of." Said aloud, all the reasons that had made some skewed sense in the moonlit courtyard seemed foolish. "You have been kind to me."

"You keep saying that, Sidi," Daen said in exasperation, "but it isn't true. I'm not kind."

"Would you believe then that I did it because the Queen has taken so much from us over the centuries that it seemed only fair that I take something of hers?"

"If that was your goal, you'd have had the wit to choose something she values."

"I assume the Queen values her possessions because she possesses them, not because they have any intrinsic worth," I replied. "You were not obligated to accept, Lord."

"Is that what you hoped? That'd I refuse?"

"I hoped nothing, except that the Queen would cease to ask me and let me go home. Forgive me for seeking to help you. I can tell the Queen I have changed my mind."

"It's too late for that, Sidi. Neither of us has a choice now."

"You could have said no," I said, remembering the Queen's words about price and consequence. *Her iron world will kill you*, she had said, and it was true. Iron might not, but mortal life would, eventually. I was appalled at the magnitude of the choice I had forced on him so cavalierly. "I would not have been offended."

"I couldn't say no," he replied. "It is the only chance I'll ever have to be free of her."

"What happens now?"

"I've no idea, Sidi." He looked down the corridor at the closed doors. "Is there anything in this place you'd see a last time?"

To my surprise, there was.

There was autumn in the air in Isbayan, though the trees still held their leaves and the flower fields still spread beneath the blue, blue sky. The far-off hills were tinged with pale red, like dusty carpets heaped on the horizon. In the yard of the stone house, a dog barked briefly.

What would it be like, I wondered, to have the whole world—or a thousand of them—a single step away?

And why did the fey bother with the doors, when it seemed they never bothered to take that step?

"How far away is Isbayan, in the real world?" I asked.

"Months. Oceans and mountains and deserts away."

Not that far, I thought, but did not say. Not so far that Euskalan soldiers could not go there and come back. I remembered the Isbayan captain in the moonlit alley; that memory sparked others, more recent. I kept my face turned to the sun and pretended it was only its heat that I felt.

"Where will you go?"

"Damned if I know."

"To Varansheld?"

"Everyone I remember in Varansheld has been dead for a hundred years, Sidi. No one is waiting for Sigur Firebeard's son and all the welcome I would get would be a sword in my guts."

I looked at the fields, the hills, the lines of trees. He might one day ride that straight road through the valley but I would never see this place again. I took off my hat and found the faint trail that led down the fields.

"Sidi." Strange how he could make that word hold so many meanings. This time, it was a warning but I ignored it. After a moment, I heard him swear and then the sound of his boots on the path behind me.

The purple lavender smelled sweet but dry, of closed rooms and old chests. I picked a stalk or two and tucked them into my robe, the scent clinging to my fingers. I heard the dog begin to bark again. The door of the stone house opened and a woman came out, wiping her hands on the apron she wore.

She was older than I, with black hair and tanned skin and dark eyes that widened when she saw us. Behind her, the door filled with children, shadows of their mother. She turned and pushed them back inside, her gaze never leaving us as she set her body as a gate, to hold her children in, to hold us out.

I clasped my hands at my breast and bowed to her. She did not move, but only watched us warily as I bent to touch the yellow flowers in the first field. They were a little like the lilies of Deshiniva, though smaller, not so lush with rain and heat. I picked two, their stamens scattering crimson dust.

I bowed again and started back up the hill, Daen at my heels. "You'll be a story now, Sidi," he said. "They'll take you for one of the fey."

I almost denied it—I was too ordinary for that—then realized with my bronze skin, shaven skull and foreign clothing, I no doubt seemed as strange as the fey to that woman. Perhaps the fey felt as ordinary as I did, the mortal world being strange instead. Thinking of Madelon, the Queen, the fantastical fey who looked through me as if I did not exist, it seemed singularly hard to credit.

"I cannot be the first. Is this the door you rode out of when you came here?"

"Yes. But that woman would have been a babe in arms then. Why did you want those flowers?"

"To see if they were real," I admitted. "To take back something of this place with me. It would be easy to think it was all a dream."

Which was perhaps what the Queen would prefer, I thought uneasily. In all the years the Euskalan had been in Lushan, no one had ever gone to the Court, much less returned from it. At least, no record, no story, no whisper survived of such a thing. It seemed hard to trust that the Queen meant to let me go back to Lushan with all that I had seen of the Court's magic and wonder and all that I knew of its politics and dangers.

On the other hand, it was all too easy to imagine the ways—magical and otherwise—that the Queen might choose to keep her secrets.

"You must have strange dreams, Sidi," Daen said as he led the way between the trees and found the door in their shadows. "Though maybe

I should thank you for not calling it a nightmare."

"It has had its moments," I replied, thinking of the duel, the ractors, and the carrion creature in the white forest behind one of those numberless doors.

"I won't ask you which were which. Some things it's better not to know."

I laughed at that, a little, but realized with no small disquiet that he had been in almost all of them, dream and nightmare both. And I was taking him, dream and nightmare, back to Lushan with me.

CHAPTER 41

Teresine

Given the Queen's penchant for demonstrations of the glory of her Court, I expected to be summoned to another extravagant banquet to celebrate my departure. But there was no knock on my door, no flower exploded over my bed, no finery, welcome or unwelcome, appeared. Perhaps, to the Queen, I was already gone.

I indulged in one last shameless soak in the luxurious pool, shaved my skull of its latest bristle of dark hair and then packed away my belongings. That task was done in a matter of moments, for I was walking out of the Court with what I had brought into it: one change of clothing, Chadrena's gift of cosmetics, a bag of barley, nearly empty, a copy of Aurelian. The blooms of lavender and ilvenia I had picked that day, I left tucked into the pocket of the robe I would wear home.

I did not expect to sleep well, from anticipation and my lingering belief that the Queen would find some way to prevent my departure or keep the letter of her promise while subverting its spirit utterly, but I closed my eyes on darkness and opened them again with my face striped with the sun from behind the shuttered windows.

One last gift had been laid across the foot of the bed, a heavy coat of russet fur, a heap of shawls and scarves in bright wool, a knitted cap, and a pair of skin boots, furred inside, on the floor. At least the Queen did not mean to turn me out into the snow to freeze.

As usual, there was food and tea waiting but once I had dressed and eaten there was nothing to do but wait. It seemed to me I had spent a good deal of my time in the court that way, waiting here in the strange false familiarity of my room or in the unchanging summer afternoon of the mosaic courtyard.

I looked around the room, at the evocation of Jayasita that had never gone away, though over time bits of Lushan had bled back into it.

The chest of drawers was now painted wood, crimson and black and purple, and the hangings over the bed had thickened from translucent silk to black wool. But the window had stayed the same, carved wood screening southern sunlight.

I had nothing left to lose, I thought, or to fear. But my fingers still shook a little as I undid the little latch and pulled back the screeen. The river was a wide, slow swirl of brown. On the far shore, the jungle was a wall of a thousand colours of green.

I closed the window and sat down until my breath steadied. It was just as well I had never looked before; it would have made it no easier to endure the Court knowing how deeply into my past its magics could reach.

I was still sitting when there was a knock on the door.

The Queen might have meant the soldiers for a guard of honour, but I could not help the feeling of being led to execution just the same. We passed through the corridors, their torches flaring and dying to light our way, until we reached the place where I had first entered the Court. The room had seemed large enough to me that night; now its size seemed to have doubled to hold the multitude of fey that filled it. The doors stood open and beyond them I could see a swirl of snow against a dull sky. None of it passed the threshold, though, and no cold breeze stirred the scented air of the chamber.

The Queen was wrapped in white fur and pearls, diamonds gleaming in the torchlight, lace like cobweb frost up the white stem of her throat. Beside her splendour, Daen loomed dark and forbidding, in his black leather and grey fur. Only his face was pale, tiredness etched around his eyes. He looked grim and wary, as if he waited for the crack in the ice of the Queen's promises. Or perhaps it was their glacial immovability he feared; it was easier, after all, to play at exile than to be forced to it.

"I give you back to your Little Queen as I found you, as promised," the Queen said, as I bowed to her.

"I thank you for your kind hospitality," I replied, and heard the echoes of Daen's annoyance at the word in my head. He was right; it meant nothing, a platitude I mouthed along with all the other empty words I said to keep me safe. I wondered if we both meant our polite phrases for irony, the Queen because she knew I could not be as she had found me and I because I knew she had not ordered my seduction from any kindness at all. Whatever either of us meant, it was dismissal;

she clearly required no more of me. I had no idea what was to happen next and was grateful when I saw Bastien gesture to me from the crowd. I crossed narrow space in the centre of the room and let him bow over my hand. "We shall miss your company, child," he said kindly.

"And her claws," Ilene drawled, less kindly, from his side, with a glance at Lindel.

"I thank you all for the company and the conversation," I said, honestly this time. "My time here would have been much less pleasant without it."

"But not so pleasant that you are not eager to leave," a cool voice said and I turned to see Madelon behind me. She was in white as well; white feathers and furs, and her horned headdress was birch. Her wings shimmered opalescent behind her.

"I am happy to be going home, Lady, as there are no doubt many who are happy to see me leave."

She laughed, the sound like dark chimes. "No perfect politeness for me, mortal? No diplomatic compliments? I was not aware I had so offended you."

"You did not offend me and I hope I did not offend you. What offence can there be in truth?"

"Why, none." Her smile suggested amusement edged with malice. "But you should remember who of all of those here ever told you the truth." With that, she turned away, the flicker of those extravagant, alien, magical wings as sharp a dismissal as a raised fan in the Jayasita court had been.

"We shall look for you at the fair," Bastien said, as if our conversation had never been interrupted.

"Bring Daen with you," Lindel added with a grin.

"I do not imagine Lord Daen will stay in Lushan," I replied. "There is too much iron in it and too great a world beyond it."

"He could have had the world from here," Ilene said.

"But always with a leash to pull him back."

"We all are bound, mortal," Hilare said, "and not always reluctantly. It is easier to wish for things than to live with them."

"Be careful what you wish for," I quoted. At his curious glance, I added, "That is the moral of most of our tales of you."

"You did not heed it then."

"But I did not wish for myself, you see. There is nothing here I wanted."

Lindel laughed out loud at that, then Ilene. Even Bastien smiled. Hilare merely looked contemptuous. I knew what they thought, what all the court must think. It did not matter, I reminded myself, but wished suddenly for the cold wind beyond the open doors, that it might steal the heat I could feel beneath my skin.

"Goodbye, child," Bastien said, as if taking pity on me. "Your escort looks impatient not to lose the mortal daylight so we will let you go."

I glanced around to see Daen waiting by the open doors, glancing restlessly between the snow-flecked daylight beyond them and the torchlight chamber. When I turned back to bid a final polite farewell, Bastien and the others were gone. I saw a flare of jewels, a shimmer of wings in the darkness of the one of the corridors but otherwise there was no sign that the chamber, now back to its former size, had ever held the fey court. I had thought their departure would have caused nothing but relief; to my surprise the receding of the fey tide made me feel abandoned, like driftwood on a cold shore.

I felt the wind then, a blast of chill air that brought snow skittering across the stone floor. When I turned, I saw Daen's gaze linger where mine had been, down the empty corridor. I had heard no farewells for him, no last words from the Queen. I wondered if he had hoped for them. The torches in the corridor went out and I saw Daen take one step towards them, then stop, as if he had thought to test his power to light them again and then decided better of it.

"Well, Sidi," he said, "are you ready to go home?"

"I have been ready for that since the moment I walked through these doors," I replied, pulling my fur coat around me and stepping towards the cold glow of freedom.

I lifted my face for a moment, eyes closed, and drew in a breath of the sharp air, felt the cold touch of snow upon my skin. *This is real*, I thought with sudden exultation. It felt like the first real thing I had known in months.

"It *would* be snowing," I heard Daen say behind me and I laughed.

"But it's real snow."

"It's a pain in the ass either way, Sidi. But at least she kept her promise."

I opened my eyes and looked at him, then followed his gaze to the jumbled ruins to the left. From behind them came the sound of runners on snow, the faint jingle of bells and then our promised transportation appeared. It was a sleigh, elaborately carved and embellished in dark wood, and more than big enough for two. The seat was heaped with furs and there were brightly painted boxes tucked beneath the curve of the front.

Drawing it were two creatures that bore the look of fey horses, long-legged and elegant, but their elongated, not-quite-horse-like heads were crowned with sharp, twisted crowns of antlers. Their hides were as glossy black as the sleigh's wooden frame but the antlers were white as bone. The amber eyes, green half-hidden in their depths, were familiar. I wondered if one of them had once been a great black horse, or if fey magic gave all its creations that amused, knowing look, those gold-green eyes. I was relieved to see their breath steam in the cold air, just like any other mortal creature.

Their harness was bright, the vivid saffron, scarlet and purple tassels matching both the painted boxes in the sleigh and the shawls tucked into my bag. Fey magic also left nothing to chance, it seemed.

The equipage was undeniably beautiful and seemingly real enough to bear us through the mountains, though I was not certain that the sleigh had been designed for the narrow paths through the passes or the creatures' long legs for icy trails.

As if sensing my thoughts, one of them tossed its head, antlers raking the snowy sky. The bells on its bridle and harness rang beneath the wind. "Can we remove the bells?" I asked, the question directed partially to Daen and partially, I admit, to the gold-eyed creatures before me. "There is always the risk of avalanches."

"There won't be any avalanches," Daen said. Because the Queen had sworn my safety, he meant.

I thought of her dismissal and what I was taking from her. "Still."

He looked at me for a moment, and then found a knife somewhere in his clothing and cut the bells from the harness. The creatures rolled their eyes in amusement but suffered him to do it without resistance. He left the bells in the snow, gave me a glance that held a glint of the same mockery as the creatures, and then went to examine the boxes in the sleigh.

One was his, containing all that he was taking from the Court that was not on his back. The rest, their lids lifted, released the tantalizing aromas of hot food into the breeze. It seemed the Queen was not only willing to provide us with transportation but with sustenance for the journey. All we lacked now was shelter for the nights but I had little doubt that the sleigh contained some provision for that as well.

The wind would be at our backs, I thought, but already the cold had begun to seep into my toes, my fingers. I pulled the knitted cap over my bare skull, pushed my hat down on top it, and then climbed up into the sleigh. The wide bench creaked beneath Daen's weight as he settled in beside me. There were enough furs for both of us; beneath their weight, it was warmer than I had expected. Another gift of the Queen, I thought, and looked toward the Court. It seemed hard to imagine I spent three months in that ruin of tumbled walls and roofs cracked open to the sky. I wondered if somewhere in that maze there was a wall now covered in a re-imagined Aygaresh mosaic.

I saw Daen look around automatically for reins, then snort wryly as he realized there were none. "Well then," he said, to the dark backs of the beasts, "take us to Lushan."

I half-expected them to leap forward into the wild, unearthly pace his black horse had set across the plateau those three months ago. Instead, they shook their horned heads and set out in a stately trot, circling in a long curve to set our backs to the Aygaresh ruin and the wind-driven snow.

"How are we going to cross the crevasse?" I asked suddenly. "The bridge is gone."

"Sidi, I don't have the faintest idea."

That made me laugh, though I found the euphoria of leaving the Court was falling away behind me even as the ruins themselves vanished into the snow. I did not want to think about crossing the crevasse, or of what the passage through the mountains might hold, or what I would do when I reached Lushan.

Neither Daen nor I were pleasant company during that first long day of travel, too deep in our own thoughts to manage more than desultory conversation. If the Queen had been kind, she would have provided reins for the sleigh, to at least allow him the illusion of control.

The world passed in a whirl of white. At some point, I must have slept, for I woke to find myself curled on the bench, my head against Daen's arm, the furs wrapped over my shoulder damp from the steam of my sleeping breath. I sat up, straightening my hat and looking around at mountains whose peaks and cliffs seemed completely unfamiliar. "Where are we?"

"I don't know," he admitted and I heard the edge of suspicion and unease in his voice.

"There must be other ways through the mountains to Lushan that do not require crossing the plateau." He nodded, not convinced. The horned creatures (reindeer, of a sort, Daen told me, when I asked him if he had ever seen their like before) were moving at a steady, tireless pace, seeming not to notice the upward slope of the ground as they climbed towards a pass I could see glittering in the sun that was hovering just above the peaks behind us.

There was tea in one of the bright boxes, hot and fresh as if newly made. I sipped it gratefully, my mittened hands wrapped around the lacquered cup. The other box held thick soup studded with yeasty dumplings. "Do we need to ration it, do you suppose?" I asked as I found bowls and spoons.

"Probably not," Daen said, accepting the bowl I passed to him. "But only probably. Don't hold me to it." I scooped another generous helping into my bowl and he laughed. "It does not seem like you to be so trusting, Sidi."

"Perhaps I am too tired for suspicion. And I still have some barley, if it comes to that."

The reindeer kept their steady pace upwards, while the sun slipped away and the darkening sky above the eastern ridge of mountains sparked with stars. I wondered if they would keep moving through the night but just as the last red line of sunlight vanished, the reindeer found a place behind a jut of rock, somewhat sheltered from the wind, and then stopped with emphatic shakes of their antlers.

One of the boxes contained grain and feedbags, which Daen offered to them and they accepted as if they were indeed only beasts and nothing more. When I opened the food boxes again, they seemed as full of tea and soup as before. I supposed it was too much to expect that the fey magic would summon a varied menu, but it seemed churlish to complain of quite tasty soup twice in a row.

Eventually, of course, the consequence of the meal was another physical function. The wind and cold was enough to make the curve of the back of the sleigh an adequate screen for privacy. Daen followed my example, though I suspected he had considerably less modesty about such things than I did.

"Do you suppose the Queen thought to supply us with a tent?" I asked, as he climbed back into the sleigh. A search beneath the bench yielded some poles and several flat, wooden planks but no tent. In the twilight it was possible to see, but not for much longer, and there was no possibility of fire to provide either light or heat. Daen stood in the sleigh for a few moments, staring at the poles and planks, then shooed me off the bench to stand on the runner. He banged about with planks, poles and furs, swearing with enough genuine ill-humour to keep me silent after my first offer of assistance was declined.

With however little grace he managed it, the end result was a crude windbreak of furs, fastened to the poles and angled out over the sleigh's bench, which had been extended into a narrow platform by the planks, these having evidently been designed for a such a purpose. What had been a seat was now a low cave, with enough room for two bodies to lie, wrapped in the remaining furs, provided neither body had an overwhelming desire to turn over.

Though it was late afternoon—at the Court, I would still be at work on the mosaic—the darkness left us little to do but huddle into the cave and try to rest. There was room beneath the bench for our boots and the outer layers we wore could be used as secondary blankets. The fey magic would keep us warm but not so comfortable we could afford to disdain the heat of another body beneath the furs.

"Take the inner spot, if you want," Daen offered, as he loosened the buckles on his armour and added the grey fur to the pile of shawls I had already shed. I tucked my hat into the corner but left my knitted cap on; on such nights I wished for the hair I had shaved off that cold morning by the lake.

"Thank you, Lord. I will. My Deshiniva blood is still thin."

"Whereas my Varansheld stuff should be hardier, is that your argument? I offer you the warmer spot in self-defence, Sidi, lest you keep me awake with your shivering."

"That was wise of you then," I replied and slid into the nest of furs, shawls and robes before the wind could go all the way to my bones. The planks creaked as Daen moved in beside me, his bulk blocking my view of the white mountainside, the dark backs of the reindeer.

I shivered for a while, but it passed. We talked to pass the time: more stories of his travels, mine, more circumspect, of life in Lushan. At last, the spaces between the stops and starts of our conversation grew longer. I turned carefully in the space I had, to put my back to the night, and to him. He shifted as well, taking the space I had abandoned and I felt the press of his shoulder and back against mine.

Daen seemed to fall asleep almost immediately, his breathing turning to faint snores. I, unused to either the warmth of another body in my bed or snoring, found rest more elusive. At last, between considering elbowing him surreptitiously and summoning the nerve to do it, I fell into sleep.

CHAPTER 42

Teresine

The morning came, somewhere beyond a heavy veil of cloud that cocooned the sleigh. I lay in my own cocoon of furs and clothing and the heat of our bodies, waiting for Daen to wake. At last the increasingly urgent demands of my body compelled me to shake his shoulder carefully.

"At least it's not snowing," he grumbled, sitting up out of the nest and hunting for his coat.

"Do not say that too loudly."

"What, afraid of the malice of the mountain gods? I thought you had no faith, Sidi."

"I don't. But why take chances?"

He laughed and shifted stiffly out of the shelter to disappear behind the sleigh. I wrapped my own layers back about me and when he returned, took my turn. We drank our first cup of tea beneath the makeshift canopy after which he disassembled our shelter and I fed the reindeer.

Finally, all of us prepared for travel, the creatures started out on a path that only they seemed to see. I still did not know how the sleigh was going to make it through the mountains, whose switchbacks were now hidden beneath the ice-crusted snow. Perhaps the cloud was a gift after all; I would not be able to see the gorges and crevasses that might swallow us.

When the cloud lifted an hour or two later, it was to reveal a pristine slope that lay between us and our destination. The fey creatures did not even pause but began to climb. I tried to look at where they placed their broad-toed feet to determine why both antlered heads remained level on a slanted trail but I could see nothing. The snow beneath their feet and beneath the sleigh's runners seemed to waver in and out of my vision, as if the cloud had lowered into mist that obscured them.

It hurt my eyes to look at it and my mind to think of it. "Don't try,"

COLD HILLSIDE

Daen advised me, when I mentioned it and I noticed he was careful to keep his own gaze averted. As the sleigh made its first sharp turn, I gasped and closed my eyes. When I opened them again, we were still moving, still level, as impossible as it seemed.

It took hours to climb that slope. I could not decide which I found more terrifying: to be on the outer edge of the sleigh, with the empty space of the valley hanging beside me but with Daen's greater weight to anchor us to the hillside, or to be on the inside, with the slope beside me but that same weight now promising to pull us down.

I knew it made no difference and it was only fey magic that kept us there at all, but my stomach paid no attention to my mind. The thought that the entire process would be reversed on the other side was disheartening; I imagined that going down the slope would be infinitely worse.

Halfway up the pass, Daen began to tell a convoluted story about a pair of thieves he had met in Bijahur. I did not trust a word of it but it passed the time and gave us both something to think about besides the prospect of tumbling to our dooms. On the way down it was my turn and I, sadly, had not his gift for telling tales. I managed a muddled version of the epic tale of the war between the gods and demons that ended in the founding of Deshiniva, punctuated by the occasional in-drawn breath I could not suppress.

At last, the reindeer made their final turn and the snowy ground beneath us became level in truth was well as illusion. The clouds had cleared and I could see white peaks I recognized: The Snow Knife, the Floor of Heaven, and, closer, the Mother Mountain. From here, the path was not necessarily easy but there were no more dizzying passes to cross. At the pace the reindeer made, we would be in the city by the next day.

As much as my heart leapt at the thought of Raziel, of my own world, I could not pretend I was not also afraid. I had to plan a dozen things: what I would tell Raziel, how far I would let Daen accompany me, what we do with the reindeer and the sleigh. At least the journey over the pass had kept me from worrying about anything except dying there. I wondered if I did not prefer that worry to wondering what I had done, what I was bringing with me to the only home I had.

When the descending dusk caught us, and I was preparing myself for another night on the dubious comfort of the bench, I saw the house. It was more than a simple herder's shelter, though the roof above the second floor had collapsed and the once whitewashed walls had faded to grey stone. I could see the ghostly remnants of bright paint along the lintels of the open doorway to the windowless ground floor.

If we were lucky, there might yet be some fuel left inside for a fire but at the very least it would provide an escape from the wind. The reindeer seemed to share my hope for they veered from their course and headed for the house. I was grateful for that as well, as I could not imagine how we might force them to do it.

As it was, they obligingly drew the sleigh to a stop in front of the doorway then suffered themselves to be unhitched, leaving the sleigh to block the wind. They then found a sheltered spot behind the building, accepted their bags of oats, folded their long legs down and closed their eyes—a dismissal as regal as the Queen's.

We unloaded the boxes and furs into the darkness of the single room.

"There are candles there somewhere, in the box," Daen said

"I have no flint," I said, to the shadow blocking the doorway.

"I do," he replied. "If we need it." I heard no flint striking but the candles flared and I saw the flash of his grin. "One of the bits of fey magic I've always been good at."

There was no firewood—I should have known no Newari would abandon such a treasure except in direst emergency—but there was a cache of dried dung in one corner, left for the herders who might use this as a shelter in the summer. Daen looked disgusted at my explanation of its use, then left me to arrange it while he dragged the sleigh to block a little more of the wind that found its way through the open doorway.

A little while later, we were settled beside the fire, furs wrapped over our shoulders, the bounty of the lacquered boxes set between us. "How long will it take to reach the city?" Daen asked.

"We could be there by tomorrow by midday, if the paths are clear."

"Try to sound less reluctant, Sidi, or I might think you regretted your generosity already."

"It complicates things," I admitted. "I had the right to ask for your release but I have none to invite you into the city. That choice is the Sidiana's, not mine."

He snorted. "She would not make it easy, the Queen. That I take you into the city is a condition of my freedom. So it is entirely up to you, Sidi." He said the words easily but I could hear the shadows beneath them;

he could not like being at *my* mercy. Though I supposed compared to the Queen, it was a bit like being at the mercy of a housecat, when one has felt the claws of a tiger. Still, it was a strange thought, that I might have power over him.

"It would be best if I went alone first, to see Raziel and gain her consent. The fey are not loved in Lushan," that got another snort of laughter but I continued, "and your presence might cause the people some concern."

"And to arrive in such disreputable company in a sleigh drawn by magic beasts would do your reputation no good, either, would it?"

"No."

"What will you tell her?"

"The truth."

"All of it?" he asked, with a glance my way. I bent my head over my tea.

"There are things I would not say, if it is not required of me. She needs to know that you are the Queen's son and champion but . . ."

"Not that I was her lover."

"I can make no promises."

"I wouldn't ask you to, Sidi." He did not ask if I would tell Raziel about the Queen's command to him, about the night of the hunt, for which I was grateful. I did not have an answer.

I fell back on practicalities, to fill the silence. "There should be other shelters farther down the mountain. We could stop at one and I could take the sleigh on to the city. Once I have spoken to the Sidiana, we could return for you."

"Whatever you think best," he said so mildly I distrusted it immediately. He packed the boxes away again and then found a cinquegrass stick in his coat. A dry twig of old hay poked into the fire served as a wick. "You said you do not miss Deshiniva. Was that true?"

"Would I lie to you?"

"Of course you would." He exhaled a plume of smoke into the air. "Though why you would about that, I'm not sure."

I knew why he was asking. He had fled the court countless times but, I suspected, always knowing she would bring him back. He had lost one world in a choice that was no choice; now he was losing a second one.

"I do miss some of it. I miss the heat and the sun and smell of flowers. I miss being . . . ordinary. Being invisible, because every face you see is the same colour as yours. I miss the spices and the sound of the words.

I haven't spoken Deshinivi in many years. Do you miss Varansheld?"

"Yes. I miss the sound of waves on the shore. Being on the deck of a dragonboat when it leapt through the water. My father laughing in the Hall, while the men cheered." He paused, his gaze searching the fire. "Believing in what you were destined to become."

"Where will you go?"

"I don't know."

"It is hard not to feel . . . exiled," I said carefully, "even when one has chosen it. Because you have not really chosen a new place, but have chosen to leave the old one."

"The difference between landing on a shore and being washed up on one." I nodded and poked another flattened round of dried dung into the fire. The smoke made my eyes water but the smell of it was sweeter to me than the flowers of Deshiniva. Sometimes the shore you were washed up on was the place you were meant to be.

Daen finished smoking in contemplative silence. I watched the fire smoulder and let my thoughts drift with the distant moan of the wind.

We laid the furs on the far side of the fire, away from the door, wrapped ourselves up and settled down to sleep. Daen let me have the space closest to the warmth without comment.

"I thought the sleigh was uncomfortable," I muttered, shifting my hip from a rock that seemed to have materialized through the ground beneath me.

"It's not so bad, this place. I think I rather like it."

"Why?"

"Because it's not the Court and it's not Lushan. It's between. Anything can still happen."

"It does feel that way. As if we're outside time." Strange, I thought, after all the time in the Court, truly outside time, that I felt it here, back in the world again. "Outside ourselves."

"If you were not yourself, who would you be to end up here?"

"A shepherd," I replied promptly.

"Sidi, you've no poetry in your soul."

"An Asezat then, on retreat."

"You *are* an Asezat."

"A good one."

"Something else," he insisted.

COLD HILLSIDE

"An explorer, crossing the mountains from the great lost kingdoms to the north, the last of all the brave souls who had set out a thousand days before." Surely that was enough poetry to satisfy him.

"Well, if you're the last explorer, what does that make me?"

"My last porter." He laughed at that. "Your turn, if my tale does not meet your approval."

"No, Sidi. I don't imagine I could better that for poetry. Though perhaps you could be *my* porter, instead."

"We'll take turns at it," I said sleepily, the heat of the fire on my face. My mind, drawn back during the conversation, began its slow drift again. I shivered and burrowed into the furs.

I heard Daen shift and then he put his arm over me, his chest against my back. There was no sound but the wind and my own suddenly self-conscious breathing. I could feel his breath on the back of my neck but it was not as warm as my own skin, the heat rising up my throat to the beat of the blood in my ears. There was a tightness in my chest breath did not loosen, a weight deep in my belly my sense could not dissolve.

He meant it for comfort and warmth—but that was not all. I could pretend I did not know it and sleep the night beneath the shelter of his arm, tucked against the warmth of his body and we would both behave as if that was all that had ever been offered.

No matter what we had said, what fancies we conjured, we were not outside time, outside ourselves. This was place was real and Lushan lay less than a day away. But it was so easy to think it elsewhere and elsewhen, beyond the rules of the world. It was easy to stop thinking at all, in the sudden rush of things I had always believed I could not feel.

I turned, into his arms.

This time it did not hurt at all.

CHAPTER 43

Teresine

In the morning, we woke in our separate bundles of furs, a sword of cold air between us. We did not talk about what had happened the night before, not even to agree to silence. We did not need to; it had happened elsewhere, elsewhen, and had no more meaning in the light of the cold dawn than a dream might have had.

It was Daen who discovered the sleigh and reindeer were gone. In their place were two sets of snowshoes and a sled to which his belongings had been tied. "Well," I said, after a moment, "I did wonder how I was going to explain them. Perhaps the snowshoes are magic."

He made a sound of disgust and we set about packing up the remainder of our food and furs. If the snowshoes had been bespelled, the magic was very weak, and we floundered and fell and swore until we sorted out the best way to walk over the snow, Daen pulling the sled.

As the morning wore on and we tramped down the gentling slopes, the snow began to thin and then to disappear until we had to abandon the snowshoes and drag the sled over rock and dirt.

"We should not have to do this," I said, panting as I steered the runners past another rock. "I was only gone for three months. I kept track of the days. This part of the pass should still be snowbound."

"Remember what I told you, Sidi. Time in the Court runs at the Queen's pleasure. Let's hope that when we arrive in Lushan, it's your Sidiana you find there and not her great-granddaughter."

His words gave me another problem to worry at, though the Queen's promise that either I or word would be sent, suggested that my return would be tied to the world's time and not her own.

At last, we passed over a rise and there was Lushan below us in the distance, its golden roofs in muted glory against the snowy hills. I admit I breathed a thankful prayer at the sight, to whatever deity might care to hear. I glanced at Daen but his face was shadowed by his hat; I could not tell if he was relieved or daunted at the sight.

Just beyond the rise, there was a lonely cluster of buildings, part farm holding, part way station on the path down from the mountains. We had agreed that it was best for me to go into the city alone and for Daen to claim to be a traveller from the north, chance met coming over the passes as I returned from the monastery, which was close enough to seem plausible. His pack yielded some foreign coin, which the farmer accepted with some suspicion. It bought Daen a space by the smoky fire and a corner in which to pile his belongings and me a ride into the city on the back of a wagon driven by the farmer's son.

"I'll be back today, if possible. If it is too late, then tomorrow morning," I told Daen as we stood outside waiting for the wagon. "Be careful. The folk here are used to seeing travellers when the pass is clear, but it is early for that. Do not give them more to wonder at."

"Meaning do not talk too much, and especially do not drink and talk too much," he said, with just an edge of annoyance. "Trust me, Sidi, I have managed in places far more dangerous than this."

"I am not concerned with danger to you," I replied. "I'm concerned with my own reputation in this. *You* will be gone soon."

"Then for your sake, trust I will be careful." His hand moved as if he meant to touch me, but he caught the gesture and turned it into casual salute. "Be careful yourself, Sidi."

The farmer's son seemed daunted enough by the signs of my vocation to do no more than bow me on and off the wagon, and press on me some bread and cheese clearly sent by his mother. It soon became apparent a return that night seemed unlikely. When he left me at the edge of the city, the sun was close to the high horizon on the mountains.

I started up the streets of the city as the shadows lengthened. No one gave me a second look as I walked towards the gate. It seemed both familiar and unreal—as if I had never been away, as if I were still in the Court and only dreaming a memory of this road. In the winter light, the whitewashed walls gleamed, though the snow heaped at their bases was dirty with grit. The guards at the gate spared me only a cursory glance and if their eyes snagged on the bright, foreign patterns of my shawls, my black robe and sash, the wide-brimmed black hat seemed to smooth their gazes past me.

No one knew where I had been, so of course no one would remark on my return, but still it seemed strange to pass beneath the iron with no ceremony. I felt nothing as I did it; all the air I had breathed in the court, all the fey food and wine I had consumed had left no trace for the iron to touch. I wondered what Daen would feel when he walked beneath it. I wondered if he *could* walk beneath it.

In the upper streets, faces became familiar, one or two heads nodded as I passed. I nodded back, half afraid someone would speak to me, half hoping someone would, as if that would break the strange spell of dislocation I felt. No one did, until I reached the palace gates and guards who knew me, but at least I now knew that the Queen had not sent me back years in the future. "Good afternoon Azi," one said and the other gave me a curious look.

"Did you walk down from the monastery? It's early for the pass to be clear."

"Not early enough when one has spent the winter there." My voice sounded normal and he laughed, as if my words made sense. "Though I suppose my teachers would say that accepting that is part of the lesson."

"Better you than me, Azi," the first guard said. "Welcome back."

"Thank you. Do you know where the Sidiana is?"

"No. But if we see her, we'll say you're back."

I thanked them and went on, into the courtyard and then to the dark corridors of the palace. I thought about where Raziel might be: the council chamber, her rooms, her office. It might be wise to dispose of my shawls, I thought, and put the iron back on my naked fingers, my empty earlobes. Raziel would come to find me, if she heard the news of my return, and there would be more privacy in my rooms than in the hallways.

It was quite sensible, which made it easier to pretend it was not also cowardice.

My room was as I had left it, though the bed hangings were drawn and there was the dry, musty scent of abandonment in the cold air. I shed shawls and hats and gloves and rubbed the bristle on my skull, regretting the loss of the perpetual supply of warm water in the Court. I found the little bag I had sent back from the fair in the top drawer of the chest and felt a moment's disorientation when I remembered that same chest set against the false Jayasita of my Court chamber.

I shook the contents out onto the chest and touched the rings and bracelets, earrings and amulets. In the long sunlit afternoons in the courtyard, the sight of my hands had sometimes startled me from the trance of my work. I wondered whose fingers I saw, with the lighter bands around their bases, places sun had not touched in years. A false sun it might have been in that courtyard, but it had tanned those traces away and the fingers I now spread looked as if they had always been ringless.

I put it all back on, all the symbols of mortality, and spread my hands again. They still looked like a stranger's. I felt no sense of safety, though now nothing of the fey could touch, or be touched by, those stranger's hands.

There were voices in the corridor, footsteps on polished wood, and I opened my door just as Raziel arrived. She had grown during my time in the Court—she had been sensible enough to bring her guards—but not so much that she did not fling her arms around me before they had time to stop her.

"It is good to see you, Tera," she whispered, hugging me hard. "I was afraid she would never let you go."

"It is very good to be home, Sidiana. And I admit to a moment or two of fear on the same account."

She let me go and I saw her glance flicker to my hands, my earlobes. She should have looked there first, I thought, but said nothing. "But here you are. How did you get here? Have you eaten? Are you thirsty?"

"I walked, at least down from the pass, and I would be very grateful for some honest Lushan dumplings and a pot of tea, plus a warm fire to sit beside the rest of the day. But I left an obligation back there and I must speak to you about it."

"Talking can be done over dumplings and tea—what *did* you eat there?—and there's a fire in my room. What sort of obligation? Did the Queen send you back with treasure?"

"Not precisely," I said with a laugh, and let her draw me down the hallway towards her rooms, aware of the wariness behind the guards' smiles. They would not wish to leave her alone with me, which was only wise, but there were things I would rather not say in their presence so I did not argue when she ordered them to wait in the outer rooms. She did consent to leave the door open, a gesture of compromise so like her sister that it squeezed the old knot of grief beneath my breastbone.

There was a fire, as promised, and servants were dispatched for food and tea, and then we were alone. "Is it done? Are you safely and truly returned?" Raziel asked, her gaze intent.

"The Queen declared the bargain fulfilled before the Court, so I think the matter done."

"Next fair, I shall have my pockets filled with stones. We all will," Raziel said and I felt a chill inside, far beyond any fire's warmth. I had not thought so far ahead, that I would have to stand at Raziel's shoulder before the Queen and bear the weight of that black, knowing gaze.

"I will not argue with that precaution, though I doubt it will be necessary. This had nothing to do with the stones. It was Court politics." At her curious look, I went on. "There are factions within the court, some opposed to the Queen's fascination with mortals. Though no one ever said it, I believe this whole business was meant to show them that she would do as she chose—and that she controlled mortals as much as she controls the fey."

Raziel's look turned bewildered as I spoke, leaving me baffled in return, for nothing I said should have surprised her. "What did you say? What language was that? I could not understand any of it," she said, when I was done.

"What did it sound like?" I remembered my fears on leaving the Court, my disbelief that the Queen would let me leave with all I knew of her world.

"Like another tongue entirely, no word that I could recognize at all."

We experimented a little with it: I tried to explain in more and more abstract terms, but in the end, that it was Court politics was all the Queen's geas would allow. We even tried having me write the words, to no better effect. I wondered what this meant for Daen, whether I could tell Raziel what she needed to know. Did the geas bind his tongue as well, I wondered, and tried without success to imagine a bridle on his uncensored ramblings.

But that thought brought me back to the fact that he was sitting in a smoky hut awaiting my return. "I would gladly sit here drinking tea and trying to find some way around this spell, but there is still my obligation to settle," I said and she nodded. "You recall the fey lord who came to retrieve me."

"Yes. He called me "Sidiana" from the back of that greathorse."

"Well, he is only half-fey, his father having been a lord in some distant northern land, and he has spent much time in the mortal world. He has long wished to leave the Court for good and the Queen granted him permission to do so, on the condition he bring me back to the city safely. But I would not let him come even outside the iron without your consent."

"If I refuse it?"

"Then it might be best to send soldiers to see him to the southern pass. Otherwise, he will be at the gates whatever you say."

"Is that what you think I should do?"

There was a part of me that longed to say yes. "He was my escort at the Court. He was kind to me." *Kind.* That word, that word he denied, that word that said nothing at all of what had passed between us. But it was the only word I could safely use. "If we can help him find freedom at no risk to us, then I am honour-bound to ask. In truth, it is partially my fault he is here. The Queen afforded me a reward for completing the mosaic—but only one that did not touch on the agreement."

"And you asked for him?" Raziel asked in astonishment. I felt my skin burn.

"No. I asked that she let him go. She gave me no time to prepare and I could think of nothing to ask for myself that was not meaningless or open to treacherous misinterpretation. I did not expect that she would put that price on it."

"I suppose I should meet him then, before I make a choice."

"Not alone."

"Do you not trust him?"

"I have trusted him with my life," I replied truthfully, "but I am not certain I would trust him with yours."

"Best to keep this discreet," she said thoughtfully. "Chadrena is in the palace. And Kirit Acton will be in his archive. The four of us and a company of guards should suffice." It was not a question, for all the faint lift in her voice, and I felt a pang of loss at the realization before the fair it would have been. She was growing into her power and I had missed it, trapped in the endless days of the mosaic courtyard. I could not even argue with her choices—Chadrena was one of the few who knew where I had gone and the archivist was the palace expert on the fey. The four of us riding out together might cause comment, I supposed, but there was very little that would not.

Despite the six months, she was waiting for my agreement, and when I nodded, she went to the door to dispatch one of the guards to fetch

Chadrena, Kirit and Savean, the captain of the Sidiana's guard. "There is something else you should know," I began uneasily as she returned to her seat. I could not help the drop in my voice, my glance at the empty doorway, and she leaned forward attentively.

"He is her son."

"The Queen's?" she asked in astonishment. The spell had not prevented me from telling that truth then. I nodded. "And she let him leave?"

"Their relationship is . . . complicated. I suppose she has grown tired of his rebellion. She has no use for a son, not even one full fey. But, in truth, I do not know why she let him go."

"And you mistrust her motives?"

"I mistrust everything about her. But whatever you decide, I think it would be best to keep this part of it quiet."

She nodded thoughtfully. This was the moment, I knew, to tell the whole tale; the Queen's order, Daen's initial refusal, the duel, the hunt. What came after. I did not think the Queen's geas would prevent it.

But I said nothing.

And then the captain was at the door, and Chadrena, and the moment was gone.

It was clear we would not be able to reach the inn and return by nightfall, which led to a debate on whether to leave and break the journey part way or wait until the morning. Raziel, characteristically, was in favour of immediate departure, but allowed herself to be overruled by Savean and good sense. Fortunately, the Sidiana had been in the habit of leaving the palace to visit the local towns, even in the winter, so our passage would excite less notice than expected.

It left me with more hours to worry, and more time to answer Raziel's questions.

Chadrena and Kirit joined us and listened with fascination as my answers slipped from ordinary Euskalan to gibberish and back. Uncomfortable though I found never knowing what might emerge from my mouth, the process did establish the parameters of the Queen's binding. Any discussion of the mosaic and the splendours—or even the discomforts—of the Border Court was perfectly intelligible but the names of the fey I had met, my speculations on the politics of the Court, and any mention of the doors to other places, other times would come out as nonsense syllables.

COLD HILLSIDE

I waited for the right moment to tell Raziel about Daen but it never came. I told myself it did not matter, that she knew enough to decide if she would permit him to fulfill the Queen's conditions.

We made the return journey much more quickly than the wagon had brought me down and it was just after midday when we saw the smoke from the farmstead and inn. Savean sent two of her guards ahead; they trotted back a few moments later and after a brief discussion, the captain looked at Raziel.

"The yard's too small for all of us," Savean said. "I would suggest you wait out here." I half-expected rebellion but Raziel nodded and let the guard take their places around her again as we rode on. "You said he was the Queen's champion, Azi Teresine. Was that title courtesy?"

I shook my head.

A sensible distance from the buildings, two of the guard dismounted, loosing their swords from their sheaths. Savean and the others remained mounted. The Sidiana looked at me and I looked at the empty courtyard.

There was nothing to do but go and look for him, I supposed, and my foot was leaving the stirrup when the door of the house opened and he walked out. I saw the flash of curious faces in the doorway, but when they saw the line of guards, the door was quickly shut. Daen walked out of the courtyard, with the economical, casual grace I remembered from the duel. His sword remained strapped across his back, his gloved hands loose and open at his sides. I knew he saw the guards, the unsheathed swords. I wondered if he could feel the iron in them, the iron that girded all of us.

He bowed, flawlessly correct. "Sidiana."

"Lord Daen." He straightened and met her curious gaze. "Our positions are reversed, it seems," she said after a moment. "You seemed much larger on horseback."

He looked nonplussed, then laughed. "So do you, Sidiana."

"Teresine says you have chosen exile from the Court and were charged with escorting her to the city. And that failure to fulfill that order would mean the Queen will claim you back."

"That's true, Sidiana."

"If I say that your duty is discharged here, my companion being safely returned to me as your Queen promised, would that constitute failure?"

"I assume so, Sidiana. I will not know for certain until you say it and I find myself back in the Court."

"And if I give you leave to ride with us to the city, can you pass its gates?"

"That is another thing I will not know until I try. I've walked most places in the mortal world without trouble." Which seemed unlikely, though I suppose it depended upon your definition of "trouble." "Though I admit it has rarely been in places with so much iron. I doubt that I could enter your palace."

"If I were disposed to invite you to, of course."

"Always of course, Sidiana."

"And once you have fulfilled the Queen's conditions and set foot in my city, what then?"

"It is a very large world, Sidiana. There are places without so much iron in them." I heard the "damn" he did not say. Give it another few moments and he *would* say it, I thought.

"Is there any reason I should grant you this favour?"

"None. Sidi Teresine made me no promises."

"Would it please the Queen if I refused you?"

"Sidiana, I've long since given up trying to determine what will please the Queen. Though I know if it did, it would not be from any love of me."

Raziel looked at him for a long moment, frowning. "Grant me a moment's consultation, Lord."

He bowed in acknowledgement of the courtesy and Raziel turned her mount to trot beyond hearing range, Chadrena, Kirit and I trailing after her, the guards left behind, a fence of armour, horse and swords.

Raziel cast one look backward as we drew up around her. "He's not what I expected," she said.

"He has a gift for that," I replied dryly.

"There's little enough fey about him," Kirit observed. "You are certain he is half-fey?"

"I've seen him use small magics, to light fires and such. He has said his only true gift is for battle. I saw him best a full-fey warrior in a duel, so yes, I believe he is half-fey, for all he is so ordinary in appearance."

"Ordinary is not precisely the word I would choose," Chadrena murmured, with a glance at me.

Raziel's mount tossed its head and she patted its neck absently. "There is likely no harm in letting him try to enter the city. Either he will manage it, or fail. Repaying kindness with cruelty seems churlish, even to the fey."

"There is no debt," I protested. "Or if there is, it is mine, not Lushan's."

"Then I have one, for returning you to me. But don't fear, Tera, I've not forgotten everything you taught me. Captain," she called, turning her horse to face the captain as Savean approached. "I trust you could find some accommodation for him in the barracks, outside the iron."

At the answering nod, she rode past her, back towards Daen. It was a reasonable plan, I admitted, answering to both security and a certain rough courtesy.

The guard parted to let her find her place among them. "My tutor claims I have no debt to you," she said to Daen. "But I am willing to count her safe passage through the mountains as a favour—and I imagine it *would* please the Queen to send you away so close to your escape. So you are welcome to lodge with the soldiers outside the iron gates. You are welcome to walk beneath them with us, if you can."

It was an offer hedged with conditions and limits; she had not forgotten he was half-fey. He bowed, a much simpler gesture than his last one. "Thank you, Sidiana."

We had brought a pack horse for the last lacquered boxes and a mount for him. "Better than making him ride on the back of *your* horse this time," Raziel had said, back in the city, and I had laughed despite my memories of that night.

One of the guards headed into the yard and knocked on the door of the house. After a moment, the farmer and his wife emerged, accepted a few coins and luck tokens from the soldier and bowed carefully in our direction. I supposed there would be talk; a monk and a foreigner coming out of the mountains, the Sidiana herself coming to collect them.

Savean's guard spoke to the soldiers and then returned to swing into their saddles and resume their positions at Raziel's back.

The ride back was slower, a pace made leisurely by Kirit's questions (not always answered) and Raziel's (more diplomatically deferred). We stopped once while food and tea were unpacked, physical needs attended to, and horses rested. It was once again darkening to evening by the time we reached the edge of the city, and it struck me that this had been Savean's intention, if not Raziel's, to minimize the curious eyes that might follow us.

"Come with us to the gate," Raziel said, "then Captain Savean will see you to the barracks."

"I'm honoured," Daen replied politely but he gave me a glance that conveyed that he knew quite well it was a test that she meant him to pass or fail in front of us all. I wondered what would happen if he could not pass it and how such failure might manifest. And what story they would tell the guards to excuse it. It seemed altogether too public to me—I would have had Savean take him there in the darkest hours of the night—but it was clear Raziel had chosen her course.

We reached the gate just as they were lighting the torches, after the last flurry of homeward bound workers had passed and they prepared to pull the great doors shut. The guards saw our approach and kept them open. I looked at Daen, riding beside me. There was nothing in his stance or shadowed face to suggest he felt any fear at all.

Then we were beneath the gate. It seemed I could feel the weight of the iron myself, like a stone on my chest, in my throat. I was beyond its unseen shadow in a heartbeat—but Daen was not. I turned awkwardly to see that he had half-fallen from his saddle, hanging against his horse's side as he hauled at the reins to pull it back, away from the iron. The guards moved, to shift their mounts between his and the gate, between him and Raziel, and then I heard him take a great, shuddering breath and swear violently.

He reappeared, heaving himself back up into the saddle to slump there. I pushed forward, the guards letting my smaller mount pass. "Are you—?" I began.

"Let's not do that again," he muttered then shook his head and sat up. "I'm sorry, Sidiana. A touch of dizziness. It might be best if I went to the barracks immediately."

"Of course," she replied graciously, as if dealing simply with an ill guest and not the proof that the ward we had all taken for granted actually worked.

The small troop split—Savean to escort Daen to the barracks—the rest of us to continue up the road to the palace. "How interesting," Kirit said. "Not quite what I expected."

"What did you expect?" I asked, more sharply than I had intended. "That he would burst into flames or turn into a toad?"

"Teresine," Raziel said. "Leave be. It appears to have done him no lasting harm. And it's useful to know what his tolerance for iron might be."

"Assuming he was not feigning," I felt compelled to point out.

"Always assuming that, of course. But now he'll be safely stowed with Savean, who will make sure there is enough iron judiciously placed to be useful, and tomorrow we will find out more. This has all turned out to be very interesting."

She flashed me a smile and put her heels against her horse's side. I followed her up the street and this time it was the weight of my own misgivings that seemed like iron across my shoulders. Interested was not at all what I wanted her to be.

CHAPTER 44

Lilit

And suddenly, there was no more time. All Lilit's indecision and fear had brought her to the week in which she would have to choose. After this, Aunt Alder would not give her the herbs necessary to end her pregnancy. She could find someone who would, if she tried, but she wanted no more alley prescriptions.

There was only one thing left to do.

It seemed easiest to meet in her father's rooms in the morning, before the day's demands claimed her mother. Her parents were there when she arrived, engaged in awkward conversation. "What is this about?" her mother asked, without preamble.

"You have us worried now, child," her father added.

Lilit sat down opposite them. She wanted to pace, to release some of the tension winding through her, but she also needed to see them, to force them to see her. She decided to start with the only incontrovertible fact in the entire mess. "I'm pregnant."

"Is that all?" Amaris sounded so relieved Lilit wondered what exactly she had feared.

"Is that why you were asking about the Kijholds?" Hendren asked.

"The Kijholds? Is the father a Kijhold?" It did not appear the prospect pleased her mother, though Lilit had no doubt her mother was busy calculating advantages even as she spoke.

"Maybe. I suppose he must be."

"You don't know?" Amaris looked distinctly less pleased at *that* thought.

"He's the only one I've been with recently." Which was true, as far as it went. Lilit was not at all certain, even now, if she were prepared to say what her dreams suggested about the night of the fair.

"Well, then yes, I suppose he must be the father. And what have you decided to do?"

"I haven't decided anything. That's why I need to talk to you both."

"You know that you have our support no matter what you choose," her father assured her.

At least now, Lilit thought. At least until I say the words. But the words must be said, if she were ever to find her way to an answer.

"I need," she began, found her throat closed on the words, and then began again. "I need to find whether it's possible that I have fey blood."

"So that's behind all the questions. Lily-girl, why would you think you have fey blood?" her father asked.

"Is it possible?"

"Everything I told you about our family's past is true. There has been no fey child in Kerias for a hundred years."

"Is it possible there has been any fey blood in Deshiniva?"

"Lilit, this is ridiculous." Amaris's impatience was shaded with a darker edge of anger.

Her father put his hand on her mother's arm, stilling her.

He knows, Lilit thought suddenly, *he knows something she does not*.

"Lilit," he said gently, "why would you think you have fey blood?"

"I went to a faerie tester. I thought Feris Kijhold might be . . . it was foolish, I know. But I went and she told me the only fey she could feel was me."

"How could you be so gullible?" her mother demanded. "The woman was a charlatan, that's all. I cannot believe you would do something so idiotic. Imagine if someone had seen you."

"That would be embarrassing for you, I know, Mother." Lilit snapped. She caught her breath and forced herself to go on. "I don't think she was lying. She didn't care, you see. She didn't care if she ruined me."

"So because you slept with some low-city boy peddling fey glamour to get gullible girls into his bed, you went to a faerie tester." The scorn in her mother's voice made her want to cringe. "Even after, I assume, your father told you the Kijholds were no more likely to be harbouring part-fey sons than Kerias is. That seems remarkably foolish, even for you. Is there something you're not telling us?"

"I fainted," Lilit admitted reluctantly. "At the fair, I fainted when the Queen came. And then," she swallowed, remembering Teresine's instructions that she tell no one but Raziel what had happened at the fair. But the words were said and she could not bear to keep the rest inside.

Only Teresine's own secret about her trip to the Border Court would she keep. "There was a fey lord who talked to me. He told me he remembered my great-aunt. He told me to be careful. That night I woke up at the bridge. I'd walked in my sleep right to the bridge. And I've been having dreams, awful dreams."

The words spilled out, while she stared at the floor, unwilling to meet their eyes. There was a long silence.

"We will go to Alder right now and she will deal with it," her mother said at last. "You have made yourself hysterical with worry and you will not repeat a single thing you've said to anyone. Tomorrow the matter will be over."

"No." Lilit shook her head helplessly. "I can't do that."

"Don't be a fool. There is no reason to have this go on. Are you imagining you can have this baby?"

"Why not?"

"You as much as accuse your father of hiding some terrible secret about Kerias, you babble nonsense about the fair, you go to some charlatan in a back alley and you think you can have a child? Tell me, if you are so eager to believe this idiocy, what will you do if you bear it and it cries at the touch of iron? What do you suppose happens then? Do you want to watch your aunt take it away and do what must be done? Or will you smother it yourself so no one will know?"

"Amaris!" Hendren said sharply.

"Lilit, there is no choice. You must end this."

"Or what, Mother? How do you propose to make me?" Lilit heard her voice scaling up, petulant, afraid.

"Will you have the thing just to spite me then?" Amaris asked caustically. "When did you become a child again?"

"Amaris, this is not helping."

"You speak to her then. You reason with her, since it is apparently only you she listens to now. But this *will* be done. And when it is, Lilit, you will stay here until whatever madness has possessed you has passed."

"Until the election is over, you mean," Lilit countered. "You cannot force me. Alder cannot force me, unless you mean to hold me down and pour her potions down my throat. I will not end this because it doesn't suit your political ambitions, Mother."

"Both of you, stop it. Amaris, you cannot dictate what Lilit will do—

she is an adult. Lilit, you cannot make this choice to spite your mother. That would be as foolish as she claims you are being." There was nothing conciliatory in her father's manner. Lilit had never heard him sound so stern.

"You asked me once if I would disown you for going to the fair with the Austers," her mother said, rising to her feet. There was no expression in her voice, all anger and contempt drained away to leave nothing but cold resolution. "I said no then but if you disobey me in this, you are no child of mine, from this day on. It is your choice. Do what you wish."

Amaris did not slam the door as she left; her words had closed a door between them more solid than the physical one.

"Lilit, she did not mean it."

"She did."

Hendren sighed. "Yes, she did. I'm sorry, Lily-girl. Your mother is . . ."

"I know." Her father came to sit beside her and she leaned her head against his shoulder. "What am I going to do?" she whispered.

"I don't know. It might be better if you did as she asks, not because she asks it, but because you have so much uncertainty in your heart for this child. Maybe it is not this soul's time to come back into the world."

"But what if it is? And what if that woman was right? What if I am part fey?"

"What if you are? You have passed all the tests. You touch iron and walk under the gate. It does not matter what a dozen faerie-testers say. You are a daughter of Kerias. You are *my* daughter."

"And hers." Lilit sat up and looked at her father. "What didn't you want me to say in front of her?"

"What makes you think that?"

"Years of watching you deflect her anger or trying to keep the two of us from fighting."

"I did not manage that so well tonight." He smiled a little but it faded when she did not echo it. "Let it be, Lilit."

"I can't. I have to know the truth."

Her father sighed and then nodded in resignation. He rose and held out his hand. "Come, then."

"Where are we going?"

"To the only person who might know it."

CHAPTER 45

Teresine

The following night, the court of Lushan descended upon the barracks for dinner.

That is an exaggeration, of course. It was only seven members of Raziel's inner circle. Of the company gathered around the long table set up in one of the training rooms to serve as a makeshift private dining room, there were only five who knew the truth: Chadrena, Kirit, Savean, Raziel and I. The rest had been told Daen was a traveller I had met on my journey back from the monastery.

"Do you suppose any of them will believe that?" I had asked Raziel, when she told me of the plan.

"That is one of the things I would like to know," she replied. "And why should they not? He can pass as mortal."

"Mortals do not usually cross those mountains before the late spring. And none of them have ever looked like him."

"He is clearly foreign, true enough. But the mountains have seen foreigners before."

"There will be talk. It seems unnecessary to encourage it if he is leaving in a day or two anyway."

"There will be talk if I ride out to bring him here and then hide him the barracks. There will be talk no matter what I do," Raziel said and I caught the edge of a glance much less confident than her tone. "Do you fear what they will say?"

"There is nothing they can say about you," I said, willfully misunderstanding.

"I did not mean about me."

I could have told her then. We were alone, or near enough so. "They can say what they like, I cannot stop them." Which was true, but meant nothing at all.

COLD HILLSIDE

"Besides," she said, "I am curious." I saw the faint flicker of her smile. "Sarit would have had dinner alone with him."

"No, she would not," I said, appalled that the thought had occurred to her, appalled that it was true. Sarit might have, in the days before Perin, though she would have gone well warded with iron. But Raziel was not Sarit.

"Maybe not the first night," she conceded. "So you cannot criticize me. I go safely chaperoned by an army of upright citizens."

In the end, it was eight upright citizens and one six-year-old girl. Ayriet had attached herself to the party, Raziel having previously promised her sister-daughter that she would spend the evening with her. None of us cared for that, but Raziel did not rescind the invitation. "She'll tire of the boring adult company before the dinner is done," she assured me, "and I'll send her home with a guard. Besides, isn't it time we started training her to be Sidiana?" She meant it for humour but there were shades beneath that: resignation, bitterness, resolution.

So the group of us arrived at the barracks to dine with Savean, our nominal host. She was careful, if Raziel was inclined not to be. The seating arrangement found Daen at one end of the table, Savean to his right, Kirit to his left and Raziel well down the table. The rest of us could fend for ourselves as far as the captain was concerned; I found myself sitting on Kirit's side of the table. Raziel looked vaguely disgruntled at her own place, with Ayriet tucked in beside her. Daen, who appeared to recognize the gambit for what it was, gave me a grin and a bow. I nodded back politely.

There had been clothes in one of those lacquered boxes, it seemed. I recognized the long coat and cinnamon-coloured shirt. His sense of occasion matched that of the other guests, though their finery was black robes and bright belts, the heavy wrapping of carnelian, turquoise and silver around throats and wrists. Ayriet and I were the exceptions: she because her robe was a child's blue and I because my only adornments were Chadrena's bracelet and my iron.

There were introductions and polite greetings, then the party began the serious business of digging into the platters of food and asking questions of the guest. "How was your journey through the mountain, Nasi Daen? Did you take the Tjezerbet pass?" Reshen asked. He nodded. We had concocted a story, Raziel and I, and given him the geography he needed to make it believable. "It is early for it to clear. The caravans from Majesthan will be here soon then."

"Most likely not. I was fortunate, that is all. It was a tedious slog punctuated by moments of terror." Which was the truth, in its own way. Reshen was Izmaret, with ties to the Majesthan traders. She did not look like she entirely believed him.

"And where is your homeland?" This was from Trine, current head of the Engineers, who were the custodians of the maps that sketched the world from the border of the Empire of Teraso to the forests of Jurget, north of the fabled, lost home of the Euskalans.

"Varansheld."

"You have travelled a very long way," the engineer said.

"You've heard of it?"

"Only through tales. A northern land, I think, known for its fierce warriors."

"Which is a polite way of saying known for its marauding berserkers."

"So the tales say," Trine replied diplomatically.

"And so we are, Nasi Trine, at least the last time I was there."

"Perhaps you will do us the favour of reviewing our maps while you are here."

"It would be my honour," Daen promised, with no trace of the lie in his voice.

And so it went. The Euskalans were suspicious, polite, and curious. Daen was bluntly charming, with an answer for every question, even if it did not provide the information they'd been seeking. As the evening went on, and the jugs of liquor emptied, the atmosphere lightened. Stories were told on all sides, curiosity turned to interest, questions turned flirtatious. I said less than the others and drank much less, watching Raziel, watching Daen. She laughed as much as the rest, her eyes bright, but I saw her decline more beer when it was offered.

Daen drank more, though without the dark desperation I had seen at the Court. Here, among mortals, I saw the fey in him for the first time. In him, the bright glamour of their beauty became force of personality, a burning vitality that made him seem the fire around which the rest of us hovered. I felt it even as I recognized it; it frightened me into looking at anyone but him, stiffened my spine against the tight clench of my heart.

Despite Raziel's predictions, Ayriet did not seem to tire of the adult company and conversation. She sat quietly, seemingly perfectly content to eat and play with the slate and colours brought to amuse her. She watched Daen with an open curiosity none of the adults dared and an innocent fascination none of them could own. For his part, he seemed oblivious to her presence, moderating neither his language nor his conversation. I was relieved by his indifference until I caught a glance between them, the drop of his lid in a swift wink, and her clumsy echo of it.

As her elders did, she grew bolder as the night wore on, slipping from her place by the table to wander around the room until her careful circuit brought her close to the empty space on the bench beside him. He did not look at her, but shoved the coat he had shed into the corner with a casual gesture. She sidled over to the edge of the bench, hitched herself up onto it and sat as if enthroned.

"Ayriet—" Raziel said in warning, though against what I could not tell. Ayriet kept her head bent over the slate on which she was drawing, pretending she did not hear.

Daen looked down at her, tilting his head to study her work.

"That's a good cow," he said.

"It's a horse," she replied, with lofty disgust at his ignorance.

"Are you sure? It looks like a cow to me."

"It can't be a cow. It doesn't have udders."

"It could be a boy cow," he pointed out. He would, I thought in despair, say that.

"It doesn't have a penis, silly."

There were hastily stifled snickers. Raziel put her hand to her mouth, her cheeks flushing. Daen lifted his brows. "I'm sorry. You're right. How stupid of me. It's a girl horse."

"Is your horse a girl or a boy?"

"I don't know. I've never presumed to ask it."

"You don't ask them, silly. You look."

"Well, then I've never presumed to look. I think it would kick me." I thought of the amused golden eyes of the great beast we had ridden to the Court and hid my own smile.

"I'll do it for you, if you'd like," Ayriet said graciously.

"That's very kind of you. But it's not here."

"I can draw it for you then. What colour it is?"

"Black."

She frowned, looking at the black slate and the selection of chalks on the bench beside her. "I'll just draw around it then."

"It has gold eyes, if that helps."

"What colour is the saddle?"

"Black." She gave him a look of disappointment and he gave her an apologetic grin.

"I'm sorry, sweeting. It is. But it might like it better if it was gold. That would match its eyes. It's a very vain horse."

She accepted that and set to work, head bent over her slate, scribbling with a will. The adult conversation resumed, punctuated periodically by Ayriet's insistent demand that her drawings be approved. Daen unfailingly did so, until she tired of the game, curled up in the corner of the bench against his coat, and went to sleep.

It took longer for the rest of us to admit to our own weariness, but after one of the soldier's hastily covered yawns, Raziel stood up and announced it was time to leave. "Thank you, Captain Savean, for the kind hospitality. We'll let you and your soldiers get some sleep."

More polite noises followed, and several seemingly sincere pleas that Daen consider spending the rest of the spring in the city—"The southern passes take so long to clear, after all." He made noncommittal noises in return. One of Raziel's guards scooped up the sleepy Ayriet and then we were trooping noisily to the gate of the barracks.

"Sidi," Daen said, when my turn at farewell came. "If you've time to spare tomorrow, can I claim it?"

I nodded and we settled that I would come to the barracks in the afternoon. Then, bundled against the night, I followed the others through the quiet streets. Snatches of conversation sifted back to me, as each of them took their turn to tell Raziel what they thought.

"I am amazed he made it through the pass." That was Reshen. "The last person I knew who did that lost three toes."

"We did not ask to see his feet," Raziel replied. "Should I?"

I lost the next comment but the shout of laughter suggested the nature of it.

"It is just as well he's leaving. There's no reason for him to stay. The southern passes are safe enough for someone claiming to have journeyed across the Northern ones."

"You're very untrusting, Reshen."

"I mistrust charm."

"Did you think him charming? I thought he was quite coarse."

"For some, that's more potent that grace."

Another muttered comment, another laugh.

"Well, I'd rather he stayed until I could stick a map or two under his nose. Assuming you think he'd tell me the truth," Trine said. Raziel appeared at my side, having drifted back through the group.

"I can see why you like him," she said quietly.

"I said that I owe him." My voice was sharp; I saw heads turn and lowered it. "It is not precisely the same thing."

"I ought to let Trine have his map interrogation." It was not quite a question.

I nodded, which was not quite an answer.

The next day I arrived at the barracks at the appointed hour, to find that Daen had charmed the soldiers out of two horses and permission for an unescorted ride. As they finished saddling the beasts, I stood with Daen at the edge of the courtyard.

"I have a gift for you," I said, finding the parchment tucked into my robe. I passed it to him and watched his smile widen as he unfolded it. He turned it to show me: it was a drawing of a black horse-like beast, with a golden saddle that matched its big golden eyes.

"Thank her for me. No one's ever given me a drawing before."

"You made a conquest. She is utterly smitten."

"So was I," he said with a grin. "Though I don't think I was quite as successful with her elders."

"Were you trying to be?"

"I'm wounded, Sidi. Couldn't you tell?" I laughed, unable to help myself, his mock outrage blunting the memory of my uneasiness at his dark charm the night before. "Though I suppose I should ask about the Sidiana, since it's her goodwill I need."

"She is not so easily seduced as her niece." The words were sharper than I had intended.

"I would wager not," he replied. "I'm not enough fey and much too male for her." I looked at him in astonishment. I knew Raziel found the fey beautiful but had never bothered to wonder where her passion in mortals might lie. "I do know I'm here on your bond."

Which was true, though it frightened me. "We should go, while the sun is out," I said, to change the subject.

Neither of the borrowed horses was black, and our saddles were dull brown leather, but their eyes were those of beasts and I trusted them more than the reindeer. It was a relief not to feel like I was being laughed at. Beyond the edges of the city, the wind blew in from the ice-fringed lake, but the sun was warm and I was well-wrapped in robe and shawls.

"Do you ever miss the courtyard?" Daen asked, as we rode along the trail that wound behind the stony dunes along the lake. The skeletal rhododendron branches rattled in the wind as we passed.

"There was something to be said for perpetual warm afternoons."

"You love the sun too much for this place," he said with a laugh.

"I love this place enough to give it up," I replied.

That silenced him, for a moment, and when he spoke again the humour was gone from his voice. "She has put a price on my going I don't think I will be able to meet. And when I go back the courtyard will be empty and snowbound."

"What price? You have brought me to the city."

"There was another test. To prove that I am more human than fey. I have to spend one night beneath the palace roof. I can't do it. There is too much iron there, too full of spells and strength and intention for me to pass it."

The trail bent towards the lake and I could see the Asezati pavilion on the far side of the small bay. "The Sidiana might consent to let you try it."

"And if I fail? Can she then let me ride away, back to the Queen?"

"She is willing to let you ride away now."

"She will not let me in the palace, Sidi. You know that. You would not let me in, either."

I wanted there to be something I could say to that, some comfort I could give, but nothing came. He was right. She would not let him in. As I would advise her, if she asked me.

Daen set his heels to his horse's sides and set it to a reluctant trot, then a grudging canter across the flat stretch of dun grass that circled the bay. My own mount followed without being told, jolting me through the trot into a gallop that left me clinging to the saddle. I caught up to him near the pier for the bridge to the pavilion. He had already dismounted and was walking towards the pier, leaving his horse to crop at the thin grass. I did the same, trusting that soldiers' mounts were well-trained enough not to force us to walk back.

At the edge of the ice, he turned back to look at me and the bleakness in his eyes stopped me. "I am sorry—" I began.

"Don't," he said sharply. "Don't be sorry. It's not your fault she's right."

"She is not right."

"For every drop of my father's blood in me, there's one of hers. I'm as much like her as I am like him. I cannot choose to be one thing or the other."

"Yes, you can. She bore you but he raised you. You can always choose."

"Because you did? It's not the same, Sidi."

"Do you suppose it is easy for me? To not know at any moment whether I am Deshinivi or Euskalan, whether my oath to one power outweighs my oath to another? I do not say it will be easy, Lord. If you want that, go back to her."

"And if you want to help me, Sidi, spare me the platitudes. Get me into the palace." It was graceless, angry, more dismissal than challenge. He turned away and tossed the rock in his hand out onto the ice, where it bounced and slid, making no difference to the ice at all.

"Yes." I heard the word, heard my voice saying it. He looked back, as surprised as I was. "I'll help you. I'll find a way."

CHAPTER 46

Teresine

The answer came to me quite suddenly, while we walked on the stony shore. We had plenty of time to ride to the far side of the palace hill, for me to point out the place in the wall. He would not even have to pass the main gates again, if he could make his way to the base of the hill outside the iron. The slope was steep, home to mountain goats that foraged in the gardens at the edge of the city.

All he would have to do would be to climb that slope, avoid the guards who passed on their rounds along the narrow track below the wall, and then scale the wall itself. Sarit had once done that, in reverse, with me as her accomplice.

Daen stared up the hill at the whitewashed balustrade to which I pointed, his eyes narrowed. "I have done much harder things than that, Sidi."

"It will have to be after dark," I pointed out, and then remembered he had the fey gift for seeing where a mortal would have been blind. "Can you leave the barracks?" He nodded, still scanning the slopes, the places where the city blurred into the barren landscape in a jumble of little houses and barren gardens.

"Thank you, Sidi. I know that this is not easy for you."

"It seems a shame to have come this far and then fail because of a little iron," I said awkwardly.

"I think that was the Queen's point, but I am still glad you are willing to do this. You are very kind, Sidi."

I gave him a sharp look, at which he laughed, and we set the horses back towards the barracks once again.

I had a few hours to make preparations and I spent them trying not to slink furtively through the palace, attempting to look as if it was my ordinary business to carry bundles into the storage areas at the far side of the building. Fortunately, many of the things I required were already there and the rooms were unlocked. I collected a brazier and candelabra from one room and blankets from another.

The outer storeroom was as I remembered it: small and vaguely musty, the windows sealed by shutters and a heavy felt hanging. There were iron amulets on the hanging and two strings of charms dangling on either side of the wooden window frame. It took a somewhat precarious climb up a pile of boxes, but I removed the hanging and took it into the next room. I left the charms where they were: I would have plenty of time to take them off the window and hang them on the outer knob of the door.

I cleared a space amid the boxes and chests, in case he should want to sleep. I made a not-so-comfortable seat on one of the chests and set the candelabra, the cards and the books I had brought beside it, because I would not allow myself the dangerous luxury of sleep.

The tall shutters were stiff and it took all my strength to throw the bolts and push them open enough to allow myself to slither out into the narrow garden. It was long abandoned and what plants had grown there had died. Now there was only the last remnant of snow lingering where the sun did not touch and the hard, rutted dirt.

The night Sarit had used this way out of the palace, we had crept through the corridors in our everyday clothes, ropes stuffed into our robes. I had pushed her up the wall, she had pulled me, and we had used the rope to climb down the outside wall. We had left the rope hanging there, in the shadows of the balustrade, and none of the guards had seen it. Once we were back in the palace, conscience and prudence had compelled Sarit to confess and Kelci had painted the walls white once again and doubled the guard. Time might have relaxed that renewed vigilance but I could not count on it.

I did not know how Daen would climb the wall but I knew I could not put a rope over it. And when this was done, I was going to have to think of some way to warn Raziel about the weakness in the palace defences.

After darkness fell, I made my way to the storeroom again. It was too cold to wait outside and seemed foolish to squander the brazier's heat by leaving the window open, so I settled for sitting by it, the hanging drawn around me, starting anxiously at every distant sound.

After two false alarms, I heard a thump and crunch, then a stifled grunt. The shutters moved more easily now but by the time they were open, a dark shape had materialized before them. A faint line of light from the parted curtains laid a blade across his face.

I pushed the hangings aside, pulling down the string of iron wards and stepping back to let him climb through the window. The wind found its way through the shutters, slid cold fingers into the lamps and fluttered the flames.

He looked at me in the wavering light.

Though many times I have wished to, I cannot lay the blame for what happened next at the Queen's door. For all that she was guilty of, in this we obeyed no will but our own and in these long years that knowledge has brought me both comfort and despair.

This time, he did not talk. We did not undress, except to push aside whatever clothing was in our way. We did not even lie down, my back against the wall and his strength holding me up was enough.

When it was over, I straightened my clothing with shaking hands and went, with shaking knees, to find the wards where I had dropped them and hang them on the window once again. (How long ago? Five minutes? Ten? Too few, surely, to matter.)

"Sidi," Daen said, behind me, in that wonderful, terrible voice. "Teresine."

All my preparations, all my plans, had been a lie I told myself. The space I had made was enough for two, the books I had brought would go untouched, and neither of us would sleep. I knew it was all we would ever have but I could no longer pretend I did not want it.

I turned back to him and began to undo my robe.

The hours passed in our little world, bounded once again by iron, defined by walls of boxes and the flicker of the lamps. When we were cold, we wrapped ourselves in blankets and drank tea, or burrowed beneath them and drank in each other's warmth. He talked again and I listened, not caring what he said, but treasuring the sound of his voice, the feel of it in the chest beneath my cheek.

Sometime in the hours before dawn, drowsing on my stomach in the nest of blankets, I felt the chill of air on my back as he drew away, then the colder ice in my spine as his fingers traced the line of the old tattoo on my shoulder. "This is pretty," he said idly. "I wouldn't have expected it of you, Sidi. But they do this in Deshiniva, don't they. I remember—" He stopped, fingers pausing. "I remember this. On the Lotus Island, the women have tattoos like this."

"The mark of the House," I acknowledged. I kept my face turned away, my forehead against my arm. "The House of Falling Leaves."

"But—" He stopped again, words failing him a second time. I would have laughed, if my heart had not been pounding so hard, if my throat had not been so tight with fear and shame.

"That is where I was a slave, in Deshiniva. That is what I was."

He said nothing, but his hand moved again, sliding across my shoulder blade softly, as if for comfort. He would not ask, I realized. So I would have to tell him the story I had not told since the night I had knelt at Kelci's feet.

"Deshiniva is rich in many things," I said at last. "One of them is the poor. Who sometimes have beautiful children. Who sometimes believe or pretend to believe that the well-dressed woman who gives them money really is taking those children away to a respectable job in the city. Because it is one less mouth to feed, one less dowry to pay."

"How old were you?"

"Thirteen."

"Fucking hells."

As if he had never gone to Lotus Island himself. As if he had never done what soldiers over the world did. I did not imagine he had always asked the age of every beauty he had bedded.

"It could have been worse. I was beautiful, which meant the House did not waste me on common patrons. They needed beautiful girls, for they were seeking to raise the House's stature. They gave me a year's grace, to train me, to clean the mud of my peasant birth away. I pretended well, better than some girls who were more beautiful than I. I could be dressed in gold and taken to court gatherings and give the noble patrons a perfect, polite blankness onto which they could project their own desires."

"So that is where you learned it."

"Lushan taught me too, but yes. When I was not required for service, they found other tasks, but easy ones, genteel ones. That is where I learned to repair mosaics. Then Sarit's ship came and I escaped."

"So that part of the story was true. I did wonder how an ordinary slave came to know so much about the palace."

His hand was on my back, warm and solid. His body was against mine, his weight on my hip, my thigh. But the ice was still in my spine.

"Are you angry?" I asked.

"Why should I be angry?"

"Some men would be. At suffering to protect false virtue."

"I may be a drunken, inconsiderate, selfish ass, but I'm not *that* much of one. Who am I to judge, after all?"

"The night of the hunt," I said carefully, my eyes closed against the hot skin of my arm, "was the first time since Deshiniva. The night in the shepherd's hut . . . was the first time of my own will."

He was still for a moment. So was I, my breath held in my throat. Then I felt his lips against the old marking on my shoulder, the weight of his body as he moved over me. "And what is this?" he asked, against my ear.

"Madness," I whispered.

Our laughter was swallowed in a kiss. Sanity would come soon enough, as surely as the dawn. Jennon preserve us if it did not.

He left at the first touch of light in the sky behind the mountains, when there was still enough darkness to hide his return to the barracks but the letter of the Queen's command had been fulfilled.

"Good night, Sidi," he said at the window, now bare of iron once again.

"Goodbye."

"It's not that. Not yet."

"Yes, it is," I said. Because it was. Because when I saw him again, my mask must be in place, all my hard-won armour restored. Because I would have to watch him ride away forever and hide everything, from everyone.

He looked out into the empty garden for a moment, swore wearily, and then caught me in one last, fierce embrace. "Goodbye, then," he whispered, "Teresine," and my name, said so rarely, was one last secret, one last caress.

He went through the window and was gone.

I pulled the shutter closed, replaced the iron wards, and set about restoring the room to what it had been. By the time the dawn truly came, I was back in my cold bed, waiting for the comfort of sleep to find me.

CHAPTER 47

Teresine

The knocking drew me from restless sleep. I scrambled from the bed, retrieving my robe, the unexpected sound touching all the guilty chords in my heart.

One of Raziel's guards was at the door. "Sidi," she said. "The Sidiana needs you." I nodded and followed her, fastening my sash, swallowing the sudden sickness in my throat. To my surprise, she did not lead me to Raziel's rooms but beyond them. The sickness turned to fear, as I realized whose room we were approaching. *Not her*, I thought, almost a prayer. *Not Ayriet.*

But it was her room we stopped at, her door the guard opened to usher me through.

Raziel was there, and Meade, the court physician. Raziel's arms were wrapped around herself, as if holding more than her robe together, and her face, behind her tumbled hair, was white. "I had a dream," she said. "It was so frightening that I came to see her, to be sure she was—" her voice broke.

"What has happened?" I asked, my own voice unsteady.

They looked at the bed, their gazes drawing my own after them.

Ayriet lay there, as pale as her aunt in the shadows of the hangings. Something sparked in her eyes from the lantern at the bedside. I put my hand to my mouth, to cover the sound there, as the light reshaped her face. It was the shell of her, the bones still echoing Sarit's, the skin still child-smooth. It had her brown tangle of hair, her sturdy shape.

But it was not her.

"It cannot be." There had not been a changeling child in the city in twenty years. There had not been one in the palace for more than fifty. And then it had been babies they had taken, not children.

The thing on the bed smiled and I saw malice and contempt, sharp as fangs. It knew, I thought in terror. It knew of the moments when the wards had lain abandoned in a corner, while Daen and I rutted against the wall.

"I've sent for Savean, told her to find him, to hold him. He will know how to get her back," Raziel said and it took me a moment to realize that she was speaking of Daen.

Had he known? The thought seared through me and for a moment I thought I would be sick.

"Teresine?"

I had to tell her the truth, tell her everything, but my throat was sealed as tightly as if the Queen had laid a spell upon it. I nodded mutely and forced myself to look away from the creature on the bed.

It was almost as terrible to look at Raziel, at the confused dread beginning to shape itself around her eyes.

"We cannot bring him here, if he is part fey as you say, and I am loath to take this creature through the streets," Meade said, practical and oblivious.

"You're right. We must keep this quiet, until it can be undone, or there will be panic." Raziel looked at me again. "I've sent for Kirit and Chadrena but there will be questions if we all stay here."

"There is a place." The words felt like broken glass in my throat. "There is a garden on the cliff wall, by the storerooms. The wall will not stop him and the wards can be taken from the windows and doors." I looked at her squarely then, the spell gone, my voice my own. My doom my own. "That is how I let him in last night."

"You let—" She stopped. "Teresine—"

Whatever question she might have asked died with Kirit's arrival and a repeat of the horrifying revelation. Then it was Chadrena's turn. I found a place to lean against the wall, as far as I could from the Ayriet-thing, and let the waves of questions and decisions rise to drown me.

Had he known? That was the only question my traitorous heart seemed to be able to ask. Had it all, every word, every touch, every moment of it, been the deepest and cruellest of fey lies?

A guard was sent with instructions for Savean. A passable story was concocted: an illness, possibly infectious, forcing the removal of Ayriet from her room. Guards went for Diamet, to take her to the storeroom and begin the whole terrible business again.

COLD HILLSIDE

It was early enough that the halls were nearly empty. No one wanted to touch the changeling, but it had to be done and one of the soldiers did it, bearing the blanket-wrapped body through the hallways, its face concealed.

Diamet was there, outside the door. Meade explained, until Raziel broke in: "So here we are, awaiting Savean. Is this the place?" The last was to me and I nodded. "Did he enter through the window or the door?"

"The window, though the door is there, behind Kirit. It seemed safer."

"Unlock the door to the garden," she ordered and then put her hand on the door to the storeroom. "Shall we go in and you can tell me what happened last night?"

It was not a question, of course. We went in, Chadrena and others exchanging curious glances.

I had tidied the room: closed the felt curtains, restored the blankets to their trunks, taken away all evidence of our presence. But it was there still; a lingering smokiness from the brazier and beneath it, another scent. The smell of flesh and sweat and sex.

I thought I was too cold, inside and out, to blush, but I could feel the hot surge of shame in my skin. "He said she set another price on his freedom from her; that he spend one night in the palace," I said, to Raziel, looking only at her, afraid that to see the contempt in the others' eyes would render me helpless before the contempt that might show in hers. "I remembered the garden: Sarit and I slipped out of the palace once that way. I took the wards from the window to let him in. It was just for a few moments."

"It was enough," Trine said.

"How long?" Raziel asked.

"I did not count."

"Because you were fucking him." It sounded more than obscene in her mouth, that word.

I nodded and made myself say the words out loud, each one a wound. "Yes. Because I was fucking him."

The sound of the guard's voice was a relief, until I realized it meant Savean had arrived. Raziel led the way outside, into the chill dawn air. She stood in front of us, her arms resuming their protective clutch across her body, as if to hold herself together.

Savean had brought a rope ladder, but it was still an awkward

345

business. In the end, the captain, four soldiers and their "guest" stood on the bare ground before us. "Remind me to deal with that wall," Savean said before she saw the look in Raziel's eyes.

Daen, unbound, took a step forward and the guards moved with him, automatically protective. "What's happened?" he asked. His gaze caught mine briefly; whatever he saw there must have been as bleak as what was in Raziel's. He bent his head. "Sidiana."

"Bring it."

It had shown no inclination to walk, which was a relief, so the guard carried the Ayriet-creature out and set in on the ground. As the blanket fell away, it bared its white child's teeth at Daen in a smile that staggered him.

"Fuck." It was a whisper, a shaping of sound. "Not her, fuck, not her. Oh, that bitch."

"Your Queen has done this," Raziel said. "I want it undone. I want her back."

He shook his head, still staring at the changeling as if hypnotized. "It's too late."

Raziel took a step forward and hit him, a hard blow against his jaw and he straightened and looked down at her, bewildered. "I want my sister's child back," she said, slowly and clearly. "I will do whatever is required, but I want her back."

"Sidiana . . . Raziel . . . it is not possible."

"No. You're lying, just as you have lied about everything else. The Queen will take her creature and return Ayriet."

"The Queen does not care about the creature."

"Then she can take you in exchange."

"The Queen does not care about me either." The sound he made was a bitter echo of his usual laughter. "I am already dead to her."

"We will see," Raziel said stubbornly. "We will go to the Court and we will see."

"Sidiana," Chadrena began, then let the argument die at the look on Raziel's face as she turned back to us.

"I will not leave her in that place. I will not. If I must go and break down the walls of the Court, that is what I will do."

It was impossible, of course. She was unreasonable, irrational. But she was also magnificent, and Sidiana, and if she dragged us over the passes, we would go.

"The passes aren't clear," Daen pointed out. "You'll never make it. Sidiana, please, don't risk yourself as well for a lost cause."

"Why should that matter to you? Or do you only fear that you'll have betrayed us for nothing, if freedom was ever what you truly sought? Give me one reason I should believe a single thing you say."

"If I were lying, Sidiana, I'd tell you what you want to hear. Because then you might not kill me."

The blunt words were like a blow, another strike to my bruised heart. For a moment, there was the faintest indecision in her face, the faintest softening of her jaw. "If that is the price of getting my sister's child back," she said at last, coldly, and looked beyond him to Savean. "Captain, please prepare to ride. If you can find shackles that aren't iron, use them. If not, do not put them on bare skin. That much grace we will do you."

Savean bowed and the soldiers moved, as if to take Daen's arms. He stared at Raziel for a moment, then made his own bow to her, and stood passively while they laid their hands on him. It was necessary theatre, I thought distantly, to signal his change from guest to prisoner. I did not think they could stop him if he chose to fight his way free but he would not do it. That would be too easy an end for all of us.

Raziel looked back at the group of us standing by the door. "We will leave within the next hour. We will say Ayriet has become ill and we are taking her to the Chitsa Gorge monastery to recover."

"All of us?" Kirit asked. "That will cause talk."

"Let it. Unless you prefer not to come."

"No, Sidiana, I will go wherever you ask. But the passes are not clear."

"He crossed them." She looked at me. "You did."

"By the Queen's magic."

"Shall I abandon her then? Stay here and do nothing simply because the way is hard?"

I shook my head. "The way will be hard but we have no choice."

We both knew I was not talking about the pass.

It would have been easier for me, I thought after, if we had possessed the magic to transport ourselves to the mountains. It might have been easier to bear the brutal cold, the unforgiving winds than endure every endless moment of the process of preparing to make the journey.

Raziel, having made the decision, seemed to lose the certainty that had haloed her. Her shoulders hunched and she shivered even in the warmth of the hallways. I thought someone might try to persuade her against the folly of going to the Court, but no one did. Diamet took charge, issuing practical commands that would procure us horses and supplies, sending everyone off with a duty.

I had none, except to pack what I wished to take. I also had an escort, one of Raziel's guards. I did not dispute that decision or embarrass the guard by speaking to her.

I had little enough to pack, just as many warm clothes as I could manage and, in a burst of bitter humour, my copy of the *Meditations*. At the appointed hour, my escort and I were in the courtyard waiting. To my surprise, most of the cobbled square was still in shadow, untouched by the rising sun. It seemed as if a lifetime must have passed since the summons to Ayriet's room, but it had been no more than an hour or two.

It was a strange assembly for a trip to the monastery, too many packhorses and too many councillors, and I saw the curious glances our way from the people who made their way around us in the courtyard. Raziel paid no attention, just as she paid none to me, staying deep in conversation with Diamet over the preparations.

To spare anyone the ordeal of prolonged contact with the changeling, someone had rigged a basket on one of the packhorses and then covered it with a blanket, as if against the cold. But a soldier rode on either side of it, guarding that obscene but precious cargo. It and Daen were all we held to bargain with the Queen for Ayriet's life—but I feared he was right. Even if it had all been a lie, a plot between them, she had abandoned him to its endgame.

But if he was guilty, then so was I. So was I.

We met Savean and the soldiers outside the city, by the lake. They seemed to have found shackles without iron, for they were invisible beneath the sleeves of Daen's coat. He looked at the party and dismissed all of Diamet's plans with a shake of his head. "Sidiana, please. Be reasonable. The passes are closed."

"Give me another choice then," Raziel said shortly as she drove her horse past him, her guards behind her. Daen looked at Savean.

"Captain—" he began.

"You heard the Sidiana. Say something useful or be quiet."

I would have made a joke of that once, I thought miserably, teased him about the impossibility of him ever staying silent. I saw Daen look down the line to where I rode. Our eyes met for a moment. It was like holding my hand to a flame. I looked away, put my heels to the placid horse's sides and startled it into a trot. Better he was behind me, where I could only feel the imagined weight of his gaze, where I did not have to watch him riding to whatever end awaited us.

The road to the monastery also led to the pass, so the first part of the journey would excite minimal comment. The snow was gone from the valley floor and the road was not busy. We would be in the hills quickly enough, into the snows again by the afternoon. I did not know what Diamet had planned for that. We would have to abandon the horses then and go on foot. I thought of the great ridge we had crossed in the sled and knew that all the planning in the world would not get us over that obstacle.

Surely Raziel would see that. Surely after a day or two slogging over the snow she would realize it was impossible and turn back.

A day or two in the mountains was enough to cost us all more than just Ayriet.

But what other choice did we have?

I remembered suddenly: the banks of the false river beside a false Jayasita, a question I had never finished, an answer he had never given.

I pulled my horse out of the line and waited for him to reach me.

"Sidi," he said, a thousand meanings shifting beneath that single word.

"Where's the door?"

"What door?" Savean asked, drawing up to us. Ahead of me, the line slowed. I saw Raziel look back.

"If we go into those mountains, some of us will die. There's another way, I know there is. Where is it?"

"I've never gone through it."

"But you've opened it."

"Sidi—" he began and I pushed the horse forward, between the guards.

"You owe her this. You owe me this. Do you want me to ask? To beg? I will. Please, for every lie you told me, please give me this one truth."

He looked at me for a long time, long enough for Savean to shift restlessly in the saddle, for questioning voices to lift from the group ahead of us. "It's on the other side of the lake. There's an abandoned building there, like the shepherd's hut, but larger." His voice sounded weary and remote, like that of the polite stranger he had never been.

I looked at Savean, half expecting to see incomprehension in her eyes, his words turned to gibberish by the Queen's spell. But the captain was looking back, across the grey expanse of the lake on the plateau below us, and it seemed the Queen had no more interest in either of us.

I turned my horse and kicked it into a reluctant trot, my assigned soldier wheeling her own mount to follow me. Raziel's guards did not seem inclined to move until she gestured, then they only pulled their horses off the path a little, to let me approach. "There are doors in the Court that open into other lands, other times," I said. "One of them opens on the far side of the lake."

"Or so he says."

"Yes. But if it's not there, we can always try the pass."

"Can he open it?"

"I don't know, Sidiana. Everything in the Court is what the Queen commands it to be. Doors opened there, for me, but that may have been her will. He said once that sometimes he would open a door in some other place and be in the Court once again, without ever wishing it."

"Is this one of the things you could not tell me before?" *Or would not* went unspoken between us.

"Yes."

"Why do you suppose she allows it now? To keep us from showing up on her doorstep?"

"I don't know that either. But I think that in this much, he is not lying. She no longer cares what we say."

Raziel looked over her shoulder at Diamet and Chadrena. "Sidi Teresine is correct that we can always try the pass if this way does not work," Chadrena said. "We will lose no more than half a day."

Raziel's gaze went past me, down the hill to where Daen sat on his too-small horse, surrounded by Savean's soldiers. He looked back, his expression unreadable. "We'll go to the other side of the lake," she said at last, "and see what he can show us."

As we sorted out the change in direction, I realized that none of us had said his name aloud, not once since the morning's terrible discovery.

It would have been quicker to return through the city, but it would have caused too much talk. Instead, we pushed the horses hard, to the far end of the lake and around it, and then up into the foothills that were heaped at the base of the mountains. Raziel consented to a brief stop at midday. It was a quiet party that dismounted to let the horses drink, then crouched over the cold stones and ate a spare portion of provisions. When we took our turns over the small rise that gave some semblance of privacy, no one went alone; Daen and I because we were each under our own sort of guard, Raziel because Savean would not allow it, the rest because no one wanted to be alone anywhere near the silent, covered presence on the packhorse. As if the Queen would snatch us away while we relieved ourselves, I thought with bitter amusement.

When we resumed, it became apparent that Daen was less certain of the destination than he had seemed. Our process was slow and wandering, punctuated by consultations that became increasingly less polite. At the crest of one hill, Daen abandoned his horse and walked back and forth for a few moments, staring at the valley below us. "Well?" Savean asked, at last.

"You'll know when I know," Daen snarled back as he stalked to the edge of the hill and looked down. I knew he had found it before he even turned back; it was in the sudden straightening of his shoulders, the tilt of his head. "There, now you know," he said shortly and started down the trail. Savean cursed and set the soldiers after him and the rest of us followed, picking our way down the edge of the hill to a second rise.

The house was there, set against the hill. The roof and walls seemed intact but the paint had weathered away, leaving the building no more than a grey shape against the barren hillside.

From the lower slope of the hill, the lake was visible and, far across it, the white bulk of the palace as it rose above the city. Raziel looked at Daen and then around the barren landscape. "Where is this door?" she asked.

"Here. Somewhere." He turned slowly.

"Open it."

I saw the protest start; then he closed his mouth, and shut his eyes in concentration. Something flared in the air a few feet away from him. For a moment, there was black space limned by fire where only air had been then it was gone.

He opened his eyes and looked at Raziel. "I can't."

"You could try again."

"I can try until the end of time and the door will not open if she does not want it to."

"Can she hear us? See us?"

"If she chooses to, Sidiana."

Raziel nodded and dismounted. She walked to where that blackness had been and stood still, staring down the valley. For the first time, I could not read the language of her body, her stance. It was not just the months I had spent away, the months she had been growing into her power. The weight of this moment, of all the choices she would be forced to, was remaking her.

She walked over to the packhorse that bore the changeling and unwrapped the blanket from its basket. She looked down into it, at that face that was the mockery of one so dearly loved, then straightened and covered the creature once again. She walked back towards where Daen waited and looked at Savean. "Hold him."

They obeyed, with swift efficiency; a boot to the back of his knee to force him to kneel, hands on his arms, a sword at his throat. I did not imagine that even he could stop that blade if it bit. For a moment, there was no sound but the long moan of the wind and crunch of stone beneath hooves.

"Will she hear me if I order them to cut your throat right now?"

His chin was lifted, the silver of the sword very bright against the dark stubble down his throat. This time the crunch of stone was beneath my boots as I dismounted. Neither of them looked at me, but I heard my guard's horse take a step forward in time with mine.

"She doesn't care what you do to me, Sidiana. I told you that."

"I don't believe you. You're her son," Raziel replied and I saw Savean's surprised glance, imagined it was mirrored by the rest of the party who had not known.

"I think that if I say your life is forfeit if that door stays closed then it will open."

"No." The word was a surprise to me, as much as my feet on the stones were, as they had been on the night of the ractor hunt. "Sidiana, do not say it."

Raziel looked over at me, her expression as unreadable as her body had been.

"I do not know if the Queen values his life or not," I said, "but I know that for her there are no idle threats. If you make this one, you must carry it out. And if you kill him now, then we have lost the only bargaining power we possess."

"And do you give me this advice because you value Ayriet's life—

or his?" It was a fair question and I tried not to flinch beneath it.

"I give you this advice because it is my duty to do so. We cannot use him to get her back if he is dead. We cannot get her back if we die in the mountains."

"She is right," Chadrena said from somewhere behind me. "We must use this coin the best way we can and I think now is too soon to spend it."

I heard Diamet second that opinion and felt a surge of relief so strong it dizzied me.

"Every moment we lose, we lose more of her," Raziel said at last, wearily. "I know that. I know we cannot cross the mountains in time for there to be any of her left." She looked at Daen. "Your life is the only weapon I have. And there is still a crime to be answered for."

"Great Queen!" She shouted it, to the air and the wind and the place where black space had been. "You have taken our sister's child. We have your son, who has betrayed our trust in him. For that, his life is forfeit, unless you return Ayriet unharmed and unchanged. We will stand here at dawn tomorrow and wait for your answer."

The echoes of her voice were lost in the wind. There was no way to tell if the Queen had heard her ultimatum or not. Most likely, we would never know. For all my counsel, I believed he was right that his life meant nothing to her.

She had let him go, just as she had promised.

CHAPTER 48

Teresine

We went to the ruined house to wait for the morning.

There was enough of it left to keep the wind at bay and provide a roof over our heads. It was divided by rough walls into three sections; a broad room across the front, and two smaller chambers in the back. One was given over to the changeling and its guards, the other designated as a temporary prison for Daen and his.

Fires were lit in all three rooms and dinner was assembled from Diamet's supplies. To my surprise, the enduring sickness in my stomach did not preclude hunger and I ate as eagerly as the rest, seated on the far side of the fire from Raziel, my unofficial guard Janith at my side.

When the meal was done, Raziel spoke quietly to Savean. The captain rose and went to her lieutenant. I watched as the Sidiana's orders unfolded: most of the soldiers sent out into the night (though what shield they could be if the Queen chose to send her own warriors through the door, I did not know), Daen and his guards fetched from the dim room behind us.

He had to stoop to keep from banging his head on the door lintel and then keep his head down, beneath the low roof, though that discomfort did not last long. The guards pushed him down to his knees in the circle, where Raziel could see him clearly across the fire. The others shifted away, leaving a space around him. Janith moved uneasily, as if she were not certain if she should keep to her place or set herself between us. In the end, she stayed where she was, another body between Raziel and me.

"This is not the Hall of Justice but there are enough of us here to pass legal judgement," Raziel said. "I am not the Queen. There are rules and I will follow them."

Daen gave a short laugh. "My life is already forfeit, Sidiana. You told the Queen that, you cannot unsay it now."

"There is more guilt than yours in question," she replied.

No one looked at me. I kept my gaze on the fire. For the first time in that long, terrible day I realized my own life might end on that windswept hill. The sudden rush of terror I felt shamed me; earlier that day I felt as if death would be preferable to misery, but I did not mean it. No one ever truly meant it, not when the moment came.

"She is blameless." His voice was urgent, low, as if it were only he and Raziel in that room. "No one wins against the Queen. She never had a chance."

"So you say."

"If whatever I say you will take for lies, what's the use of a trial? You may as well let us all get some sleep and then kill me in the morning."

"You are capable of persuasion. You have nothing to lose by trying, "Raziel said with a trace of bitter humour. "Except your sleep, of course."

He looked at her for a moment, his expression opaque, then he grinned and lifted his chained hands in a gesture of surrender. "Spare me some of that wine I see passing around and I'll answer your questions."

Raziel nodded and one of the guards edged from the circle to pass him the wineskin. He tipped it back, drank gustily, wiped his mouth and settled himself into a more comfortable cross-legged position. "At your service, Sidiana."

"Why?" The simple question sounded raw.

"Which one?"

"Why take Ayriet? She was innocent."

"Which would make no difference to the Queen. If it matters, Sidiana, none of this has anything to do with mortals. Not that the Queen bothers to discuss politics with *me*. She never gave me a reason for anything she commanded so this is only my best guess. There are rivalries in the Court. The Queen has a cousin," the weight he gave the word made Raziel straighten; it was clear he knew the significance of the word. "There are factions who have no use for mortals, who view the Fair as a corruption, who view me as a monster she should never have borne. I think she saw a chance to demonstrate that she had no fondness for mortals—and that she could force her critics to endure one's presence in the Court if she chose."

"But why Ayriet?"

"Because it is the old way. Because it brings you grief and fear."

"What has she done with her?"

"I don't know, Sidiana. That's the truth. She might keep her. She might just let her die." It was like him, I thought, that blunt honesty.

"I wish I thought you were lying," Raziel said at last, painfully. "But I do not."

"I am sorry, Sidiana."

"And you claim that you knew nothing, that you simply obeyed her commands."

He gave a brief, bitter laugh. "That was the genius of the Queen's plan. I could pretend I was refusing her. I could believe I could get what I wanted without paying her price for it."

"What did you want?"

"To be free of her."

"Enough to betray us, to betray a child."

Enough to betray me.

For a moment I thought he would dispute that, but he simply took another swig of the wine, and nodded. "That's what it came down to, Sidiana. I don't imagine it makes one fucking bit of difference that I didn't know what she intended. I would not have let her harm Ayriet. Not if I'd known."

Raziel glanced my way but the firelight flared in her eyes and I could read nothing there. She looked back at Daen. "Begin at the beginning. Tell me all of it."

So he did, as if it were only the two of them in that firelit darkness.

"I did not know what she had sent me to do when I arrived to fetch Sidi Teresine." Did his voice tremble, just a little, on my name? I hated myself for noticing, for wanting it to be true. "I suppose that was clear. The Queen told me only that another price was required and that I was to bring it back to the Court. Once I had done that, she told me that I was to be her escort, her guard. That I was to seduce her."

I knew this. Of course I knew this. But it was hard to hear it, said so plainly, to feel the weight of curious, prurient eyes upon me. As if they would have resisted, I thought with sudden, vicious anger. As if any of them would not have had him, given the chance.

"Why did she—of course, she did not tell you."

"Of course not, Sidiana. I did not agree, if that matters, but she was used to that. She insisted and I refused. It was an old dance between us, even if she always won in the end. When she commanded a duel that turned out to be to death rather than blood, I realized she was not prepared to accept my refusal. Even when I told Sidi Teresine what I was supposed to do, which I expected would rather neatly prevent it from ever happening, the Queen did not relent. She arranged another demonstration that might have been fatal."

He paused for another gulp of wine. "As I told Sidi Teresine, anyone can be seduced. The irony of it is that while she could not be seduced by vice, she was susceptible to virtue. What she would not do from desire, she was prepared to do to prevent the Queen from killing me. She was betrayed by her own decency."

"Did the Queen know that?"

"Decency is not something the Queen understands."

"But you knew."

"Yes, I knew."

"And when the Queen had what she wanted?"

"She told me she would let me go at last. Let me leave the Court forever and promise never to drag me back as she had done a dozen times before. She would set me free. All I had to do was escort Sidi Teresine back to the city and spend one night beneath the palace roof. To prove I was more mortal than fey, she said."

"So you persuaded Teresine to let you into the palace, to take the wards from the windows, and while you fucked her, the Queen's magics entered and stole my niece away." The crude words were shocking from her; she said them with something like bitter relief, as if welcoming the wound they were meant to give. It was a place for her to put her anger and betrayal, I thought, and put a neat wall around what had happened between Daen and me.

"Yes."

That bald, blunt assent was an unexpected bolt through my already aching heart; until that moment I had not known how much I had wanted to believe it had been more than that.

"Let's be clear about this, Sidiana. If it hadn't been her, it would have been someone else. As I said, anyone can be seduced." He smiled, dark charisma and male sexuality charging the chill air. Then he sobered and the moment was gone, along with some measure of his bravado.

"I didn't do it because I meant to keep the wards open. That never occurred to me." His voice turned urgent, with the first edge of desperation I had heard. His gaze never left Raziel, but I knew the words were meant for me. I wanted to flee, I wanted to cover my ears, I wanted to be anywhere else but here. But, most of all, I wanted his next words to take back that traitorous "yes."

"I never had to lie, only omit truths. Since I was refusing to obey, I was not required to play the part of a seducer. I only had to get to know a woman I found interesting. When she offered to let the Queen win to save my skin, all I had to do was make love to a woman I found beautiful. I spent the night in the palace to get my freedom, but the rest I did because I wanted to. Like all fey bargains, the Queen cheats you by giving you what you most want."

Oh yes, I thought in anguish, she does. She does. I had wanted those words and now they burned through me until there was nothing in my throat but ash and pain and sickness. I was on my feet before I knew it, out into the night before Janith could stop me, on my knees on the cold, sere ground before I could stop myself. I, who had always stopped herself, who had always known how to hide everything, now crouched spewing her dinner onto the frozen earth.

I had wanted him. Even back in the Court, I had wanted him.

I had *loved* him.

I still did. Even with Ayriet lost forever, even with my heart now laid open to every unfriendly eye, I still did.

"Sidi—" Janith's tentative voice.

I wiped my mouth, swallowed bitterness.

"Sidi?"

"I am here. I am not going anywhere. But I cannot go back inside. You will have to guard me out here," I said, wearied and sickened into bluntness myself.

"As you wish," she said softly and I heard her footsteps as she backed away. When I glanced back, she was crouched at the edge of the faint light coming from the doorway. The moon and stars were bright enough that she could see me where I sat. For the first time, I noticed the dark shapes of the other soldiers at their posts, silent witnesses to my humiliation.

It did not seem to matter. What future did I have now anyway? I knelt on the ground, shivering against the wind, and let its chill blow through the emptiness inside me. I wondered when Raziel would send someone to fetch me, to ask me for whatever truth they thought he might have missed. It would the prudent thing to do, though true prudence would have demanded we be questioned separately. Someone should have told her that, I thought absurdly. I should have told her that.

But when a voice called me back from the abyss of my thoughts, it was Raziel's, saying my name.

I heard a guard's half-voiced objection and I turned. Raziel lifted her hand to her. "We'll not go out of sight," she promised. I rose awkwardly, my knees gone stiff with kneeling, and followed her into the night, where the wind would take our words. We stood in silence for a moment, her gaze out across the hills to the distant glimmer of the lake and the far-off fires of Lushan.

"Give me," she said at last, "a reason to be merciful."

"You should not trust any answer I give you."

"But I do."

I was blinded briefly by the vision of eloquence that would somehow undo everything that had been said and done over the last day and night. What did truth or justice or honour of any of it matter, if somehow I could keep the sword from his throat? What honour did I have left to lose?

"There is no reason," I said at last, though whether it was from cowardice or courage I still do not know. "And you have made a vow before the Queen."

"You did not know, either of you, what would happen."

"We should have. He, most of all, knows what she is. I should have told you the truth from the first. But he wanted to be free and I wanted him. Would you be looking for reasons for mercy if it was one of the others who had let him in?"

"I hope so. He says he is dead to her—what good does killing him do?"

"Justice matters. Strength matters. So does the appearance of both."

"She does not care what we do."

"It is not only about her."

"What good is being Sidiana if I am so powerless?" she said at last, for the first time sounding as young as her years. I had no answer for that, because she knew them all. "I was so angry, at both of you," she said. "Now I am only tired, and sick at heart. She is gone. I cannot bring her back. I cannot bear to lose you, too."

"You have no choice."

She nodded and looked up into the starred sky for a long moment.

"Did he tell the truth?" she asked, at last.

"In that, truly you should not trust me," I answered, astonishing myself with my laugh. "The facts were true."

"Do you lo—" she began, then, remembering mercy, stopped. She put her hands to her cheeks for a moment and then drew a breath; I heard its tremble even above the wind. "We must go back."

I followed her, back into the warmth, the firelight, the curious gazes of those waiting around the fire. Raziel nodded to Savean, who disappeared into the darkened prison room and re-emerged once again with Daen in tow. They must have sent him there while they debated his fate. It seemed a bitter farce, a hollow enactment of the rituals of a trial that had only one end.

He found his place again, knelt down with a semblance of his old grace and bent his head to her. "A few hours ago I would have put a knife in your heart myself," Raziel said without ceremony, as if his bluntness had infected her as well. "You have struck one into ours and have admitted you knew that some evil might be done through your actions. I believe you would not have meant harm to Ayriet—but you should have known it might come. You chose to gamble with her life for your freedom.

"I would be merciful, if I could. But I cannot. I made a vow before your Queen and it cannot be undone. Even if I could, justice demands I hold to it. My judgement stands: if my niece is not returned to us tomorrow morning, your life is forfeit."

"I never thought otherwise, Sidiana. But thank you for the thought of mercy. Now," he shifted back to his feet as the guards gathered themselves around him, "if you will permit me," he bent to catch up the wineskin that he had earlier abandoned. "I will go and spend the rest of the night getting drunk."

I wished I could do the same, but that solace was not offered. Instead, I found a wall to set my back against, put my head down on my arms, and tried to find—or feign—sleep. The endless, grinding circle of my thoughts was painful, but not as painful as it would have been to endure both those thoughts and the careful glances of my companions. With my eyes closed, at least I was spared that.

In the end, I must have slept, for the touch on my arm startled me out of slumber. I lifted my head to find Raziel crouched beside me. She put her finger to her lips to signal silence then rose, drawing me after her.

COLD HILLSIDE

By the firelight, I could see the rest of the party slept, except for the guards at the doors to the outside and the prison room. Curious, I followed her across the room, stepping as quietly as we could. I thought the night beyond the door was our destination; the realization that it was not stopped me until she turned back and gestured me on.

We passed the silent guards who sat at the door of the prison room and took a few steps into the darkness. The fire had burned down and was now little more than a heap of embers. I shivered and looked past it but could not be sure which shadow at the far end of the room might be Daen. I looked back at Raziel, her face just visible in the faint light. "There will not be another chance to say farewell," she said softly.

I shook my head. "I don't need—"

"Give me one less thing to regret, Tera. Please. I know what it is to have no final word." She had me at that, her grief for Sarit and Kelci making refusal impossible. The Queen was not the only one with a gift for giving you what you wanted, even if you could not admit to it— but at least I could believe Raziel did it from kindness.

I nodded and made my careful, reluctant way into the room. Darkness shaped itself into a figure seated on the low stone bench that ran across the back of the room, then something in the fire flared and the light found pale skin, sparked in an eye. I glanced back but could see only the hunched silhouettes of the guards at the door. "Sidi," he said and there was nothing I could read in his voice.

"The Sidiana thinks it kindness to let us say goodbye."

He gave a faint snort of laughter. "She's young, isn't she?"

I nodded, then remembered the darkness. "Yes."

"Then have a seat, Sidi. If you think they'll let you."

"I don't know what they'll allow," I replied but stepped forward and sat carefully beside him. "Are you drunk yet?"

"It's come and gone, sad to say. And there's no more wine. I'll have to face the morning sober after all." He leaned his head back against the wall. "I am sorry, Sidi. I hope that you believe I never meant any of this to happen."

"I do. I wish I didn't, but I do. I wish it had all been a lie, all of it, from beginning to end. I wish you had planned it all with the Queen from the start."

"Why would you wish that?"

"Because then it would be an enemy I must watch die tomorrow morning." I found the shapes of the guards again; I wondered if Raziel was there as well. I wondered if they could hear our quiet conversation. "I am sorry, too. I could not give her a reason to be merciful."

"I know. Don't blame yourself, Sidi. The Queen would say I am simply getting what I wanted. I wanted to be mortal, after all."

"Do you want it so badly, then? That you'll die to prove it?" I asked "I know you could end this if you chose. They could not stop you."

"There's a little of my father left in me, even after all these years. I do remember what it meant to be a man, to have honour. I would like to be worthy of him, at the end."

I took a breath and heard it tremble, betraying the ache of tears behind my eyes. "Don't cry, Sidi. Please," he said softly. "Be merciful." We sat in silence for a moment, while I found a place beyond the threat of tears. "Do you suppose they'd let me kiss you?"

"Could they stop you?" I managed with a laugh.

"Would you let me?"

"Could I stop you?"

"Yes."

But I didn't. His hands were still bound, but he cupped my face with them, kissed my forehead, the salt at the corner of my eye, and then my mouth. He said my name, once, before he let me go.

Then it was I who kissed him, one last harsh press of my mouth against his, before I walked away, from one darkness to another, from one pain to another, clinging to that last taste of the thing for which I had thrown away every future I had ever believed in.

CHAPTER 49

Teresine

Then it was dawn.

The sky was dull, featureless grey, as if no other kind of sky was ever possible again. There was a fierce wind from the north, tugging at robes and scraping chilled skin. I shivered in my layers of coat and shawls, my arms wrapped around my ribs, wishing it colder, the wind crueller. Wishing for anything that would blot out that colder dread, that crueller pain inside.

The faces around me were as grim as the day. I do not imagine anyone had slept well; there had been no appetites for the provisions Diamet had brought. Raziel's face was white, except where the wind burned her cheeks and brow. Daen was weary, red-eyed, slump-shouldered, as if the grey sky was an iron weight bearing down on him.

We assembled at the mound of rocks the soldiers had left to mark the door's location on the barren hillside. No one spoke, except for Savean's murmured commands to her guard. No one knew what to say, I thought, or what to do. Raziel's fierce resolution had brought us here but even she did not know how this farce was supposed to play. The fey sense of time was notoriously elastic; was it even dawn at the Court? With only the dull sky above us, was it dawn for us? When did it end? When we all grew tired of the cold and the wind and accepted that there was no salvation for Ayriet or anyone else?

It was Daen who broke the silence, of course. "She's not coming, Sidiana. Just kill me and be done with it. I'm tired of waiting."

Raziel did not look at him, her gaze trained on the emptiness above the rocks. "Great Queen!" she called. "The dawn has come. Give us back our child and we will return yours. Or else he dies."

I knew she would not come, would not return Ayriet, would not save him. I knew that—but when the air began to darken, to shape itself into a doorway of light, hope went through me like a blow.

The doorway expanded, pearly-white against the grey sky, the sere ground. There was a sudden scent in the air; the heavy sweetness of flowers, the cool balm of trees.

The door opened. Beyond it, there was only the grey sky, the sere ground.

My breath turned to a sob. Daen's turned to obscenity.

The door vanished.

There was sudden laughter, raucous and biting, like the contemptuous caw of crows. It was the changeling, shaking off the blankets that wrapped it as it sat at the feet of one of the soldiers.

For a moment, we were all frozen by that jeering sound, by the obscenity of that sound in a mouth that still held the memory of Ayriet's sweetness.

"Savean," Raziel said, her voice breaking. The captain took two steps to reach the changeling and slit its throat.

"Thank you," Daen said solemnly, with a bow in Raziel's direction. "I did tell you, Sidiana."

"I am sorry."

"I know." He straightened and set his shoulders then lifted his bound hands to reach inside his coat. The soldiers tensed, their hands on their swords. For a moment, I thought that he might change his mind and take this one last chance to escape.

But he only withdrew a small folded piece of paper and held it out to Raziel. "I am sorry as well," he said, as one of the guards took the offering and passed to the Sidiana. I watched her face as she unfolded it and knew what it was. "I would have gone back to the Queen if that would have saved her."

Raziel swallowed hard and tucked Ayriet's last drawing into her robe. He knelt neatly on the cold ground and looked at Savean. "I assume you know how to do this cleanly." She nodded. "A new knife would be appreciated, though," he added and she gave a sharp, involuntary laugh. The soldier at her side offered up his blade and took the other, red with the changeling's blood, from her hand.

"Is there—" Raziel began, then her voice failed. She began again: "Is there some funeral ritual among your people we should follow?"

"We burned our lords in boats out on the bay. But you don't have a lot of boats here."

COLD HILLSIDE

"No, we don't." Raziel looked past him, to the distant lake where the wind drove the leaden water into white-edged waves. The moment stretched. I waited for her command with each breath, held helplessly between the prayer for one more moment of life for him and for the sword to fall. For it to be done.

I knew why she hesitated. Pity and mercy and guilt, and the knowledge that the fall of the sword ended all the impossible unavoidable hopes for Ayriet as well. At last, she nodded and Savean stepped up behind him.

His head turned a little, his eyes meeting mine. My hands clenched on cloth, on flesh, to hold me still, to hold the wail I could feel like broken glass in my throat.

Then he bent his head to let Savean's blade find the swiftest path through muscle and flesh into the fierce beating of his heart.

There was blood. I looked away quickly, but not before its bright blossom was seared in my mind. I saw Raziel put her hands to her cheeks to wipe away her tears.

The pain was like the sky; leaden and limitless, as if there was no space for anything but it inside me, as if it would crack me open and spill out to fill the entire world. My only clear thought amidst it all was that I could not stay.

And so I left. I found my horse, pulled myself blindly onto its back and set its head away from the hill, the silent figures there, the huddled shape on the ground. No one tried to stop me. That was Raziel's gift, I guessed, but when I looked back, I saw Janith moving towards her own mount.

It didn't matter. Let her follow me. I did not know where I was going. *Away* was all that mattered. I was content to let the horse go any direction it chose save back to its fellows. After an attempt or two at that, it found the trail back to the city.

I don't know when *away* became final, when I realized it meant more than the hillside. By the time I reached the city, I knew I could not spend another night under that roof, within the walls I had violated. I knew there was no choice for me but exile. It was a favour to Raziel, after all, my own last gift: to go before she ordered it. It would spare her scandal. It would spare me that as well, spare me the lingering dissection of my shame and guilt and whatever other punishment Raziel might be forced to give me. I could add cowardice to my list of crimes.

Janith followed me all the way to the city, to the palace and through its halls to my rooms. Savean would have stopped me, but Janith, having no other orders, merely watched while I packed my satchel with what little I could not bear to leave behind.

She trailed behind me back to the stables. I was willing to walk, reluctant to take more than I must from the city, but cold pragmatism stopped me. I would make much better time on horseback. If my conscience bothered me, I could leave the horse at the last inn before the pass. I saw Janith speaking softly to another guard and then she was saddling her own mount. We rode out of the city as we rode in, she my unacknowledged shadow.

I slept that night in a wayside inn, while Janith stayed in the stable, as if she thought I might flee by moonlight. But I didn't and she followed me into the dawn. The sky was blue, so bright it seemed as if it could never have been any other colour. I shed shawls in its warmth but the world stayed grey to me. I tried not to think or to feel. I simply rode on towards the jagged hole in the mountains that was the pass down into the green world I had left behind so many years ago.

Savean caught up with us some miles before the last outpost at the beginning of the climb. Her guard swept around us in the pounding of hooves and Janith melted back into it gratefully. The captain looked at me for a moment. She nodded and the troop eased back, leaving us some grace.

"The Sidiana has said she will burn his body on the lake," she said at last.

"That is gracious of her."

"Where are you going, Sidi?"

"I don't know. Over the pass. Back to Deshiniva. Does it matter? I am a liability to her, Savean. You know that. She has been forced to make a terrible choice. I am trying to spare her another."

"You are running away," she said bluntly.

"What orders did she give you, when she sent you after me?" I asked, because I did not want to argue with her, because it was the only question that mattered.

Savean sighed, unhappily. "To be sure you know you can come home, if you want to."

I thought I had no more heart left for breaking, but I was wrong.

"Tell her," I said at last, when my throat could let the words go, "tell her I am grateful for that."

COLD HILLSIDE

She nodded and turned her horse away, releasing me. Before she reached her guard she looked back. "He died like a soldier, Sidi. Whatever went before, *she* could not take that from him."

She meant it for comfort. I think he would have taken it as praise.

I set my horse up the empty road towards the pass, where only the sky and the mountains could see my tears.

CHAPTER 50

Teresine

It had taken me three weeks to reach Lushan, those fifteen years ago. It took me four months to return to Deshiniva. I had forgotten in those years what life outside the Euskalan world was like. For all I had felt superior to the cousins for their assumptions of freedom and power, I had grown used to those things. I had forgotten that in the world beyond the mountains I was nothing but a woman, alone and unprotected.

I kept my shaved head, my robes, and the trappings of my amulets and beads. A holy woman, even a barbarian one, was still allowed some latitude. I used Euskalan coin to pay for my place in caravans and groups of pilgrims and whatever passage I could find southward. I was grateful for what work I could do and the distance my travelling companions kept. I moved through the days as I had once skated with Sarit across the icy lake; trying to keep my mind only on the next step I must take and not on the black depths that lay beneath my feet.

My numbness was so complete that it was not until I reached the northern border of Deshiniva that I realized I was with child. I had ignored my first missed bleeding and then my second, my thickening waist, my periodic illness. It seemed impossible that I could be pregnant. Just as it had seemed impossible that I could desire the Faerie Queen's son, that I could love him.

When I finally reached the river, I shed my robes and traded some amulets for the cheap cotton skirt and blouse of a Deshiniva peasant. With a cloth wrapped around my head, I walked the riverside road like any common wife on her way home from market.

Even in Deshiniva, there were ways to end a pregnancy. Not as many as Lushan, to be sure, not as safe, not as sanctioned. But there were always ways that women knew, that women used, no matter what the priests or the gods or their husbands might dictate.

COLD HILLSIDE

I was carrying a child one-quarter fey. In Lushan, they buried the bones of such children in the mountain caves.

I was carrying the grandchild of the Faerie Queen, who had borne and seduced and destroyed her own son.

It was quite clear what I should do. I should drink a potion and be rid of it. If that did not work, I should bear it and drown it. I would not be the first poor woman in Deshiniva to let the river take her baby and I would not be the last. There was nothing I could offer this child, no love or faith or power that could take away the curse that would be bound in its blood.

Except it was my child, as well. And his. It might have its grandmother's cold heart—or it might have his great one. It might have his hunger for life, his stubborn courage. His blood and mine might be strong enough to bind the child, our child, to the mortal world.

Except it was all I had left of him.

So I did nothing but continue to walk in the humid grasp of the Deshiniva summer. I was still days away from the place I had been born. It was not my destination, in truth I had no destination, but my feet kept carrying me that way as if it was still a home to which I could return. Perhaps if I had stayed on that road I would have come to a remembered bend in the river, a still-known door to a still-known hut, and walked in to see my mother at the table, chopping vegetables for the evening meal. Perhaps I would have stayed, invented some story to cover my state, and had a child that would grow up as I did, with the sound of the river beneath her in the night and the long days of work to ensure she slept soundly despite it. Perhaps there would have been safety there, and love, in a place so insignificant the fey would never know it existed.

But well north of that bend, that door, I saw a symbol nailed to a tree; wooden hands shaping a lotus. And so I turned off the road and walked up the narrow trail that led to the House of the Holy Hyanatha, whose sisters took vows of poverty and took in the women who had nowhere else to go.

I found myself in the company of women again, as I had been in Lushan and in the Asezati school, as I had been in the brothel in Jayasita. There was work to do, to offset the bed and board the Sisters gave as charity, and even though it had been years since I had scrubbed the floors in the Asezati refectory, I still remembered how. I was as grateful for the work as I had been then, grateful to fall exhausted onto my cot beneath its shroud of netting and sleep without dreams. I was even grateful for the worship that was also part of our payment. If I did not pray, I still managed to find some place of refuge from my thoughts, to find some way to lose myself in the lifted voices and the drift of incense.

It was early autumn, the nights now pleasantly cool, the days no longer quite as steamy, when I bore the child. It was a hard labour. I wasn't brave, remembering Sarit, half-wishing both the child and I would follow her into the red darkness, half terrified we would. But at last I heard the first hesitant cry and the attending sister placed a warm, sticky bundle into my arms. Weakly, I fumbled for the iron amulets in their little bag beneath my pillow. They spilled out and my shaking fingers found one, pressed its cold circle to the infant forehead.

The baby squirmed, screwed up its eyes and wailed—but the iron left no mark. As I held my daughter against my breast and wept helplessly, the stone over my heart lifted away for the first time in months.

I stayed for a year. The nuns had some respect for my foreign vocation, for the skull I still kept shaved, and they let me stay beyond the normal term—though I suppose it might also have been my willingness to scrub floors and manage accounts that bought my peace there. For a time, I allowed myself to believe it might be possible to find a permanent place for me—and for the child I had named Amaris—there, in that place apart from a world to which I no longer belonged.

As the year moved on, and summer lay across the land in damp inevitability, Keshini arrived at the House. I noticed her because she shared the name of my youngest sister. She was well along in her pregnancy, her belly a burden that seemed too heavy for her fragile frame. She didn't talk about what had driven her there, as some of the girls did, or spin tales of rescue by lovers or families, as others would. She worked quietly and diligently and, to my surprise, Amaris, who had demonstrated an unbendable will even at that age, liked her.

When Keshini delivered a stillborn child two months before it should have entered the world, it was Amaris who comforted her, Amaris who would crawl to lie beside her in the heat of the long afternoons. I was grateful, because it left me time for my duties, and jealous, because she was mine, my child born of loss and grief and I could not bear the thought of sharing any of her attention.

COLD HILLSIDE

Amaris's first birthday came and it was celebrated in the Deshiniva fashion by anointing her forehead in jasmine oil and the Euskalan fashion with the gift of one of my iron amulets. I sewed it to the collar of her shift, while she squirmed in my lap. I held her still and with fingers turned suddenly unsteady I turned the little iron hand until it touched her collarbone. She twisted, her face screwing up for a squall of outrage, but the skin beneath the iron stayed smooth and perfect.

In a spasm of energy she squirmed from my grasp long enough to tear the amulet from her collar and throw it in the dirt. For a moment we stared at each other. She looked Deshinivi, I thought, as dark-eyed and dark-skinned as I was. There was nothing of Daen in her look, except perhaps the set of her shoulders as she stood there, daring me to stop her.

Then she toddled off to find Keshini and I retrieved the amulet from the ground.

The next day, the soldiers came.

For months we had heard rumblings of unrest, tales of bad harvests to the south, of corruption in the capital, of troops unpaid. The House Mother worried, we buried what coins we had a little more carefully, and we waited, because that was all women could do in Deshiniva.

There were ten in the ragged troop, headed by a lieutenant with a patchy beard and a hard look. They accepted a meal and a small bag of coins but I saw their eyes as they watched the nuns and the pregnant girls who served the rice. We tried to keep the prettiest ones, the most delicate ones, out of sight but I did not imagine it mattered. We were women, we were alone, we were fallen. We were prey.

That troop moved on but one night, not long after, there was one that did not. And I, having laid plans with cold deliberation that would have done the Queen proud, dragged my daughter and Keshini away from the flames and screams down the path I had chosen.

With the coins I had taken from the sisters' carefully hidden hoard, I bought passage on the next barge up the river.

I told myself I was only seeking the next sanctuary I could find but I think even then I knew. The first time I told someone Amaris was Keshini's child, I told myself it was because it was a scandal for a woman passing as a nun to have a child—but I knew. The first time another woman nursed my daughter, I wept in silence—but I bound my breasts until they dried and went on. The first time Amaris called Keshini "mother," I stopped pretending there was any other place for us to escape to than the mountains. To Lushan.

Once the choice was made, the rest was, if not easy, then straightforward. The last of the stolen coins and my shaven head bought us a place in a trading caravan through the pass. They were Malabens, traders from a minor House in a southern town, and if any of them recognized my name, they did not show it. Keshini I claimed as my sister and Amaris as my niece and they had no reason to disbelieve us. While Amaris was still happy to sit in my lap around a campfire, or ride one of the pack horses beside me as we trudged up the pass, it was to Keshini she went for comfort, for nursing, for love.

And every time she did, it was a blow that left me winded, breathless with pain. But the pain always passed, as did the doubts that kept me awake in the cold nights. There is no place else for us to go, I told myself. I will find some place far from the city where we will be anonymous, safe.

The Queen will never know. Raziel will never know. Amaris will never know.

The things we do for love, the prices we pay again and again and never learn how not to want, not to need. The lies we tell ourselves and the world.

We left the caravan a day from Lushan. There was a monastery in Keryn, across the valley. I was, as far as I knew, still an Asezat. They would give us shelter until I could find someplace for us to settle.

We stopped the next night in a little village. There was no inn, but one of the farmers offered space on the floor of her common room and I accepted gratefully. It was no more uncomfortable, and considerably warmer, than many places we had slept.

It was the night of the Soul Moon Festival, which I had forgotten until the farmer asked if I would add a blessing to the boats as they released them into the stream that ran like a silver ribbon through the village. Keshini and Amaris came as well, wrapped in borrowed blankets, and watched curiously as the villagers knelt to release the paper boats with their fragile lights—most no more than a smear of wax and a twig—into the water. One of the old women said words in the old tongue, I said some in the new and we watched in silence as the boats swirled and slid and sank away. Then the villagers left and we three were alone in the moonlight.

There were three boats left, granted at my shameless request. I crouched on the bank and struck my flint until the fire found the wicks.

I placed them gently in the stream, whispering the names: Sarit, Ayriet, Daen. I thought of what Savean had told me and saw in my mind's eye a boat burning on that cold grey sound I had seen beyond the door in the Faerie Court. Had it been enough, I wondered, for his father's gods? Had they taken him in, a warrior-son fallen in a strange land?

Behind me, I heard a sound that became the end of a series of sounds, half-heard in my grief. The jingle of a bit, the heavy whuff of a horse's exhalation, a footstep. I glanced at Keshini, who was staring behind me, her arm wrapped around Amaris, who had fallen asleep against her.

I rose, turning, and saw Raziel. She was standing on the bank, her head bare, her golden hair, so like her sister's, blown across her face by the wind. I bowed my head. "Sidiana."

"Teresine." There were guards some paces behind her, holding the horses. "I heard you had come back."

"I meant to send you a message, when we reached the monastery at Keryn."

"We?"

"My sister, Keshini, and her daughter." She looked at them for a moment then her gaze shifted to the three boats caught in an eddy in the stream.

"I should be at the palace, for the festival," she said at last. "But I did not think I would ever see you again."

"We had nowhere else to go." It was an apology, an explanation, a plea. "I thought to find a village. Somewhere quiet. We could farm. Or I could teach. If you give us sanctuary, Sidiana."

"Sanctuary." She said it as if the word were in a foreign language. "Your sister and her child are welcome here, Teresine. You are welcome here."

"You know that isn't true," I said but found it funny, suddenly, and could not help my smile. Her own curved, hesitant, hopeful.

"No, you're right. But I welcome you. I missed you." She held out her hand. I took it and let her help me up from the river to the bank. "I need you," she said quietly as the assistance became a quick, fierce embrace. "Come back to the court."

"I can't. You know I can't."

She drew back and even in the moonlight I could see the change in her. It had been Raziel who had smiled and embraced me, it was the Sidiana who stood before me now. "You may have a house, outside the city if you wish. A safe place for your family. But I need you back."

"Raziel, I am a traitor. No one will trust me."

"You are not a traitor unless I say you are. I told you then I have no hate left in me for what happened. And I trust you. I always have. I always will." She said it loudly enough that the guards, hovering with the horses father up the hill, must have heard. Her voice lowered, she went on: "I need you. The city needs you."

"And that is to be the price then?"

"Yes."

I thought about leaving, thought about the long trek back over the mountains, thought about the world below in which none of us might ever be safe. I thought about how it would be to sit with her in the council once again, beneath the bitter, contemptuous gaze of those who knew what I had done. I thought of what Sarit and Kelci had meant me to be—the one person who would have no interest but the Sidiana's, because she could never belong to the Houses or the city.

"I know what I am asking," she said. "And you know why I must. You taught me, after all."

I nodded, thinking that all along she had been wiser than I, who had once told her that she had a choice. She had learned the hardest lesson of all; that power gave her no choices at all.

I had embraced Raziel, my dearest friend. I knelt to the Sidiana as I thanked her for her mercy.

CHAPTER 51

Lilit

Lilit had not really believed her father intended to go to the palace until they arrived at the outer gate. "We don't have an appointment," she pointed out as they entered the courtyard. "What if she cannot see us?"

"Then we will make an appointment and come back," Hendren replied sensibly. "Besides, avoiding Kerias for a few hours is likely a wise option for both of us."

Lilit could not argue with that and so trailed her father through the corridors until he reached an office presided over by one of the Sidiana's aides. The woman took their names and disappeared down the hallway, leaving Hendren and Lilit to join a small gathering of petitioners waiting to see the Sidiana.

The aide reappeared a few moments later and gestured for them to follow her. Raziel was waiting for them in her office. "I've ordered tea," she said, rising to embrace Lilit and accept Hendren's brief bow. "Please sit down. How are things in Kerias?"

They settled into the chairs in the little sitting area and Lilit let her father manage the polite conversation until the tea arrived. Raziel nodded to the young man who brought it, waved him away from serving it and he bowed and closed the door as he left.

"Now, tell you me why are here?" she asked as she leaned forward to pour the tea, as casually as if she were no more than any woman welcoming friends to her home.

"I would have gone to Teresine but without her I must hope you will do whatever you believe she would have wanted. Lilit," Hendren's voice faltered for a moment, "went to a faerie-tester who told her that she has fey blood. She fears it is true, and fears for the child she is carrying. Amaris is insistent upon her ending her pregnancy."

"That is Kerias business, unless she forces her," Raziel said, after a moment. Her voice was calm but there was no longer any possibility of mistaking her for simply an old family friend. "And I assume you assured her that faerie-testers are not to be trusted and there is no possible way that she can be fey."

"I told her there is no more taint of that in Kerias than in any other House," Hendren replied. "But as House Archivist one comes across many strange old stories. I think it would be better if no one else had a reason to remember them. My daughter has said she wants the truth and will not stop looking for it."

It was odd to be discussed as if she were not present, Lilit thought. It seemed as if there were layers of meaning under everything they said, some parallel conversation that Raziel and Hendren understood but she could not.

"I see. Thank you for bringing her here. I think it would be best if she and I spoke alone for a while."

"Shall I wait, Sidiana?"

Raziel shook her head. "No, go on home. Everything will be fine." She saw him to the door politely, closed it behind her, and then turned to look at Lilit.

"Well," she said, suddenly the Raziel of the long days at the mountain house, the formal weight of the Sidiana seeming to slip from her. "I suppose you'd better tell me what is going on. All of it—and start at the beginning."

Lilit did, as honestly as she could: the night with Feris Kijhold, fainting at the fair, the fey Lord Bastien, sleepwalking to the bridge, the ominous dreams that had plagued her, Teresine's confession of her time at the Border Court and finally, her trip to the faerie-tester and the argument with her mother.

"And then Father insisted that we come here," she concluded.

"Quite rightly, too. How much of this did you tell them?"

"Everything except what Teresine told me about the Border Court."

Raziel took a sip of her tea and then refilled her own cup and Lilit's. The tea was cold but Lilit suspected her actions had less to do with refreshment than with delay. "I ought to tell you that your mother is right," Raziel said at last. "I ought to advise you—very strongly—to end this pregnancy and forget the lies of a fraudulent seer. That would be kinder to us all."

"But it wasn't a lie, was it?"

"I don't know. But if I go any further, you must understand that you are bound to silence on everything I say. You must swear to it and know that if you break that oath, you have committed treason, not only to me but to Teresine."

"I understand." Lilit put her hands to her heart and bent her head. "I swear I will never tell anyone."

"I will hold you to that. Now, I must ask you to wait here for a few moments. I need to retrieve something that may help me to give you the truth."

There was nothing for Lilit to do but sit and wait. It seemed bad manners to wander around the small office unsupervised and she did not want to give the Sidiana any reason at all to distrust her discretion. She felt a numb astonishment at the turn the day had taken, that her conversation with her parents had brought her here to the edge of a secret she had not even been certain existed.

Raziel returned, carrying a book bound in red silk and tied in black ribbon.

"Now I will tell you a story," she said as she settled back into her chair, holding the book in her lap. "I have never told it before, so you must forgive me if I do it badly. At my first fair as Sidiana, the tribute was one stone short. The Queen demanded of us another payment. There was an Aygaresh mosaic in the Border Court and she wanted it restored."

"And so Teresine went."

"Yes. She went to the Border Court and every day for six months I prayed to Jennon for her safe return. I feared I had sent her into terrible danger, because I had not been clever enough to save her from the Queen's service.

"Then, on the 10th day of Nahase, she came back, but not alone. The Queen had sent an escort, the same fey lord who had taken her away after the fair. His name was Daen and he was half-mortal. He was also the Queen's son."

As Lilit listened, a knot of pain twisting tighter and tighter beneath her breastbone, Raziel told her of Daen's arrival in the city, the devastation of finding Ayriet gone, the revelation of Daen and Teresine's relationship, the trial in the abandoned house, and the Queen's abandonment of her son to death on a cold hillside.

"Teresine left the palace that day. I sent Savean to find her, to tell her I forgave her, but she fled the country anyway. We burned Daen's body on a boat on the lake, because that was the custom of his father's people. I could not hate him for what had happened; he was the Queen's pawn and her victim as much as any of us.

"Two years later, Teresine came back with Keshini and Amaris. All she wanted was a little farm, she said, or a place she could teach. But I would not give her that. I made her return to the city and sit in the council with some of the very people who had heard Daen's confession, who knew what she had done. I made her endure that because I needed her. I flatter myself that she did it for love of me, but I know it was for love of your mother and then of you. To buy you both a place of safety, she would have done anything."

Raziel picked up the book and began to undo the ribbons. "On my last visit to the mountain house, the day I met you on the path, she gave me this. After all those years of silence, she wrote it down, all of it. I've read some of it, as she gave me leave to do. There were so many things I never understood before, about her life and her past. But some of it, I think, is meant only for you."

She paged through the book for a moment and then held it out to Lilit. "Read this to me."

Lilit looked at the familiar scrawl of her great-aunt's handwriting and found a sentence. "'On the dais sat the Queen. I lowered my eyes but the image of her remained there, as if burned into my lids: the white hair, like a cascade of moonlight that fell past her knees, spilling over the dais to pool on the ground,'" she recited and then looked at Raziel.

There was sorrow in the pale blue eyes and in the faint sag of her shoulders, as if some expected blow had finally landed.

"I would have read the whole thing," Raziel said, "but I could not. The Queen cast a spell of silence and to me the words are meaningless scratches, just as back then Teresine's explanations of life at the Court were gibberish to my ears."

"But I can read it."

"Yes, you can."

For a moment, Lilit couldn't breathe past the iron weight on her chest, in her throat. The thought that had been taking shape during the Sidiana's story was no longer possible to deny.

"She wasn't my great-aunt, was she?"

"No, I don't believe she was."

"And I can read this because—" But she could not say it.

"Because you are the great-granddaughter of the Faerie Queen."

"It's not possible. How is it possible? I passed all the tests," Lilit said, disbelieving. She held out her hands, fingers spread. "Look at the iron on my hands. My mother . . . my mother is going to be head of House Kerias." It was the most powerful proof she could think of against such an absurdity.

"She probably will. Your mother is a formidable woman."

"But how . . . how can you allow it? How can you trust us if . . . ?" The words would not come; she abandoned them in a helpless gesture.

"I have known you both almost all your lives. I have watched you and I have had you watched. All these years, I have never had a cause for alarm."

"Until now," Lilit said and Raziel nodded.

"What will you do about the child?"

Lilit shook her head. "I know what everyone thinks I should do. I know they're probably right. But there's something . . . I can't explain it. . . ."

Raziel leaned forward and laid the book in her lap. "Take this. Go somewhere safe and quiet and read it. I cannot tell you what you will find there but Teresine wanted you to know everything. I think that once you do, you will know what choice to make."

"And if that's to keep this child, will you let me?"

Raziel looked at her for a long moment. "Lilit, I have loved you as if you were my own grandchild," she said at last, "but I will always do whatever I must to protect Lushan." Her voice was gentle—but it was the Sidiana's voice once again, the voice of the woman whose whole life had been spent in the service of the city. The voice of the woman who would order the end of an unborn child if she believed it was necessary to fulfill that charge.

Lilit nodded numbly and drew the book to her chest, hugging it there as if it could keep her from dissolving into tears and terror.

CHAPTER 52

Lilit

She could not stay in the palace nor could she go home to Kerias, not with the book of her great-aunt's (who was not her great-aunt, she reminded herself, but her *grandmother*) in her possession. Not while her mother (who was not just her mother, but was the *Faerie Queen's granddaughter*) was convinced she was hysterical and required potions and isolation.

In the end, she went to the lake, to the same spot she had sat over a month ago, trying to decide what to do about her pregnancy. There was a cold breeze from the water but the sun was warm enough and within a few pages into Teresine's memoir, Lilit felt neither cold nor heat.

When she was done, she sat back, wiping the last traces of half-dried tears from her face.

The words had been so vivid that she had heard her grandmother's voice in her head as she read. She had recognized the woman behind those words—her tough, bitter humour, her unexpected gentleness—but there had been so much more, all the passion and love that she had hidden; for a friend who died too soon, a lover whom she had watched executed, a daughter she was forced to deny.

It was a miracle that she had any faith left for love, Lilit thought, fighting fresh tears. *But she loved me. I never realized how much.*

She looked down at the book in her hands and saw the dark bands of the iron on her fingers. It did not burn her, no matter who her great-grandmother was. Just as it did not seem to touch her mother, who had more fey blood than she. Did Amaris know? Did she even imagine such a thing was possible? Lilit thought of her mother's obdurate will and her long resentment of Teresine, the mother she did not know she still had. She could not know, she decided. Even Amaris would not be able bear her own strength, her own cold power, if she knew from whom she had inherited it.

COLD HILLSIDE

Lilit's gaze lifted across the choppy waters of the lake to the shape of the far hills. *He died out there*, she thought. *My grandfather. She* let him die. They all had: the Queen, Raziel, Teresine.

She saw it in her mind, conjured by Teresine's words; the grey sky, the door opening and closing, the blood falling. And suddenly she knew where it had happened.

She remembered going with her great-aunt . . . her grandmother . . . on one of her trips on the Sidiana's business to visit an irrigation project under construction in a far village. They had ridden through those hills. Teresine had seemed withdrawn and snappish, but Lilit was already aware of the vagaries of her temper and her dislike of travel. (Ironic, now that she knew how great her grandmother's travels had been.) She remembered Teresine halting their little party at a stream with a small shrine to Jennon beside it and vanishing up one of the hillsides with a stern injunction that she wanted to be alone. The accompanying guards had made a crude joke or two about an old woman's intestinal difficulties, silenced when they remembered Lilit.

It was a long time before she returned. The guards said nothing. Lilit had looked at her face and kept silent as well. They had ridden on as if nothing had happened.

Lilit looked across the lake, her imagination firing a boat there, watching the red flames rise in mosaic tiles to an indigo, pearl-starred sky. She still had no idea what she was going to do, her heart and her mind still too full of her grandmother's story to consider how her own was supposed to end.

She could not return home and she had left Kerias to go the palace with no money to buy a place to stay. There was only one place left to go. She went to the Austers and begged a bed of Toyve. "My mother," she said with a shrug and Toyve nodded knowingly and found her a spot in a spare room. She joined the other apprentices for dinner but they accepted her silence and early retreat without too many questions, ascribing her distracted mood to her fight with the formidable Amaris Kerias.

Lilit lay in the darkness, holding the book across her chest, thinking of her grandmother walking down the hill with her face full of a sorrow Lilit was too young to recognize or understand. She thought of the fair and the things that had haunted her; her faint, the sleepwalk to the bridge. Had that been the response of her blood to a call it could not deny or had the nearness of the fey awakened something in the scrap of life slumbering inside her? She wondered if they had felt it, as they walked about the fair, that tug of their own kind where none should be.

In the morning, she went to the workroom and did her best to keep her mind on her tasks but at midday, Jerel sent her away. "You're worth less than a first-day sweeper," she said acerbically. "Go on before you break something." Lilit didn't argue with the unexpected kindness.

She did not have to decide where to go; she had made that choice during the long hours she had not slept.

At the stables they had not asked her any questions, simply accepted her Kerias token and given her one of the House horses. She followed the lake road, trying to reconstruct that long-ago journey in her mind as she went. On the far shore, all the paths that led up into the hills looked the same.

What are you doing? She thought as she drew the horse to a stop and looked up yet another trail winding away from the road. What do you think this will prove? There was nothing here that would answer her questions, just the wind and the empty hillsides.

Then the outline of a scrawny, wind-bent tree snagged something in her memory. Just a little way along, she told herself. Just round a corner or two. Just to see if I'm right. It was four corners, but then there it was, the stream and the neglected shrine. She urged the horse up the hill and, at the top, dismounted and looked around. In the shadows cast by the waning sun, she saw the ruins of an abandoned house in a shallow valley to the left.

Halfway down the hillside the ground levelled a little into a stretch of flat land. She paused there and the horse bent his head to mouth the sparse grass. The air seemed charged and Lilit thought of the fair and the feel of sparks and unseen breeze on her skin. The horse's reins dropped from her hands and she was dimly aware of it tossing its head and backing away. There is still time to leave, she thought, but knew she would not.

"Hello," she said tentatively, feeling both foolish and frightened. "Is someone there? Can you hear me?"

She took a step forward.

"Great Queen, can you hear me?"

There was no sound but the wind. She saw nothing but the dun-coloured hills beneath the pale, late afternoon sun.

"Great-grandmother, are you there?"

There was the faint sound of chimes, the faint scent of flowers on the wind that was suddenly warm on her skin. Something began to shape itself in the air in front of her. It was not a door but a column of white that shifted from mist to smoke to silk and then the Queen was there. Lilit trembled and dropped her eyes, the words of the old story echoing in her mind.

A woman it hurts to look upon. But Teresine had looked, she reminded herself. Teresine had defied her. She slowly lifted her gaze.

Before her stood the Queen, clad in white furs, her white hair a mass of braids and loose waves that did not move in the breeze. The air was dark and smoky around her.

"So," she said at last, her voice soft and cold. "Mortal child. Do you claim kinship with me?"

"Would you have come for someone who only claimed it, Great Queen?"

"You have his blood and his unruly tongue." Her black eyes shifted over Lilit, scouring her. "I felt you at the fair this year, mortal child."

"Did you make me faint? Did you make me sleepwalk to the bridge?" She did not have Teresine's gift for concealment or indirection. She could only blunder on and ask what she needed to know.

"What interest have I in fainting or sleepwalking?"

"I'm pregnant. Do you have an interest in that?"

The Queen looked at her for a long moment, until it took all Lilit's will to hold her gaze. "What is in your womb is not of my doing. It is no concern of mine." Against the cool dismissal in her voice, all of Lilit's unvoiced fears about the fair seemed like nothing more than absurd imaginings.

"If it's no concern of yours, will you promise to leave us alone?"

The black gaze grew stonier. "It is *you* who called *me* to this hillside. I make no promises to mortals." Mist wreathed its way around her feet, swallowing the white fall of her fur robe. Through the air above her head, Lilit could see the darkening sky once more.

"Farewell, great-granddaughter." Not *mortal child* with its anonymity and distance, but a salutation chilling in it possessive acknowledgement.

"Why did you let him die?" Lilit flung the question at the fading image, because she had nothing left to lose. "He was your son. Why didn't you save him?"

"He wanted to be mortal. That is what mortals do. They die."

The smoke turned to darkness and then to sky and Lilit was alone, listening for any echo of sorrow in her great-grandmother's voice.

Her strength seemed to vanish with the Queen and she crumpled helplessly onto the cold ground to sit weeping in the place where her grandfather had won his wish and lost his life.

CHAPTER 53

Lilit

She knew it was folly to take the path to the mountain house in the dark but Lilit led the horse on a slow trudge up the switchback paths, lit only by the uneven light of the low, cloud-shrouded moon. She was tired and numb and could think no further than reaching the warmth of the one place she had always gone for comfort.

Urmit and Filiat would be in bed, of course, but that did not stop her from picturing herself sitting in the kitchen while they made her tea and clucked over her and called her "Lily-child."

Mortal child, the Queen had called her, and then *great-granddaughter*.

Meaningless words, Lilit thought, and a meaningless heritage. It hadn't kept her from having a life in Lushan, for which she was grateful, but it also hadn't gifted her with any extraordinary powers either. She could not start fires or light paths or stop time or even decide whether to have a baby or not.

It is no concern of mine, the Queen had said.

Lilit remembered Teresine's words, on the visit she had not known would be the last. *They cannot be trusted. Oh child, never forget that.*

The Queen had sacrificed her own son to the politics of the fey court. Even if she declared she had no interest in it, were there other powers in the fey that would consider a child of the Queen's blood a valuable pawn in their unending game?

Lilit climbed over the last rise and saw the house waiting below her. She pulled the horse the final distance and forced herself to the necessary tasks of unsaddling him in the dark and tying him up by a bale of feed. She slipped through the unbarred door into the kitchen, where the embers in the hearth cast enough glow that she could find the lanterns. She was stoking the fire for tea when Filiat arrived, trailed by Urmit. Both of them carried knives, which made her laugh aloud.

"Lily-child! What in the Mother Mountain's name are you doing here at this hour?" Urmit asked.

"I'm sorry. I didn't mean to wake you. I needed someplace quiet to think."

As she had expected, Filiat looked after the mechanics of tea while Urmit concentrated on those of comfort; finding her a blanket against the cold, disappearing to light the braziers in her bedroom. Lilit took the tea and accepted the comfort and then told them both to go to bed. They told her to do the same but she went to the terrace instead and sat in the dark, wrapped in the blanket and warming her hands around the mug of tea.

She thought of that day by the lake, when she had imagined she could add the reasons for and against up like mourning flags and know her answer. She knew now that the questions and the answers were not as simple as a line but a tangle of possibilities, a complex equation of "ifs" and "thens."

Imagine the worst, Lilit told herself. *Imagine the most terrible endings and see if you can endure them.*

To bear the child and have it cry at the first touch of iron, to have Aunt Alder take it away to die and to know you would never, ever dare to have a child of your own body again.

To bear the child and have the Queen's fickle black gaze settle on it with interest, because she made no promises to mortals.

To be forced to end it by the woman she loved almost as much as she had her grandmother, because the Sidiana could not risk any of the other outcomes.

Every path except the easy one, the rational one, the one urged on her by her mother and her ruler, promised pain. She was not as strong as Teresine, whose life had been shaped by harsher hands.

But inside her lay all of the living legacy that Teresine might ever have. It might not have been conceived in love but it was the child of it nonetheless. It was *his* last legacy as well, her unknown grandfather she could not help but love because her grandmother's passion for him had been in every word she wrote.

It might have its grandmother's cold heart—or it might have his great one. It might have his hunger for life, his stubborn courage.

She did not know what legacy its father might bring to the child, but she knew what hers might be: not only Teresine's strength and

Daen's vitality, but Hendren's compassion and even Amaris's single-mindedness. Was that enough, all that mortal, damaged, enduring love and courage? Would it be enough to protect it from both cold iron and the colder intrigues of the fey?

Was all of that enough to give *her* the strength to stand against both mortal and fey power?

If she did not believe it was, then her only choice was to go to Aunt Alder and end the pregnancy.

The edge of the mountains began to pale with the dawn. Lilit rose, cramped legs complaining, pulled her blanket around her and went to the edge of the terrace to look down the valley towards the city somewhere beyond the ridge. She had not slept but sometime in the night she had passed through exhaustion into a new wakefulness.

Noises came from the house behind her; Filiat and Urmit beginning their normal routines. She thought about them, the familiar faces against the familiar stones, the people and a place she loved and might lose.

She put her hand against the curve of her belly and waited for the sun.

CHAPTER 54

Teresine

The years passed. I endured the city until finally Raziel set me free of it. Keshini died too soon, too far from the world she knew to survive, and Amaris grew up believing me to be the aunt who had failed her. In her ambition, her will, I saw the icy echo of her grandmother, but she wore the iron that was required and fought her way into the heart of the city, beneath the gates, without its wards rejecting her so I suppose my blood was as strong in her as the Queen's. Though I have been as ruthless in my own way as the Queen, so perhaps that too is my fault to bear.

And then there was you, Lilit, whom I loved far more than I could ever show. Whom I feared to love, because my love has never done anyone any good, not even me. You have been the one pure joy in my life.

I never told Raziel the truth, perhaps my last betrayal of her, but I have always suspected she knew it anyway and did whatever she felt necessary to protect the city.

I am old and now I feel it. I can feel death coming for me and all the things I have never been able to say can no longer go unsaid, remembered only in the temporary patterns of colour and shape. I don't know if you will be able to read this, if the Queen's magic will render it nonsense, but I owe you the truth of how you came to be in the world, especially now that you have been to the fair.

There will be no burning boat on a grey lake for me but Raziel has promised me a pyre and not the caves. I am still superstitious enough to find that comforting. I do not know if there is anything—or anyone—waiting for me beyond the smoke.

I suppose I will have to wait and see.

APPENDIX: CHARACTERS

In the Palace, listed by ruling Sidiana

Kelci – mother of Sarit and Raziel
Maudrian – former head of the Palace guard
Neith – Kefir's consort
Teresine – Deshiniva-born companion to Sarit, tutor to Raziel

Sarit – daughter of Kelci
Ayriet – Sarit's daughter, father never identified
Perin – Sarit's lover, member of the Engineer's Guild
Roshan – General in Sarit's time
Savean – captain of Palace guard for Sarit and Raziel

Raziel – daughter of Kelci, succeeds Sarit
Chadrena Rumah – House Head and council member, Newari
Cserin – Priestess of Jennon
Diamet Auster – House Head during Sarit's reign/early part of Raziel's
Janith – one of Savean's guards
Kirit – Archivist in Raziel's court
Lakshi – another candidate for Sidiana
Meade – Physician at Raziel's court
Reshen – one of Raziel's council
Trine – Engineer/Map maker on Raziel's council

The Merchant Houses

(Note: generally, all adults are considered aunts/uncles, and all contemporaries cousins regardless of actual blood relation.)

Kerias
Alder – house healer during Lilit's time
Amaris – Teresine's niece, married into Kerias

Bizat – aunt during Lilit's time
Charlot – mother of Teras and Teril
Hendren – Amaris's husband
Irah – cousin during Lilit's time
Jihan – House Head when Hendren married Amaris
Lilit – Amaris's daughter, Teresine's great-niece
Neven – Lilit's brother, died as a baby
Sitran – cousin during Lilit's time
Tannis – aunt during Lilit's time
Teras and Teril – cousins, twins
Ursul – Kerias House Head during Lilit's time
Vinesh – cousin during Lilit's time

Auster
Colum – cousin, goes with Lilit to the fair
Dareh – House Head during Lilit's apprenticeship
Diamet – House Head during Sarit's reign/early part of Raziel's
Hazlet – uncle, goes with Lilit to the Fair
Jerel – head of the Auster gem studio
Toyve – cousin, goes with Lilit to the fair, Dareh's daughter
Wilheh – aunt, served on clan council

Other Clans
Crisfan sa Alladis – sister of Perin
Feris Kijhold – Lilit's lover before the fair
Anil Vachos – friend of Amaris
Hyanith Vineret – attends fair

Other City Folk

Aurelian – Euskalan philosopher (dead)
Zayan Bevan – Asezat teacher (dead)
Yeshe Bukoyan – Asezat monk, Teresine's teacher
Hekat – Teresine's fellow student at Asezati school
Jenet Kalins – woman in bar, rumoured to be part-fey
Somchin – Newari waiter
Zayan Bevan – Asezat teacher (dead)

At the Mountain House

Urmit – Teresine's housekeeper
Filiat – Teresine's cook
Keshini – mother of Amaris, Deshinivi

At the Faerie Court

Bastien – Lord, scholar of mortal ways
Daen – half-mortal, Queen's Champion
Ferrell – Queen's advisor
Garrich – young lord
Hilare – companion of Bastien
Ilene – companion of Bastien
Lindel – companion of Bastien
Madelon – Queen's cousin and political rival
Veradis – the Faerie Queen

ACKNOWLEDGEMENTS

In the almost twenty years it took me to finally finish this book, I've racked up a large number of debts I can never hope to repay.

For listening to me whine, ramble or protest and for either staying silent or providing advice as the situation demanded: Darlene Storey, Maureen Brewer, Marilyn Kielly, Maria Mendes, Susan Antonacci, Carole Leckner, Michelle Sagara, and Jean and Bent Nielsen.

For telling me not to give up and for making me cry in the Queen Mother Café: Terry Sellwood.

For providing the most supportive environment a traumatized writer could ever hope for in sharing her work: The Bellefire Club, being the incredibly talented Gemma Files, Sèphera Girón, Helen Marshall, Sandra Kasturi, Michael Rowe, and Halli Villegas.

For reminding me that Art Saves: Liisa Ladouceur, Christine Stait-Gardiner, John and Sandra Huculiak, Kayla Dobilas, Tanya Schreck and everyone from the late, lamented Royal Sarcophagus Society.

For magic, moss, martinis, cats, photos, inspiration and much more: David Keyes.

For listening to me tell this story (somewhat edited, of course) since she was a child and for letting me watch her grow into a talented writer, artist and creative soul: Elisabeth Nielsen.

For showing me how to finish the book (sorry about the swearing): Gillian Holmes.

For faith, wise editing, good counsel and for taking the leap that has given us ChiZine Publications: Sandra Kasturi (and, of course, Brett Savory).

For always being the best person in the world with whom to share coffee, cable cars, and long conversations about writing and anything else: Kim Kofmel.

For believing that I could do this—and for loving me even if I couldn't: Richard Shallhorn.

ABOUT THE AUTHOR

Nancy Baker is the author of three vampire novels (*The Night Inside*, *Blood and Chrysanthemums*, and *A Terrible Beauty*) and a collection of short stories (*Discovering Japan*). She lives in Toronto and avoids writing by working with numbers, gardening, and making jam. You can find out how any or all of these things are doing at nancybaker.ca or on Facebook.

EMB
RACE
THE
ODD

A TERRIBLE BEAUTY
NANCY BAKER

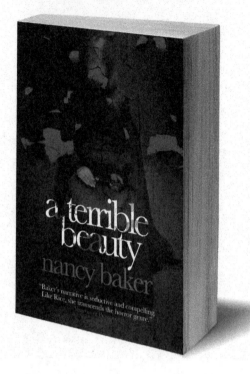

"Will you give me your blood to drink, though you die of it?" In an unexpected twist on a fairy tale, an artist goes into the wilderness to fulfill his father's debt and finds himself the prisoner of a dangerous, aliently beautiful monster.

AVAILABLE NOW
eISBN 978-1-77148-188-5

THE NIGHT INSIDE
NANCY BAKER

Dependable grad student Ardeth Alexander finds herself trapped in a nightmare as the unwilling blood source for a captive vampire. When she discovers that her fellow prisoner is not the worst monster she faces, she realizes that the only way to survive is to make an irrevocable choice.

With a brand new introduction by Suzy McKee Charnas, author of *The Vampire Tapestry*.

AVAILABLE NOW
eISBN 978-1-77148-189-2

BLOOD AND CHRYSANTHEMUMS
NANCY BAKER

Becoming a vampire was terrifying but learning to exist as one is harder than Ardeth Alexander ever imagined. As she and Rozokov try to find a way to live in their new world, an ancient vampire from a far different tradition is searching for them.

With a brand new introduction by Suzy McKee Charnas, author of *The Vampire Tapestry*.

AVAILABLE NOW

eISBN 978-1-77148-190-8